THE GIRL IN THE BOG

Also available by Keith Donohue

THE GIRL
IN THE
BOG

A NOVEL

KEITH DONOHUE

CROOKED
LANE

NEW YORK

Published in the United States by Crooked Lane Books, an imprint of The Quick Brown Fox & Company LLC.

Crooked Lane Books and its logo are trademarks of The Quick Brown Fox & Company LLC.

Library of Congress Catalog-in-Publication data available upon request.

ISBN (hardcover): 978-1-63910-849-7
ISBN (ebook): 978-1-63910-850-3

Cover design by Elizabeth Yaffe

Printed in the United States.

www.crookedlanebooks.com

Crooked Lane Books
34 West 27th St., 10th Floor
New York, NY 10001

First Edition: August 2024

10 9 8 7 6 5 4 3 2 1

For Melanie

A HELPFUL NOTE

O FTEN CALLED THE Irish *Iliad* or the Irish *Beowulf,* the *Táin Bó Cúailnge* tells of the clash between Cúchullain, the Hound of Ulster, and Queen Medb (Maeve) of Connacht in a first-century war fought over a bull. More or less. The *Táin* plays a role in this book, so we thought to provide some tips when encountering the characters from that epic pagan myth.

Irish is a tricky language, never mind Old Irish. Certain characters of this book are Irish, but the spelling is more phonetic than it seems. Siobhán, for example, is "shio-**van**"—the *b* and the *h* are run together with a bit of air behind them, making a "v" sound. Go ahead, try it when nobody is around.

This is a loose approximation of how the major characters' names are pronounced. Stressed syllables are in **bold**, and *italics* indicate a breath:

Ailill: **al**-il
Cúchullain: koo-**c***h***ull**-in
Fedelm: fe*dh*-elm
Láeg: **loy**gh

Medb: mayv
Táin Bó Cúailnge: toyn bow **koo**-ling-e

You need not concern yourself with silently pronouncing the other occasional Irish words in the text. People may stare at you if you move your lips as you read. We suggest buying two copies, using one to jot down little reminders and exclamations in the margins to look up later while keeping the other copy pristine. You have come this far. Plow on!

CHAPTER

1

Leaper

W*HO'S UP THERE NOW?*
Somebody was walking atop her grave. At last, a visitor had chanced upon the desolate spot. The squelch of boots made her dry heart quiver, for she had been alone for such a long time. She brightened at the promise of a break from the monotony of being dead.

Three feet under in the peat, she listened intently, trying to discern who was about. A bull of a man, judging by his slow trod, bearing the weary weight of all Ireland. Whistling to himself, off-key and absent-mindedly, the same few bars of an airless melody, like a bird who could not carry a tune. She wondered what he looked like, young or old, fair or dark, and decided he must be middle-aged, cap tilted to expose a broad-beamed widow's peak hiding not a single thought. Unshaven chin, pepper whiskers, the eyes watery blue, and two deltas of broken capillaries spreading across the nose, the map of a longtime drinker. A farmer of sorts, though not the real workingman of yore, but a retro enthusiast keeping alive the old customs, a weekend traditionalist who still cut his own turf to spite the modern world. She remembered him from the spring before. *Back again, are ye?* He was searching for the seam he had carved a year ago. No doubt accompanied by the obligatory work-obsessed border collie.

A brief debate knotted her thoughts. She considered casting her spirit into the dog for a spell and romping about the land on four paws. Years had passed since she had last stretched her legs, and the village must have changed in the interim. Always good to get out and see what Ireland was like these days. The little bitch whimpered, confused by the faint scent of an ancient aroma wafting on the breeze like sour shoes. *By the gods*, thought the girl in the bog, *don't let the little monster take a piss above me.* Back in her day, hounds could not be trusted, might steal your baby or let the wolves slaughter your lambs. Look at your modern dog, living with folk inside the house, imagine, begging for a nip of kibble and sleeping at your feet, no thank you. She would not be fooled by the wag of a tail. The farmer barked a word, and the dog trotted off to worry some distant sheep. Dogtrotter, bogtrotter.

The man dropped his tools with a clatter and sighed into the cool morning. Putting off the work, he unscrewed the lid of a jar of strong tea and took a long swallow. *I could murder a cup meself,* she thought. *Get on with it, sor. What is your business here?* Dallying as the sun spread across the empty valley, he seemed to be anticipating a divine sign, just as she had been waiting these endless centuries for someone to notice her.

When her killers threw her in the water and weighed her down to the muddy bottom, she had no idea that meant she would be stuck in the same position forever. The sphagnum moss and watery plants would die and decay, knot and fuse, and then harden to encase her like a thick, wet blanket. Sewn into the turf and pickled by the tannins and weird chemicals till she was nearly indistinguishable from the peat itself, her body stewed for two thousand years, the lifetime of two whales. Decade by decade, century by century, the waters receded, and the peat dried to fix her in place, unable to rot and disintegrate into pure nothingness. In her day, a dead person was thrown on a pyre and burned to ash or left inside a cairn to dry to bone and dust. But here in the wet now, she was sick of her own company, and the gods know, there's only so many times you can replay the same story of your life, long or short. True, for good stretches, one can reside instead in the present space, but that, too, is circumscribed by the grave. More than once in those twenty centuries, she had thought it would be grand to quit the whole matter of death altogether. Nobody ever came for a chat or a cup of tea, only damsel flies and midges, wayward songbirds, and occasionally a lost fox or blundering sheep, bawling for rescue from this godsforsaken place.

Out of sheer boredom, she had discovered the trick of the leap. On a fine Irish spring morning such as this, the heather perfumed the air and the land hummed with new life above. An explosion of hares romped and fattened on nature's bounty, mad for the tender new clover and grasses, the watercress floating at the edges of puddles and pools. Huge bucks boxed for the rights to the harems. Two rabbity lads stood upright on their long hind feet, giving each other what-for with their tiny fists. Nothing better than an Irish bantamweight, man or hare. From her murky grave, she longed to see the roister of crazed hares leaping across the valley like those armies of her youth, war-ready men and women clattering shields and swords, riding in their spangled chariots behind their warhorses, out for blood and bounty. She wanted her life back with such ferocity that she cast forth her spirit and bumbled directly into the body of the nearest hare.

Every newborn, whether cracking through an eggshell or being expelled from its mother's watery womb, is startled by the immense light of the world, the first drafts of cold oxygen, a gasp for life. Leaping into another being was no different, a jarring big bang into immense freedom. Pulsing with the drumbeat of blood in her veins, she felt the sunsplash on her whiskers. The smell of dank and decaying turf was replaced by the forty green aromas of the Connemara countryside. She leapt again, this time with a hare's sinews and muscles, and astonished herself by how high and far she could go. Testing these big new feet, she hopped more softly. Ah, she bounded, zigging and zagging, elated by the power of her limbs. She vaulted into new life with such vertiginous extravagance that all the other bunnies froze on their haunches, puzzled by what had gotten into their comrade. The old joy of life filled her heart, and she stretched her big thumpers, pawed the sunshine, and wriggled her long velvety ears, giddy with all she could do in this young, new body. She could not stop wriggling the puff at her bottom, as if it had a mind of its own, and the paradise of the great outdoors thrilled her beyond expression.

The neighborhood had certainly transformed in the centuries since her death. Gone was her home village on the crannog. Indeed, the little island built in the lake had vanished altogether, down to the last stick. The huts and halls and wooden walkways had rotted away. Nearby the stand of oak and ash had fallen or been felled, and where the lush forest had once stood was a stretch of flat, damp, endless marshland. At the crown of a hillock, she surveyed the whole valley. Far off in the west, the great ocean rolled timelessly. To the south lay protrusions of gray rock after rock, as barren as the moon. Only the lake and the distant hills to the northeast were the constants of the Connacht province she once knew.

Where are my people? she wondered. My father and mother and those I loved best? *Vamoosed to the other side. Left me at the rest stop and drove away.* What had happened to the great kings and queens? Dissipated into airy nothing. No home, no welcoming arms. Only the ghosts of what had been. She let out a long cry, an infant squeal that pricked up the ears of the other hares chewing their clover and shamrocks. Out on the Atlantic, the whales answered her lament, and gulls and seabirds echoed her melancholy call. She loped back to her human form entombed in the peat. As quickly as her new life had begun, it ended with a short hop into the grave. Her spirit settled into her own leathery skin, and she rested miserably, disappointed by her brief sojourn and the relentless tick of the eternal tock.

Seven hundred years passed before she forgot her grief and dared try again. A dragonfly hovered and landed on the tip of a bog asphodel to lie in ambush for other insects attracted by the sweet smell of nectar. She felt the slight quiver of its wings and cast her spirit into the strange bug. The leap was not so ecstatic the second time around, though she did admire her slender emerald body and the marvel of flight.

The world had changed yet again. More farms had taken root, and dirt roads etched the land. Mysterious white lumps moved in the faraway hills, but they were only sheep, oblivious to her wonderfulness. Settling on a reed bent above a small stream, she viewed the panorama through her dragonfly eyes, hypnotized by the kaleidoscope of colors and patterns, so bedazzled that she nearly ended up in the belly of a frog, darting to escape the long flick of its sticky tongue. The natural world is a dangerous place for a delicate creature. If the dragonfly who contained her spirit were to die, would she die with it? Best flit back to her own place.

Halfway home, she heard a nearly forgotten sound drift-
ing along a fair breeze. She tracked the song to its source, a
stone wattle house clinging to the side of a craggy mountain.
A man sat cross-legged on the doorstep and lifted his voice
above the ocean. The melody enchanted her, but the singer
was a revelation, her first encounter with another person in
eons. She hovered close, but the man took no notice. His eyes
were squeezed shut in some private consideration, as though
the song took his full concentration. A seer, she thought, a
mystical conjurer of the gods. Although she could not fully
understand his mangled and incorrect Irish, she knew the
other signs of the divine affliction. Transfixed by the beauty
of his own hymn, he failed to notice the dragonfly light upon
the reddened rim of his ear. She felt the notes rise from the
gutter of his throat and the rhythm of the bellows of his
lungs. Bending to the cavity of his earhole, she whispered to
him in her own ancient and correct Irish: "Be not afraid. The
spirit of a dragonfly is upon me, but I am a prophet like you."
He swatted at her with a finger snap, all the while crooning
praises in a bastard tongue. "Some priest you are," she said.
"Out of tune with life." Had he been a real holy man, surely
he would have heard even the tiniest transcendental whisper.
She buzzed back to her grave and cast herself back into the
buried body, crestfallen. The good part of a century passed
before she could forget the godseeker in the beehive hut.

One fair September day, having nothing better to do, she
leapt into a magpie skulking over her tomb. The bird
squawked at being taken over, and she wrestled his birdiness
to assert her identity. High in the morning air, she spied the
rutted cattle trails leading to a modest village that had
cropped up at a crossroads. It was market day, and the streets
were full of people. Shepherds led their flocks of sheep and
goats. Pigs grunted in pens, and fowl heckled from coops.

Drovers poked their beef cows, the beasts mooing in protest. Long ago, a spat over a prize bull had brought war and nearly torn the country in two. The bull of everlasting trouble.

Dogs circled the margins of the crowd, herding the chaos. Women at crude tables hawked turnips and honey mead and loaves of fresh warm bread, the aroma enough to drive a poor bird mad. The wee children found ready mischief, laughing and shouting and chasing the magpie till, overwhelmed by the hubbub, she flew to the gable of the highest building and landed on a stone windowsill. From there she watched more buying and bartering, the sneak thieves pocketing apples, the sellers weighing down the scales with dirty thumbs. Beer and cider sealed many a deal, accompanied by a clap on the back of a dusty coat, the bonhomie of fair trade, and great laughter at some poor sap being swindled.

The magpie listened carefully to the sound the people had on them and recognized slowly, syllable by syllable, the occasional old words, the familiar patterns of sentence and paragraph, and thus she came to understand the new Irish, although it was not as pleasant or musical as the old tongue of her youth. Still, she was glad to be able to decipher the language in the banter and blather of the plain folk below. For the best part of a week, she stayed inside the bird, visiting villagers' homes and picking up more news from open doors and windows. The gossip and pointless conversations warmed her heart and reminded her how much she missed the simple pleasure of companionship around the hearth. The *craic*, stories told for a laugh, puns and witplay, and compulsive stretching of the language for sheer fun. Had it not been for the scruffy gang of lads who threw stones at her, she might have stayed till winter. She shat on the ringleader's head before zipping back to the bog. Life as a bird had its advantages and its limits. Getting so close to real people was almost too much to bear.

A fox might suit her better, she thought, and waited two hundred years for one to happen by. A loner, silent, exiled, and cunning. On the glassy surface of a black pool, she admired her reflection, the sheen of her red fur, the white tip of her brushed tail. Her ears cocked at a small voice crying from a nearby ditch, and she trotted over cautiously. The young lad was little more than a bundle of bones dressed in scraps of rags. He lay on his back, facing the clouds, oblivious to her presence. His mouth and chin stained green from eating grasses and cress, the child was dying from starvation, and he spent his last moments singing to his mammy, a near skeleton herself, who had already perished by his side. The fox sniffed one and the other and blanched. Making the rounds of the countryside, she soon discovered the whole of Connemara gripped by the famine. Death's odor fouled the air and drove her back to her comfortable tomb. She shuddered in her old body, relieved to be hidden from the hungry sorrows.

Empty Ireland. Where had everyone gone? When she dared leap again, this time as a harmless sparrow, she found a ruined land. Abandoned houses sat like broken seashells. Stone walls had collapsed in heaps of rubble. After a day of flying about the parish, she hopped through the open door of a pub. Old souls, stricken guilty for having survived whilst so many perished, nursed their pints in dark corners. But a lively bunch of young men were jabbering away at the bar in an incomprehensible language. *Field and farm*, they said. *Ships. Goods. Over to Liverpool. Across to Amerikay. Pull the divil by his tail?* To her ears such contortions were *fuaim riastartha*, a twisted sound. Those young fellers dribbled gibberish, might as well have lost their tongues. The modern Irish she had learned over the centuries had nothing on the old Irish, but at least they were sisters of the same family. These ugly imported words signaled a wholly new way of speaking and thinking and considering the meaning of it all. She listened the whole evening, sustaining herself on spilled porter and crusts from *hang samiches*. Around midnight, the truth dawned on her: *Saxanach*. The fiends from over the sea. Or worse, Irishmen who were speaking the King's English, by the gods. How on earth had such a catastrophe befallen the good, plain people of Connacht?

The English had been in the province since Cromwell's time or before, murdering and putting down the peasants, speaking in a simple and unmelodious language to keep knowledge and power for themselves. They were only one type of the many visitors to this fair island—the Norsemen and the Normans, the black Celts, the blacker Spanish from the lands beyond—a polyglot of seafarers who learned the Irish language or made a dumbshow to trade with the western world. Miscreants and criminals were given the chance of hell or Connacht. Never in two thousand years had she considered that her own people would be speaking English—exclusively—in a public house.

She spent a pair of summers, first as a honeybee and then as a jackdaw, trying to learn this Hiberno English with its borrowed words and syntax, working in a state of despair over its ascendancy and leaping back into the body in the bog when she had enough of the bloody language. How were the people of Ireland supposed to understand one another when English pinched their tongues? She had better conversations in her hidey-hole, even if she was only talking to herself.

"For feck's sake."

As he bent to his work, the farmer muttered to himself in English, an old Saxon curse between his teeth. He grunted each time he sliced a moist brick of peat and threw it over his shoulder to the gathering pile. In the good old times, she thought, a real man would have forged a razor-sharp *sleán* in the morning and carved a winter's worth of turf by the end of the day. Men were men. And some men were even more manly than that. In all her many years of being dead, she had never once thought of leaping into the occasional man out on the boglands. She had known so many temperamental *scibirlín-*swinging men, walking over anyone who got in their way. Yet, men had convinced themselves they ruled the world. Who knows, perhaps she could find a masculine body for herself. Might be interesting to be the bully fella up above. No, not this one, no. A bit weakish, she surmised. A little thick. He was busy anyway, hacking away at dear old Ireland. The sleán slid into the peat like a broadsword through a belly. She could feel the blade draw closer to her. Careful now, she said, though she knew he could not hear an underground word.

C H A P T E R

2

Diggers

A T FIRST LIGHT, the bitch pressed her cold nose against his bare leg. "Feck off," he bellowed, and she whimpered and hung her head, the hurt registering in her soulful brown eyes. Under the comforter, Mullaney remembered his ex-wife planting her icy toes on his warm bum on a winter's night. "Good god, you're cold. Are yis dead?" he had often asked her. Not dead, no, but gone now as surely, over to Liverpool. And then his daughter, Flannery, skedaddled off to America first chance, leaving him all alone on the farm. Talking to himself, or worse, holding conversations with the dog who would always tolerate him, thus was the nature of her love and devotion. During the night he had managed to twist the blankets around his torso, and he struggled to free himself. The collie watched for clues of the work ahead. Mullaney planted his feet on the wooden floor and absently scritched behind her ears, and they were friends again. He looked at the window for the weather. The sun peeped between the hills, and the morning promised to be dry and clear. "A fine day," he told her, and Bonnie wagged her tail.

After a quick wash and a shared breakfast, Mullaney prepared a jar of tea and wrapped two hard-boiled eggs in a kerchief for his next meal. The collie trailed him to the old shed and watched him gather the proper tools, a pair of garden spades, and his father's sleán, ancient but kept sharp. He loaded the equipment into the lorry and whistled for his boon companion to join him in the cab. They drove over the rise in the road, putting the house behind them. The ground was still soft and spongy from the steady rains that for weeks had bedeviled his plans for one last dig to lay in a supply of turf for next winter.

Not a soul could be seen from any of the four directions. Farmer and dog walked to the scar in the earth that marked last summer's labors, the rows carved and taken. Mullaney welcomed the serenity and thought of nothing but cutting long rectangular bricks like black butter and flinging them to the bank above him. The turf smelled of promised smoke. A lost art, soon to be forbidden by *Bord na Móna* in the name of climate change, but Mullaney took a perverse satisfaction in the backbreaking work.

The earth has a wet heart. If he dug deeply enough, through the layers of peat and on past the bedrock, he would hit a vein reeking of damp rot and decay, the water seeping to the soft center, fecund as a womb. Where else would the rain go, then, if not into the earth? The constant rain, nine months out of twelve, lashed in curtains and waves in Connemara. Endless rain, weeklong showers, or soft days fogging the mornings and hazing the early afternoons from September to May. The wetness from the great Atlantic, swollen and windblown in drear winter. The streams flowed from the mountains and fed the blue lake behind his house. He could feel the water through his soles. The gray misery of bygone months was barely offset by the greening of the land and the springtime burst of wildflowers, ramsons and vetch, wild orchids and gorse and thyme, harbingers of the brief dry spell that allowed him to get his digging in. His father had always been able to read the signs in the land, the hours of light in the sky, when to sow and when to reap, but Mullaney himself relied upon the weather lady on the news. Sommersby her name was, a lovely young lass swooning over a forecast showing a row of five yellow suns with smiley faces. Perfect weather for the dig, and time enough to let the bricks dry.

The pile of turf grew at a steady clip. Kinks in his neck and shoulders worked themselves out, and the sun warmed his back in such a pleasant way that he nearly forgot his troubles. Push his boot against the blade, cut through the twisted plant fibers, and then toss the wet slab in one continuous swinging motion. He dug again. The sleán crunched against a hardness and met resistance. Once long ago, his father had unearthed a huge twist of bog oak that had been perfectly preserved by the acidic stew. Together they dug out the limb, long as the boy was tall, and later fashioned sections into a shepherd's crook and two gnarly walking sticks. Mullaney knelt to inspect what he had struck.

Sticking out from the raw edge of the earth were what appeared to be the tips of four blackened human toes. He instinctively tore at the brick he had cut a moment ago and found the severed pinkie.

"Sweet Jesus," he said. His stomach grumbled like a cow's.

Mullaney stood and scanned the horizon for the border collie. The moment he needed her, the damned dog was nowhere to be found. Nothing but green fields and stone walls, the far-off mountains and the rocky bogland. He considered trekking to the farm to call the authorities. The *Gardaí*, he assumed, would want to know about the foot, no matter how long it had lain buried in the peat. But he was curious. Suppose there was a whole body? What harm in taking a closer look?

He brushed the dense fibers away from the other toes, and digging with his fingertips, he exposed the bottom of one sole. By the size and shape of it, the foot belonged to a young woman or a child, he felt sure. In the bright sunshine, the map of lines crossing the sole was clear and distinct. He ran a fingernail against the dark-brown, nearly black skin and scored the pliable curve of her instep. Working tenderly over the course of the remaining morning hours, he removed enough of the matted turf to find the other foot, tucked against its mate, and he deduced that the body was lying on its side, like a shy bride in a marriage bed. He cupped a heel in one hand, toying with the birdlike lightness of it, all the while doing the spatial geometry, visualizing how she might be positioned beneath the layers of decayed vegetation. A job, surely, if he was to free her. He wiped the sweat from his forehead. The day had grown unpleasantly warm.

Careful not to park himself above her, Mullaney sat on the bank and unscrewed the jar for a swallow of strong tea. From the rucksack, he took one of the hard-boiled eggs and cracked the shell against his elbow. The dog, he thought, would hear him peeling the snack and come bounding at the mere possibility of food. She was an old bitch but keen of ear. She would doubtless tell him what must be done. No, that's not right. The dog would not actually speak to him, that would be mental. But Bonnie would give him a sign. Slant of the head, questioning eyes. A warning bark, a wagging tail. The last connection to his father, who had raised her as a pup, she was his oldest and most steadfast confidante, but nowhere to be found at the moment. He ate his snack, mindful of the dead girl.

Above the spot where he imagined she was positioned, he skinned away the top vegetal layer to reveal the bare ground.

Anxious to not nick another toe or worse, he kept the blade under tight control and dug from the edges inward, guessing how and where the corpse was arranged. Not till the late afternoon hours did Mullaney uncover the contours of its form. Taking a hand trowel from the back of the lorry, he dug carefully, exposing the hunch of a shoulder, the rise of a hip.

The body revealed its secrets slowly. She lay on her left side, legs drawn up slightly, hands joined together as in prayer but bound by a rope at her wrists that stretched to her neck. Her long cloak and tunic had been preserved and clung damply. Mullaney hesitated before uncovering the head, fearful of seeing the face. On his hands and knees, he pulled away the last inches of peat, stroking the dirt softly so as not to awaken her. Worn by his long labor, he paused to wonder whether he had missed his tea. He felt eyes upon him from overhead. Stray thoughts darted through his brain: what if the girl's people had come and caught him in such a situation? Worse, what if the police had shown up?

Five sheep stood on the lip of the ditch, staring at him dumbly through vaguely satanic eyes. Their elongated pupils unnerved him, as much now as when he was a boy and had been absolutely frightened of their gaze.

"Ach, go on then!" He echoed his father's voice note for note. The sheep made no move. He chucked a broken clod at them, but they were frozen in place.

"They'll tarry as long as that bitch of yours is at their heels." The sentence arrived before the man. Up strode Thomas Burke, his father's longtime friend, blathering as he drew near. "Fine work to have them round up and brought on, she's not lost the knack—"

The old fella swallowed his word and took in the entire scene. The sheep eyeing the excavation, the man up to his knees in peat, the black body half exposed in the dark earth.

Burke drew the back of his hand across his mouth. "Good Lord. Are you after burying the girl or digging her up?"

The absurdity of his question lingered above the grave.

"What would make you think I was burying a body out here in the bogs? What sort of eejit do you take me for?"

"Did you murder her then?"

"I found her this morning as I was cutting the turf."

Burke flushed to a bright rust, and then gathering his wits, he stooped to inspect the remains. The sheep wandered away as the collie circled the dig to investigate the fuss. At the sight of the half-buried woman, the dog lay flat on the ground, ears pinned, whimpering and anxious. Resting his weight on the shovel, Mullaney offered a reassuring whistle and held her in place with a glance. Burke crept closer.

"Black as the night," he said. "Is it not the Nigerian girl from the chipper's over in Roundstone? I'd heard she had gone missing ages, but word was she went back to Lagos on account of the pissing rain day after day. Longed for the sunshine, she did."

"It's not the Nigerian girl, you fool."

"An honest mistake. Who else would it be then?"

"I dunno." Mullaney stared at the corpse. "One thing for certain, she's ancient. Older than yourself, even. One of the bog people."

Balancing revulsion with the urge to know, Burke stepped into the hole. "Are you sure, Michael? Wouldn't she be nothing but bones? Look at the skin on her. She might been stashed there yesterday."

"Aye, take a closer look at her clothes, man. Would your friend in the chipper be wearing a tunic made of deerskin? She's an old one. Hundreds of years, thousands maybe."

Mad with curiosity, Bonnie crawled on her belly. Guided by her nose, she stood to have a good sniff. She whined at the scent and backed away, puzzled, and took refuge behind her master's legs.

Burke waited for the dog to finish. "Do you not think it would be a good idea to call the *Garda Síochána* in to have a look? Have the experts verify your theory?"

Eager to get back to his work, Mullaney spat in his hands and rubbed the grime into his palms. "Time enough to bring in the authorities. Since I was the one who found her, seems only right to take a proper look at the girl before the whole area is taped off like a crime scene. Are you not interested in history, Tom? See her for yourself before we are overrun by police and whatnot? Will you not help me, at least, to uncover her?"

"You're a damn fool, Michael Mullaney. Have been ever since you were a wee chuff." He peeled off his vest and rolled his shirtsleeves to the elbows. "Still. Where angels fear to tread. Now, where do you suppose is the head of her?"

The men worked quietly in the full light of the long afternoon and exposed the corpse by inches, reluctant to touch her pliable skin. She had met a violent end. A willow cord bound her wrists together, and the other end of the rope encircled her neck. Someone had slit her throat just above the noose, and she had been bashed in the skull. Murdered surely, three different ways. Made sure she was dead. At her breast, a metal oakleaf pin kept her cloak joined against the elements. Her scalp had been shaven but for a whorl of red hair spiraling from a knot fixed on the left side, and most astonishingly, her dark face was unmarred and at peace, as though she had merely fallen asleep, dreaming of her freedom as the bog waters claimed her. With his thumb, Mullaney brushed the last flecks from her eyelids and then sat back on the damp ground. Burke fetched his pipe from his filthy vest and kept a silent vigil over the grave.

Mullaney stared at her body, curled like a toddler down for a nap. "She looks all of seventeen, maybe younger."

"A handsome lass," said Burke. "What sort of savages would murder a poor slip in such a mean way?"

Trails of pipe smoke whitened the golden air. A soft western breeze carried the salt smell of the ocean. The sunlight cast the men's elongated shadows, making them look as if they belonged to giants. Alone with their thoughts and the ache of a day's toil, the diggers did not speak for some time. The body lay between them, resting, as if the girl might awaken and wonder, too, why she had been abandoned in such a barren part of the world.

"You were right, so," Burke said. "To have a chance to see her first and before all the gawkers. Keep her to yourself. Ourselves."

"I was only curious." Mullaney paused to consider what they had done. "Maybe we should have let her be."

"The authorities will have their say on the matter. There will be an investigation, naturally, by that lot. They will seal off the place for miles with their tape, and then the reporters come up to have a look, and by the by, they'll call in the whaddyacallits, the archivists, is it?"

"Archaeologists?"

A deep furrow creased Burke's brow as he contemplated the correct answer. "I suppose you're right. They will take her away, surely, to study her. A museum in Dublin, so the nation might recall yet another violent chapter in our cruel history. Do you think our names might be on the plaque, Michael? The Connemara Girl, discovered by Michael Mullaney and Thomas Burke in the empty West?"

"I had not thought of a plaque, Tommy. I had not gotten as far ahead of myself."

"There's a bit of light left in the day. Let's ring the telly news down here. Local heroes and all that. Perhaps there's a bit of cash in it. Have a go at our fifteen minutes of fame." Burke tapped out his pipe and retrieved from his back pocket his old smartphone. While his friend's back was turned, he took three quick snaps of the body. "How about a selfie, the three of us?"

"Are you mental? Don't be taking pictures of the dead. Desecrating the poor girl." Mullaney reached for the camera, but Burke shoved it in his trousers. "Don't go touting those photos, Tommy. There'll be crowds around, the last thing she would want."

"Desecration? All right for you to dig her up, and me taking on the labor, my age. What do you know anyways about what that mummy might want?"

"Keep those photos to yourself, for now. Don't be blasting them over social media."

Burke spat on the ground and feigned penitence. "Sure, lookit. I'm too old for that shite."

"If the dead could only talk, they would have a word for you. We will leave her be till the morning. One more night's peace for the lass and promise tomorrow first thing, call the police in to solve a two-thousand-year-old homicide. Help me cover her again, enough to keep the foxes and rooks away." Mullaney reached for a spade.

With a world-weary sigh, Burke heaped loose earth over the body. "A fox would be scared out of its socks if it stumbled upon your girl in the night's dark hours, and I'm sure my own sleep will be overrun with nightmares."

"Murder and banshees and ghosts rising out of the bogs." Mullaney shook his head at the old man's superstition. "You mustn't tempt the fairy world."

Once they had finished their grisly work, they said their goodbyes, agreeing to meet for a drink after their tea and a good wash. No good showing up at the pub knackered and dirty as, well, a pair of graverobbers.

*   *   *

After he had seen Burke safely home, Mullaney snuck back to the gravesite. Best to keep her to himself. Fighting a wave of apprehension, he stooped to cradle the dead. She was as light as his own daughter at eight or nine when he had last lifted and held her in his arms. The unexpected featherweight threw him off-balance, and he collapsed to one knee in the earth, soaking his trousers. Out of breath, he struggled to his feet and carried the bog girl a few yards to a blue tarp spread above the ditch.

"There now," he said. "That's better, isn't it?"

Laid out, she looked smaller and more vulnerable. In the move, the frayed rope had snapped in two, releasing the bonds between her neck and wrists. A sigh of relief, though he could not tell if it came from his lips or hers. The grave robbery, if indeed it could be called as much, preyed upon his imagination. Even the dog was undone and nervous, making a chain of whines linked by a few barks. As if to say what the hell are we doing here and let's run off whilst we can. With the sleán and hayfork, Mullaney broke apart a hank of loose peat to cover the body and keep it moist, and then he rolled her up in the tarp tight as a burrito, shrouding her face last. He laid the body in the back of his truck, wary of someone discovering them. Even his own footfalls gave him the quivers until she was settled in. Then he fetched his tools to fill in the empty ground. He prayed that the old fool would keep his trap shut. With the body gone, Burke would have only an empty story. Bonnie sauntered around the hole for one last check.

A pair of rooks flew across the pink-and-orange setting sun as Mullaney finished the job. The reek of wet fur permeated the lorry, so he rolled down the window to let in fresh air. Each rut in the road jostled the old suspension, and he worried about his cargo wrapped in blue, hoping she would not mind the bumps. He listened for any grunts or groans.

In the driveway, he sat behind the wheel to consider his plot. Accidentally finding the girl was one thing, but the long day's exhumation troubled him, as if he had disturbed the natural order of the past. Why had he felt such a need to see her whole and recovered? Her presence in the tarp unsettled him. By nature, he was not a superstitious man, but it is not every day one digs up a two-thousand-year-old murder victim. Who had put her there, murdered three ways? The least he could do was give her a decent and more proper resting place than the mire. Acts of atonement, even the best intentioned, often have unintended consequences. But he had come too far to worry about waking the dead. And for her part, the bog girl had not made a peep.

"We're home," Mullaney said. Gathering his strength, he heaved the rolled tarp to the toolshed and laid her in a shadowed corner, damp and dank. You'll feel at home here, he thought, and stood above his parcel, contemplating his decision to hide her. Out on the bog, she had been on her own, but inside the shed she felt like his secret. For the one night, she would be under his care. Weariness leached into his back and limbs, and he was filthy with mud and peat, leaving behind a trail of dirty footprints to his bedroom. An hour remained till he and Burke were due to meet for drinks. He would just rest his eyes for a minute.

CHAPTER

3

Red Hags

THREE BABIES BORN six days apart was an unusual occurrence in the parish, but each one arriving as a red-headed girl was a downright omen. Some of the local wags said the girls must have shared the same father, while other more devout villagers blessed themselves and said an extra Hail Mary in hopes of preventing a curse upon the community. During those early months when the babies were largely confined to their bassinets and playpens, the gossip merely simmered, but when summer arrived and their mothers took to strolling the streets with the little darlings in perambulators, the whispers began in earnest over the lasses' uncanny resemblance to one another. *Didn't I just see you at the shops? That's the second redhead in two days. Three gingers together in the front pew of the eleven o'clock Mass, I would not want to tempt the devil.* Siobhán Flaherty was often mistaken for Eileen Magill, and both were confused with Mary Catherine Burke. The toddlers were alike as three oranges.

As the three red-haired girls grew older, they suffered their share of double and triple takes. To the untrained eye, the resemblance was uncanny. Same size, same fair complexion, same bridge of freckles across their noses and cheeks, same fiery temper. Red Children of the Corn. By the time the girls entered school, their manes had come in thick and curly, and the threesome grew partial to one other. It came as no surprise that each preferred the company of the other two. Behind their backs, the townsfolk referred to them as the Ginger Sisters. Sometimes spoken with a shudder.

Had adolescence been avoidable, their benign sorority might have continued innocently enough. But everyone must endure the angst of teenhood. Their classmates mercilessly culled the gingers from the pack. The popular girls made the first move to separate the outliers, calling them the devil's daughters, the pale ones, wee vampires, and carrot tops. *Do not pet a redhead lest you burn your hand. Watch out for the temper on that fiery lot. What is the difference between a shoe and a ginger? A shoe has a sole.* The constant teasing drew Siobhán, Eileen, and Mary Catherine closer and tripled their growing resentment at being so ostracized in the little town.

At age fourteen, the friends decided to take a blood vow.

It began as a joke at first, a break from their Irish lessons near Halloween. Siobhán waved her hand before the class formally began: "Excuse me, sir, but what is the Irish for witches? You know, the Halloween kind."

"Well, that's a surprising question," Mr. Ó Suillebhean said. He usually had the austere demeanor of a man who had devoted himself to a hopeless cause, but given the rein of a query, he let himself run wild. "Don't you remember your vocabulary? A witch can be simply *cailleach*, but depending upon the context, it might also mean old woman or hag, a midwife perhaps. *An cailleach dhubh* is a nun: the woman in black, eh? The same name is also given the cormorant. The *cailleach na clúide* would be your granny in the chimney corner, and the *cailleach na luatha* is a sit-by-the-fire. Or as she is better known: Cinderella. Woman of the ashes, you see. And the owl is the *cailleach oiche*, a woman of the night—"

The boys in the back row hooted and giggled. Ó Suillebhean flushed and began to lecture the class on decorum. ". . . if ye hooligans wish to make anything of yourselves at all." Siobhán tossed back her hair, triumphant that her question had taken five minutes off the school clock. Her ginger comrades in the front row silently applauded.

That evening, the girls met in the Burkes' attic, the *sanctum sanctorum* they had created over the years. Strands of colored fairy lights ran the length of the eaves, and two floor lamps illuminated all but the far corners. They had brought up an old futon and an easy chair, laid out a fake Indian rug, and covered the walls with their own pictures, ideas for books and films, the images that inspired the stories they told one another to scare or charm. Eileen was the visual artist, tending toward a dark gothic vibe with her monsters and giants and fair maids in danger. Siobhán was the writer, yammering away with a thousand unfinished ideas. Mary Catherine, whom everyone called Emcee, provided the meeting place and the occasional bottle of cider to split three ways.

They were in high spirits, recounting how they had derailed the lesson, and they snorted over the back-row *amadána*. Women of the night, indeed, as if any one of those boys would know what to do with a girl, day or night. Scare the shite out of them with a naked thigh. They hooted in the rafters, calling for the lads, but the night remained silent. Even the *cailleach oiche* had fallen asleep.

"We should be witches," Siobhán said. "Weird sisters."

"Amn't I already set to go out as a Galway hooker?" Emcee said. "If I can elude my mammy's eagle eye before the Halloween parties."

From across the room, Eileen tossed a pillow that clomped Emcee in the shoulder. "You're a feckin' eejit. A Galway hooker is a red-sailed boat. What you are is a Galway hoor."

"I don't mean for Halloween dress-up," Siobhán said. "But for real. Witches. Not the warty-nose kid stuff, but proper witchcraft. Make a study of it. Teach ourselves all the old ways. Everyone in town is already a bit frightened of us as it is. Why not give them a taste of what they deserve?"

"You're daft," Emcee said.

Siobhán leaned into the possibility. "C'mon, girls, what's the harm in it? Wouldn't it be grand to learn some spells and potions? Sure, you could pass your exams with a simple hex. Or make your mammy blind to what you're wearing out the door in the morning. She'd think you're a nun when you are a plain tramp out to a party."

"I won't have to ride a broom, will I? Fall off one of them things forty feet in the air, and you're bound to bash your brains out on a stone. I seen it all the time, like, in the murder mysteries. Two people having a scuffle, and one falls over and cracks his skull on a hard edge, so. The head is a deathly thing to be fooling with."

"No broom riding then," Eileen said. "Only black magic and maybe seeing the future, like in *The Wizard of Oz*, staring into a crystal ball to learn what your enemies are about. 'I'll get you, my pretty, and your little dog too.' That's gas."

"I'd like that," Emcee said. "But no green skin neither."

Taking a penknife, Siobhán pricked each palm and held out her hands. They made a blood pact, giddy over their bold decision. "We'll call ourselves the *cailli rua*. The Red Witches."

Grinning like a carved turnip, Eileen said, "Aye, better yet, the Red Hags."

Off and on for three years, they studied witchcraft, sneaking books on the occult and spelling manuals to the attic hideaway, pinning and chatting on dark corners of the internet, sharing videos about the latest curses. Eileen spent hours on pen-and-ink drawings of witches and warlocks, painted lurid watercolors of druids and the ancient kings and queens of Ireland, carved woodblock prints of ravens and hemlock, and festooned the vaulted ceilings and walls of their mad museum. Boys from the county were transformed into princes who then failed to arrive on golden steeds and had to be punished. Teachers and priests became acned ogres who menaced and threatened to steal them away. Words and music crowded the available space. Poems painted on the attic door, long trails of staves and notes roped around the gabled window. Siobhán added a contrapuntal melody in red ink. Emcee hid dirty limericks about their classmates behind the ceiling beams.

The garret was off-limits to anyone not a Red Hag. Out of desperation, Mr. and Mrs. Burke had ceded control over the upper story to the house ages ago and tolerated the strange ginger girls who climbed the stairway with barely a greeting or farewell, coming and going at odd hours, playing their syncopated tunes in the attic, a hint of grass wafting down now and then, an odd bottle of hard cider in the recycling. The room was where the weirdness happened. "I would rather Mary Catherine was a witch," Mrs. Burke told Mrs. Magill. "Long as those girls are safe here and not hither and yon about the countryside, gallivanting with the village lads."

Twin beds were brought up and lined the east and west walls, and on overnights, Emcee slept between them on the floor. Dormers at either end let in scant light, and atop an antique desk, a pair of widescreen monitors glowed. The girls grew an herb spiral in the Magills' garden, dried mugwort and hazel, sought arcana in the shops down in Galway. Tinctures to cure spots, make the next boy who sees you fall in love. Pinned voodoo dolls of their enemies. On the Magills' great horses, they rode down to the sea to wail and keen at the tides and scramble across the headlands of the western world, where incantations could be loud and unfettered. They tried every trick in the magick books: a goth phase, with their pale speckled skin and fiery hair set off smartly by dark clothes and kohl eyes, multiple piercings, and knotted rings on every finger. Pricking their thumbs. Ouija boards that never said yes. A stone pentagram hidden under a throw rug. A black cat, shanghaied from a local barn, lived in the attic for a long weekend as their familiar, till Mrs. Burke complained of the unholy yowling after midnight and the gift of a dormouse at her feet. They sent away for witches' kits from England and America, joined a listserv for the Wiccans and Pagans of West Ireland, searched for the nearest coven, and even toyed with the idea of going to a druid cosplay convention in Strabane. They had their palms read at the summer Fun Fair, and over Emcee's objections, had a go with the tarot deck, though neither Siobhán nor Eileen could properly interpret the symbols. No matter how many times they were shuffled, the cards always revealed the Ace of Cups.

But nothing seemed to work. The potions turned rancid within a week. Boys failed to be enchanted. If anything, the lads grew more fearful of encountering one of them, leaping over to the other side of the street, blessing themselves with the sign of the cross. The other girls were no better. They laughed at the would-be witches behind their backs and isolated the redheads even further. No party invitations. Shunned in the hallways. Laughed at, scorned, ignored. Each girl privately thought, at one time or another, of chucking the whole business, but each dared not disappoint her sisters. By

the spring of sixth year, as they prepared for the uncertain
road to uni, the Red Hags clung to the belief that the dark
mysteries might yet be cracked. Or at the very least, they
would find some answer to their shared yearning for something, anything, to take them out of the ordinary and into
the scalding desires of their hearts.

* * *

Emcee's younger brothers raced each other to see who
could more quickly gobble their pizza, enduring the blis-
tering mozzarella without crying out or flinching. Emcee
did her best to ignore their antics. Even at five years old,
the twins seemed to have absorbed the macho competitive-
ness of their species. *Boys.* She checked her phone as her
slice cooled. A barely perceptible trail of olive oil marked
her thumb swipe on the screen, but she did not stop scroll-
ing through the special offers designed especially for her.
How did the internet know she had been talking to her
mammy about a new pink swimsuit for the summer? That's
where the real dark magic lurked, deep in the algorithms
that listen to our conversations and read our thoughts and
precisely deliver the goods we do not yet know we want.
She nearly zipped past her grandfather's message with its
attachments to download. Ever since he had given her the
mobile phone for her seventeenth birthday, they had been
exchanging texts, a quick hello or some cat video three years
behind the times. Online chats, though he lived over the
next hill. It would have been easier to talk in person. Cute
at first, but lately they had ramped up the game. She sent
him jokes a shade blue. He sent her memes that pushed the
limits of humor and good taste. Sacrilegious puns. Double
entendres. She wondered what disgusting photos awaited
her. Obscene old man.

The three images slowly unspooled as she took a bite, the hot tomato sauce burning the roof of her mouth.

TOP SECRET in the subject line and then straight to the point:

> You will never guess what the cat dug up. We were out for the turf this A.M. and found a body out on the bogs. Mullaney says it may be an Iron Age lass. All day digging her out. Keep it under your hat, MC. Highly confidential. If you want to see her for yourself before the county is crawling with the police and the TV vans, meet me on the old lane near the Mullaney place at half-past eight tomorrow morning.
>
> —Pops

"Holy shite," she said.

The first of the attachments was a selfie. Dirty and smiling, her grandfather's face filled most of the frame. Below him, obscured by his shadow, lay a dark mass in the background. Even when enlarged, the splotch looked like hardly more than a trick of light. "You are only having me on," she muttered to herself.

Her mother gave her a disapproving look. "What's that you're gawking at?"

"She said 'holy shite,'" a little brother squealed on her.

By reflex, she gave the chancer a quick slap on his shoulder. "Another one of Pops's jokes."

"Don't tell me." Her mother sighed toward the ceiling. "I don't want to know."

Slanting her phone away from prying eyes, Emcee wiped her greasy fingers on her jeans and then scrolled to the second photograph. No mistaking the girl half-submerged in the peat. The late sunlight bathed the corpse, strongly enough to reveal a rope stretched between her neck and joined wrists. Something awful had happened to her. The final picture made her gasp. Close-up of the serene and still face. Eyes shut, lips drawn together, a tangle of red hair in contrast to the deeply blackened skin. She was lovely, but dead all right.

Her little brothers were clamoring for more pizza.

"Shut your traps, you pagans," said their mother. "I will bring you a slice each if you cool out."

Ignoring the twins, Emcee forwarded her grandfather's note and the three images with her own message to the other Red Hags. Come right over after your tea. Lookit, an ould wan of ours. Dead witch found in the bog.

Not fifteen minutes later, the other two arrived on a pair of the Magills' giant horses. They found Emcee in front of a monitor that was glowing like a bubbling cauldron. She had all three photos queued for their inspection. As the Photo-shop expert, Eileen controlled the keyboard, while the other two kibbitzed over her shoulder as she zoomed and cropped, lightened and desaturated, auto-enhancing and fiddling until the images had been sharpened clear as could be. "He should buy himself a mobile with a decent camera," she said. "And the lighting was crap."

The selfie of the old fellow revealed little, for the girl lay in shadow. After tinkering with the exposure, Eileen thought to reverse to negative, and the body became apparent in ghostly white. The girl's bare feet and clasped hands regis-tered lighter than the surrounding peat, but even at ideal resolution, her features were indistinct. The other two pic-tures provided more detail to rebuild her byte by byte: the twist of the rope, the filigree carvings on the bronze pin at the close of her ornate speckled cloak, the peaceful set to her mouth, and even the lashes at the ends of her closed eyelids. Tanned by the bog acids, she was forty shades of black and brown, from the ends of her fingernails tinted sepia to her earhole dark as a cave. Most striking of all was her red hair. A ginger all right, one of them. They could not look away from the arched gash at her throat behind the noose.

"Connemara CSI," Emcee said. "Multiple injuries. Cause of death: strangulation, or was it a knife to the throat?"

Siobhán pointed to a spot behind the auburn hair. "Bit of a smash there, you see? An indentation where they stove in her skull with a blunt object."

"Something heavy. It's always something heavy on the telly, as if you could crack a nut with a feather." Eileen rubbed the spot near her temple where a pony had once delivered a good kick.

"Geez, they made sure our girl was well and dead," Siobhán said. "That's a grim end to anyone. Cut her throat, bashed her head, roped her like a steer, and threw the body in the bog. How many ways does it take to kill a person?"

"Maybe she was a witch or sorceress," Emcee said. "Everybody was afraid of her powers, so they could not risk her rising from the dead. Pops says to never leave the door open from this world to the next, for you cannot tell who might be trying to sneak in."

"The poor thing," Eileen said. "I wonder who she was."

"She's right down the lane," Siobhán said. "Let's go find out for ourselves."

4

Killers

S HE BLINKED.
    For the first time in two thousand years, she opened her eyes. Sure, she had seen plenty of the world in the form of a hare, a dragonfly, a magpie, but this time she could see through her own eyes, and though the view was merely the dim blue fabric of the tarp, she was dazzled by the color, astonished to be making any movement at all. Her lips parted in amazement, and her small gasp sounded like an ocean's storm. Alive, alive-o. No longer in the peat but drinking in oxygen. Her chest swelled and ebbed. Despite the close air of the little shed, each gulp tasted as sweet as mead.

    She twitched.

    The quake traveled across her shoulders, and she laughed at the electric jolt in her limbs. Wrapped tight as a pig in a blanket, she hadn't the strength to break free, but she could flex her fingers and wiggle her toes, suddenly aware that the wee one on her right foot had gone missing. Right, so, amputated by the clumsy oaf with the spade. An accident to be sure, but the man could not stop apologizing for the damage he had done, talking to her corpse as if he knew she had feel-ings. After the mistake he took his time digging her out. *Careful now*, he'd whispered to himself again and again. The gentleness in his rough hands surprised her. He was prim as a curate's wife, brushing the bits of peat stuck to her face, reluctant to touch her. Then the other fella showed up, full of blather, inebriated by the sound of his own voice. The kind who could not abide silence. And last to the scene was the suspicious dog. That bitch could smell the truth wafting off a body. Ach, there was a terrible ache in her neck and a stiff bow of her spine from being scrunched these many years, reminding her of girlhood mornings when she woke from deep sleep and needed a good stretch like a cat waking in a patch of sun.

She yawned.

She let her jaw drop and then coughed out bog water, thick as syrup. The staleness of her own breath alarmed her. The smell off her. Leather, blood, the roughness at her throat. By the gods, she thought, if I could only move. An apple would be brilliant. A bit of fresh watercress would be grand. Nothing to be done, unfortunately, till the ould fella came back to unwrap her from the cocoon. Outside, the birds sang the day to its end. She could only wait patiently, but what was one more night after the thousands she had suffered alone? The turf cutter would be astonished, no doubt, to find her alive come morning. *Hello there*, she practiced, *how are ye? Where's the craic?* Or she could take a more obtuse approach, let him slowly discover the truth. And then? Who knows, perhaps he might explain how and why he'd unlocked the door and pulled her through.

She remembered.

Unable to rise on her own, she recalled her last thought upon earth. The quick end and the absurd circumstances that led her to this most unusual place and time. In retrospect, she had missed all the signs, beginning with the lad who came to warn her.

The blind boy had fanned his palm, revealing five small round calluses on the tips of his fingers, a talisman for his secret sight. He swiveled his head to the northeast, listening for a sound only he could hear. Despite her own powers of envisioning the future, she had no foreboding of the disaster. Perhaps this poor waif had read the signs incorrectly. Blank as the moon, his face bore the same untroubled countenance he presented to one and all. His chapped lips twitched as he mumbled, counting under his breath.

"Run," he said. "They are after you. Three men, not far."

She did not believe such a thing could be possible. What had she done, after all, but tell the dire truth? What fault of hers that the queen failed to take heed? For a moment, she considered standing her ground. Let the warriors come. They would surely listen to reason. They might be fools, but they were her people, her kinsmen.

The boy stepped to her, latching his fingers on her shoulder. "They are going to kill you, Fedelm. Run, as fast as you can."

She grabbed his wrist and felt the blood pulsing through him. "Where will I go?"

"To the edge of the western world," he said. "And if you must, leap into the sea. Ask the three great waves to take you to the Otherworld till these troubles pass. Quickly now."

When she laid her hand on the lad's cheek to thank him, Fedelm felt the warmth of his blush, the pressure of his face nestling into her touch. A cloud of warm breath escaped into the frosty morning. "Make haste."

Beneath her feet the boardwalk trembled, and she feared the whole village would hear her clomping across the wooden path. There was one only one way off the crannog to safe passage through the dangerous marshland. If she could escape the little island before the three men arrived, she reckoned her chances were good. Beyond the wild and bleak landscape, a half mile away stood a stand of oak and ash where she might conceal herself from her pursuers. What madness this was, a war over a bull. As she hurried toward drier land, she replayed the story in her thoughts.

After a year away, she was going home. Even the rough chop of the sea had not subdued her excitement to be returning to Connacht. Fedelm knew her mammy and da would be thrilled with all she had learned at the feet of Scáthach on the Isle of Skye. The year abroad had expanded her mind: martial arts in the morning, poetry in the afternoon, and in the evening the mistress passed on the secrets of the *imbas forosnai* and the gift of prophecy. And she could not shake the vision of the future she brought with her. Bright as a newly lit lamp, she foresaw that Queen Medb had been scheming to steal the Brown Bull of Cooley. Sure, hadn't Fedelm spied the great horned beast himself on her way through Ulster? Grand, he was. Well-endowed, a real fine specimen that could service all the cows of Connacht, but hardly a nonesuch worthy of men's lives. Medb had mustered a great army for the raid, not only men from Connacht but mercenaries from Leinster and Munster as well. In her mind's eye, Fedelm saw them assembling for the incursion: legions of chariots, shields and spears and swords glittering in the sun, horses and men to the horizon, and at the front rode Queen Medb, battle-ready and out for blood.

A scout had brought word that the queen would like to meet this seer heading home. For her appointment with the royal army, Fedelm dressed in her finest clothes, her favorite tunic trimmed with the red embroidery, the dappled cloak fastened by the golden oakleaf broach, and the shoes with the matching gold buckles. Her charioteer had helped fix her hair: triple plaited with a knot on each side and a braid down her back, bouncing against her calves. Leaving her shield and sword in the chariot, Fedelm stroked the nose of a black stallion in the harness. *Don't be afraid*, she told herself. Medb was her queen, after all. Striding through camp, she cast a long shadow that rippled in the fires' flames. A fat guard led her past the soldiers, whom she refused to look upon, anxious to avoid the doomed men's stares.

A roaring fire kept the chill off the royal party. Even the queen's white mares drew close for the warmth. The horse on the right twitched in the harness, and the horse on the left scratched an itch with a raised hoof. Firelight sparkled in the chariot's gold trim. Flames glowed in Medb's ebony eyes. "They tell me your name is Fedelm and that you have been studying poetry in Scotland."

"On the Isle of Skye, m'lady, and I am on my way to my parents' home in Connemara in Your Majesty's province of Connacht."

"I am pleased to meet one of my people. And when we return from the triumph, you must say to me your poems. But tell me, Fedelm, what else did you acquire in your seasons over the sea? Have you the second sight to foretell the future?"

Apprehensive of the question to come, she nodded.

"Well then, prophetess, tell us: how easily may we take the Brown Bull of Cooley? Look into the future. How fares our grand army?"

Fedelm closed her eyes. Signs of the slaughter swirled in her imagination. She spoke from a trance: "Of your great army, I see crimson, I see red."

Medb laughed in her face. "Impossible. I have it on good authority that the armies of Ulster are afflicted with a sleeping spell, debilitated by an ancient curse. My spies inform me that every man of them is abed and unable to fight. Must we slaughter them in their dreamlands?"

Three times the queen asked the poet for a winning prophecy for the armies of Connacht, and three times, Fedelm replied, "I see crimson, I see red."

The loitering generals were perturbed by the mere sound of her voice and the unvarying refrain. Fuming at the girl's reticence, Medb raised a hand, determined to slap some sense into her. Instead, she spat into the fire. Through a shower of embers, Medb edged closer and whispered her question. "For my army, prophet, what lies ahead?"

"I see crimson, I see red." Fedelm opened her eyes. "I see a great warrior uncursed by the deep drowse upon his fellow Ulstermen. A blond, good-looking strap of a lad, with a fierce light in his eyes, a soldier who wears his wounds as easily as the belt across his broad chest. Seven gems sparkle in the black pools of his eyes. His teeth are sharp swords, and he is deadly handsome. A real beauty of a he-man in that red tunic, but do not mistake his delicate features, for he fights like a monster."

"Who is this paragon?" Medb asked. "What is his name?"

"I cannot say whether this is the one called Cúchulainn, the Hound of Ulster, but I know this: his every foe in battle will be stained red, and none can best the dire mankiller. I see a great open plain, the armies of Connacht and our brother kingdoms on one side awaiting this single Ulsterman on the other. He readies four swords in each hand. He carries the *gáe bolga*, a killing machine that springs with barbs once inside the chest of his enemy. I see his chariot rocket into the crowd, his red cloak waving like a flag, the man twisting and slashing terrible blows to your dear brothers and old fathers and beardless sons. Avoid him on the warpath, my queen, for he will sweep over you like a winter storm. There will be carnage in crimson and red."

King Ailill and the other leaders of men had gathered behind Medb, hanging on every word, though the lass was a mere girl. The queen drew her short sword from her girdle and threatened to stop the blasphemy.

"No one will be able to number the dead," Fedelm continued. "He will kill every man he faces, and others will flee like rats from a fire. Three thousand three hundred and fifty heads will be lopped off, and the bodies will be piled in a great mound for the ravens and vultures and dogs to violate. After the Cattle Raid on Cooley, women will keen for seven years and wander Ireland to bury their scattered dead beloved. They will curse your name forever. All due to this Ulsterman, this thunderbolt from hell."

"Enough, witch!" The queen was unaccustomed to this sort of address. "You say you have the second sight? Bah, one man to vanquish the army of Connacht? Why, my own seven sons have seven divisions each. Brave soldiers have joined us from the east and the south, not to mention a battalion of Ulster exiles. Surely, we can defeat a single Northerner with a ridiculous name. The blacksmith's hound, all bark and no bite. On your way, child. I will bring his head to you, and you can write a poem about his pretty lips and sparkly eyes. I will hear it when I lead the Brown Bull of Cooley by the nose to tup your father's cows. Go now, girl, you unsettle me."

After the war was over, those who survived limped back to Connacht with stories of crimson and red and the unholy tornado of the blacksmith's hound. Worse, they said, than all predictions. On the retreat from the Swineherd's Plain, as Medb stopped to wash her monthly blood in a stream, she was surprised by the man himself. Caught with her drawers down. That Cúchulainn spared her was seen by some as testament to his chivalry. But Fedelm had her doubts. She knew he was an incorrigible hound, and Medb an easy mark. Perhaps that's what doubled the queen's shame. She lost the bull and was spurned by the man. In the long years after the disaster, she would often confess her rue at failing to heed the prophetess and thereby spare many men the loss of their heads. And Fedelm regretted she could not persuade the queen.

Now the Connachtmen were after her.

The blind boy had warned Fedelm that a prophet is often without honor in her own land. The queen's men would have her life for not warning them more forcefully. *My fault? she thought. I could not make them listen.*

Just a girl, she was. A convenient scapegoat to be sacrificed for their failures.

The boards trembled, three sets of feet stomping on the walkway, the killers chasing her. Panic spurred her on.

A hundred yards ahead, the forest glowed with red, yellow, and gold leaves. But the thicket would be dark enough to hide her in its heart. She could lose the murderers if she could but outrun them one last stretch. A stroke of good fortune, she thought, for in two weeks' time, the cold days would be upon the west, and those trees would be November bare, no more protection than the bones of a skeleton. Luck, at last, was on her side.

Halfway on, she saw a shrouded figure step out of the woods and stop in the middle of the path. Clad in a long black robe cinched against the chilled air, an old woman waited silently. Hands hidden in her sleeves, she had the regal bearing of a queen or priestess, and for one brief second, Fedelm thought it might be her spiritual mentor, Scáthach, come across from the Isle of Skye. But as she raced closer, she noticed the woman was much older, a granny perhaps, or a mother awaiting her child's return with a welcoming smile.

Fedelm stopped directly in front of her, desperate for air. "Thank the gods," she said. "Will you help me?"

"What troubles are on you, child? Come closer and catch your breath."

Fedelm rested her arms on the old woman's shoulders. "Three men are following me. They mean to kill me."

The woman in black glanced at the landscape behind the girl. "Why, there's no one at all."

As soon as she looked back, Fedelm realized her mistake. Swift as a wolf, the old woman slipped the noose around her neck, planted a knee in the girl's back, and drew back to tighten the knot. Fedelm's hands clawed at the rope, and she tried to remember her martial arts moves, but her wits deserted her.

The assassins arrived, red-faced and angry. The largest and strongest, big as a hut, lifted a wooden cudgel and struck Fedelm in the head, knocking her to her knees. The second pulled the rope taut and looped it around Fedelm's wrists, so that with any movement of her head or hands, she would choke herself to death. The third man drew a knife from his belt and slit her throat. Fedelm's last thoughts flashed unbidden: the Brown Bull and the beautiful Cúchulainn. It was an absurd picture to carry to the grave.

The deed took mere moments. Her exit from the world came much more quickly than her entry. The fiends waited, splattered with blood, their weapons ready to strike should she stir. Convinced she was gone, one killer lowered his cudgel, and another dropped his knife. On her knees, the spry old woman leaned close to listen for another breath that never arrived. She rose and wiped the gore from her hands. With their daggers, the men cut two braided tresses for souvenirs. The executioners stood watch over the corpse until the villagers began to arrive.

Alone or in pairs, men and women and children old enough to walk assembled at the deadly spot to bear witness to the sacrifice. The curious were followed by the fearful, but no one dared venture too close to their kinswoman, none being willing to catch the roving spirit of the newly murdered. The woman in black drew the hood around her face as a cold mist drizzled and dotted her cloak like wet diamonds. She spoke softly to her conspirators, and with a nod of thanks to the crowd, she retreated into the dark woods. The people watched the old woman go with a kind of reverence stirring in their hearts. They saw through her disguise.

The three despatchers lifted the body and led a procession onto the soft ground of the bog. They knew precisely where to deposit her and waded into a reedy marsh till the waters rose to their chests and drenched the burden in their arms. The tallest of them shoved the body to the bottom of a black pond, barely keeping his whiskers above the waterline. From the boardwalk, a woman handed over sharpened V-shaped willow stakes. Two men took a deep breath and ducked underwater to pin Fedelm in place. Soaked to the skin, the killers had to be helped out of the mire. They smelled of shame and sulfur. A chant began to slowly circulate through the crowd, a soft and sad song to mark the occasion. Bubbles broke the dark surface of the pond. No one dared leave, but then an icy rain began to fall in earnest. Over the next hour, the crowd thinned to a handful of witnesses, making sure the deed was truly done. At last, only a pair of boys remained, the blind lad and his brother.

"Let's hope she can't swim," said the brother, and he laughed as the rain hardened to sleet.

5

The Empty Grave

CAKED WITH DRIED mud, his trousers nearly stood upright where he tossed them in the corner. Burke remembered a story by Dr. Seuss that his granddaughter used to love hearing when she was a little girl, about a pair of pale-green pants. He couldn't remember the title, but she liked to call it "The Pants With Nobody Inside Them." A little fella (a sort of talking bear, was it?) meets up with a pair of bewitched empty trousers running all by themselves across the fields and into the woods, and the lad follows them hither and yon. There's a bicycle chase and so on, all deliciously thrilling to a six-year-old. Seems these britches are as afraid of us as we are of them. A gas tale, and Mary Catherine squealed at each page and drawing, laughing at those pants who had a life of their own.

"Stay where you are," he admonished his dirty trousers, and he trudged to the shower. As he washed and changed, Burke thought back to the girl in the bog, who had once had a life of her own. As he ate a bit of cold stew for his tea, he imagined her all alone, disturbed from her rest, probably as afraid of the two men handling her as they had been unnerved by her. Mullaney did not mind as much, but he had always been an enigma of sorts, the kind who never gives more than a hint of himself. We all have a kind of buried life that we hide from one another, but Mullaney had catacombs in his heart.

Burke studied the clock and counted the hours before they were to meet for drinks to discuss how to handle their discovery. Time enough, he decided, to have another look-see, check in on the girl to make sure she was tidily covered for the night. Poor dear out on the lonesome.

At half six he set off. No sign of life at Mullaney's: shades drawn, probably having a wee nap before their appointment at the pub. Burke watched the windows in case they might blink, and then continued west to the bogs, his pipe smoking like a steam locomotive. The grass was already bone dry along the center hump of the lane, ideal conditions for airing out the turf bricks. Beneath the passing shadows of a few stray clouds, Burke considered himself most fortunate to be from such a place of green beauty and desolation.

At the rise in the road, the plain revealed itself anew. Little pools seeping through the sparse vegetation. Quagmires disguised as solid ground. Ditches healing scars where the turf had been cut generations ago. He loved the familiar landscape. Home, he thought, as much a part of his identity as the buried girl's. Tomorrow the place would be flooded with curiosity-seekers from the four corners of the nation joining the plain folk of the parish. Nothing grander had happened here in his lifetime. He and Mullaney would be famous, after a fashion, their names engraved on a brass plaque on the museum wall in faraway Dublin. Reporters clamoring for a word. His face on the telly. The pair of them forever linked to the discovery of the Connemara Girl. Puffing mightily on his pipe, he chugged quickly to the gravesite.

But the corpse had vanished. Nothing but a girl-shaped nothing. No ancient bog body, only signs of absence. The mark of the sleán hard against the banked peat. The earth chewed away by a toothed beast. Bootprints in the damp soil. A path of flattened vegetation, as if something had dragged away the body. He lingered at the empty hole, like the hole in his heart, hole in his head, draining his hopes and filling him again with a blankness. He poked for clues around the lip of the dig, wondering if perhaps they had misplaced her. But no, someone had absconded with the body. Or had she risen from the dead and scrammed, like the pants with nobody inside? Dark questions crossed his mind: Should they not have unlocked the door between this world and the other? Who knows what trouble waltzes in? Where the hell is she?

Dumbfounded, he did not notice the invaders till they were upon him: two Draught horses, one gray and one black, clopped over the rise, carrying on their backs the three witches, their red hair blazing in the slant light. Mary Catherine rode the darker stallion and her two uncanny friends the gray. The conflagration atop their heads unsettled him. His granddaughter on her own was ginger enough, but add two besides, and the sky seemed afire.

For the life of him, he could never remember which was Siobhán and which was Eileen. The young lasses had changed considerably over the past year or two, transitioning from plain schoolgirls to lovely young women. The joke around town was that not even their mothers could tell them apart. As they slid off the steaming flanks of the beasts, the girls with their bright redness and fair freckled skin seemed more like sisters than best friends. Perhaps there was something to this witch business after all. He guessed immediately that Mary Catherine had betrayed his confidence.

"Ladies," he said, bowing at the waist.

"What are you doing here?" his granddaughter asked.

"I might ask you the same, missy. We'll have a word later, won't we, about the meaning of *top secret*."

One horse blubbered a wet sneeze. The hags walked right past Burke as if he weren't even there, curious to see what he was guarding. Siobhán and Eileen perched on the edge like a pair of cats looking over an empty nest. This bird had flown.

"There's nothing there," Siobhán said. "A great big nothing."

Emcee hopped into the hole, picking through bricks of turf. The faint smell of sulfur, kicked up by their explorations, rose from the spot. The victim had fled the scene of the crime. Without a corpse, was there even a death?

"She's buggered off," Eileen said.

"Where is the bog body, then, Pops?"

"I do not know. Believe me, I am as flabbergasted as you. We were digging the whole day through." He fished his phone from his pocket and swiped through to his messages. "I sent you them snaps. You sent back three exclamation points and a wee happy face."

"We seen those pics, but where's the girl herself? Did she run off, like?" Siobhán asked. "No proof, and no pudding."

"Me and Mullaney decided to cover her up, like. So as no wild creatures prowling in the night come across her and scavenge our work. You don't suppose some boyos were watching the whole time, making a play to steal her and win the glory? You see what I seen when I got here after me tea. No body."

"Bloody hoax," Eileen said.

"No, lass, I assure you she was realer than yourself. Did you not have a close inspection of them jpegs?"

The conspirators kept a reply to themselves.

"Whose is this land?" Siobhán asked. "You are not supposed to be digging up the peat. It's one of the best natural absorbers of all the carbon in the atmosphere. It's bad as chopping down the rain forests. Or do you not care about destroying the planet altogether?"

"It's Mullaney's fields, if you can call it so. He's the only one for miles still cutting turf for next winter's cold. I have told him about leaving things alone till I was blue in the face, but he's a man of long tradition, that one. *The old ways is best.* I had no part in it. I was minding me own business till his collie come pestering my ewes. I chased that dog till I come across Mullaney hisself, up to his oxters in the raw earth. Had the girl half-excavated."

"Tradition, my arse." Eileen swiped a smear of wet earth from her left cheekbone. "And why did the two of yis not consult the proper authorities? Anyone else would bring in the Gardaí straight off. Have DCI Vera take a look for clues."

"That is another complete conundrum. We talked it over, but he had a change of mind, you see. Been a quare old lonesome bird ever since his wife went over to England for the divorce, and the one and only daughter emigrated to America, nary a word nor Christmas card. I was all for the proper authorities, but he was insistent that her honest countrymen dig up the creature themselves, and by the time we were finished, it was too late to make the evening news. Best save her for the sunshine. What's one more day when you're dead?"

The gray horse nickered and nodded its great head.

"Come morning, this whole place will be a no-man's-land, and any chance for a close look at the dead girl will be out of the question. That's why I sent you the text, Mary Catherine, so you could have a gander before the gossips spread and caused conniptions around the parish. Or before you saw the dead girl in the newspaper or on the whaddyacallit on your phone. But I see you let the cat outta the bag with these two, when I distinctly said to tell no one at all." He tried to glare at her but found it impossible to keep feigning anger. Mary Catherine was a rip, all right, and he could not stay mad for long at such an audacious girl.

"Pops, I only shared them photos with my best friends. But now you have me looking like a right goose, not a body to be found."

"Well, don't let bad news stew. Let's go straight to the horse's front teeth, in a manner of speaking. Mullaney should know she's gone missing. And he might know the whyfor."

Burke hitched his trousers and began walking down the lane with his granddaughter. Leading the two giant horses by the reins, the other hags followed in single file. A few black-faced sheep hung about the lane, staring and chewing, watching the strange procession. The farm had changed little since Michael took it over from his father, the old Mullaney. A new iron cattle guard, fresh whitewash on the stone house and the little shed behind, but otherwise the land was slowly sinking in neglect. Not a crop in ages, not even a vegetable patch. A ramshackle fieldstone wall blocked off the end of the driveway from the shore of a small lake. Nearby, a wee rowboat lay keel up against the incessant months of rain. From behind a wooden gate, Bonnie loped out to greet them, barking at the indifferent horses and circling the ginger girls, breaking the eventide stillness as Siobhán and Eileen tied the reins to the gatepost.

When a polite knock at the door produced no answer, Burke gave it a mighty pounding. Emcee strayed around the far corner but found not a soul out in the yard. The place seemed deserted, though a single table lamp shone through a back window. Burke tried the doorknob, and the party spilled into the front room, nervous as a flock of sparrows. Stray patches of sun lit the kitchen and a pair of filthy wet boots stood by the door. Keys to the lorry rested on the table next to piles of newspapers and old bills. Mullaney's damp jumper hung from a hook. A bachelor's idea of cleanliness ruled the roost. Tidy-looking at first glance, but puffs of dog hair lurked beneath the sofa, the ash of several fires powdered the hearth, and a thick layer of dust fuzzed every surface.

Treading heavily on the lino, Burke twice called for Mullaney before opening the bedroom door. "You have visitors, Michael. Are you decent, man?"

Curled like a baby in his crib, Mullaney was still dressed in his mucky clothes, lying atop the quilt and blankets. He did not move a muscle.

"Is he feckin' dead?" Eileen asked.

Burke shoved at the hump of his hip. "Rise and shine."

"Dead drunk," Siobhán said.

"Merely done in," Burke said. "Worn out entirely from a hard day's labor, but sweet baby Jesus, the stink rising off him. Get up, you wallowing pig."

The lump in the bed muttered and stirred. Batting his eyelids, Mullaney woke slowly from deep sleep. The strangers in his room did not seem to startle him, as he moved his gaze from face to face to register their presence before landing on the familiar mug of his old friend Burke. Bone weary, he struggled to his elbows, leaving behind an imprint like the Shroud of Turin. A watery cough escaped his mouth.

"Tommy," he said, and then cleared his throat. "Girls. I seem to have dozed off in my clothes. Give me a chance to clean up a bit. The kettle's full, tea in the cupboard."

"Have you been asleep this whole time we got back from the turf?" Burke asked. "In such a disgraceful condition."

"Fell over dead."

"Them sheets and blankets will need a good wash."

"So I see. Be right with you, Tommy, and your harem of gingers."

"My granddaughter and her coven."

"*Gabh mo leithscéal*, girls," Mullaney apologized. "Caught me at an inconvenient moment."

"Make yourself presentable, but be quick about it. We have a job on." Burke escorted the hags into the kitchen.

Mullaney peeled off his rancid clothes and stepped into the shower. Half of Connemara, the water black with peat, filtered through the drain. All the while he hoped they might be gone by the time he dressed. A job on? A coven? Burke showing up early was never a good sign. And the Ginger Sisters were always unnerving when he chanced upon them in the village.

They were waiting for him in the parlor, even the dirty dog Bonnie at Burke's feet. The strange girls chatted amiably over tea and biscuits, their young fresh faces expectant.

Best he could, Mullaney offered a smile. "Sorry for the mess. What brought you here?"

"It's alive! You clean up nicely, Michael."

He raised his chin at the girls. "Do yis always go about together?"

"My understanding is that they're some sort of club," Burke said. "The Red Hags."

"Like-minded souls hang together," Emcee said.

A cup was poured for their host, and they all stared at him, anticipating an explanation, but Mullaney sipped at his tea and offered not a word. They were playing conversational Russian roulette.

"The girl in the bog," Siobhán said finally. "We are here about the witch you found."

Mullaney glared at Burke. "I thought you agreed not to tell anyone about her."

"Honest, I only texted Mary Catherine. And despite my very clear instructions, she blabbed to these two. They're good girls and have kept mum, haven't you?"

Not a peep from the three of them.

"Anyway, it's not like Sky News is sending a helicopter over the valley. I merely wanted to give my granddaughter a close look before all the fuss in the morning. But it turns out it didn't matter a damn. She's gone, Mick. Left an empty hole in the ground."

"What do you mean, gone?"

"We were out there not a minute ago and saw the empty tomb for ourselves. Thought I was hallucinating, but not a twig of her, as if she had never been there at all. What do you say about that?"

"Gone, is she?" Mullaney added a lash of milk to his tea and drained the mug before answering. "That I do not know. It's a mystery to myself as well."

"Is that all you have to say for yourself? You know nothing?"

"I'll tell you three times if you like and deny it thrice. I have no idea what you are talking about. She was there when we left her."

Disbelief circulated like crackled lightning through the room, but no one had the courage to challenge his veracity. They were a long time speculating over what might have happened, who might have chanced upon the bleak and deserted gravesite. Who would have stumbled across the location in those few hours since the men had left her? The odds hovered near zero. In the end, every explanation was as puzzling as the original mystery of the girl. Here and gone. Dead but alive enough to walk away, like the pale-green pants with nobody inside them.

"Maybe she'll show up later," Eileen said. "Come knocking at your door after a stretch of the legs. Speaking of which, we best get going. The hour is late, and those horses should be home for the night."

"Horses?" Mullaney raised an eyebrow.

"The horses what we rode in on," Eileen said. "From my parents' place. The old wauns don't like us riding after dark."

"I see. Well, I'm sorry to have disappointed you, and I promise when we find her, if we find her, you'll be the first to know."

They walked out to the yard, where the tethered pair munched on the grass growing at the edge of the shed wall. The horses wagged their ears and huffed at the girls, as if they had a bit of gossip to share. Keeping himself between the shed and the horses, Mullaney smiled at the animals. "Lovely specimen of the horse."

"The gray is Macha, and the black is Sainglend. Crosses between the Irish Draught and the Irish Sport," Eileen said. "Strong and swift. Anything bigger and we'd need a ladder to climb to the saddle."

"Aren't you the fine ones." He stroked the muzzle of the gray, and the beast showed his long teeth. The black one shook his mane.

When the girls tried to mount, the flustered horses pawed at the ground and rocked unsteadily, disturbed to be leaving. Eileen cupped Macha's left ear in her hand and whispered soothing words. *Steady on.* The beasts cantered sideways and then allowed themselves to be mounted. She flicked the reins, and off they trotted, leaving Burke and Mullaney squabbling like an old married couple.

* * *

Agitation twitched in the horses' muscles. The riders had to spur them on away from the farm, but the animals kept pulling on the reins, fiddling with the bits in their jaws, protesting to go back. It took a forceful hand to keep them from being spooked. Macha and Sainglend eased into a measured stride, guided side by side so the riders might more easily talk. Mullaney's farm receded in the distance, and they followed an old trail through a meadow, startling the flying insects in the summer air. When they were safely out of earshot, they felt free to test their theories.

"That fecker is hiding something," Eileen said.

"Did you see the face on him when my grandpa said the girl was gone?" Emcee asked. "Guilty as a babby with his wee mitt stuck in the sweetie jar."

From the black horse, Eileen nodded. "That Mullaney fella took her. And hid her somewheres else, so your old pops wouldn't be snooping about, disturbing things."

Siobhán pressed closer and laid her head against Emcee's neck. "Or the both of them together are up to no good. Can't be trusted. I say we take matters into our own hands. After we put these horses away, we come back after dark. Unless he stashed her under his bed, there's only so many places to hide a body on the farm. We'll find her, even if we have to dig her up again ourselves."

6

The American

A GRANDFATHER IS ONLY as good as his stories.

Not quite eight years old, Bridget Scanlon slid her glasses to the bridge of her nose and pinned them with one finger as she waited for her grandfather to begin. She made a tent of her nightgown, tightening the fabric over the hump of her knees and pegging the hem with her toes. Her grandfather read to her, stretched out beside her on the bed, sharing the pictures when they appeared. Or if he had no book, he simply told a tale from memory, stories drawn from the well of his own childhood in Ireland, sixty years or more since he left for Philadelphia.

Every night, he filled her head with wonderful nonsense. Fairies and leprechauns and banshees when she was just a tyke. Later the long stories of the Children of Lir, turned into swans. Or the exploits of the giant Fionn mac Cumhaill, who sucked his thumb whenever he needed wisdom and who built the Giant's Causeway as stepping stones to Scotland. Her grandfather spent a week recounting the battle of Cúchulainn, the Hound of Ulster, versus Queen Medb of Connacht, who coveted a prize bull. A war between a great hero and an equally ferocious queen.

Bridget's favorite was a story about a mysterious island off the western coast where people take their dead but do not bury them. There they remain for all time as they were in life. "You can go and see them, if you dare," her grandfather said. "I once paid a visit. Rows of my long-gone ancestors were arranged neatly in the grassy sod, their faces turned to the western sun, working on their tans. A gentle breeze, sweet with salt air, ruffled their hair and collars."

"Weren't you scared?" Bridget asked.

"I was not," he said. "Not at first, anyways. It was peaceful-like, searching for my grandfather among the restful people. At last, I found him, right down to the pipe tucked in his pocket, just as I had seen him seven years before. His face and hands were brown as walnuts, and he looked more relaxed than ever. 'You look grand,' I joked. 'Death becomes you.' Didn't his eyes pop right open with a start, as if he had an urgent bit of wisdom to share about the meaning of life. 'I will tell you a curiosity,' he says. 'There's not a mouse to be found on this island. Go on, search high and low. Mice do be driven mad if they set one foot upon the soil. If you try to sneak in a mouse hidden in your pocket, it will hop out and scurry to the nearest cliff to throw itself into the deep, blue sea.'"

At a good stopping point, he folded his hands over his belly or closed the book, a signal for a kiss on his cheek and time for bed.

Sometimes Bridget could hear her parents clucking at her grandfather.

"I wish you wouldn't encourage her," her mother said. "I'm going to be the one she'll call for when the nightmares come."

From the living room, her father's voice rose like smoke. "You and your fairy tales, Dad. She has her head in the clouds as it is."

Bridget stretched out perfectly straight beneath the sheet, crossed her arms over her chest, and pretended to be dead. She would not have been scared to talk to her ancestors on the island with no mice. Dead men would have great stories to tell.

She had always been a morbid child. She used to dress her dollies in their finest clothes and then bury them under her pillows. Pet goldfish were dispatched in solemn ceremonies at the toilet. Any bird or small animal that had passed away was given full honors in a shoebox and laid to rest beneath the red maple trees in the backyard. She liked to pretend she had been shot and left for dead on the morning school bus, till the driver bawled her out. She loved Wednesday Addams and Edward Gorey's *Gashlycrumb Tinies*. She kept a list of favorite cemeteries, riding the train into Philadelphia to have a chat with the bones of Ben Franklin or stride through the gravestones at Laurel Hill. On a dare one Halloween, she broke into the deserted Mount Vernon Cemetery, full of tangled brush and neglected graves, and a Philly police car passed by and its headlights gave her a delicious scare.

But most of all she loved the dead at the Mütter Museum tucked inside the graceful College of Physicians near the city center. She had been all of ten, jumping out of her skin and awhirl with questions, when her grandfather first took her there on the subway. "You might be a little scared," he said. "But not to worry. Nothing is going to spring to life and get you." Hand in hand they walked through the doors, and the main gallery thrilled her with its strange antiquarian beauty, the bright glass and dark burnished cabinets packed with old medical instruments and, best of all, anatomical specimens and models. On the train ride home, Bridget told her grandfather, "I could live there."

She haunted the Mütter for years. The staff loved the weird girl in glasses so much that they offered her a job as a part-time docent when she was in high school. Her favorite task was to shepherd school groups through the oddities and watch the children's reactions to the collection of 139 human skulls arranged in a floor-to-ceiling glass case. Most of the kids would cringe at the sight. A few sensitive souls might be frightened to tears, and once a little red-haired boy fainted straightaway. But there was always a small group, her people, who loved to study the bony faces as much as she did. Eleven-year-old boys were the ideal patrons, but she was never happier than when she met a young sister of the macabre. She regaled them with microscope slides stained with bits of Einstein's brain and shocked them with the plaster cast of Chang and Eng, the famous Siamese twins. By the end of the tour, nearly every child was brave enough to take a photo next to the skeleton of the Mütter American Giant, all seven and a half feet. Only the most intrepid, however, would follow Bridget to the Soap Lady.

"She's not really made of soap," she explained. "But her skin is covered by a greasy substance called adipocere caused by hydrogenation of the tissue fats. A kind of 'grave wax' can form when the circumstances are right. It sure looks like soap."

Even the bravest were duly grossed out. One of the children was bound to peer closely at the mummified corpse and ask why her mouth hung open.

"She's been waiting to get in the bathtub for two hundred years."

The Mütter was a second home in Bridget's teen years. It wasn't so much the allure of the dead; she was fascinated by the past held in their bones. The bodies told a story of who they were, how they looked and loved, cared for their children, fought their wars, and raised their questions to their gods. In her senior year of high school, Bridget announced to her folks that she wanted to become a mortician. Many a teary conversation ended in a stalemate over this proposition, though parents often indulge their only child's dreams, no matter how odd they might find them. *Why don't you go into something more suitable?* History is all about the past. Or how about working in a museum like the Mütter after you graduate? What sort of degree would you need for that? Or: you will love college, and the chance to meet other people. *Living people.*

So that was how she fell into archaeology. A junior semester abroad at Trinity College in Dublin doing fieldwork put her even deeper under the enchantment of Ireland. The good fortune of her grandfather's Irish passport enabled her to get one of her own and later secure a graduate degree and a junior post at University College Dublin, where she could teach others to fall in love with the dead. Late one spring afternoon, she was lecturing to a class of a dozen first-years, running through a slide show of some of her favorite people. On the projection screen was a picture of a body found preserved in a peat bog.

"The Tollund Man. Discovered in the spring of 1950 by two brothers in Denmark who had been cutting turf. You will notice the noose around his neck. Hanged, I'm afraid, as the X-rays later confirmed. At first, the local police thought he might have been recently murdered and dumped in a shallow grave, but the poor chap was killed in the fourth century BCE." Dr. Scanlon nodded at her unseen graduate assistant. "Next slide."

A desiccated fellow with a deeply tanned skin and red hair, his head weirdly angled, and a grimace on his face. "The Grauballe Man. Looks peaceful, doesn't he? Another young Danish man. A pair of assailants killed him. One man gave him a knock to the back of the head so the other man could cut his exposed throat."

The greatest hits of bog bodies quickly followed: the Windeby Child, the half-torso of the Lindow Man. The Huldremose Woman and her severed arm. Red Franz of Lower Saxony, a red flame of hair still attached to the skull. Queen Gunhild, the Girl of the Uchter Moor, the Yde Girl strangled with her own belt. And Ireland's own Clonycavan Man and Gallagh Man. She wished that just one of them could talk to her and share the secrets of the grave.

A young man in the front row cleared his throat. "How do they not rot to dust like the rest of us?"

"The secret is the bogs," Bridget said with a smile. "Peat acts like a preservative. Sphagnum moss is one of the few plants that flourish in such wet and cold conditions as we have across northern Europe, and its life cycle is responsible for the slow formation of the bogs and their capacity to preserve the bodies hidden there. As one layer of plant growth dies off and decays, it reacts with the bacteria in any freshly dead organic matter—a body, for example—to prevent ordinary decomposition. The chemicals turn soft tissue rubbery and give the skin that deep-bronze hue and redden the fair hair. For hundreds and thousands of years, imagine, they are perfectly unspoiled and buried layer by layer by the moss.

"Marvelous stuff, moors, bogs and fens, the wasteland. For centuries, farmers and whole governments have sought to drain these 'dangerous' wet places and convert them to useful land. *Don't venture out on the moors. Tread not in the Dead Marshes.* Turns out, ladies and gentlemen, they store twice as much carbon as all the earth's forests combined. That's why places here in Ireland and abroad are now preserving the peatlands. No more mass harvesting of turf. Save the bogs, save the planet! Not only that, you will save these poor bog bodies from being chewed up by machinery. We must remember to save the dead."

From the back of the class, her teaching assistant was frantically pointing to an imaginary watch on her wrist.

"Ah, time, ladies and gentlemen," Bridget said. "Papers in by Friday. Final examinations are right around the corner." The undergraduates moaned and shuffled off, leaving her alone in the lecture hall. She packed up her notes and checked her phone.

Without the *#bogbody* hashtag, she would not have known about the Connemara Girl. Usually, the tag was from some Goth trying out Halloween makeup. Once there was a link to a photo of a preserved rhino dug up in Poland. Occasionally a post from a far-flung colleague on some new discovery or call for papers for a professional conference. But most days there was nothing at all, and Bridget often forgot about looking for bodies in the flotsam and jetsam of information that rides the daily flood. The message was another blip in a remote corner of the internet, invisible unless one was deliberately searching for such things. "Connemara Girl" followed by brief and mysterious tags. *#bogbody, #pops*. Four "likes," if such a count could be believed. Posted by someone who called herself the Red Witch of the West. Three dark images the size of postage stamps appeared on the screen. Bridget laid down her cell phone and clicked on her laptop to get a better look.

Could be, but doubtful, she told herself, remembering her undergraduate days at Penn and lectures on the great archaeological fakes. The Piltdown Man. The Cardiff Giant.

The Ossuary of James, brother of Jesus. Or the local wrecks that turned out to be false trails. And people got excited over bits and shards, hoping they had found valuable treasures. Arrowheads, animal bones, and bric-a-brac from the last century. She had been to Connemara once, as a junior member of a dig team sent by the government Turf Board when a tractor driver noticed an arm sticking up from a boggy field he had rolled over. The arm, black as a tire, was unfortunately all that survived the blades of the mechanical reaper. When the lab analyzed the specimen, they determined that it could be dated to the late Bronze Age. More's the pity, the rest of the fellow had been chopped to bits by the turf cutter, with not enough pieces to put the puzzle back together.

Certainly the past seven years in Ireland, Bridget had been waiting for some dead thing to dig up. Some fieldwork to take her out of the classroom and get her hands dirty. So far, the finds had been entrusted to the stewardship of the senior archaeologists at UCD and the National Museum. Only fair, given this was their land, not hers. There were other long-term digs out on Achill, the *Brú na Bóinne* at Newgrange, the caves at Rathcroghan, but she dreamed of a discovery all her own.

Could be, she told herself after staring at the pictures. The first shot was a selfie, an old codger proud of his work. The dig appeared to be the work of an old-fashioned spade-man, the marks in the earth consistent with a hand-drawn sleán. Whoever this digger was, he had been careful in the exhumation. The second image seemed more lifelike, a young woman curled like a sleeping child, but it was the third image, a closeup of her face and hands, the brooch, the girl's terrible wounds, that looked real, not staged. Still, Bridget had her reservations. Might be another practical joke, an elaborate dummy. Her first year on the job, a group of students in Dublin insisted they had discovered the remnants of a Viking village at a construction site, but it turned out to be a hoax. The tip of a horned helmet was from a bull in an organic farm off the M1 towards Drogheda. The clay cups had been turned by a potter in Dalkey, and a bronze medallion buried in the dirt was nothing more than a fake coin bought off a Romanian counterfeiter down by the quays. The Irish, she had found, were quite subversive. Some merry pranksters with nothing to do in the West might have rigged this Connemara Girl. A kind of mocking fiction for the gullible. Cogging the Yank. But why would the Red Witch make such a meager effort to spread the news?

She scrolled to the posting again and gave it a simple red heart. Arrowed to the Red Witch's profile to have a look at her history. Bits and bobs of folklore and the occult, standard stuff among a certain crowd, and further back in the witch's life, more photographs of the western countryside. Two youngsters in a foggy cemetery. A video clip of a youth choir singing a rousing "*Sláinte na nÉanach*" for local friends and family. And picture after picture of three redheaded girls as they grew from toddlers to teenagers. Several shots of a madly decorated room—an attic, judging by the light and slanted ceiling—the walls covered in art and graffiti. One beautiful panorama on a windswept beach with two massive horses. A pinned recipe for a lemon-based potion to rid yourself of unwanted freckles. Perhaps the Red Witch was one of the three recurring teenagers. Perhaps her friends were witches too, curious about the other side of reality. Much as Bridget had been at the same age back in Philadelphia, looking for some magic, drawn to the myth and romance of the past.

The Red Witch of the West had been circumspect about her true identity. Not much in her bio to peg the real person.

Age: Older than the hills
Lives in: A hut in the Wild West
Interests: Hexes, myth, cake

Nevertheless, Bridget elected to follow her posts and sent a direct message about the girl in the bog. Loved these photos. Is she real? Where did you find her? I am an archaeologist in Dublin and would love to hear more about your discovery. Can meet you anytime.

She called a friend in the IT department and invited him for drinks, knowing he would not refuse. Plied with a tall tale and a pint of stout, he was able to pinpoint from the metadata that the images of the farmer and the body were from a speck of a village in Connemara.

"I thought as much. Can you get me any closer?" she asked.

"Would be like trying to find a needle in a haystack in a field of haystacks surrounded by a lot of other fields," he said. "With their own haystacks. Each with a needle."

"How about this mug?" She toggled back to the farmer's selfie.

"Old Joe Murphy," he said. "The chancer."

She wasn't sure if he was having her on. "You know him?"

"No, sure, one culchie looks like another. Needle in a haystack, Brid. But a needle has a sharp point, easy enough to find, if you don't mind pricking your thumbs."

Her phone vibrated against the wooden bar.

The Red Witch had an answer for her: You better hurry. Try the Crúchaun Inn if you're coming tonight. The bog body will be revealed early in the morning! Last chance!

The message tortured her. Could be, might well be, she could not make up her mind.

"Bad news?"

"No, it's the girl who posted the photos. I can't decide if the whole thing is a joke or if it's real. She wants me to drop everything and come out there tonight. Says it is my last chance to see a corpse they dug up before anyone else. None of it seems real to me. It's like one of those leg-pulling stories my grandfather used to tell when I was a child. Gods and monsters and islands that drive mice crazy. You never could tell when he was having us on. Probably a wild-goose chase, don't you think?"

"Anything is possible in the Wild West," he said. "Besides, never miss a last chance."

The adrenaline leapt into her like a surprised hare. *Go,* said the little girl inside her, *go now.* She pushed her glasses up the bridge of her nose, drained her pint, and left her friend with an unexplained goodbye. On her way to her car, she dashed off a message to her teaching assistant to cancel classes for the next day. If she hurried, Bridget could make Connemara at a decent hour.

Cat Burglars

S UMMER NIGHTS FALL slowly in the West. At ten o'clock,
the violet sky threw a ghostly light. Downstairs the telly
blared from the sitting room, the last fading hour before her
parents would go to bed. Siobhán had made her good-nights,
gone upstairs to her room, and turned off the lamps, waiting for her eyes to grow accustomed to the dark. Quiet as a
cat, she padded softly across the floor and shimmied through
the open window to the small roof above the garage. With
a practiced swing of her legs, she lowered her body till she
was hanging by her fingertips from the edge and let go with
an *oof.* Her parents had never heard her slip away before, but
she was alert to the slightest noise from within the house.
Shrouding her red mop beneath a black hood, she moved like
a silhouette against the night sky.

Emcee's mother was on the night shift at the Inn, leaving
her father in charge of their three children. He'd readily
believed Emcee when she told him she was spending the
night at Eileen's, and Eileen had said she was staying with
Siobhán, an elaborate game of musical sleepovers they played

because Mr. Burke was not likely to speak to Mrs. Flaherty, who would not dream of bothering Mrs. Magill after eight in the evening. The parents would swallow almost any scenario.

As arranged, the witches rendezvoused at the crossroads on the village's western edge. Very few people were about at that hour on a weeknight. Tourist season was a ways off, and while the spring had been warm and pleasant, most folks were still indoors bingeing and streaming or going about the ordinary business of the quiet life. A few hardy and feckless regulars were down the pubs, so nobody noticed the three witches huddled around a tiny cellphone screen. The close-up of the bog girl glowed like a candle in the pitch dark.

"She's beautiful, isn't she?" Siobhán said. "In her own way, dead like. Good bone structure. Sweet about her face. Who would have done her in so brutally?"

"Vicious bastards." Eileen grabbed the phone to have a closer look. "They really wanted to be sure she would never get up. Strangled with a hangman's rope, slit her windpipe, and tossed her in the bog. The crops gone bad or some such, and she paid for the hunger with her life. Ritual sacrifice to the gods."

"The virgin offering," Emcee said. "It's always the virgins. There's no use saving it."

"I still say she was murdered for her beauty," Siobhán said. "Drove half the men wild and was punished for it. The other woman found in the arms of the cheating husband by a jealous wife."

"That's a juicier story," Emcee said. "Better than a virgin's lot."

"Did Mullaney run off with her, d'ye think?" Eileen asked. "He's an odd one. Wouldn't put it past him. Going mad out there without a soul's company, save that dog."

"And the odd sheep or two," Emcee said.

"Lights off, you hags," Siobhán said. "We have a body to find."

The witches kept to the ditches in case a motorist or bicyclist happened along. At the old miller's, they crossed the Rubicon of a small, winding stream and reached open ground, taking care to avoid a cow pasture, slinking alongside the stone fences like black cats on the prowl. Communicating through signals and gestures, they stayed close and kept quiet. Siobhán, who led the way, stopped and held up a hand.

"The Good People," she whispered.

Barely discernible in the moonlight, a fairy ring encircled a hawthorn tree.

"You don't believe in that shite, do you?" Emcee said.

"We'll go around. To be safe, like."

"Afraid of being kidnapped, are you? And made to dance till your feet drop off?"

"Don't say it, Emcee. They're always listening."

"*An síoga.* The fairies coming to get you, boogidy, boogidy."

"Why, I oughta pound you—"

Eileen inserted herself between the pair. "That's enough." Flipping on the flashlight app, she traced the arc of stones and mushrooms. "You do what you like. No use tempting fate." Taking Siobhán by the hand, she followed the light, while Emcee stomped straight through the center.

"If I meet any leprechauns, I'll be sure to ask after a pot of gold for yis."

Attracted by the blue light off her phone, a swarm of gnats and midges went mad for the girls' eyes and ears, and a ghostly brown moth fluttered by, tapping at the screen and banging into the hags one by one.

"Dousen that mobile, would you," Emcee hissed, a bug in her left nostril. "There's your feckin' fairies, and I'm being dive-bombed by Mothra over here."

With only the stars to guide them, they footed through the darkness, slowing their pace when the small triangle of Mullaney's peaked rooftop came into view from the road. A faint halo shone above the house. They paused before any further trespass. Nobody wanted to go first.

"The lights are on," Eileen said. "What if he's home?"

"No, he's down the pub with my grandfather," Emcee said. "They'll be there all hours over the Guinness. Pops will pry the truth out of Mullaney if it's the last thing he does."

"What if the doors are locked?" Eileen asked. "Suppose he has the body hid inside?"

"Nobody locks their doors around here," Siobhán said. "Sure, aren't we good country people? When we were here earlier, did you notice that wee rowboat upside down by the lake? I say he has stashed the body under there. Remember how spooked the horses were? Like they could sense the dead nearby."

"What if she's not here at all?" Eileen asked. "What if he simply moved her to another hole on the bog?"

"Or maybe he's telling the truth," Emcee said. "Suppose someone else came along and dragged her off? Did you ever see that film *Young Frankenstein*, where the graverobbers come to dig up enough parts to make a monster and the doctor's servant drops the jar with the genius brain and substitutes the one tagged ABBY NORMAL? They sew the brain in the head anyways and zap it with a grand dose of electricity from the thunderstorm."

"It's alive!" said Eileen. "Poor feckin' monster, didn't know what to do with himself."

"It would have worked if they only had the right brain," said Emcee. "Didn't the ancient people have the power to bring back the dead to life? I read that a killed weasel can be made alive again by the cry of its mother, and lions resuscitate their dead whelps by breathing upon them. Wasn't there a spell for this sort of thing, the ashes of the phoenix or the skin of a snake? Maybe some druid came along and claimed the girl in the bog for his own."

Siobhán rolled her eyes. "There's not some mad scientist in Connemara trying to reanimate the dead. And what would be the sense of simply putting her in another hole? Never mind the fact that he would have to dig an entirely new grave. I say she's hidden about the place. If he was so concerned about graverobbers or wild animals scavenging the body, where else would he put her but in the safety of his home?"

From her side pocket, Emcee pulled out a small flask. "A drop of courage, ladies?"

Each took a swig before climbing the dark lane to Mullaney's front gate. From the two front windows and the gaping-wide front door, bright light glistened. Insects loitered in the entrance. The Red Witches waited for some sign of life, but the place seemed as deserted as a ruined castle. At the stone wall separating the yard from the lane, the girls froze and waited.

"Who would forget to close their own door?" Eileen asked. "Is anybody home?"

"Something's not right," Emcee said. "Unless Mullaney took that dog with him to the pub. Where's the collie and her mad barking?"

Siobhán laughed. "Probably run off to harass your grandfather's sheep. Speaking of which, why are the sheep so quiet too?"

On the hills, pale clouds of white, the sheep had nothing to say. Normally they would have been baaing their heads off at the approach of strangers.

Jammed between two stones stood the long thick blade of a scythe used for clearing brush from a hedge. The salt-pocked metal was bent and twisted into an S from being plunged into the rock and crumpled by sheer force. Each girl tried to pry the Irish Excalibur from its rock, but they could not budge it.

With a groan, Emcee gave up. "Fair play to the fella that stabbed the wall with this here machete. Must be strong as a bull."

They made their way up the walk. In the wooden front door, the face of a sléan had been buried, its long shaft perpendicular like an empty flagpole.

"Jaysus," Emcee said. "I don't like the looks of this place." She grabbed her friends by the sleeves of their hoodies. "Do you not think we should feck off whilst we can? Call in the police?"

Determined to find out more, Eileen pushed her aside. "Mr. Mullaney, it's us, the Ginger Sisters. Are you here at all?"

The house was as quiet as a Sunday morning. They stood for a while on the threshold, uncertain about transgressing what felt like a veil between two worlds. Trembling, they stepped into the foyer. A carving knife bisected the linoleum like a threat.

In the kitchen, the drawers and cupboards had been thrown open, the crockery smashed on the countertops, pots and pans strewn across the floor. The draperies were in shreds, and great gashes marred the wallpaper. The points of all the sharp objects had been embedded in random surfaces. Buried to their hilts, knives stood out at crazy angles. An augur poked through the bread box, screwdrivers punctured the microwave, and a splatter of nails festooned the teakettle. A pair of scissors had been split in two and thrown like darts into the wall calendar. A cleaver chopped the front of the dishwasher. It looked as if someone had been trying to kill the room.

"Bloody hell," Siobhán said as she took hold of Eileen's hand. "What a feckin' mess. Like some crazy man in a frenzy stabbed everything in sight."

Trailing her friends, Emcee entered and gasped at the wreckage. "Looks like they couldn't find a knife sharp enough to cut whatever needed cutting. Oh, but Christ, the poor dog."

The girls glanced around the room, dreading the possibility. Siobhán whistled. "She might be about, hiding somewheres, afraid to show herself. Come on out, girl."

From another room, an anxious bark relieved the pressure in their chests.

"C'mere, Bonnie. Where are you, lass? It's okay, just us girls."

When the collie did not answer their calls, Emcee reached for a butcher's knife that had been slammed into a cutting board and wriggled it free. Siobhán grabbed the garden shears, and Eileen found a boxcutter and flicked its razor blade. The three witches tiptoed from room to room.

"Mr. Mullaney, are you there?" Siobhán called. "We're only after the dog, so no harm."

Outside the bedroom door, Eileen stopped and drew a deep breath. "Wait, suppose he's on the floor in a pool of blood? Stabbed thirty-nine times?"

"What makes you think that?" Siobhán said. "Why do you always go there to the worst? Blood and guts and gore. Things are never as bad as they seem."

"Knives sticking out like voodoo pins make me a wee bit nervous. Are you not afraid of being murdered? Whosoever played with the silverware means serious business. Suppose the murderer is hiding behind the door. Suppose there's more than one monster inside the house."

"If there were any psychos about, they would have stabbed us by now."

"Isn't that the very thing about killers?" Emcee rubbed her hands together. "They strike when you least expect. You're having a nice shower, and in comes the cross-dresser to cut you to ribbons. Have you never seen those fillums where your man in the mask is sneaking up on the poor babysitter while she's on the telephone, ringing for help? Creeping behind her back, but it's too late? The voice is coming from inside the same house. A quick yelp and then *Heeere's Johnny*." She looked back over her shoulder.

"Would you both be quiet?" Eileen said. "Help me find poor Bonnie." She pushed open the bedroom door, and from beneath the bed, the dog whined mournfully. Her wagging tail thumped the mattress slats, but she would not budge. The girls dropped to their knees to coax out the collie.

"Dear old thing," Emcee said. "You're all right now. Did those hooligans scare you, girl? That's the lass. You're safe, c'mon then."

Bonnie refused to move. Eileen offered her the smell off her fingers, and the dog licked her salty skin and crawled from beneath the bed, keeping an uneasy watch on the open door. "Frightened out of your wits, you are. Shaking like a baby."

The witches surrounded the bitch to comfort her with caresses and kisses. Bonnie sneezed at the dust bunnies stirred up by their relentless petting. With her nerve restored, she broke free of her rescuers and headed off to search for the exit.

"What happened here?" Siobhán asked. "Do either of yis speak dog?"

The collie led them to the kitchen, where she crouched on the floor, ears flat against her skull, daring the sharp objects to make a move.

"Sons of bitches," Emcee said. "Who would terrorize a poor dear so? Bonnie, love, we'll find a treat or a bone, take your mind off your troubles."

Bonnie pricked up her ears, hearing voices from the road moments before the girls did. She barked and whimpered and chased her tail three times.

"What the devil got into her?" Siobhán put her finger to her lips. Just outside the house, two sets of footsteps approached the house. "Someone's coming this way."

Eileen stared at the crazed dog, torn between flight and fight. "You don't suppose it's the killers come back to finish the job?"

"Run," Siobhán said, and they scurried through the ruined kitchen and out the back door. Pinned in by the small lake to the east and the bog to the west, the witches had no choice. They slipped inside the toolshed. Swollen with moisture, the door had to be forced shut with a thud. Aromas of fertilizer and oil mixed in the damp air. A thin chain, disturbed on their way inside, swung in front of Eileen's face, and she pulled it. The glare of a single bulb overhead provided them a measure of calm as their eyes adjusted, and their ears were attuned to any possible movement from the house. The glow intensified, illuminating the corners of the cramped shed. A stepladder leaned in one corner, beside a battered cardboard box labeled CHRISTMAS in a child's handwriting. Farm implements, scythes and saws, hung neat and orderly on one wall. Opposite, a cabinet held more tools, hammers and nails, pots of paint, a broken weathervane, and an ancient coil of rope. A few trunks sat on the floor beside a hank of roofing thatch and a red wheelbarrow. At the back was the only window, garlanded with cobwebs, the dark pane of glass mirroring their reflections. Beneath the window, a blue tarpaulin lay in a tidy roll.

They drew their hoods over their heads and huddled together, knee to knee to knee. In the close atmosphere of the shed, they waited for the door to fly open or, at least, to hear voices raised in shock or surprise at the jagged chaos in the kitchen. All was quiet but for their own heavy breathing, like playing hide-and-seek with a madman or two.

"What will we do now?" Eileen whispered. "We're trapped like mice in a tin bucket."

Outside in the darkness came the sound of a horse and cart crunching over the gravel drive. More visitors were arriving at Mullaney's.

"You just had to do it, didn't you?" Siobhán hissed. "Didn't I tell you never to cross a fairy ring? See what trouble we're in now. You barging through like some feckin' Bigfoot, not thinking, tempting fate."

Forgetting their predicament, Emcee raised her voice. "You don't honestly think it is the little people from the Otherworld. Who knows what's out there in the house? Maybe it's Bonnie and Clyde come to Connemara."

"Keep quiet," Eileen said. "Don't you ever listen?"

A moan drifted through the shadows, a human sound, soft and plaintive. The three witches stole quick glances into one another's eyes, searching for courage, and joined hands. Someone else was with them inside the shed, and for a few marvelous seconds, they lingered at the edge between silence and another stirring. A second groan pinpointed the location. From inside the rolled tarp came the muffled noise again, desperate, awake, and alive.

8

The Black Stuff

THE CRAIC WAS on at O'Leary's. Nursing his first pint of the night, Burke listened to the musicians gathered around the big table at the window. A pair of old fiddlers raced each other through the reels. Ó Suillebhean, from the secondary school, tickled the concertina. Jimmy McKenna beat the goatskin bodhrán, and Sean Mannion tooted the tin whistle. A nice-looking blond girl sang a Cranberries tune for the young ones, a catch in her throat, and half the fellas in the bar tiptoed to the verge of true love. A taste of "Carrickfergus" and the grandads would be ready to swim across the Atlantic for their sweethearts gone to America. As if. Here and there, young people conversed in Irish, oscillating between modern life and the almost-lost past. O'Leary himself lorded over it all, happy to be draining another keg of the black stuff.

"Two pints of plain, Mr. O'Leary, if you please," Burke said as Mullaney arrived at his side. "It's your only man for the troubles what ails you."

They took their stouts to a snug as far as possible from the music. The lass launched into a lament a cappella, and the whole place listened with an overarching sadness at the sorrowful lyrics and the pathos of the minor key.

"Damn, that's a beautiful song," Burke said. "Too bad I don't understand a word of it, no more than those Germans at the bar. Look at them crying in their lager, you'd think their hearts were breaking. Try an Irish pint, lads."

Mullaney sipped the cream off the top. "It's the story of a woman who wants to be brought home to be buried, for she is soon to die. The English is something like 'Carry me home to Mweenish Island, so I might be buried with my own people.' But sadder still in the Irish."

Burke took a long slug from his pint and with the back of his hand wiped the milky foam from his lips. "Fair play to her. You wouldn't want to be dead away from home, so. What a comfort to lie there next to the old folks. If you're going to spend eternity in the same spot, may as well be beside someone who knows and appreciates you from when you was something. I remember when my da took sick with the cancer, wasted away to sticks and skin. Once he was gone, the picture of those last days faded straightaway. We remembered his glory. Big fella, he was, strong as an ox, and it's almost that other thin man in the hospice never existed at all, d'ye follow me?"

"Aye, as soon as you're dead, we'll plant you next the rest of them Burkes, your mother too. The only person who could outtalk yourself. Your mammy be right happy to see you again."

"That girl singer. Delicate, every word and note." Burke swallowed the stout left in his glass.

"You ought not to have told those Red Witches, Tommy, what we found in the bogs. It was supposed to be a secret. We agreed, did we not, to wait till morning?"

An uneasy silence passed between the two old friends, Tommy contrite and Michael unforgiving. They had been mates for years, despite the difference in age. After Michael's father passed away, Burke had been like a second father to him, always offering a helping hand or a word of advice. As compensation, Mullaney looked after the old geezer, driving him over to Galway to the eye doctor, minding his sheep when the weather shifted wet and cold, keeping him company now that most of his kin had long fled Connemara. Just the one son and daughter-in-law left, the red-haired granddaughter and the twin grandsons. Who else did Burke have in the world? But now, on the cusp of the most momentous event in the history of the village, he could not be trusted with a simple confidence.

"Mary Catherine says she only told the other two, then them's all that knows. I cannot take the suspense a minute longer. Why did you have to go and hide her, Mick? Do you not trust me?"

The Guinness had softened Mullaney, brought a tear to his eye. "Put it down to my keen understanding of human nature, or at least what I know about you. You're a cracked teacup."

"What can I do to make it up to you?"

"Fret no more. She is safely tucked away for the night. Those girls can see the body in the morning. I've a plan in mind, a certain order as to how to spread the news. First, we have a private viewing, like. Take some good photographs to archive our discovery. Put her back where we found her, call in the experts, then notify the press and tell them to hightail it over to the spot. Finally, the Gardaí for crowd control. You and me at the center of it all. It's a once-in-a-lifetime moment, Tom. Let's not blow it by another careless word."

Relieved that the subject was closed, Burke finished his pint and held up two fingers to the waitress navigating among the drunks and the tables. No more than a tilt of the chin, and she knew what he wanted. With practiced skill, she balanced the empty glasses on her wee tray, and his gaze followed the swish of her backside as she went to the bar. The more he drank, the closer Burke leaned into the person at the other end of the conversation. His breath reeked of oaty stout and old stew, and the tang of sheep never completely left his clothes. "I feel a real spiritual connection with that one. A black-haired, blue-eyed Galway lass. Reminds me, I wonder what color eyes on the one we dug up this morning. Black, do you think, like the rest of her? Maybe hazel or blue, given the ginger hair."

"A good question. Maybe you can ask the archaeologists in the morning."

Burke held his glass to the light. "Did you know the Guinness is not black at all? A deep red, so dark it appears black to the untrained eye. Hold up your glass to the light when it gets here, you don't believe me. You'll see. Thick red like your blood pudding."

Two pints arrived and were set before them. Before the Galway girl could get away, Burke grabbed her wrist. "I've an important question, miss. Would you say this stout is black, or is to more of a blood-red black?"

She looked at him as if he were the man in the moon.

"And what part of Galway d'ye hail from anyways? Spiddal could it be, or perhaps on the banks of the Corrib by the Spanish Arch? There's a grand Italian restaurant there on Quay Street, if you ever fancy a lasagna dinner with a distinguished older gentleman."

"I am Romanian," the waitress answered, slipping from his grip like a wet mackerel.

Mullaney hid his smile by lifting the full glass to his lips.

"Transylvania, more like it." Burke's voice trailed after her. "Sure, she is having us on. Your black Irish."

The session musicians snapped to an abrupt end. They had been stomping their way through a medley of jigs, the fiddlers frantic. When the whistler piped a sharp note at the end, they all let out a fair whoop. The absence of a tune created a void. Into that silence Burke's voice boomed, asking the odd query: "Which reminds me, *a mhic*, where on earth did you hide the body?"

From the back of the room, someone shouted, "In another man's bed!" and as suddenly, the pub sparkled with hearty laughter and backchat. Mullaney set down his glass with a wet smack against the water-ringed wood.

"That mouth of yours is going to get us into trouble before the night is through," he said. "It's been a long day, and I'm dead tired from the digging."

"Fair play. One more after this one. And then I'll steer you home."

Laying coins on the table for the waitress, Mullaney pushed away his glass. "No, I've hit my limit on the black stuff. Or the blood-red stuff, if you like."

Burke quaffed the rest of his stout. "Let's go then. What are you waiting for?"

The fresh air sobered them a bit as they stepped away from the vapors of ale and beer and the clump of smokers on the sidewalk. Aside from O'Leary's, the only lights on in town were from the Crúchaun Inn down the main street. Cars were arranged haphazardly, some nearly on the sidewalk and others cocked at makeshift angles well out from the curb. Irish parking, Mullaney always called it. Stop anywhere you please. They toddled off, unsteady on their feet, Burke crooning memories from the evening's songs. A half mile up the road, an animal ran in the darkness. A streak of black and white charged straight at them. Bonnie spiraled around the pair and then lay low in the street, trying to herd them away. When Burke tried to shoo her, she barked a warning.

"What's got into you?" Mullaney asked. "Who let you out of the house?"

When they rounded the corner, he had his answer. The front door was blown open to the world, and lights shone from every window.

"Looks like intruders been here," Burke said. "Vandals and Visigoths. Do you want me to phone the constabulary?"

The dog glued herself to her master's leg, but he pushed on. "Let's have a look for ourselves first."

They hustled to the front door and examined the sléan handle protruding from the wood at an angle of forty-five degrees. Mullaney gave it a tug, but no go. They stepped inside and found a mess of pointed instruments jabbed everywhere.

"Holy good night," Burke said. "Is anyone about? I'd take a care if I were you, Mick. Hello, hello?"

A quick tour of the rooms revealed no one. They walked slowly through the wreckage, testing whether they could free the blades. Mullaney's father's old fountain pen had been darted into the cover of his favorite book. Pinking shears had halved a throw pillow bought on a Spanish holiday. A letter opener speared the family photograph on the mantelpiece, straight between Mick and the rest of his family, till death us do part.

"Punk kids," Burke said. "Dirty teenagers down the school. What purpose does this serve, I ask you? It's not as if you ever done anything to anybody. No, there's no more a gentleman in the county than Michael Mullaney, ask around, they'll tell you. Unless you're not cluing me onto some arch-enemy. Lookit here, a set of fish forks crammed into the toaster. Not that anyone has a need for fish forks, but it was a perfectly grand—"

The dog woofed from the side of her mouth. Raising her head from the floor, she stared at the front of the house, hearing a commotion out on the lane. With not even a barked fare-thee-well, she raced away, nails skittering on the floorboards, and headed straight into her fortress under the bed.

From the yard came the clomp of hooves in the gravel. A pair of horses nickered and blew through their nostrils like an engine backfiring, and then a clatter of metal on metal dragging across the driveway. Burke and Mullaney listened for a knock.

Battered open, the front door nearly flew off its hinges. Suspended in midair over the threshold was a bare foot the size of a badger, each callused toe flexing as if testing the temperature. In stepped the man who belonged to that foot, a bigger-than-life figure in a blood-red tunic belted at the hips by a thick leather strap. A fine example of masculinity he was, each arm big as a leg, each leg thick as an oak. His muscles rippled like ocean waves, and his chest was broad enough to block the night stars from view. A giant of a man, sculpted like an American footballer, and handsome too. His wavy blond locks tickled his shoulder, and his boyish chin, cleft by a bottomless dimple, was smooth as an egg. Light shone through his blue eyes, which wandered independently in their sockets, taking in the environment with gravest interest. His plump lips hid two rows of white teeth, perfect as a movie star's. His smooth wide brow looked hewn from fine Italian marble, and his nose quivered like a hound's at the strange smells wafting from the men sitting, pieholes agape, at the kitchen table. Fastened to one arm was a bronze shield, decorated with two serpentine dogs. On each wrist hung metal cuffs, each fashioned as a fierce wolfhound in profile, the eye a dazzling ruby. In his free hand he held a broadsword, glinting with sharpness, half the size of an ordinary man. A golden aura enveloped him from his blocklike head to his supple toes. He looked as if he had stepped off the pages of a storybook.

A second young man trailed behind, not nearly as well formed, but nevertheless a fine-looking lad in his own right. He was burdened with a quiver and bow as well as a spear in each hand. Tied to his girdle were four swords of various lengths and purposes, and he wore a kind of skirt below his bare chest, which was crossed by a bandolier holding even more weaponry. He gave the impression of being a servant or a sidekick, a calf to the first man's bull. The metal on the fearsome pair rattled as they stepped into the foyer and stared at the drunk men glued to their chairs.

The taller youngster addressed them in a torrent of gibberish, rising and falling, before concluding with a spittle-filled demand for something or other. The warrior's flushed face grimaced in a twisted spasm, and he snarled and bared his incisors. Dumbstruck and afraid, Burke and Mullaney could not understand a word of it, though they intuited that he was as angry as an Ulster preacher, and they feared worse yet to come. The half-naked sidekick stood on his toes and whispered into his ear. The muscle man's shoulders drooped, and he slowly shook his head in some private disillusionment. "Try English," his assistant said.

A storm of confusion swept across the shoreline of his gaze. Streaks of lightning crossed his eyeballs as he scrutinized the faces before him and grumbled at the prospect. The foreign words mangled between his ears and forked his tongue. A single scalding tear splashed to the floor, big as a cup of hot tea.

"Where is she?" His voice had the hard edge of a Northerner, and each word trembled as it escaped the cage of his teeth.

Burke clasped a hand against his chest to still his hammering heart, and Mullaney grabbed the arms of the kitchen chair to stop from fainting. Petrified as pillars, they offered no reply.

"You heard your man," the younger one said. "Do not trifle with his patience or test his temper. It is a good thing you were not here earlier for the first go-round when he was truly upset. This havoc was merely the overture. When he has a temper on him, death and destruction are the major movements of his symphony."

The giant took a stone from the pouch at his hips, deposited it in a leather sling, and then whirled the contraption like a yo-yo before letting the missile fly. The stone whizzed between their heads and crashed into the oven door in an explosion of glass smithereens. He lifted a woolly eyebrow in their direction to indicate that he meant business. Waves of heat rose from the big fella's forehead.

"There's no need for violence, lad." Burke puffed out his chest and tried to bluster his way through. "You boys mustn't be from around these parts, for we are peaceful folk. We will tell you what you want to know, but please let's all calm down. Who else could use a friendly drink?"

For the first time since he'd burst into the house, the great warrior allowed a smile to grace his lips. With a quick nod, he gestured to his aide to fetch a bottle. A noggin of whiskey was quickly produced, and three glasses were poured. The tall Ulsterman abstained while the others imbibed, and instead he took an axe and pruned a strip of veneer from the kitchen table. With his hands and bare feet, he fashioned a hoop. Using the nail of his big toe as easily as another man might use a knife or awl, he inscribed some primitive slashes along the outer face. Satisfied with his writing, he casually tossed the band around the liquor cabinet, sealing it. His way of preventing a second round of drink before their business was settled.

"Where is she?" he asked again.

"And who is it that you're looking for?" Burke asked.

The sidekick swallowed the last sip of the hard stuff. "Fedelm."

Emboldened by the whiskey, Burke answered back quickly. "We don't know any Fuh-dell-um, if that's how you say the girl's name. Is it a Protestant name? I've never even heard such a quare sobriquet in these parts. Was it you two come by earlier looking for this lass? Breaking and entering and smashing the place to bits? Malicious mischief, that's what the law will say, and you'll have to pay every cent in damages, not to mention those dangerous knives and forks about the place. A new cooker will be most dear. I'd be surprised if there's not a session in gaol as well. Your generation is all the same. Well, we seen your faces, bucks, and it won't be hard for the law to catch two dirty long-haired miscreants such as yourselves."

In one fluid motion, the Ulster warrior pulled a great broadsword from his belt and swung, the blade whistling loudly in the air. With a single stroke, he lopped off Burke's head. It bounced like a football across the kitchen floor and came to rest at Mullaney's feet.

"Bloody hell," Mullaney said. He swallowed the strong acid that had risen to his mouth. The violence was so sudden and unexpected, he was dumbfounded.

Burke's head had landed chin down and his doleful eyes stared at the ceiling. His torso remained motionless in the chair, his hand wrapped around the empty whiskey glass. The cut had been so clean there was no blood, only the thinnest leak of stout from the esophagus. Burke's eyes danced in the lopped-off head on the floor, desperate to find the headless torso. He could only blink at the sorrow of his separate circumstance.

The soldier casually wiped the black stuff from the blade and again asked Mullaney. "Where is she?"

"Why did you have to go do that for? Are you off your nut?" Mullaney gasped at the head staring back at him. "Ach, Tommy, I'm so sorry."

"Lookit," the sidekick said. "Your man there talks too much. We poured you a dose of a nice friendly whiskey. We asked politely, but this ould fella would not shut up."

The head on the floor mumbled but could not move its lips to allow for proper speech. The giant wriggled his toes in Burke's face, getting ready for a corner kick.

Mullaney leaned in for a close listen. He was confused by the muffled sounds escaping from the head but knew he must act before something worse occurred.

"Leave him be," he said. "I found a body in the bog this morning as I was cutting turf, if that's who you are looking for. This Fedelm, as you call her."

The great warrior withdrew his foot and sheathed his broadsword. Resting his dog-knotted Celtic shield on an empty chair, he let out a sigh windy enough for hawks to glide upon. The ice in his eyes thawed.

"I'll take you to the spot," Mullaney said.

Burke managed a grunt from the corner of his mouth.

"But only if you can do something about my headless friend here. Can you work your magic, wherever or whenever you're from, and give the man the use of his head?"

The giant's lackey said something in the ancient tongue, older than Old Irish, a singsong of clacking consonants and phlegmy throat-clearing. Mullaney thought he recognized the word *ceann*, which he knew meant head, though the rest of their dialogue remained obscure. In the end, the big fella nodded and stuck out a great paw. In that monstrous mitt, Mullaney's own hand disappeared entirely.

From his armory, the great hero took a javelin and jammed the point into the floor, then he scaled it like a monkey and balanced on the blunt end. Scrunched against the ceiling on his perch, he supervised as his secretary maneuvered the head in place, screwing it on like a cork in a bottle, till Burke was neatly restored. Burke sputtered and swore as he craned his neck from side to side several times.

"Guys those are who?" he asked, aware as he spoke that something was wrong with what he was saying.

"Your plumbing was put in backward," Mullaney said.

Burke's hands flew to his throat, checking for the proper fit. The two young soldiers laughed at his misfortune, and Burke took a moment to understand he had been the butt of a practical joke. With a flick of his finger and thumb, the warrior gave the head one final clockwise spin. Burke coughed out a wee frog, which hopped toward the sink.

The two yokes collected their swords and spears and began girding their loins. They took a final look in the mirror by the door to adjust their tunics and comb their golden locks with their fingers.

"Who are those guys?" Burke asked again.

"Have you never cracked open a book in your life?" Mullaney asked. "Not even a comic book when you were a lad, if only for the pictures? Do you know a thing at all about your native land? Look at his shield and those bracelets. What do you make of those knotted hounds? I'm telling you, these fellas are straight out of Ireland's bloody past."

The valet swept his arm like a maître d'. "Your chariot awaits, messirs."

In two long strides, the marvel was through the doorway, his servant on his heels. Burke and Mullaney reluctantly brought up the rear.

"That's Cúchulainn," Mullaney whispered. "The Hound of Ulster."

Pausing in the doorway, the sidekick said, "Nobody asked, but my name is Láeg—pronounced LOY-egg—his right-hand man and official charioteer for the Hound. And we are here to find the girl who opened the door to the past. If need be, we'll fight every last man of you in the West."

9

Westward Ho!

ALL THE WAY west, Bridget pondered human sacrifice. Beyond the Pale of Dublin, the traffic thinned out, and sunset lasted from Kilbeggan to Athlone, but even the long glory of pink-and-yellow sky could not distract her from speculations about the body out in Connemara. She surmised it had been some sort of ritual killing. The quick slash across the throat, wrists tied to the neck, the victim dumped in a liminal space—all were clear signs of an appeasement to the gods. A prayer token for a good harvest. One life to protect the whole society. As far back as the Paleolithic era, ancient cultures all over the world had done it. The Great Death Pit at Ur, the Inca, Maya, Aztec, the cult of Osiris. The infants at Carthage. The Gauls had their colossal wicker men, the great effigies they stuffed with living men and then set afire. The Semnones gathered in the sacred forests between the Elbe and the Oder with hollowed idols of their gods and opened their crop-sowing ceremonies with a human sacrifice. Other cultures specialized in hangings and floggings, sacralized drownings and immolations, and sometimes the threefold death. If the Romans could be believed, the Celts were particularly barbaric axe swingers, head loppers, child butchers, and cannibals, their trees and altars stained with blood. Of course, old Caesar and even the Greeks were notorious for projecting their own practices onto foreign peoples outside the Empire, not just the Gaels and Celts but Jews and Christians and infidels alike. The gods, after all, were an equal-opportunity bunch. As to whether the Irish were as bad, the archaeological evidence was paper thin.

The dead girl would speak to Bridget and provide another piece of the historical puzzle, far more reliable than Roman propaganda. Forensics would reveal her age and physical condition. Her clothing and hair, even her fingernails, would provide clues to whether she was rich or poor, esteemed or neglected among women. X-rays, CT, and MRI to inspect her organs, check out her gut for signs of her last meal, gruel and buttermilk and griddlecakes, perhaps. One of the other bog people—was it Grauballe Man?—had toxins in his gut caused by ergot in the grains he consumed. That stuff was enough to kill a person but not before driving them mad with convulsions, burning sensations, and hallucinations. Some scholars theorized that the girls of Salem had eaten tainted grains and suffered visions of witchcraft, a mere bit of mold leading to wild accusations and hangings.

Or maybe jealousy or fear drove otherwise decent folks to weed out the undesirables. The crew at the university would check the bog girl's spine and bones for abnormalities, find out if she had any tattoos. An endoscopist would peer inside her skull and take a tissue sample of the brain. Her tunic pin would be dated by the electrochemist's skill. Threads from her clothes and the rope around her neck and wrists would go under the microscope. They would prod and poke and cut until every last scrap of information could be gleaned. She was a dream girl, a gift from the gods.

After such thorough examination, the college or perhaps the National Museum would put the preserved body on display in a climate-controlled glass case. Sleeping beauty, marked by a plaque with her new name, where and when she was found, and a few lines about her archaeological significance. Perhaps her death could be given some meaning at last. Bridget would write a paper, present a hypothesis at an international conference, and add to the corpus of literature on the subject. They would be linked forever in the footnotes. Bog sisters.

Television reporters would want to interview her, and the story might be picked up back in the States. *American archaeologist makes spectacular find, changes modern understanding of ancient Ireland.* Don't forget, she told herself, to mention her grandfather and his stories of talking with the dead. Her family back in Philly would be proud of her at last. Though they had never said so to her face, her parents frowned upon her chosen profession. One Thanksgiving morning in Bridget's final undergraduate year, she had overheard them in the kitchen fussing over the turkey and sweet potatoes. Wrapped in an old throw blanket, she had one ear on the TV commentators describing the floats in the parade and one ear on her parents sharing their misgivings.

"Well, I don't know what she plans on doing," her mother said. "Grad school? It's so impractical. You won't find archaeology jobs just anywhere, you know."

Her father forced a reassuring grunt. "She will go where the work is."

"I blame your father, always going on about the past. Dear old Ireland and those who stayed behind. Like living with a ghost sometimes."

"At least she's not an undertaker. Remember that phase?"

"Who cares about the past? You dig up some pottery shards or a few coins and then stick them in a museum." Her mother punctuated each phrase by cramming a handful of stuffing into the bird. "Let's not get started on her obsession with the dead. Honestly, I don't know how she became so morbid."

"Death becomes her," said her father. He was secretly delighted by her dark side.

"What a family," her mother said. "Bird's ready for the oven."

The closer she came to Connemara, the more Bridget felt on the edge of something big and important that would show them all. She tightened her glasses to her temple. The department would invite her to join the senior faculty. She would write a book.

The GPS guided her around Galway City and onto the narrow roads, past fields and meadows. She was careful not to scrape the mirrors of her rental when she had to scoot over to let the oncoming cars get by, or wait out a flock of stubborn sheep crossing the road. Sometimes she spied a slice of the Atlantic brooding in the distance past the windscreen, but mostly the countryside was windblown, green, and desolate. The stretch of dry weather had not changed its raw character. The earth seeped from its core, and she could well understand how a body stayed a body in such surroundings.

Her grandfather had come from a village nearby and spoke of the land with a melancholy air. "Rain and more rain," he reported. "Wears down a soul, especially the winters, when the sun hides behind the gray clouds for weeks on end. I swear Noah must have asked the good Lord to send the filthy weather our way in exchange for a promise to sin no more. Forty days—try *eighty*. Or nine out of ten. I might have stayed with my own if not for the rain."

He had emigrated to Philadelphia at eighteen years of age, yet he always spoke of coming home one day for a visit. Late in life, he booked a ticket, made plans to first see his sister in London before hopping the ferry to spend some time with Bridget in Dublin. But he took ill at Heathrow and went straight back to the States the very next day. Beginning of the end for him. Bridget glanced at the empty passenger seat and filled it with his ghost. How he would have loved the journey and applauded her resolve.

The closer her destination, the more doubts had begun to corrode her fantasy. What if the story was a hoax? She would be the laughingstock of the department if word got out. Many a lonesome night since coming to Ireland, she had wondered if she had made the right choices. Not just living and working in a strange country, so far from home. Perhaps her mother was right: What sort of life is spent studying the dead? If she turned around, she could be back in Dublin in a few hours. She could finish the semester and think about some more affirmative direction for her life. Clouded by self-doubts, she nearly missed the village altogether and was surprised to find herself stopped in front of the run-down hotel.

The parking lot of the Crúchaun Inn was empty but for a pair of beat-up service vehicles near the staff entrance. A good sign, she thought, to be the only one sniffing the trail. Tomorrow every room in the inn and for miles around would be taken by the gawkers and archaeology nerds, and she would be lucky to find a manger in a stable. She checked her messages, but there was nothing further from the Red Witch of the West. The *#bogbody* tag had not garnered any additional likes. Dropped into the well of the internet with nary a splash.

Done up in shades of brown, the tired lobby was deserted. No one answered the bell at the front desk. Around the corner in the hotel's tidy pub, a bartender stared at a Gaelic football match on the overhead TV. A fortyish woman kept him company, her head propped on one hand. In a corner snug, the only other patron was fast asleep against the wall. The

Wild West, Bridget told herself. "Excuse me," she said. "I have a reservation."

The bartender tore his gaze away from the match and nodded at the new customer. "There she is."

"Ah, love, right so," the woman at the bar said. With a coy smile, she slid off her stool and led the way back to registration. "We weren't sure when you'd arrive. Slow night in the middle of the week. Would you believe the place is packed with Americans in July and August?"

"Traffic was bad getting out of Dublin, but I'm glad to be here at last. Who is winning the big game?"

"The Lord only knows. Them brutes bashing the stuffing from each other. Sure, I only watch to pass the time. I don't even understand the rules of the game." The innkeeper fussed with a computer. "Ms. Scanlon, you'd be. We have you down for the one night."

"Bridget," she said. "Seeing as I'm the only guest apparently, we might as well be on first names. I might need to stay a bit longer if things work out."

"Stay as long as you like, love. As you can see, we're not busting at the seams. What brings you to our far little corner?"

"I'm not sure if it isn't all a wild-goose chase. I have come from Dublin—"

"Ha, I had you down as a Yank."

"Philadelphia, originally. But my grandfather's from this part of Ireland. Do you know Kinvara?" She flushed. "You wouldn't happen to know anyone who calls herself the Red Witch of the West, would you?"

The innkeeper stopped entering the credit card number. She scrunched her lips together and tapped her nails on the counter.

"She's the one who steered me to stay here," Bridget said as she dug her phone from her pocket and scrolled through her messages, stopping at the selfie of the old man at the excavation site. She held up the picture. "How about him? You ever see this man around here?"

"Holy shite." The woman laughed. "Pardon my French, but that's my father-in-law. Tom Burke."

"Your father-in-law? He's the man I've come to meet."

"Small wonder she sent you here. I'm Natalie Burke," she held out her hand. "And that message is from my daughter. One of the so-called Red Witches. Hah, she's not a real witch, mind. There's no danger of any black magic. How on earth did the two of youse hook up?"

Bridget toyed with the idea of telling the whole story to ingratiate herself with the woman and her family, but she decided to keep it secret till the morning. The fewer people who knew the details, the less likely a mob would be out scouring the bogland before dawn. "Well, as I said, it may be a great big nothing. She didn't tell you about it?"

"I am lucky to get the time of day from that one. Teenagers."

"Could be a small matter of archaeological interest. Anyway, I have always wanted to see where my grandfather came from." She offered a conspiratorial smile. "Perhaps you could ask her to contact me directly? Or tell me how to get in touch with Mr. Burke?"

"My daughter is spending the night over at her friend's, but I'll have her call in the morning. You might find Tommy Burke down the end of the street at O'Leary's." She looked at the clock and handed over the key card. "Still a chance he's not dead drunk for the evening. What's that amadán got himself into this time?"

"Thanks so much," Bridget said, waving the key. "O'Leary's?"

"If you hurry, you might catch a tune or two. Trad Night, not to be missed."

*   *   *

On the sidewalk in front of O'Leary's public house, a pair of rough-looking hard chaws loitered, drinks in hand. The taller boy wore his long hair in a ponytail, and his friend had on a wool cap despite the warm weather. The two country bucks, handsome and dangerous under the arc lights, followed every step of her approach. How ridiculous it was to feel such a stranger in a strange land, unaccustomed to the local men with their unblinking stares. If she oversaw the sacrifice to the gods, her prime victims would be lads such as these. Sweet talkers, players, and charmers.

"How's the form?" the smaller one said as he tugged the brim of his cap.

She nodded a greeting and looked for the best path between or around them. The taller one moved closer, blocking the way, and she stopped, annoyed by his aggressiveness. On second glance, she was slightly stunned by his beauty and the way the lamps reflected and shimmered in his eyes. Bold as can be, he was inspecting her, head to toe, his eyes lingering at her breasts and hips. He said not one word, but she felt like a kitten meeting a pit bull.

"Don't mind him, lass," his short friend said. "He don't like to waste a word if he can spend a smile, but I am afraid you have tied his tongue in knots. You remind him of someone we used to know. We have not seen such a beautiful Connemara girl in a long, long time. We've come down from the north for the night and are not from these parts."

"Neither am I," Bridget said, as she aimed to push her way past the brute. "I'm American."

Puzzled, the lads parted, grumbling to each other in a foreign dialect, spraying invective and mutual blame.

Inside the pub, two session players remained, a tin whistle and concertina dragging one final tune to the finish line. A raven-haired waitress collected empties from the tables and wiped away the rings. The crowd had dwindled to the hard and committed, and Bridget saw no one about the place who resembled the man from the photo. She bellied up to the bar.

"What can I do you for?" O'Leary asked.

"I don't suppose you have any limoncello. I have a hankering for a Lemon Drop martini."

"You don't suppose correctly. House wines in white or red. A cider, maybe, or an American beer? Or a drop of the black stuff?"

"Red would be fine." Her foot started tapping involuntarily in time to the music. She showed him the picture from her phone. "I'm looking for a friend who might have been here. Do you know a Tom Burke?"

O'Leary squinted at the small image and then shook his head and went off to fetch a clean wineglass. Sidling up to her, the whistle man announced his presence. "Don't mind O'Leary. He's trained to say no to any woman asking after any man. Safer that way, and the fellas appreciate the discretion should the missus be looking for her mister when he is supposed to be home. I couldn't help but eavesdrip. Tommy Burke, is it? You just missed him by three hops. Came in with Mullaney same as usual, amn't I right, O'Leary?"

The bartender laid down the glass of wine and flipped a towel to his shoulder. "Mannion, you ought not to be blathering on. They left twenty minutes or so."

"Do you know where I might find him?"

"What would you want with an old sod like him?" O'Leary asked. "Wait till closing time, and I will be free."

"Honestly, is every man in Connemara on the prowl?"

The musician came to her rescue. "I'm Sean Mannion. Everyone these parts knows Tom Burke—a bit of a chancer, if you follow me. Could be home, the Lord only knows. Go west at the crossroads and follow on till you come to a lane with a large stone on its southern border. Go over the stream on a wee bridge, and his is the second house you will see, if you are looking properly. If Burke's not there, try his neighbor Mullaney's farm. Mind the dog if it's about. I'd wait till morning meself. Those two will be tucked under their covers this time of night, and sure, they were bushed from working the turf all day. They nearly fell in their last pints."

"A happier ending I cannot imagine," said O'Leary. "Drowning in the black stuff."

"I could escort you there," Mannion said. She gave him the once-over. Never trust a whistle man, her grandfather had told her, all them fingers skipping up the rigging. On the other hand, it might be worth a chance to make the trip herself and see if Burke might be awake for a chat. And to ensure he could keep a secret till the morning.

She thanked the tin whistle man kindly and sent him on his way. The concertina player, taking advantage of having the stage to himself, played a final solo on the squeezebox. A melancholy tune trailed her as she stepped outside. The two punks outside the door were long gone, and the western world was falling asleep beneath the stars. She decided it was not too late for a stroll in the country. Her grandfather walked with her through the village, silent at her shoulder until she reached the crossroads. She could smell the whiskey on his breath and hear his old story about the island scorned by all mice. *Set sail*, he would have told her, *be not afraid*. Jamming her hands in her empty pockets, she marched down the lane. *Westward ho*, to her destiny.

CHAPTER

10

Connemara Cradle Song

CRADLED IN HIS arms, she had felt almost human again. Alive, intact, and whole as she had been before they laid her in the bog and skewered her to the silty bottom. The old gent had lifted her like a baby and pressed her against his chest, close to his beating heart and breathing soul. She fell into his rhythm, inhaling and exhaling when he did, steady as the tide. Other men in other times had held her in their arms: her father singing a lullaby to soothe her to sleep, a lover embracing her, and the men carrying her into the black water. Teetering on the cut edge of the ditch, he had to snuggle her more closely to regain his footing. He talked to her in a soft, reassuring voice as he laid her down on a blue cloth, straightened her legs, and crossed her arms. Then he had swaddled her like an infant and eased her into the bed of the truck. The rocking motion nearly lulled her to sleep, till they stopped on the gravel drive, and he carried her to the cold floor of the shed. She had missed him after he left and felt more alone than she had in centuries.

Later, after nightfall, the door had creaked open. With the click of a chain, a ball of light penetrated the open ends of her wrap. Three distinct female voices chewed over their plans. Frightened, on the edge of panic. Sisters, probably, judging by their familiar bickering. Soul sisters, she hoped, who might be of some usefulness.

Two thousand years had passed since she last uttered a word. Despite the residual moisture from the bog, her lips and tongue felt dry. Worse yet, though she knew English well enough from her spirit's frequent leaps and sojourns around the West, she had never uttered one syllable of the strange and cacophonous language. Irish thoughts battled English words. In her mind, she had a whole speech rehearsed, but she could only produce a low guttural moan.

The young visitors abruptly halted their conversation, and when they spoke again, their words crackled with fear and confusion. Not sure how audible she was, Fedelm moaned again, louder and longer, surprising herself by her voice's long-repressed intensity.

The first question zipped from the other side of the room. "What the hell was that?"

"Is there someone hiding in here?"

"I don't care if we do get caught," the third girl said. "Let's get the feck out of this place."

"There's something crying from that blue oilcloth."

"Are you out of your feckin' mind, Siobhán?"

One of the girls dared to walk over and stand directly above her.

The corpse had not meant to frighten them. *Be a sister, Siobhán*, she pleaded silently, and unroll me. Brave lass, good on you. She tendered a mewling cry, innocent as a kitten, to entice the girl to follow her tender instincts.

A pair at each end moved the tarp to the middle of the shed, bonking her feet on the edge of a trunk and nearly stepping on her belly. As a present is unwrapped, there comes a moment when enough paper has been removed to reveal the surprise inside. The girls had not quite finished the job when all at once they stopped.

"It's her," one said. "The girl from the pictures on your phone. He hid her in here, the old fool."

You've one more layer, the bog girl thought. C'mon, you've nearly finished, don't stop now. She grunted encouragement.

"Did you hear that?" Siobhán asked. "Is it coming from her, do you think?"

"It's the gas escaping," the third girl said. "A bit of chair-wheeze. Methane leaking out, like from a stuck cow."

"Doesn't sound like a fart to me."

If you silly girls don't hurry, I'll rip one that will knock you cold till next Tuesday.

Working together, the three positioned the body on its back and peeled the last layer. When they saw the full effect of the blackened body and shock of red hair, the gash at the neck and the noose, the girls retreated to the darkest corner. She had been waiting for hours, ever since the old coot had brushed the peat from her face. No, she had been waiting much longer. Centuries, it was. The lifespan of two whales. Her stint in solitary confinement, with only her imagination for company, had gone on too long. The world itself had been pressing darkly on her. The bulb shone glorious as the sun, and a halo bathed the dead girl's face.

She opened her eyes and blinked.

The three ninnies shrieked, and one dropped to her knees, reciting the "Hail Mary," her teeth chattering the while. Another one pulled her hair and shouted, "It's alive!"

Woozy from the sudden rush of air and the frightened cries, Fedelm tried to sit but had no leverage to lift her shoulders. With a sigh, she silently pled for assistance and held out her bound wrists.

One of the girls shed her hood and looked directly in her eyes. Taking a small scythe from a hook, she advanced slowly, caught between the desire to rescue and a healthy nervousness.

"Siobhán," her friend yelled. "What do you think you are doing?"

A name to a face at last, but when Fedelm tried to speak, out dribbled a glob of peat and black water, thick as stout.

Steadying herself, Siobhán stood astride the body. Up shot the bog girl's hands, ready for the slice of the blade.

"This won't work. Too dangerous. I need something else that cuts."

"I could go back in the house," the smallest one said. "Knives galore stuck in the walls."

"Best stay away from the house. We have no idea who's in there," Siobhán said. "Haven't we been waiting all our lives for something to happen? A bit of real magic, you hags. This is our chance, or else we will miss it altogether. I say we help this poor thing. She's alive. Come over here and get her set up proper."

The third girl obeyed, but the smallest one shook her head. "Who knows what this thing will do if we cut her loose? Don't! She'll be at our throats the next moment, looking for her next drop of blood."

"Mary Catherine Burke, are you one of us or not? Sure, she's nothing more than skin and bones. If it were you, wouldn't you want someone to at least untie your wrists?"

They gathered close, not entirely confident in what they were about to do.

"I am Siobhán Flaherty," her rescuer said. "And this is Eileen Magill and Emcee Burke. We are the *cailli rua*. The Red Witches. Gingers like you. We mean you no harm, and only ask that you will not kill us if we set you free."

The bog girl nodded, inspecting a strand of her red hair from the corner of her eye.

They crouched on their haunches and dared touch the vivified girl. Soft as a pair of favorite boots, her skin warmed in their hands, pliable, not stiff as they imagined, and she gasped as they lifted her by the shoulders. Her head swayed like a newborn baby till she slid her legs under her bottom to find her balance. She smiled patiently as Siobhán sawed through the ancient rope, and once freed, the girl from the bog dropped her hands to her lap and rubbed her sore wrists. All the while, she glanced from one to another, supplicating looks calculated to reassure.

The room whirled as if she were drunk, and her senses struggled to keep pace with the stimulation of sight and sound. Her limbs tingled as if a battalion of hedgehogs galloped in her muscles. She unfurled her fingers and tested her toes. A deep breath made her lungs ache, and a sharp pain in her sinuses mercifully subsided. Her jaw popped, and her teeth felt loose as a tumbledown stone wall. Her fingernails felt brittle as chalk. But the struggles for bodily equilibrium were nothing compared to the racing elation to be alive again, to have her spirit restored and trembling. The three stunned beings helping her were both strange and familiar. Human, no doubt, but at odds with the folk she remembered, talking and moving in a cosseted manner, softer, less weathered and worn than women her age. And what age was that now? Not likely to run into other souls two thousand years old? These moderns would have to do.

The witches helped her stand, and she gripped their arms with iron fingers to keep steady. Her withered form and desiccated flesh filled out to remembered dimensions. Blood in the veins, the electric twitch of life. Like a toddler learning how to walk, she hesitated, and then lifted one foot off the floor to lurch forward, shaky at her first baby step in millennia. A wobble or two before she shrugged off their assistance and walked slowly to the door, trailed by the girls anxious as new parents, ready to catch her should she stumble or fall. Once she reached the door, she could not hide the proud smile on her leathery face.

"Good job with the walking," Eileen said. "Can you speak? Can you tell us who you are?"

"Fedelm is the name on me," she said, her voice croaky as a frog's. "A hundred thousand thanks for extracting me from that shroud. What sort of witches are you? Druids in your dark hoods? Do you live in the hedges and consort with the fey? Where are your familiars? Your brooms and black cats? Perhaps you are merely herbalists. Or Wiccans. Are you good witches or bad witches? Are all redheads witches?"

Riverrun of words, the syllables and sentences poured out of her, and she felt like an Irishwoman again. The waterfall of her thoughts gushed over the edge and thundered in the pool of her mind. She had a million things to say, and the excitement of having someone to hear her thoughts made her giddy. Coming back to life was like falling in love in its hapless fear and mirth. What seemed like a heart pounded in her breast.

From inside the farmhouse came a loud crash, the shattering of glass hit by a large projectile. Angry voices argued back and forth. Something hummed like a helicopter slicing through the air. A heavy—what, football?—bounced on the floor. A man squawked. Wickedness simmered in the atmosphere. Eileen cracked the door ajar to see what was going on. Giant silhouettes crossed the lighted windowpanes. From the

gravel drive came nervous hoofsteps and the crunch of chariot wheels. Horses unnerved by some violence inside.

"Whisht," Fedelm said, and held a finger against her lips.
"I know the sound of that terrible sword anywhere. By the
gods, we must make haste. What is the way through the
backside of this hut?"

Eileen crossed to the small window. "You might be able
to shimmy through, you're thin as a reed, but our asses would
never fit through. There's only the one way in or out."

"We cannot risk being seen. Have you the charm for
invisibility, you witches?"

Emcee rolled her eyes. "Sure, and I'm Harry Potter, and
this one is Ron and t'other Hermione."

Siobhán slapped Emcee on the shoulder. "No, we don't
know any spells for invisibility. But we have hoods to hide
our faces. We will be quiet as a shadow. Over west is the
bogs"—the bog girl reddened slightly—"or maybe we go
north. Take the rowboat and cross the lake toward the hills."

Having no choice, Fedelm let them lead her away. One
by one they slithered out and hugged the wall. Littered with
thousands of empty snail shells, the shore crunched under-
foot, despite their best efforts to walk softly, as if on air. The
rowboat was heavier than they'd guessed, so all four joined
together to heave it over and slide the bow onto the black
water. Glistening on the surface, a circle of moonlight shuddered and rippled as each one hopped aboard. The girls
squeezed together on the two seats. Emcee and Eileen took
the oars and pushed off, the keel scraping the rough shore.
Hard rowing at first, but they managed to reach the shallows,
moving stealthily, the dip of the blade and drip of the water
the only giveaways. Behind them, the windows of Mullaney's
house blazed with lamplight, and they could hear the hearty
roar of men come to some agreement. The sailors followed

the shoreline, heading for the cover of a spit of land ahead. Between the strokes, the boat settled into a calm buoyancy.

A great whoosh startled them, wings ripping into the air as a crane burst out of the reeds and disappeared into the night sky. Transfixed, the rowers stilled their oars and let the rowboat drift.

"Wasn't that a thrill? Nearly sent me back to the grave." Fedelm laughed at herself. "When I was your age, we had a pet crane. They are far easier to tame if raised from an egg and you are the first thing they see. The chick thinks you're its mammy and will follow you anywhere. Oh, that bird was an elegant long-leggedy gentleman. And we never had to catch a fish on our own. Didn't he bring us a dinner whenever we asked?"

No louder than a whisper, she sent a word on the wind. In the next minute, the crane reappeared and orbited the boat before landing, stilts in the shallows, curiosity gleaming in its yellow eyes. Fedelm spoke in the ancient tongue, and the great bird seemed to follow her meaning, dipping its beak and loping among the reeds like a dancer. Whistling softly, she set it free to fly, and they watched its wings trace a straight line in the moonlit sky.

"What was that all about?" Emcee asked.

"A bit of reconnaissance," the bog girl said. "Keep an eye out for trouble."

"You can talk to the cranes?"

"Cranes are marvelous aviators. Loyal as a watchdog. When his time was over, we made a crane bag out of our fella's skin. Have you misplaced your own magic pouches this night?"

The three witches remained silent.

"No crane bags? Where do you keep your chess pieces?"

"Chess?" Eileen laughed. "None of us knows the first thing about it."

Fedelm tapped her bony fingers on the girl's knee. "Chess is a great game for settling disputations. You have your army, your knights and pawns, surrounding the royalty. Everything is black and white, and many a war would have been better settled on a chessboard than a battlefield. Mind, I haven't played in two thousand years. Long ago, I knew a fella gaga for the sporting life, and he was the devil for a game of wits. Carried his thirty-two pieces in a jeweled crane bag, and the squares laid out on an embroidered cloth. Always prepared if he had an hour to spare. The Hound took all comers, never lost nor drew a match. I'm not sure I ever saw him even sacrifice a queen at the chess. Went mad, he did, when nobody would play him anymore."

"Who was this fine fella?" Emcee asked.

"Best not to speak his name, lest he hears us talking about him. It would only swell his head." Trailing her fingers in the still water, she laughed, and her teeth shone in the night. "We had grand playthings in my day. A doll hewn from an oak limb, or the camogie, the old stick and ball—now there was a game."

"If you are from so long ago, how come you speak English and not Irish?" Eileen asked.

"I had to pick it up where I could," she said. "For a time, I went about the land as a magpie, black and white as a chessboard."

The rowers began to pull again, heading for the hills on the opposite shore. Between strokes, Emcee asked, "A magpie?"

"Aye. All kinds of birds, sparrows and robins and even a harrier for a time. Once a tree cat, a bullfrog, a butterfly. Anything that strayed too close to my spot in the bog was fair game. It took a century or two, but I figured out a spell would let my spirit leap out of the ground and into the animal, bird,

or insect. Gave me the locomotion, a chance to get out occasionally, rather than be stuck indoors in the same hole all the
time. The hard part was steering them back to the site, you
see, so I could leap back into meself. Learned this bloody
language of yours leaping back and forth. And it has been
many a year till your man with the shovel picked me out of
the peat this morn."

"Mr. Mullaney?" Siobhán asked.

"That's the name on him? Not to mention his dog too. I
thought that bitch would have my left shin for her dinner.
And then the other ould wan came along, starting in with
the questions and speculations. Supervising the business. All
talk and no shovel. I was glad to be finally up out of it, if only
to no longer listen to such blather."

"My grandfather," Emcee said.

"Ah well, lass, we can't choose our two parents, much less
the four grandparents, the gods love 'em. I meant no offense
by it, I didn't. You're a grand girl yourself, pulling that oar
like a born champion."

Seeing how the remark about the girl's grandfather had
stung, Fedelm said no more until they drew near the opposite
shore. The chop on the water pushed the boat away from a
smooth landing spot toward a fallen tree snagged in the shallows. All the efforts of the tired rowers were not enough to guide
them safely in, and every stroke further taxed their energy.

"Pull together," Siobhán said. "You'll have us wrecked on
those roots."

Eileen handed her the oar. "Not as feckin' easy as it
looks. How about you take over, princess." She rose to trade
places, and the little boat floundered and nearly capsized.

"Sit down and shut up!" Fedelm took command. "One of
youse will have to hop out and take the rope tied to the bow.
Walk us in."

No one volunteered. Her long hiss of exasperation steamed like a prayer to the heavens above. Grasping Siobhán by the back of her sweatshirt, Fedelm lifted her high in the air and tossed her into the lake in one go. Sputtering from the shock, she rose from the knee-deep water in front of the row-boat. Sopping wet, she stared in disbelief at the passengers in the boat. "Why d'ye have to do that for?"

"The tow rope." Fedelm pointed to the bow. "You're a strong lass. Heave-ho!"

Once safely ashore, they built a small fire so Siobhán might dry her shoes and feet. A mist silvered the lake, and now and then a fish or turtle broke the surface. The witches huddled together by the fire, and the bog girl stood beside a willow tree, eyes focused on the other side of the lake, watching for a sign of who might be out there, what wickedness was a-gathering past midnight.

CHAPTER

11

Boyhood Exploits

THE GIANTS STEPPED onto the front lawn and discovered that their horses had vanished, wandered off to greener pastures while the commotion raged inside Mullaney's house. Cúchulainn berated his servant with a stream of slanderous blue curses in Old Irish, emphasizing by pantomime how to tie reins to a post. Using their hands as shields, oblivious to the fact that the moon and not the sun was high in the air, the two men scanned the horizon for their missing vehicle. In frustration, Láeg kicked the ground with his bare toes and did himself a small injury. He hopped up and down like a one-legged kangaroo. "Thundering blazes! Do I chase after those horses now, or is this girl more important?"

"All the same to us which way we get there," Mullaney said. "I'd hate for your wheels to get stuck in the marsh, and besides, it is only a mere stretch of the legs. Why don't we walk?"

The Hound pointed his spear to the west. Off they sauntered, swords and shields clattering like tin pots, with Mullaney and Burke reluctantly bringing up the rear.

"That Cúchulainn lad looks like he knows where he's going," Burke said. "A natural-born leader, that one, charging off without an idea to slow him down."

"I wouldn't go around squawking near those two boys," Mullaney said. "Don't be so quick to forget the big fella's swordsmanship. Bite your tongue and save your neck."

With stomping great strides, Cúchulainn and Láeg put ten yards between them and the two men at the bottom of the driveway.

From his vest pocket, Burke produced his briar pipe and tobacco pouch and calmly began loading the bowl with Half and Half. "Let them go on and get a nice head start. They don't seem to need us at all, and I am destroyed for want of a smoke. I'm feeling a bit light-headed."

"Can't say that I blame you, Tommy. But we don't want to test the man's temper."

Burke struck a match to the tobacco and sucked furiously to get the pipe going. Up ahead on the road, the pair had stopped in their tracks and lifted their noses in search of the strange smell. Like honeybees to hyacinths, they followed the aroma back to its source, intrigued by the strange contraption in Burke's hand.

"Are ye eating fire?" Cúchulainn asked.

Clamping his teeth on the stem, Burke winked and drew in another mouthful. He blew a smoke ring at the ancient heroes. "Have you never seen a man enjoy a pipe?"

Láeg breathed in deeply. "What is that sweetly scent?"

"That, me lads, is the finest Burley mixture, straight from the plantations of ole Virginny. Have a good whiff. Perhaps you can detect a touch of anisette and the subtle hint of chocolate. I've had others, but this is the lad. Mind, it's a bit dear, but expect to pay for quality. Special order, all the way from the United States of America."

"And where is this America?" Láeg asked. "Where you can breathe in fire and blow smoke through your nose?"

"Out there beyond the sea. Follow the sun, and by cracky, you'll end up in the state of Philadelphia, America. It is the next land over the water."

"I know the place. It is where our ancestors do not putrefy after they have died but are left out to enjoy the sun and talk to their great-grandchildren should any brave soul dare sail over for a visit. It is said that mice cannot abide the place and will jump into the ocean rather than set one foot on that strange land."

"No, no. None of your fairy tales," Burke said. "America, streets paved with gold. Where all you need is tug your boot-straps and you can be the president of the whole place. Swimming pools in every yard, baby back ribs on the barbecue."

"Surely you mean the *Tír fo Thuinn*, the land under the wave? Or the Isle of the Apple Trees? You're not referring to *Tír na nÓg*, the land of everlasting youth and home to the timeless warriors of the *Tuatha Dé Dannan?*"

The pipe had gone out while Burke was listening to the lad's questions. He lit another match to stoke the fibers aglow. "I do not understand a word you are saying. Apple trees, is it? You can get your share of four different breed of apples at the Tesco day or night, and an island beneath the waves is no island at all. As for your land of everlasting youth, who would want that? Youth is best wasted on the young. No sor, a teenager again and plagued with the skin bumps on me face and the girls looking at me funny—you can put that in your own pipe to smoke. No, I'm talking about the U S of A, the land of the free and so forth. Burger King and the San Francisco Giants—"

Cúchulainn snorted at the mere mention of other giants.

Unabated, Burke continued. "I'll have you know, my good fellow, that there are more Irishmen over there than what's left here in Ireland. You cannot swing a cat in Boston without hitting a Kennedy. Sure, half the policemen are Murphys and the other half O'Briens. Why, Michael himself has a daughter in that faraway place. Ninety-nine percent of this country has a relation over there, rolling in the dough. What sort of oaf hasn't heard of America?"

The Northerners drooped their shoulders and pointed their weapons to the ground. Gobsmacked by the information coming from the little old man, they looked as forlorn as lost lambs, and Burke might as well have been the big bad wolf, smugly puffing on his pipe. The fug of smoke lay sickly sweet above their heads.

"I nearly went over meself," Burke said. "Not even you know that story, Mick. But I was a young lad like these two chancers, and there was no work to be had in all the Republic, save gathering seaweed with the women or stealing sheep like a hermit from Roscommon. I was all set to make the crossing, I was, when the Gaelic Games came to our backwater, and the lads from miles around were recruited for the local hurling team to play against the Derrymen. Pardon me, the boys from Londonderry. We were green sticks, cowboys, and culchies with no business in the matter. But somehow, we were tied dead even near the end of the match. Down the field the big Orangemen came, swinging their sticks and smacking the lashings off the ball. Me and a big left-footer in no-man's-land are the only two with a chance. So up I leaps, oh I was a rabbit in them days, and manage to swat it over to our side, and then goal and match to the boys of Connemara. And who do you think is passing out the ribbons to the winners? That's right. A girl with ginger hair and icy blue eyes, skin as pale as the moon. Kissed me square on the left cheek. We made our introductions, and that was that, as they say. Banns announced at Christmas. Married the next spring. No

Amerikay for Tom Burke. I was planted as a seed potato from the minute me and Mrs. Burke clapped eyes."

His pipe had gone out for good, so he tapped out the spent tobacco and cleaned the bowl with his thumb. Lost in their own memories of first love, the foursome remained speechless, revisiting the beauties of their youth. Overhead in the night sky, a crane flew by, the draft of its great wings folding the soft summer air. Like a petulant schoolboy, Cúchulainn picked up a rock, tossed it in the air, and swatted it with the flat blade of his broadsword. The shot barely missed the poor bird.

"Good ball," Burke said. "You look like a hurler yourself."

A naturally bashful man, Cúchulainn looked off into the distance to give them the benefit of his majestic profile. Mullaney and Burke sat in the dust to continue their appreciative listening.

"My friend here is too modest to boast," Láeg said. "But I'll tell you what sort of man you would be up against. When he was a mere boy of four years, he would like to take his hurley stick and wallop the *sliotar* so high and far that the ball would be no more than a speck in the bright sky, and when the speck would completely disappear, he would start running, a quarter mile betimes, so fast that there he'd be on the other end to catch the ball falling like a comet through the clouds. And when he tired of that, he took to batting the pill and then tossing his hurley stick after the ball, then throwing his toy javelin after the pair of them, and quick as a wink, he'd dash across the plain to catch ball, stick, and spear in one go. All day long, if you please, till his mammy called him in for his tea."

"Ah, g'wan," the giant said. He blushed heroically.

"Aye, I will. He was a grand lad for any game, you name it. No one could stop him from scoring at the Hole Game, and he never gave up a single goal. In Wrestling, he threw three fifties of opponents to the ground, all in a row. Matteradamn if them boys were husky or no. In Strip Tag, he left three fifties buck naked on the playgrounds, and every man jack failed to remove a single stitch off him. Ah, but his real love was the Gaelic football."

"I follow the Galway Tribes meself," said Burke. "Maroon and white. But Mullaney here is a Mayo man. God help us! Imagine rooting against your home team. Did you happen to catch the Connacht finals last year?"

The strapping young fellow glared at the impudence of the old sort for interrupting his story and adding nothing to the conversation. Chagrined, Burke took out his pouch and pipe and crammed in another dose of the hard stuff.

Láeg interrogated his supervisor. "How old were you, Cú, when you first took up the Gaelic football? Four, was it?"

The giant held up five giant fingers. A big fat grin on his face showed how much he enjoyed hearing the recitation of his boyhood exploits.

"So, minding his business, he was a mere five-year-old pup out for a bit of a stroll when he comes across the lads chasing a ball acrost the plain. High schoolers a-playing at the football in a real game with a real referee and fanatics in the grandstands. Little Bit here knows no better, so he lays down his toy spear and toy shield and runs onto the pitch in his short pants. The ball comes his way, and sure, doesn't he catch it between his knees, and not one of those boys on either side can tackle him before the ball is over the line for the winning score."

"Well done that," Burke said. "He's a true sporting man."

"Naturally, the referee comes over, blowing his whistle like a stuck pig and waving off the goal. You know the type. Mr. Play-by-the-Rules scolds the wee lad for not asking permission to join the match, and then he gives the high school lads a tongue-lashing about being a fine bunch of Ulstermen letting a mere pip beat them. He had them stirred to a lather, a raging mob out for blood."

"Boys will be boys," said Burke. He sent up a smoke signal from his pipe, proud of his sagacious observation.

"Three fifties of spears they hurled, and the lad caught each one in the skin of his toy shield. Three fifties of hurley balls he blocked with his chest, and three fifties of hurley sticks he swatted away with his own stick. Now, I don't need to tell you he has a temper, but it was the first time anyone seen his famous frenzy. Each hair stood on end and his head looked like a pincushion with a thousand sparking needles. Blood boiled beneath his skin and dyed his face the color of a red onion. One eye closed to a knife-slit, and the other grew wide as a tea saucer with seven spinning irises. His teeth sharpened into two rows of saws, and when he screeched, you could see his tonsils and the boiling ocean in his raw throat. His muscles had muscles of their own, and they flexed and trembled in fear of their own strength. His aura burned like a neon sign spelling r-a-g-e, and he went after those older boys, knocking out fifty with his fists and scattering the rest. Nine of those hooligans ran into the bleachers crying for their mammies and daddies, trying to escape this boy tornado, and who do you suppose our lad bumps into?"

Mullaney, who had been following the tale with rapt attention, offered a guess. "Conchobar, was it?"

"Good man yourself. Right, it was the king of Ulster himself, playing a game of chess on a bench in the stands. King Conchobar had seen the lad on the pitch and admired his nephew's skill and dexterity. Sure, wasn't that his sister's boy? The king was right busy and hadn't clapped eyes on the lad since he was a slobbering infant. With a calm hand, he

slows the dervish, then and there offers him his protection
from all harm in exchange for the boy joining up to play the
Gaelic football for our team, the Red Hands. From that day
on, we could not be beat, no sor. Soon enough, no team from
the other provinces would schedule a match against us, and
we had no other option but to scrimmage amongst ourselves.
Three fifties of the boys on one team against hisself alone.
Sure, but didn't he continue to beat them fair and square.
When those ruffians could no longer bear the shame, they
tried to unionize and give the upstart a good thrashing. He
went berserk again and knocked out a third of the lot. The
biggest footballers chased him all the way to the king's house,
and the boy hid under Conchobar's king-sized bed. All the
assembled men of Ulster went after him, even the king, even
meself. Arching his back, our Cú lifted the mattress with
thirty stout fellows hanging on for dear life and tossed the
whole bed, pillows and men, straight through the window.
Took the whole afternoon for the rest of us to corner him and
negotiate a truce. You trying talking sense to a five-year-old."

"They can be little monsters," Burke said.

A bittersweet nostalgia mixed with the burning tobacco.
All four of them fell into quiet contemplation of their lost
boyhoods, remembering those carefree days when life was
innocent and easy. When every loved one was whole and
here, before life pulled out the rug.

Wiping a tear from his eye, Cúchulainn buckled his
shield to his arm and scabbarded his sword, anxious to get
going. His valet sprang to action and similarly adjusted his
weaponry. Creaking with age and the labors of the day, Mullaney and Burke struggled to their feet and brushed the dust
from the seats of their trousers. They set off down the lane at
a more leisurely pace, trailing the two heroes, giving them a
chance to confer in privacy.

"I am surprised at you, Tom," Mullaney said. "You don't recognize the story of the 'Boyhood Exploits of Cúchulainn'? Surely every country lad went through a phase of playing with wooden swords and ashcan shields. Every boy threw a ball into the air and tried to catch it before it hit the ground. Your education is lacking in several key regards."

Wounded by his friend's remark, Burke defended himself. "Maybe I was learning my catechism and how to avoid the road to perdition whilst you had your nose in a comic book, dreaming about the pagan legends. The nuns and the brothers don't tolerate your godless heroes. Go ahead, ask me anything about St. Patrick. Did you know that Welsh snake charmer wore blue robes instead of green? Oh, I could tell you stories about that interloper, and sure, don't we have plenty of saints native to Ireland? Once upon a time, the place was crawling with martyrs and other holy joes. And I'll go toe-to-toe with any of youse over the seven holy virtues."

"St. Thomas of Burke."

"And you're a right heathen."

With a thwack, the spear landed directly between the two men's feet, the shaft vibrating like a metronome and the point driven deep into the dirt lane. Cúchulainn walked on, and his factotum jogged back to retrieve the weapon and give them fair warning.

"Quit squabbling like a pair of hens over one egg. I'll ask you to remember our business for the night." The driver joined them to continue their journey three abreast.

"Tell me something," Burke said. "What sort of name is Cúchulainn?"

"Not his given name," the charioteer said, behind his hand. "His mammy, the king's sister, named him Sétanta, the wayfarer, as soon as the babby barreled into the world. Maybe she knew he would be always on the go. He earned his nickname as a boy. Seven years old, playing chase the ball and stick and spear, he decides to take a shortcut home so's he is not late for his tea. Little does he know he's trespassing on the blacksmith's property, a man with the name Culann on him, who has one of them big watchdogs, fierce as a wolf, the kind known as Cú, the Irish for hound. A Spanish mastiff so terrible it needed three chains to hold it and three men to hold each chain whilst they took it for a walk. A pooch who would take the leg off you for just looking over the fence. Even his great mean turds would growl at you. This particular day, the beast had been let loose to guard the cows and bull in the pasture. The hound gets one whiff of the boy, starts howling and baring its fangs and foaming at the mouth, and charges straight for him. Imagine how frightened you would be. Your lad takes his bat and smacks a ball so hard it bashes through the dog's teeth, down the windpipe, and clear through the other end, dragging the guts out through its arsehole.

"Everyone for miles around had heard the ferocious baying of the dog, and the king of Ulster himself feared Sétanta had been killed. Meantimes the blacksmith Culann comes running out to the iron yard and sees his pet turned inside out. Moaning and complaining about losing his best friend in the world and how will he ever find such another loyal watchdog, but naturally he can say no more, on account of the child being the king's nephew."

Ahead on the path, Cú waved away his servant, giddy to finish the tale himself. "I says to him, 'Don't worry. I will raise you an even finer beast, and until that pup is big and strong enough to protect your land and livestock, I will stand guard for your family, your cows and bulls besides.' Some joker nearby says, 'Then you should be called Cú Chulainn, the Hound of Culann.' I says, 'Go right ahead. That good name is now on me.'"

"That certainly explains a lot," Burke said. "I am Burke, and this is Michael Mullaney. Should we call you Cú or Mr. Cullen, which do you prefer?"

A few hairs stood on end as if hammered into Cú's skull, and one eye narrowed as the other widened. It seemed the smallest slight might set him off.

Playing the peacemaker, Láeg stepped between the two parties. "Now then, Mr. Burke, Mr. Mullaney, which route should we follow?"

"Yes, where is she?" Cúchulainn asked.

Mullaney edged around the Hound to lead them astray. Uncertain about their intentions, he would not give up the girl so easily. "This way, gentlemen, to the bogs."

CHAPTER

12

Pillow Talk

B RIGHT ENOUGH TO throw shadows, the full moon shone on the winding path to Burke's farm. Bridget checked the time on her phone, the aura from the screen reflecting off her glasses. Not too late, she decided; if any lights were on, she would knock. Otherwise, back to the inn and retrace her steps in the morning. Incessant rows of waves murmured upon the faraway shore. An owl called out for its mate, and moments later a reply echoed from an abandoned barn. A churr from the hedges startled her. The single cry from a distant fox sounded like a woman being murdered. A splash from an otter out for a night swim in the nearby lake. What a strange thrill to be on her own in such an unfamiliar space and time, and rather than being frightened, she drew strength and confidence from her solitary walk. Wind carried distant voices, as if doors and windows had been thrown open for the first burst of summer and snatches of conversation escaped. The West was awake at that late hour, the scrim between the worlds parted, and all things magic passed easily under darkness.

Following the tin whistle man's directions, she found the large stone landmark, forded the stream, and started counting farmhouses. Set back from the lane, the first stone cottage was silent, buttoned in its pajamas for the night. Dark forms moved in the front yard, a pair of horses hitched to a cart and forgotten, left to fend for themselves in harness rather than the comfort of their stable. Bridget toyed with the notion of waking the farmer to reproach him for such neglect, but she pressed on with her mission, deciding that if those horses were still tethered outside when she headed back to the inn, she would have a word.

The second house was lit up like a jack-o'-lantern. Lamps beamed from every room, and the front door was ajar. The place looked recently deserted, like one of those stories where the family is suddenly abducted by aliens, half-eaten pork chops on the dinner plates, glasses of milk still cold to the touch, a cake gone to cinders in the oven, and the needle stuck on the same skip in the endlessly spinning vinyl record. What had Tin Whistle said? Burke would either be home alone or at Mullaney's for a nightcap. *What sort of mad party is going on, Mr. Mullaney?*

With each step toward the front door, she found her point of view wavering. At certain angles, the house appeared to flatten like a drawing and then shift to three dimensions with the next step, the seesaw effect a mere trick of the light or a trick of the mind. Or had the world shifted, somehow, between planes, the uncertain perspective a sign of time gone awry? A low wall separated the front garden from the lane. Jammed into a crevice by the gate, a long blade had been squeezed like an accordion. Bridget fiddled with the handle, trying to pry it free, but not a chance. A powerful force had driven the metal into the stone, and she wondered if it was supposed to be some perplexing sculpture meant to enchant visitors to the farm—beat your weapons into plowshares or something like that. Modern art often leaves the viewer guessing. She playfully pulled again, and the sword vibrated with a pleasing twang.

The bronze hilt of the weapon seemed familiar, a copy perhaps of the ancient swords she had seen in her Irish archaeology textbook as a specimen from the turn of the first millennium. First the report of a bog body, and now a possible treasure from antiquity. She'd allowed her qualms to be swept away and had willingly chased a chimera clear across the country because of a few jpegs. It's crazy, she told herself, to be knocking on the door of a dream.

Nobody answered.

Bridget stepped inside. Instead of the expected ordinary squalor of a bachelor farmhouse, she found utter disarray. Someone had ransacked the rooms. Jagged gashes scored the walls. Curtains were shredded and pillows torn open, stuffing protruding from the gashes. A desk in the parlor lacked its drawers. She stood in the middle of the rubble, quietly considering the evidence of recent violence. The horns of her dilemma were quite sharp and pointy, but some incipient boldness budded in her, some sense of her own Irish bullheadedness to press on, come what may. "Mr. Mullaney? Mr. Burke? Is anyone in here? Are you all right?"

The stillness chewed at her nerves. She half feared to find a body on the floor, blood pooling around the head, an old geezer with a blade in the middle of his back. On the balls of her feet, she crept into the kitchen. Shattered glass was strewn across the floor, and the oven had a gaping wound. Cuts and scratches on the walls and furniture. Some madmen in a frenzy had taken out their anger on the place. All the knives and forks, scissors and shavers, screwdrivers, needle-nosed pliers had been heaped on the table like a mountain of bent and broken weapons laid down after battle, the losers' disarmament or the victors' spoils.

A person flashed by her peripheral vision and startled her, until she recognized her reflection in the glass of the liquor cabinet. Belted around its middle was a wide band of wooden veneer with strange incisions. With her fingertips she traced the carvings. Runes. Ancient Ogham writing scratched into the cheap surface. What sort of madness had she wandered into? Her colleagues back in Dublin could verify her suspicion that the text was authentic. As she studied the patterns, she had the sensation that someone was watching her, and she spun around quickly, expecting the worst.

A small border collie, with a patch of white around one eye like a monocle, sat in the hallway between the kitchen and the bedrooms. Bridget had not heard the click of its nails on the linoleum. The dog had simply materialized and was now inspecting her, head tilted to one side, brown eyes following her every move. Bridget exhaled and offered the back of her hand to smell, but the dog gave her a great wag of the tail that said *This is completely unnecessary. I am delighted that you showed up.*

"What happened here?" Bridget asked. "It's okay, little fella, I don't bite. That's a good boy."

The bitch was used to the error. She allowed herself to be petted and then flipped over for a belly rub. Despite the pleasure, her eyebrows twitched the whole time as she scanned the room.

"A girl, are you? What are you trying to tell me then? Has Timmy fallen down the well, Lassie? Do we need to run and get help?"

The collie rolled over, inched forward, and barked sharply.

"Is he in the bedroom, girl?" She tried to pass the dog, but it blocked the passage, herding her back into the kitchen.

"Mr. Mullaney," she called. "Are you back there? Mr. Burke?"

A man's muffled voice shouted one annoyed word, and an old mattress creaked as someone rose. With a bash, the bedroom door flew open, and a tall young woman stepped into the hallway. A bad case of bedhead flattened one side of her blond hair, and loose knots whirled on the other side. The overhead light made her wince and scrunch her features. She wore a white tunic, fastened at the right shoulder, her left breast uncovered. Her bare feet were dark with dust as if from a long journey. Indifferent to her state of undress, she tottered toward Bridget on champagne steps, resting her hand on the wall as she gathered her bearings. Gold bracelets jangled on her wrist, and on each finger she wore rings with glittering gems.

The dog took off, leaving Bridget alone with the stranger. They eyed each other curiously. With their matching Roman noses, they could have been sisters, Irish cousins at the very least. The woman carried herself as if she were a person of privilege who enjoyed great wealth and power. Bridget thought she looked like a queen without her crown.

"Oh, excuse me," Bridget said. "I didn't mean to wake you, and I'm sorry to let myself in so late at night, but the door was wide open, and nobody answered, and here we are. I'm sorry, I should introduce myself." She held out her hand, but the woman seemed puzzled by the gesture. Instead, she buttoned up her tunic and finger combed her hair, waiting for Bridget to continue.

"I was looking for a Thomas Burke or . . ." She remembered at last. "Michael Mullaney. You must be Mrs. Mullaney." Before going any further, Bridget stopped and reconsidered. The half-naked woman looked to be about her own age. Either Mullaney had married a much younger woman or this woman was not his wife.

In the corridor, the young sybarite yawned and knuckled the sleep from one eye. A patch of whisker-burn on her nape looked fresh and raw, and her lips were swollen bee-stung red. She had the kind of self-confidence that others might read as haughtiness but that allowed her to openly inspect Bridget from head to toe, stopping at the curiosity of her eyeglasses. She leaned nose to nose and peered through the lenses. "Hmm," she said, and shook her blond curls in disbelief. "I'm sorry, darling. Why are you looking for this Burke Mullaney?"

"You see, my name is Bridget Scanlon. I'm an archaeologist from the university in Dublin, and these two may have uncovered a very significant find. The body of a girl in the bogs, two thousand years old. I'm looking for Burke or Mullaney to take me to her—"

"A girl in the bog." The news seemed to excite the woman inordinately. "Tell me, did she suffer the triple death? Bound at the wrists and neck? A bash in the skull, a slash at the throat?"

"As a matter of fact," Bridget said. "How on earth would you know that?"

From the bedroom, a man's voice bellowed, "What's going on, babe?"

"'Tis nothing, babe," she said. "A strange woman come to the house."

"Why don't you invite her in?" he sang.

The woman in the hall rolled her eyes. "Call me Medb, if you please. M-e-d-b, or as you might pronounce it, Maeve. You don't sound from these parts, I reckon. English, are you? What's the strange accent on you? What quare music plays beneath your words?"

"I'm from America," Bridget said. "Philadelphia."

"Brotherly love, is it?" She yawned. "It's all Greek to me, darling."

From the bedroom came a spicy invitation. "Are you coming or not? I am ready to be plundered."

"I'm sorry, I'll leave."

"Oh, for the gods' sake, sure that's just me old man. You can call him Al. He's a rake, but he's handsome. Met him when he was my first husband's bodyguard. Mr. Irresistible. We were after having a wee bit of pillow talk and must not have heard you. C'mon in, Bridget."

Wagging her bottom, Maeve turned on her heel and retreated to the bedroom. Bridget followed, protesting. "Do you know something about the girl—"

Her old man Al was not old at all. Propped in bed, he was as handsome and in his prime as his wife. Above his heart was a magnificent tattoo of the Connacht coat of arms: a black eagle and a raised fist gripping a sword. Curly-haired as a satyr, he wore only a lascivious grin above a smart goatee and gold rings on both thumbs. Beneath the sheets, he obviously was not wearing a stitch.

"Put a tunic on," Maeve said. "Have you no decency? This here is a respectable lass. Bridget come all the way from Philadelphia, and she'll have none of your paddywhackery."

Bridget took a step toward the door, but Maeve stopped her in the strong grip of one hand. "Tut, tut, what kind of host would I be throwing you out in the dark middle of the night?"

Pouting and muttering improprieties, Al searched for his robe at the foot of the bed. "The queen must be obeyed, matteradamn what I want. It's Maeve's way or the highway. Don't you find her a bit headstrong, Bridget? By the gods, what a lovely name."

"Pay him no mind," Maeve said. "We were having a wee donnybrook. He's endlessly palavering about whose family is richer, whose house the grander, whose fields greener, and who has the best bull—"

"Don't let's get started on that again, babe," Al said. He stood in front of the mirror, fixing his hair into a man bun.

"Would you let go of me, please?" Bridget freed her arm and backed away. "I'm lost. I thought this must be Mullaney's. I've never even been in this part of the country."

Maeve stood behind her husband and admired her reflection. "If you ask me, Connacht is the prettiest of Ireland's four provinces. No disrespect to Munster—it's charming and picturesque in its own way—and Leinster is the birthplace of kings."

"Not to mention Ulster," Al said.

"Grrr, I won't hold a grudge against those folk," she said. "But nor can I pardon their stubbornness."

"Hah! Their stubbornness? That's rich, coming from yourself. We wouldn't have half the trouble if you had a healthy respect for Cú—"

"Right, so," Maeve interrupted. "How many times do I have to say I'm sorry? What's past is past, can you not leave it?"

"I should go," Bridget said. "I caught you at a bad time."

"Nonsense, darling. Stay, stay. We share a common interest. I want to know everything there is to know about this bog girl of yours." After she pinched her cheeks red and flounced her hair, Maeve stuck out her tongue at Al's reflection. "I'd offer you a drink, only someone's locked the liquor cabinet tighter than a chastity belt. Won't we all be more comfy in the parlor?"

Following in her footsteps, Al brushed past Bridget lightly enough that she could not tell if it was an accident or a deliberate flirtation. He sashayed into the parlor and patted a place for her on the sofa next to him. She sat in the easy chair.

Oblivious to the glass under her bare feet, Maeve went to the stove to wet the tea. She kept one eye on her husband, the other on the kettle. "So, Philadelphia, how do you know this Mullaney and Burke?"

"Sounds like a solicitors," Al said. "Or the folks what does your taxes."

Maeve had the tea tray in hand. "A comedy team."

"Or a brand of whiskey," Al said. "I could murder a good Mullaney and Burke about now."

With a wink to her husband, she played mother and poured.

"I don't know them personally," Bridget said. "I'm only in Connemara because Burke and Mullaney found a girl in the bog."

Behind the back of her hand, Maeve mouthed "Fedelm?" to her old man.

Bridget donned her archaeology hat. "They pop up from time to time. The chemicals in the peat help preserve the corpse, more or less intact from the time of death. Some softening of the tissue and darkening of the skin, but the person looks much the same—"

"How long do they last under the water?" asked Al.

"Centuries," said Bridget, warming to a subject dear to her heart. "A few are actually thousands of years old. Amazing what you can learn from the body. What they ate, how they dressed, how they died."

"And who killed her?" Maeve asked. She winked and flashed a high sign, an elaborate wiggle of the fingers, to her husband, and in return, he stretched his long legs and rubbed his bare feet together against the edge of the coffee table.

Remembering the purpose of her visit, Bridget was ebullient again. "I only found out about her from the internet. The only other people to know about the discovery are Burke's granddaughter and some girls who call themselves the Red Hags."

The news flustered them, and they drank their scalding tea as if it were on ice. "Al, I'd like a word with you."

"Chatter away, my filly. I am all ears."

"In private," she said. "If Miss Philadelphia can spare us. Join me in the bedroom."

"There is no place on earth I would rather be." The smile slipped from his face when he noticed Maeve's glaring eyes. He followed her down the hallway like a boy sent to the headmaster's office. They were long absent in private consultation.

Bridget was tempted to head back to the village rather than search any longer for Burke or Mullaney. She had stumbled into the wrong house with an oversexed maniac, clearly under the woman's thumb, while the woman herself was as changeable as the Irish weather, soft as a fine drizzle one moment and full of thunder the next. They were oddly intoxicating, and she found herself thinking about what was going on behind the closed door. But what had they done to the poor dog to make her run away? And why were they in Mullaney's house in the first place?

They were gone so long that she worked out the puzzle of where she had heard of a Maeve and Al. Her grandfather's old story. The Cattle Raid on Cooley.

From the bedroom came the shattering of glass. A shoe or hairbrush flung against a mirror. They argued mainly in Irish, and despite her several years in the country, Bridget knew only a handful of words. *Gabhdán,* Maeve shouted. *You're a real old wagon*, Al replied. Tears flowed, though Bridget could not tell through the closed door who was sobbing. Perhaps they had a real donnybrook before she arrived and that's why the house was a shambles. Still, that did not explain the ancient sword in the stone, or the spade stuck in the door, or the liquor cabinet trussed by a band marked in Ogham. Her head ached with doubts. Not for the first time that day, she wondered if she had made a mistake. She stood and moved to the door, but a question stopped her: *Who is Fedelm?*

The bedroom grew suspiciously quiet. Maybe, she thought, they had forgotten about her and turned in for the night. A giggle found its way to the parlor. Al was singing, what passed for an Irish serenade. Two seconds later and Bridget would have been off, waving her hands over her head and complaining to the stars as she beat it for the inn. But out they tumbled.

"No need to run off, pet," Maeve said. She practically glowed with an aura of inner confidence. "We go at it like the two black cats of Kilkenny, clawing and scratching till all that remains after the fight are two long tails. It's the making up, isn't it? We would like to help track down this body of yours, and you can help us find who we are looking for, too. Astonishing that you happened to chance upon her."

"Extraordinary," Al said. "What great coincidence, the three of us looking for a girl."

Feeling a bit sheepish for the undeserved credit, Bridget corrected the record. "I didn't personally discover her myself, and even if I dug a thousand holes, I'm not sure I would have. After all, I cannot even seem to locate two farmers, given exact directions."

"Don't be so hard on yourself, darling. Indeed, this is Mullaney's hut. Or at least that's his name on all the bills and letters on his desk. After our long journey, we chanced upon this humble abode, deserted as the Newgrange tomb. Since no one was at home, we decided to have a lie-down in the bed, Goldilocks and Papa Bear, and that's where you found us. We have been all night hunting for someone too. A friend of ours we haven't seen in ages."

After sipping the dregs of her tea, Maeve set down the cup with a majestic clatter.

CHAPTER

13

The Graveyard

THE FIRE BURNED quickly for want of dry fuel, so the witches stirred the embers. Siobhán shoved her feet into the ashes, hoping to dry her damp shoes, and waited for Fedelm's instructions. She remained as inscrutable as a henge. Her eyes focused across the lake, trying to conjure her old trick of foreseeing the future, but the magic had deserted her when she needed it most. Behind her, those three little kittens debated in whispers whether to follow her.

"This whole situation is pure mental," Emcee said. "We must be out of our minds, traipsing all over the county with a dead girl. At least I think she is dead, and surely she was dead this morning. My pops would have mentioned the walking and the talking, you don't see that every day. What sort of resurrection is it? Back after two thousand years."

Eileen pushed the charcoal edges with a stick. "Maybe they should have never uncovered her in the first place. Waking the dead. You cannot say you are not a bit afraid, Shey."

"I'm going home," Emcee announced.

Pulling the tight laces of her shoe, Siobhán would have liked to wrap the shoestrings around their necks. "Listen, are we witches or not? You may have been pretending all these years, but Eileen and me made a commitment. Scared, am I? If the thing had wanted to do us in, she would have done so by now. Did you see how she flung me about like a sack of flour? She might be strong, but she needs our help, somehow, and I for one intend to see things through."

"Some kind of feckin' monster," Emcee said.

"I'm not deaf." Fedelm appeared suddenly beside them. "If you would rather run to your mammies and warm beds, go on then."

Penitent, the girls bowed their heads.

"Listen, when I was a girl, my father met three witches just like you. He had cut enough turf to last a long winter and stacked the bricks in a reek black and tall as a mountain. During the night, the hags snuck in and piled a share in their creels and stole away. They did so again night after night that whole frozen season until our supply was very nearly gone. But they were greedy-guts, down to the last scraps of turf, and the next midnight hour I followed them to their cave in the Pass of the Boar. They were using our fuel to keep a cauldron constantly on the boil for their potions and whatnot. I was so angry I rolled a boulder down upon them and bashed the pot and spoiled their brew. Let me tell you, girls, they were mad as wet hens and chased me to a great oak tree. I had climbed near the top to hide away, but the eldest witch turned one sister into a fierce wolfhound to keep me stuck in the branches, and then she changed the other sister into a broadaxe. First swing, she cut a third of the way through that oak and the next blow chopped another third, and just on the backswing of the third, sure, didn't the sun peep over the Maumturk mountains. The powerful rays turned those three witches into fair maidens, such as yourselves, and off they went, holding hands and singing folksongs echoing the length and breadth of Connemara."

These three Red Hags failed to interpret her meaning.

"Mind you the laws of Mother Nature, who draws a scrim between an ordinary girl and one who makes magic. If you want to be witches, you must act like witches. I can help you if you help me. Otherwise, off ye go and think no more upon the black arts."

The weight of years of friendship fell on the girls. Hesitant at the brink of a long dream's fulfillment, they dithered and dallied, passing silent pleas and threatening looks. Finally, a sign from Emcee, no grander than a shrug, was all it took for them to make the leap. They nodded in unison. Yes, they said, yes.

"Thank the gods you finally decided. We need to put some distance between us and those men we heard at the little hut. One swung a broadsword sharp enough to make the air bleed. I do not wish to encounter him again, so I'm for the hills. I only hope that those chasing me cannot find our trail."

Falling in behind her, they drew their hoods over their red manes and buried their hands in their pockets to stave off the chill. In the bright moonlight, a few whitewashed houses shimmered like stars. At a crossroads, one path meandered around the wetlands toward the western ocean, and the other crooked lane climbed to the highlands. Fedelm did not hesitate. After so many cramped centuries, their sojourn was a tonic, but her feet were sore, and the stump of her little toe throbbed. Her retinue, however, grumbled after the first mile, saying they needed a rest. At the next stone wall, she sat and allowed the girls to catch up. They moped and complained about the long trek, so Fedelm tried again to picture what was to come. Long ago such visions had arrived unbidden, the blood-red fields littered with her Connacht countrymen and the boy hero of Ulster burning hot and bright after the slaughter. Now even the thinnest premonition failed to arrive. *Some seer*, she thought; she could not even imagine the road ahead, nor was she entirely sure who was following them on the road behind.

"A bit further on," she told her troops. "We need to be hidden, not out in the open."

Behind a tangled hedgerow lay a stone chapel, a spare and simple country church, now in serious decay. The roof had disintegrated long ago, but three crumbling walls remained. Grass had conquered the nave and altar, and lichen and moss bloomed on every stone, creeping into the mortar. Two glassless windows held their grip against time, one to the south, the other to the east, framing the countryside beyond. The witches inspected the sanctuary, poking in the corners where schoolboys had smoked their mitched cigarettes and drunk their purloined beers, discarding the empty amber bottles. Fedelm went through to the other side, and surprised to see her, a sheep bleated and called for its maaa. Nearly jumping out of her skin, the bog girl let loose a stream of Old Irish curses at the poor misfortunate creature. But the dumb thing refused to move until she stomped her foot and waved her branchlike arms. To the sheep, she must have looked like a tree come to life and full of fury.

"*Tóg go bog é*," Siobhán said. "Take it easy. It's only an old bag of wool."

Fenced by a fieldstone wall, a cemetery held a few dozen graves. Headstones 'leaned in every direction, cracked or fallen on their faces. In the middle towered a Celtic cross dedicated to the Famine victims and the Great Hunger, a grim reminder to all who passed by. The three witches stayed on the old winding pathways. Cat-curious, Fedelm stalked the grounds, pausing at each stone. Years of wind and rain had erased most of the letters and dates, and the names were lost to time.

"You shouldn't be walking on top of the burial places," Emcee said. "You should watch where you tread and show some respect."

Fedelm leaned against a plinth. "What is this place?"

"You should feel right at home here," Emcee said. "Have you never seen a cemetery?"

"What is the purpose of these stones in the grass?"

Siobhán laughed. "It's an old boneyard, where they bury the dead."

"Like in the bogs?"

"No, in pine boxes, with a Mass said over them, a proper priest and the folks come to mourn the deceased. The stones mark the person underneath, when they were born, and when they died. And maybe a note saying how good they were and how they are sorely missed. Ah, what's the use? You have no idea what I mean."

"Do they not burn the bodies after the spirit is gone?"

"Is that what they did in your day?"

"If you were one of the fortunate ones to die in good standing, but who can know when the hour comes? Tomorrow catches you by surprise and throws you in a bog, ensuring you are stuck in this world and not free to go to the next."

Eileen popped a mint in her mouth. "Some folk say you are supposed to keep the windows closed when a person dies in the house, and some say to open them and let the soul fly away. My granny was the one with stories galore. Did you know you can make butter in half the time by using a dead man's hand to stir a jug of milk? Or wrap the corner of a used shroud to heal a sore thumb or toe. Always carry the body out feetfirst, she'd say, so the soul cannot tell it is leaving and refuse to go."

"It's a quare thing to run out of time in the end," Emcee asked. "My pops says 'tis the fate of the pot to lose its bottom."

From inside the church came a faint rustling and the tortured creak of an axle slowly turning. The witches hid behind the nearest wall, and Fedelm crouched beside the Celtic cross. The squeaky wheels grew louder. A pair of ghostly white horses appeared from the ruins, pausing at the dark threshold, uncertain of what to make of the new scene. On the right side, the horse's great nostrils flared and drew in the dampness and decay, and then the horse on the left let out a loud and wet sneeze. With renewed confidence, the mares moved into the graveyard, dragging behind them a small chariot, moonlight glinting off the gold trim of both wheels.

Fedelm walked straight to the horse with a shaggy gray mane, cupped its muzzle in one hand, and stroked its neck with the other. She spoke gently, in the old language, to calm it further. Unable to temper their emotions, the Red Hags rushed in to coo over the fine animals. Eileen was smitten, and she fed each horse a candy and whispered sweet nothings into the cathedrals of their ears.

"What is this contraption?" Emcee asked. She climbed into the chariot's small two-seater cab and took hold of the reins, marveling at the craftsmanship of the leather inlaid with red-and-gold knotwork. Entwined along the length of each strap was a stylized embroidery of running horses. "Where in the world did this thing come from?"

"I have seen this chariot before," Fedelm said. "I know its gilding and the careful handiwork of regal design." The left horse lifted her great neck, and the right tossed her silvery mane. "There now, my beauties. There's nothing to fear, old girls. Ah, but it has been a long, long time. *Fadó, fadó.*"

She asked Eileen to free the team from their traces and harness, and while the girl worked the buckles and straps,

Fedelm let loose a steady stream of honey words. After some difficulty with the old-style halter, Eileen managed to unhitch them. The pale horses cantered sideways, threatening to spook, as the tongue of the yoke slipped and fell with a dull thud.

"Easy now," Eileen said. "How long you been dragging that bloody chassis around?"

Fedelm pulled at the right one's bridle to settle the left one's nerves. "These alabaster beauties are Connacht mares. Now I am doubly confused, for I was expecting Ulster stallions, black as fired and hammered iron."

"Wait, now," Emcee said. "You were expecting horses and a chariot to show up? You knew about this?"

"Ever since I heard that swordplay back at the house, I have been expecting the worst. But these are horses of a different color and belong to the queen. Perhaps there is no danger afoot after all."

She ran her free hand along the shaggy one's withers and caressed its broad back. Without a warning, she smartly slapped its rump. The beast hopped in alarm, and then free of its burden, the ghostly horse trotted past the gravestones and disappeared into the night. Her harness-mate hesitated before giving chase. They all watched the pair gallop away, admiring their elegant locomotion.

"Who is this queen?" Siobhán asked.

"Medb, the queen of Connacht, who else? Those two farmers who dug me out of the underworld must have left open the door to the dark. The gods only know who else besides me is out and about this night. Those pale horses belong to my queen. My kinsmen must be out looking for me, ready to welcome me back into the clan. Do you know what this means, girls? I thought our enemy, the Hound of Ulster, must be about, but those pale horses foretell an

altogether different fate. This is a most auspicious omen."
Feeling rejuvenated, Fedelm clapped her hands and took in
her surroundings once again. "Right, we must make ready.
Our prospects have much improved."

Relief spread like a virus. The girls' spirits were lifted by
Fedelm's abrupt change of temperament, and each began to
plan for the journey home.

"I must look a fright," the bog girl said. "Dear me, does
any of you have a looking glass?"

The witches stared at her, fascinated by the blackness of
her skin, the luster of her tunic, and the raw-looking wounds
at her thin neck and delicate wrists.

"You're not too shabby," Siobhán said. "Considering."

"Not bad at all," Eileen said. "If you are partial to that
death-warmed-over vibe. Decenter than most people
who have been under the ground two thousand years. It's
a bleeding miracle you are standing on your two
feet, talking to us, like. And you wonder if you are
presentable."

Remembering her smartphone in her back pocket, Emcee
cued up the camera app and handed it to the bog girl. "Take
a look," she said. "It's like a mirror."

Entranced by the magic looking glass, Fedelm touched
her face and scarred throat and fiddled with the nest of her
reddened hair, once honey blond before her many centuries
in the bog. After all those dark years, she had forgotten what
she looked like, but she had not imagined the extent of dam-
age to her face and the ragged ends of her shorn locks. She
was a stranger to herself.

Emcee offered a practical suggestion. "You could do
something with what's left. It's a lovely shade of ginger, but
the braid's come undone, and you've the flyaways. I could
straighten the knot if you like."

"That would be grand." Fedelm parked in front of her and presented her head. Like a pair of wrens on a wire, Eileen and Siobhán watched side by side from the wall.

Her hair appeared brittle as dried flax, but it proved supple to the touch. On her left side her braid would have reached to her waist, but the right and back had been crudely hacked and chopped. Emcee's first task was to figure out the pattern and untie the knot. She separated the locks into thirds, plying and weaving, losing herself to the plain joy of a simple task. Under the girl's care, Fedelm shut her eyes. No vision or dream, only pitch darkness.

As she worked, Emcee spoke with a distracted air. "Fedelm, where are we going? What are we to do with you if we do not find your kinfolk?"

With the tip of her tongue, Fedelm wet her dry lips. "That's a real conundrum. Sure, wasn't it you three that unwrapped me from the shroud, and wasn't it your grandfathers what pulled me out of the earth? I could ask you what purpose they had in mind."

Siobhán piped up. "For the record, neither of those two farmers is my grandfather, nor Eileen's. They are Mary Catherine's pops and his drinking buddy, Mullaney."

Luxuriating in the feel of fingers in her hair, Fedelm stretched her neck and rolled her shoulders. "Why would they dig me up now? I didn't ask to be exhumed. Minding my own business, I was, snug as a bug in a peaty rug. Have a good leap every century or so to keep up with the times. Or if I was bored. What would those old fools want of me?"

Lost in the task of unweaving her hair, Emcee answered with an absent-minded air. "Aren't you the most brilliant thing to happen in these parts? They'll take you to Dublin straightaway. First, the experts will have at you, clean you up a bit and take you to the laboratory. Put you in one of them big MRI tubes and have a good look around inside and out. That brooch will go on display with all the other national treasures. Afterwards they will put you in a glass box with some fake dirt, as if you had been lying there the whole time waiting on Prince Charming. Mammies will bring their weeuns on a Saturday to have the bejaysus scared out of them. My pops took me to see the Old Croghan Man, what's left of him. Two arms connected to half a chest. No head, no legs, not a scrap below the belly button. Gave me bad dreams a fortnight. You're lucky to be in one piece, like. They will definitely want you for the collection. People would come from miles around. Think of all the Americans." She tucked the last lock into the knot. "There now, you're done. Looks like that Star Wars girl, only the one side instead of two cinnamon buns."

A second story landed in Eileen's brain. "Obviously they couldn't put a living person in a display case. It wouldn't do, not if you're alive."

"I am not sure I am alive," the bog girl said. "It doesn't quite feel the same the second time around. And I was certainly dead yesterday, and well before that. I could tell you stories about how I came to an end." She traced the rope marks on her neck.

Eileen was not convinced. "On the other hand, you are here in this graveyard real as us. None of these skeletons are rising for a chat."

"You can walk and talk," Siobhán said. "And you are as strong as a bull. Who's to say if you are alive or not if all the evidence points one way? Dead or alive. Or is it both at the same time, like that cat in the box?"

"By the gods, you speak in riddles." Fedelm patted the braidwork on the side of her head. "But one of you witches, at least, has some magic in her fingers."

14

Black and White

LÁEG WAS UP to his nipples in the peat. Flakes of turf stuck to his hairy arms, and clots of muck clung to his bare sweaty chest. The hem of his short tunic was filthy and ruined. He stabbed the moist earth again and sluiced a brick of peat to the banks of the ditch. Worn from their labors, Mullaney and Burke slagged off in a nearby hole of their own. Paring his fingernails with a razor-sharp dagger, Cúchulainn stood on high ground with an indifferent air. The night work was made possible by the glow of his hero's aura, bright as a halogen lamp. They had been at it for hours. First one hole near the actual spot where they had found the girl, but when no body turned up, they moved on to other patches on the bog. Hole after hole, to no avail. The Ulsterman did not tire from supervising their labors, for he was convinced they were bound to remember eventually where they had put her. For their part, Mullaney and Burke could only stall the inevitable.

"Mick, I cannot go on," Burke said. "I am completely spent entirely, with not the energy to wipe my own arse. I am sweating pure stout and my arms are like rubber bands. You don't have to tell me what you did with the body, but for God's sake, confess to those two goons and let's be done with it. All desire is wrung out of me. I do not care about fame or fortune, my name on a plaque. I only want to be under me own covers, enjoying the comfort of my one constant friend, me own bed."

Mullaney lobbed a spud of dirt to the top of the hole. "Tom, do you not think I have thought the same? Do you not remember they chopped off your head? Amn't I afraid of what these boyos will do to us once they've found out we have been telling fibs?"

"We, is it? Who is this *we* you're speaking of? I have half a mind to say something myself to the Hound. Look at him there, not a speck of dirt on him. Why doesn't he pull that stunt and get hoppin' mad, like? Wind him up a bit, put a sléan in his hands, and half the turf of County Galway would be stripped by morning."

Caught in the radiation of the hero's luminosity, they picked up their spades and bent to work. With a shrug, Cú shouldered his spear, like an overseer cradling a shotgun whilst minding the chain gang.

"An Irishman's lot," Burke said, raising his voice. "All we are good for is the manual labor. Let me tell you, Mr. Man, the Irishman paved England and built the buildings and dug the sewers that saved the Thames. The Irish what carved the subways of New York and sunk the legs for Brooklyn Bridge and drowned in the Hudson when the tunnels collapsed. Where would the ships go without the Irish-dug Pannyma Canal? Who but the Irish to lay the bricks, to clean the shite, to break our backs for the western world? And what thanks do we get, I ask you? Give Paddy the shovel and tell him to dig."

From the other hole, Láeg called out, "A little less gab, if you please, and a little more excavation. Are you sure, Mullaney, that this is the spot?"

"Here or there, I think. But we are bound to find her if we only keep at it."

Occasionally when he was bored, Cúchulainn would chuck a brick of turf into the air and whack it with the flat end of his sword. He would then cup his mouth and breathe out an imitation of the roaring crowd at Croke Park in Dublin or the *Páirc an Phiarsaigh* in Salthill. Mullaney admired the ease with which the big lad could keep himself entertained.

But Burke would have none of it. "Listen, even a navvy gets a coffee break," he shouted. "Or a chance to have a wee pipe, if you please, boss."

"Take five," Láeg said. "Smoke 'em if you got 'em."

Burke crawled out of the hole and sat on the top edge of the damp ditch. A mist lay over the bogland as far as the eye could see, and in that rising gauzy fog Cúchulainn's light cast a soft halo outlining the contours of his shapely form. He looked like a model for a photo shoot. Men of the Wild Atlantic Way. Burke lit his briar and walked straight over to the gorgeous Irish beefcake, who seemed to have forgotten all about the workingman. With the stem of his pipe, he poked the warrior in the chest to get his attention. The big man took a healthy sniff of the smoke in the twin caverns of his nostrils.

"Have a go, then," Burke said. He handed him the pipe, stem first.

Clutched between the giant's large finger and thumb, the pipe looked like a toy for blowing soap bubbles. The Hound guided the stem between his pursed lips and clamped it tight in his hound-sharp canines. Drawing deeply, he sucked and held in his lungs a nimbus of smoke. Blood boiled and rushed to his cheeks. His hair stood on end. One eye narrowed to a mail slot and the other blossomed like a sunflower. He coughed violently, the steam pouring out of his ears and mouth, and he hacked out clots of blood from long-ago spear wounds to his lungs. After his fit, he spat on the ground and shook his long golden hair with a shiver.

"You have to work on your technique." Burke took ahold of the Hound's fist and guided the pipe back in place. "Don't inhale all the way, knucklehead. Take the smoke in your mouth like a swally of wine. Savor the notes of licorice and Hershey bars, and then smooth as you please, let it escape like a sigh."

They nodded in unison, and Cúchulainn followed his instructions. When the bowl was spent, he handed back the pipe, expecting a refill.

"Better, isn't it? One thing you cannot deny, those Americans know how to make smooth pipe tobacco. Go ahead then, enjoy yourself."

Cú smiled like a little boy promised a lollipop.

From the other hole came a squawk like that of a foxed chicken. Debris cascading from his chest and arms, Láeg rushed over and quickly snatched the pipe from Burke's hand, leaving him with a lit match. "What in the gods' name do you think you are doing?"

"Sure, there's nothing wrong with a bowl or two. I'm after learning the youngster. Look how he has attained the hang of the matter."

Winding up like cricket bowler, Láeg launched the pipe far into the desolation. "Don't get him started on that filthy habit. It's fun and games now, but after you two are gone, I will be the one stuck feeding the furnace night and day. Mr. Mullaney, can't you do something about that friend of yours? He is a bad influence."

"I'll agree with you there," Mullaney said. "He's a mind of his own, and his mouth lets the words fly before his thoughts are finished."

"Smoking." Láeg tsked. "Cú is a man of great appetites. Have I not related his boyhood exploits? His love for the hurling and the Gaelic football? How often I had to fetch him to come inside from his sports when the snow piled to his knee-caps or on the third rainy day of five in a row? You couldn't tear him away from the pitch. Cavorting in the foggy dew from the top of the morning to the rising of the moon, always late for his tea, his mammy bellowing his name over the plain, *come in for a nice Irish stew I've been slaving over all day*, but the lad was never once on time for a meal, which irritated his father to no end."

"Old artificer." Cúchulainn swore under his breath.

"You didn't have to throw my pipe away," Burke said. "Now I'll have to go home and fetch another."

With one hand against his chest, Láeg stopped him in his tracks. "You don't get it. The boy has an obsessive-compulsive disorder. Take him for a nice outing at the shops, and he wants to go to the market every day. And he's forever buying things he does not even need. Or want, necessarily. It's the bargains he cannot resist. Look how much we're saving at this price, he says. No matter how many times I tell him the best bargain is spending nothing at all. But you can't tell him nothing, for he would fight his own shadow for a few coins."

"This American tobacco is dear," Burke said. "I'm always looking for a sale meself."

"Same for assembling—gaga as the Mad Hatter. The Knights of the Red Branch have their annual conference, and the Hound must attend every session possible, taking copious notes at the presentations, and no sooner is it over he's jabbering about the next year's convention. Loves the free giveaways. He's a divil for the craic afterwards and the who-knows-what goes on after midnight behind closed doors, if you get my drift.

"Treat him to a nice feast, and he does be wanting a banquet and a bib every meal. Suckling pigs and boiled lobsters galore, roasted beefsteaks and potatoes fried in duck fat. By the gods, I never seen such a man mad for the spuds. Mash swimming in butter. Boxty, colcannon, even fried with a chopped onion, he doesn't care. If it is a spud, it's in him. Desserts of all sorts too. Your soda bread slathered with jam and butter, apple cake with custard sauce, a good barmbrack, but leave a raisin in it and he'll run you through with his trick spear. I need a barrow to wheel him away from the table, and an hour later he's hungry again. But worse than that is when he's had so much as a sip of an alcoholic beverage."

Mullaney let a wish leave his lips. "A Guinness would be good about now."

"I won't go into it," Láeg said. "Only to say that the lad can hold his liquor. Gallons of porter, hogsheads of mead. Beer, ale, stout, matteradamn, he's a bottomless jar. Pissing rivers like a stallion and then back to the hard stuff. When the thirst is on him, he'll quaff a barrel of whiskey in one go, but even a demigod has his limits. Your man over there, when he has had too much to drink, the famous *riastradh* comes upon him, only a hundred times worse. In his frenzy and mad torque, he sprouts extra digits, so he's got seven fingers on each hand and seven tootsies on each foot. Seven irises appear in that pie eye of his, and his hair lights up like a ninety-year-old's birthday cake. Woe betides any publican who cuts him off. Many a bartender's head in the gutter with a look in the eye asking, *Where'd I go wrong?* A whiff off his hangover alone would kill an ordinary man, even you or me. Many a morn he rolls out of bed for a hair of the dog, and what does he find under the covers? Some young slip of a colleen whose name he cannot remember.

"Aye, he loves the women. Milkmaids or nuns, he's not particular. A kiss is all it takes. Or the innocent batting of the eyelashes, and he is in love with love. The great romantic moping about the hut like a puppy if he doesn't hear from her, and then if she's remotely interested, he's out carving their Ogham names in the bark of a hickory tree, and after that comes the assault of flowers and other love trinkets. Forests of roses and daffodils and enough chocolate to liquidate the Swiss. Once wooed and won, the poor lass is thrown aside. Take a good look at him. What fair maid could resist? Before he was even seventeen years old, he had a wife in Ireland and a son in Scotland by another lass. Bedad, that is a sad story for another day. Not the first time his bad habits got him in trouble. So, you understand, don't get him started on the pipe. He's liable to burn down the whole island."

Mullaney's thoughts drifted to his ex-wife in Liverpool and his daughter somewhere in America. They had been gone a long, long time, and a pint of plain would be a comfort at the moment. He was shaken out of his reverie by a spotlight in his face and a booming voice, loud as a policeman's.

"Where is she?" Cúchulainn asked.

"No luck yet," Mullaney said. "Keep digging."

"How many holes have we drilled?" Láeg asked. "Three each times the three of us, and three by three is a magic number that should have brought us luck by now."

Spasms twitching below the surface, Cúchulainn scowled at the farmers. Dimming his hero's light, he went off to consider what next to do. His loyal attendant consoled him with a few choice words in their native tongue, and the man's man seemed pacified. He removed a bejeweled crane bag from his belt and emptied the pouch on the dry ground, and the two warriors hunched over and picked at the contents. Squinting, Mullaney could make out the black and white pieces of a chess set and a checkered cloth board spread between them. With the attention only true players know, they were methodically positioning the chessmen, giving Cúchulainn white and the first move.

Heartbroken, Burke stared mournfully in the direction of his lost pipe. "We cannot put them off forever. What is your plan B, if you have one at all?"

"We could make a run for it," Mullaney said. "But we need to create a diversion and step away whilst they are otherwise engaged."

"There's nothing out here to distract a fly. If your man had not throwed away my best pipe, I could have puffed a smokescreen, and off we'd go behind a cloud."

"Too bad about your pipe. Look at them, having a game." A memory forced itself to the forefront of his mind. "You still play, do you not, Tommy?"

"I do. But I play better with a corncob between my bicuspids."

"Do you not think the strategies of chess have improved these past two millennia? Surely they never heard of the Queen's Gambit or the Fool's Mate, now would they? Could you outwit them if need be?"

Burke scratched his receding hairline. "They might have different names for those parlays, Michael. Logic is logic, after all."

Bent at their places, they studied the board, glancing occasionally at their captives.

"Could you hold off the dumb one for a while? You're that handy, right?"

"I'll have you know I earned a second at the All-County. Fifty years ago, but I still got it. You don't lose your intelligence along with your hair."

"Here's the plan." Mullaney drew closer. "Once they fin-ish, we will issue a challenge, you against Cúchulainn. Appeal to his vanity and love of sport, but make sure you insist that you play much better with your pipe. I will volunteer to go hunting for it out on the bog whilst you two start your game—"

"Match. A game of chess is called a match."

"Right, so. Whilst you have the two lunatics otherwise engaged, I will sneak back home and get the body for them."

"Aha, I knew you had it hid at the mansion, you dirty bastard, keeping a secret. Where had you stashed her then?"

"In the toolshed, wrapped in a tarpaulin, safe as a Christ-mas cracker. I'll load her in the lorry and hand over the body, quick as a rabbit."

"What about the Igor fella?"

"Láeg," Mullaney said. "He can be the referee. These hard chaws are sticklers for the rules and etiquette of a duel. I know these Ulstermen, they will not back down from a glove thrown down by the champion of Connacht."

Burke pondered the logistics of the operation. "Suppose I finish him off before you return?"

"Are you an eejit? First, you may play him to a draw, but under no circumstances should you beat him. And make like you're pondering each move and go real slow."

"Suppose I have no choice and he blunders into one of me traps?"

"Okay, he'll want a rematch. And if you let him beat you, he will be a sporting man and grant you one." Mullaney had reassured himself. "That seems a sensible plan."

"Suppose I beat him at the rematch and his face starts convulsing like a swarm of eels caught in a pot?"

"Don't lose your head again." Mullaney slapped him on the back, and they moseyed over to where the ancients played.

Láeg had him cornered, the white queen dead to rights, but moved his castle in a deliberate blunder a twelve-year-old would recognize. The Hound shook his head and tutted through his teeth, and given the second chance, he escaped. Somehow his lieutenant had snatched defeat from the jaws of victory.

"What have you two guttersnipes been going on about?" Láeg asked. His question had the snarl of a kicked dog.

"How about a match against someone who knows how the sport is played? Sure, did I ever tell you I was All-Connacht champion at the age of sixteen?"

The primitive set, carved out of bog oak and cattle horn, was laid out again, and Mullaney excused himself to track down Burke's necessary pipe. In the shadows, he circled round undetected, glancing over his shoulder with a wary eye, until he reached the lane. It felt strange to be on his own and out of their peculiar company. His worries about what Burke might do were assuaged by the clear path ahead and the belief that this strange encounter would soon be over. Half-two in the morning, and he felt he had been awake for a week.

At the front door, he whistled for Bonnie, but the little collie was not in the house. The place was still a shambles, but in the interim since their forced departure, all the knives and forks had been unstuck from the walls and furniture and piled neatly on the kitchen table. On the counter sat two dirty plates, yellowed with yolks and crusted with beans. In the sink were a pair of teacups and an empty beer bottle for the recycling. It occurred to him that the people who had cooked and eaten this midnight snack might still be in the house. His hullos went unanswered, but he could not shake the sensation deep in his bones of a second set of visitors. The scent of a woman perfumed the room. He remembered how much better the place had smelled when his wife and daughter had lived there.

He went to the fridge and saw the dark-brown bottles standing there. The first swallow of that cold pint was the best he'd ever tasted. Guinness is a gift from the gods, he chuckled. He opened another and went to inspect the rest of the house. Someone had been sleeping in his bed. One of the three bears from the Goldilocks story or, judging from the mangled sheets and artful positioning of the pillows, perhaps the mama and the papa bear having a romp. Long bleached hairs on the pillowcases, a smear of lipstick on the duvet, and the memory of sweat and cologne. Mullaney called out, but the lovers were long gone. Sleep tempted him, but he resisted. Snatching the lorry keys from his bureau, he made his way to the toolshed. It would be like picking up a parcel to take to market. They would finally be rid of the hidden bog girl who had caused so much trouble.

The moment he flicked on the light, his heart fell from his chest. Rumpled on the floor was the empty tarpaulin, forlorn as the deep blue sea.

15

Behind the Tattoo

A COLD THREAD OF sweat trickled down Bridget's spine. Menacing as a pair of Dobermans, Maeve and Al grinned at her from the sofa. They had bewitched and tricked her into saying too much. Ordinarily, she was more discreet about her personal life, and blabbing the details now seemed to her a peculiarly American trait, an eager compulsion to be liked, at odds with the wily reticence of the Irish. She turned over in her mind the two possibilities: either they were a couple of kooks cosplaying in some fantasy, or they actually were Queen Medb and King Ailill, leapt from the pages of legend, back somehow and searching for someone named Fedelm. The girl in the bog.

"Be a lamb," Maeve said. "I cannot be gallivanting around the province in this slip. Would you find me something decent to wear? Hubby can put on a pair of the old coot's trousers, but I'd sooner go around without a stitch than in this old frock. Check the room down the hall. What kind of home has no woman in it?"

Afraid to turn the knob, Bridget put her ear against the closed door to listen for any stirring within. She pushed it open and fumbled for the light switch, and the colors smacked her in the face. Two walls had been painted turquoise and two emerald, and the trim at the baseboards and windowsills screamed in purple and royal blue. A fantail peacock design stretched across the bedspread and matching pillowcases. Compared to the drab whites and tans of the rest of the house, the bedroom throbbed and bedazzled. On the dresser, artfully arranged, a row of seashells circled a small vase holding a single peacock feather. The collected works of Flannery O'Connor sat on a bookshelf, and hanging over the bed was a framed reproduction of a Gothic painting of the writer flanked by her favorite peacock. What sort of child would live in such a flamboyant space? Mullaney's daughter, surely, once upon a time. The relics of childhood. Long gone, Bridget guessed. Each object had the forlorn aspect of sitting in the exact same spot for years. She sneezed in the dust. On the corner of the dresser was a snapshot from happy days: father, mother, daughter. The bedroom was a shrine, in case she came back to stay. Bridget felt pangs of sympathy for Mullaney and thought of her own parents back in the States. Did they miss her too?

The clothes in the wardrobe had been fashionable a decade ago. Bridget slid the hangers quickly along the rod, looking for something suitable, or at least an outfit that Maeve might consider. On the mattress she laid out a yellow sweater and a pair of pale-green pants, and as a gag, a turquoise sundress printed with bright peacock feathers. Three soft knocks, and Maeve flounced into the room.

"I love it! Fit for a queen," she said. She danced across the floor, taking in the decor, before stopping at the painting on the wall. "Who is that strange chicken?"

"Surely you have seen a peacock. A beautiful bird from India."

"What will they think of next? And where is this India?"

"Have you never heard of India? Where are on earth are you from?"

"Some say Ballypitmave, and others Barnavave or Knockmaa, though I cannot be certain, for wasn't I a babby at the time. You will have to ask my mother, if you can dig her up. And sure, I was only having you on about India, lass. I could go for a nice curry and chips."

Bridget put the weird answer aside and showed her the outfits she had chosen. "I was not sure what size you are, and what sort of thing—"

Without warning, Maeve's tunic hit the floor. Her naked body displayed the same easy athleticism as her husband's. She held up each outfit in turn, shimmying in front of the mirror, unable to decide what to wear. Tattooed across her backside were two bulls squaring off against each other. As she tightened and flexed her gluteus maximus to work the dress over her hips, the creatures locked horns.

"Ta-da!" Maeve caught her staring. Turning her back, she lifted the skirt proudly. "The tattoo? So as I never forget, honey. Though why Al suggested getting them on my tushy is a mystery. Not too likely I can see my own arse."

"Maybe it was so he would remember the bullfight that caused all the trouble."

"Men. You cannot account for what goes on in their dirty little minds, if anything at all." She smoothed the wrinkles from the fabric and straightened the straps. "They are so visual, don't you find? You would never catch me asking him to have some picture inked on his bum. Imagine what a rooster would look like when he's an old wrinkly git and his bottom drops."

"You look good in that dress."

"Thanks, honey." Maeve admired her reflection, delighted she could pull off such a gaudy number. "Let's see how the old ball and chain has got hisself fixed."

Standing in the parlor, Al looked like a three-year-old wearing his father's hand-me-downs. One sleeve of his jersey flopped three inches below his hand, and the other had been rolled thick as a plaster cast up to his elbow. The bottom cuffs of his trousers covered his feet, so as only his toes stuck out. Maeve laughed at the sight of him.

"Oh, Allie," she said. "You're hopeless."

"You don't like it?"

"Let's say that outfit is not your size. Is this Mullaney a giant?"

"For the love of the gods, why can't I wear me own tunic?" Al straightened to his full height and allowed her to fuss over him.

Maeve rolled the dangling sleeve. "Now, we've discussed the matter before and agreed. All the other women would be beside themselves if they had a peek at you in all your glory. Isn't that right, Philadelphia?"

As soon as the question registered, Bridget nodded.

"Well, you should talk, in that slinky dress." He ran his fingers down Maeve's bare arm. "All the men of Connacht will be drooling."

"Stop your palaver and hold still."

"A chuisle mo chroí . . ."

"None of your fancy lovetalk." She pulled up his trousers and cinched tight his belt. His look of pained surprise gave way to a grin of pleasure. Maeve also seemed to be enjoying his reaction a bit too much as she pulled harder and harder, and they were both nearly carried away again. To remind them of her presence, Bridget cleared her throat.

With a lick of her thumb, Maeve tamed his cowlick. "There, now you're perfect. We are all ready to go as soon as you find yourself some shoes."

Wiggling his toes, Al caviled. "I've tried on every pair, and I'll not be galumphing all over the parish like a clown."

"Find you some slippers then, you silly boy."

"I'll try, but I'm famished with the hunger. I'm not going anywhere till I've had a good feed." He smiled at Bridget. "Be a good lass and rustle up a nice fry. While you're at it, see if there's any drink about."

Bridget was flabbergasted.

"You don't expect Her Majesty to cook, do you?" He flexed his eyebrows like Groucho Marx. "She couldn't scramble an egg if it cracked its own shell. Nor crisp a rasher of bacon even if it trotted to the skillet. See what magic you can conjure. Check the fridge for a pint of plain. Or at the least, something stronger than another infernal cup of tea."

"Slippers." Maeve pointed him to the bedroom. "C'mon into the kitchen, Philadelphia. Don't believe a word he says. I know full well how to put the kettle on."

In the fridge were some eggs, baked beans, and blood sausages, along with a few bottles of beer. The stovetop worked, though the oven had been smashed to smithereens. Into a dustpan, Bridget swept the glass from the floor, and then she fired up the pans. Maeve opened a bottle of stout for her man. The moment plates were set on the countertop, Al shuffled in wearing oversized moccasins.

As she watched them attack their breakfast, Bridget sat by. "I hope you don't mind, but I am still curious about that tattoo of the two bulls."

"My best work yet," Al said. "Did she tell you I designed the tat myself? Though I am sorry to say the privilege of the needlework went to another lucky chap. Had to cut his throat when he was finished."

Maeve shot him a withering look. "You're not from around these parts, but surely you have heard of the *Táin Bó Cúailnge*, or as you Americans would have it, the Cattle Raid of Cooley."

"Here we go again," Al said. "The old epic."

"A good story can be told any number of times, and a very good story is never finished at all." Her bracelets rattled as she gave him the bird. "Ain't that always the way with a man. Listen, it is a matter of simple respect. A woman can be the equal of a man in all things, and don't you forget it, bub."

Through a mouthful of eggs, he rebutted, "I'm only saying that a woman, even a rich woman, should be grateful to be married to an even richer man. It doubles her wealth. *Mi casa es su casa.*"

"Maybe a woman wasn't looking for wealth but for a man without meanness, jealousy, or fear."

"Faraway fields are greener." Al popped a whole sausage in his mouth and gave it a good chew, washing the lot down with a swallow of stout. Maeve pushed her beans about her plate.

"I don't want to be rude." Bridget interrupted their silent grievances. "But who are you two really?"

"We're just a couple having an ordinary tiff," Maeve said. "We have come this night from Rathcroghan and our home in Oweynagat, the Cave of the Wildcats."

Capturing a small burp that surprised even himself, Al wiped his gob with a dish towel. "Go on, tell her about the bull."

"Can you not say *gabh mo leithscéal*, or were you born in a barn?" She could not bear to watch him chew with his mouth open, so she turned for a more sympathetic ear. "Ailill here had this prize bull, which ironically had been the calf of one of my own cows. I ask you, wouldn't that make the bull mine to begin with? Hmm? Finnbennach, by name, the White-Horned."

As partners often do, Al took up the story. "White-Horned did not see fit to be considered a woman's property, so he snuck off in the wee hours before dawn and joined the king's herd. Slips right in, like, among the ladies—*Where's the craic, gals?* A better class of beef, don't you know."

"That's a lie!" Maeve tossed a sausage at him.

"Tut-tut, darling, mind the company." Al threw an arm over the back of Bridget's chair and leaned in closely to address her. "You see, she likes to say *Anything you can do, I can do better.* So she asks around to her wealthy friends and finds out there is a better bull in Ireland: the Donn Cúailnge, the Brown Bull of Cooley, up north in Ulster."

Maeve slammed her hand on the counter. "Here comes another damned falsehood. I'm tired of getting the blame all through history. I am no cattle rustler. Please, I asked the owners politely, may I have a borrow of that Brown Bull? But no, those selfish bastards would not come to terms. I would have paid handsomely. Those Ulster cowboys simply refused to loan out their precious stud at any cost, and furthermore, they insulted the queen of Connacht in the bargain. Never in my life have I stood for such odious treatment."

"A bit thin-skinned, if you ask me," Al said. "When she is sweet, she can talk the legs off a chicken without so much as a cluck. But when she is angry, she is cross as a bag of weasels. C'mon, admit it. Their refusal of stud services was cause for the bloody war."

"And what a war it was," Maeve said.

Al drained the last of his pint. "And that is why my darling sports a white-horned bull on the one cheek and a brown bull tattooed on the other. To remind Medb not to be so bullheaded."

A pall fell over the conversation as each person considered the matter. The tea grew cold, the butter congealed, and beans dried onto the plates. Bridget realized she had one last shot at returning to the real world.

"Look at the time," she said. "I don't suppose I could get a cab at this hour. Is there any chance you might be willing to drive me back to the inn? It's just up the road. We can meet first thing in the morning and go look for the girl together."

"What do you say, my darling?" Maeve asked her husband.

"Smashing. We did not mean to keep you so long." Al stood and pulled up his trousers. "First, a quick stop to use the loo, and I'll be ready in two shakes of a lamb's tail."

As soon as the man left the dining room, Maeve brought the rest of the dirty dishes and stood by Bridget to wash up. Lightly bumping shoulder to shoulder, Maeve let her know that the squabbles had concluded and peace was restored. She ran her fingernails on Bridget's back, looked her in the eyes, and gave her a conspiratorial wink. "We thought you might be the girl we are looking for, but now I am glad you are not. Don't you find him romantic? After all this time, he got so carried away when we found the place empty . . ."

A jaunty driving cap on his head, Al clapped from the front door. "Ready to go, girls? What's keeping you?"

They walked through the clutter to join him on the landing. A cool mist floated over the threshold. "I wonder if this dress will be warm enough," Maeve said. "Maybe I should see if Flannery left a light sweater."

"You'll be fine, darling. That furnace inside you will ward off any chill." One foot outside, he stopped, puzzled in the fog. Maeve, too, looked in both directions, scratching her head.

"Philly, darling, did you happen to notice a pair of white horses when you arrived?"

"Horses? No, not here, but I thought I saw two horses and a buggy earlier, outside the first farm on the lane."

"Where the deuce are them horses?" Al frowned. "I thought I asked you to tie them up?"

Indignation rose in Maeve's voice. "Since when is it my job to park the chariot?"

"All our stuff is gone," Al said. "Gone with the back of the cart. Everything we need for the job."

"Wait a minute," Bridget said. "What are you talking about now? A chariot and horses? Isn't that your truck in the driveway?"

Al and Maeve walked over to look at the old lorry parked beside the house. They fiddled with the door handles and kicked the tires.

"Damn fine vehicle this Mullaney fellow has, but where do you hitch the horses?" He hunched his shoulders. "A horse, a horse, my kingdom for a horse."

With a shrug, Maeve offered an apology. "I'm sorry, honey, but it looks like we won't be able to give you a lift into town after all. Maybe you can ask this Mullaney person, if he ever comes home."

Horses and bulls and kings and queens straight out of ancient history were all too much for her. Without another word, Bridget set off to find Burke's house. She took one last look over her shoulder to see if they were still there and not figments of an overstimulated imagination. Behind her, Maeve pulled out the sword from the stone and straightened the blade between the vise of her locked thighs in one mighty swipe. "At least we'll have one weapon, should we need it. Enough for you, pet?"

Al kissed her in admiration for her strength and ingenuity. For good measure, he patted the place where the two bulls locked horns.

"Wait up, Philadelphia," Maeve yelled. "Here we come."

16

The Triple Jump

T HE MEMORY LINGERED long after the white horses had disappeared like phantoms in the night. The witches rummaged through the abandoned chariot, astonished by its clever design and deadly cargo. Capped with pointed iron, the ends of each axle were menacingly sharp. Two long spears stood pinned to the cart's flanks, and stashed along the dashboard were a pair of broadswords and six smaller weapons, ranging from a dirk to a razor blade that could be hidden behind one finger. The arsenal was protected on both sides by two shields, one with a screaming eagle etched on the surface, the other depicting an iron fist brandishing a *scian* with a rounded pommel. Where a cupholder would be, a crane bag hung, filled with chessmen and amulets. The sweet smell of apples tussled with the aroma of iron and old leather. From the chariot floor, they unfurled a thick animal hide, the coat of an Irish elk the likes of which had not been seen for centuries. The fur was big enough for the three of them to crawl under and wage war against sleep. At the cemetery gate, Fedelm stuck her thumb in her mouth and tasted the air. By this reckoning, she supposed there would be three hours or so till sunrise. She let them rest.

Emcee knew exactly what time it was. Ten after three. While her friends drowsed, she kept a watchful eye on the dead girl, who paced among the tombstones talking to herself about her next move. There would be hell to pay in the morning. Her mother had pinged her at eleven and again at midnight, and Emcee would have to lie that the messages never came through. She could hear her own excuses: *My phone was off. I fell asleep talking.* The plain truth was out of the question. Her mother would roll her eyes, smell for liquor on her breath, and ask when she was going to give up this witchy nonsense. Pops was her only possible ally, and she thought of texting him or even giving him a call, but she did not want to waken him at such an ungodly hour. He never doubted her, unlike her parents, who rarely believed her, even when she was being honest. Emcee stirred the pot of her grievances, hoping resentment would keep her awake. She fought off a half dozen yawns, but sleep is often contagious, and she drifted off, snug against her ginger sisters.

Once the girls were safely in slumberland, Fedelm could test her plan. She had seen herself in the tiny mirror. The leather of her skin, her golden hair reddened by the peat, the scars that would never heal. Bog girl. Wraith. Monster. And there they were, young, beautiful, each one with a promising future. She had no way of knowing if the switch would work, having never tried in two thousand years, but an intriguing possibility existed. She could leap into one of those girls and leave her old body behind. Easy enough to remember the mechanics of the soul jump with the lower forms of life. How different is a butterfly from a human being? A hare, a magpie, a dog? In truth, a person is more complicated, their spirit on a different plane altogether. They can talk, for one, and she did not know if she could ever master the modern teenage patter. The whole idea could be a disaster or the perfect solution. Behind her in the graveyard were a hundred souls without a prayer. Bones and dust. Distant branches of a family tree, remembered only in the archives. Who, if offered such a second chance at life, would not leap?

Curling next to the three sleeping girls, she listened to their soft breathing and synchronized her own respiration. *Go on then*, she told herself. *Jump.*

The first leap

She launched her spirit, uncertain as to where she might land. The bog body went limp, lifeless, and Fedelm found herself in Emcee's dream as she slept. Their thoughts mingled. At sea. A teenage boy swam towards her in a windmill of splashes. A thin lad, pasty-faced, spots blooming on his cheeks, a shock of black hair plastered on his round head. Arms as long as the kraken's, a hairless chest, and redolent with acrid testosterone. This gangly creature treaded water next to her. She could see herself now: a girl in a pink bikini, red hair trailing in the ocean like a bed of kelp. *Emcee.* The boy intended to grope her under the cover of the waves, and he is about to force her into his arms, lips puckered for a kiss. *Swim away!* She kicked froth in his face. On the strand, other boys ogled her as she emerged from the sea, and she lets them, welcomed their stares, struck a pose not unlike that painting *Venus on the Clamshell*, naked, her long red hair discreetly covering her *Sheela na gig* and a hand across her chest for good measure. *Is this what you want, eh?* Fedelm tried to dispatch the boys and sweep the images out of Emcee's mind, but the lads kept right on coming. Three fifties of lascivious hooligans, hormonal wave after wave, a horde of zombie teenagers, and movie stars, a footballer from Manchester United, her Irish teacher. They chase but never catch hold of her, as if Emcee's imagination were limited by experience. All the boys running on the one-track mind. Fedelm tried to force her to think of other matters: the Ogham for nymphomania, a game of chess, Scottish poetry, the armies of Connacht and Ulster on the ridges above the plain, crimson and red. No dice. The slathering eejits would not leave her alone. Worse yet, not only was she enjoying the attention, but she was also expanding the circle of admirers in her own head. *This will never do.*

Gasping for air, Emcee woke with a start as if a tsunami had slammed into her. A few brief moments had disappeared and left a lacuna in the story of her life. Her thoughts had not belonged entirely to her. To her right slept her fellow Red Hags, quietly undisturbed. To her left lay Fedelm, the braided knot quivering with each breath.

Conscious thoughts uncoiled, and Emcee struggled to tie the loose ends of the dream Fedelm had left behind in her mind. A boy in a golden chariot raced home from his first foray as a killer. Staked to the front of the vehicle were the round heads of his first three foes, stunned expressions on their grisly faces. Hitched to the rear of the wagon trotted an Irish elk stag, upon whose stupendous antlers a charioteer hung for dear life. Driving like mad, the boy warrior clenched the reins in his teeth, and tied by their feet to the traces flew twenty wild swans, captured by one of his signature ricochet shots. In a brazen act of disrespect, he banked the chariot clockwise and shouted out to the guards at a fortress: "Send out your best warriors to fight, or I swear by the gods, I will have every head in the place."

A dozen women spilled out through the front doors, led by the local queen. "These hills are your foes today, conqueror." They bared their breasts and lifted their skirts to reveal their naked bottoms, laughing and giggling at the upstart. "Why, you are no more than a pup."

Blushing, he beseeched his second, who had fallen from the great elk's rack. "Láeg, help—"

But the women swarmed upon him and carried the boy, kicking and bawling, to their hut. They threw him into a barrel of cold water, which immediately burst at the seams with the hiss of his lust heat. They tossed him in another barrel, and the water boiled so furiously that the bubbles nearly knocked him out. Dunked in the third barrel, he finally cooled enough to be handled. The queen wrapped him in a thick towel and drew up his cowl, and she sat him upon the king's knee, a good little boy at last. Seven years old, he was. In the span of a decade, he would take on all of Connacht for the sake of Ulster.

Next thing, Emcee was awake, trying to shake the hero from her mind. She stole one last look at the bog girl, who hadn't moved a muscle, and fell back into a deep sleep.

The second leap

Fedelm rolled over to look at the constellations, star-dotted puzzles of the gods and heroes, legends and myths in the sky, a reassurance to a time-traveling soul. The lads will promise you the moon and the stars in exchange for a ride, the oldest story in the world. Girls like Emcee were bursting with curiosity, apparently, and Fedelm wondered if the other two were as boy-crazed, all emotion and no imagination. She made the leap again, leaving behind the empty shell, hoping Eileen would prove more suitable.

Thank the gods there was no pimply boy awaiting her. No, Eileen's point of view was dark as a grave. Only the sensation of moving forward, rocking as she sat atop the massive beast between her legs, hooves clopping, birdsong in the air, and as if rolling through a long tunnel, the landscape burst into view, a Technicolor Ireland, dig those blues and greens, bright as a peacock's feathers. By the gods, it hurt her eyes to see such a spangled, made-up country, colored in by a child. The horse trotted straight as an endless line. The sky changed hue, blue draining away and replaced by magenta, the trees and grasses now orange and cinnamon. Up in the hills, the black-faced sheep reversed themselves to white-faced sheep in black wool. Harp strings appeared in lieu of the horse's mane, and with each bob of its head, the wires vibrated and played vermillion notes that appeared in the yellowing sky. Her horse itself hummed the melody, and when the refrain came along, it sang the dithery-didle-do in a kind of Irish scat. *Bono equus.* Hallucinations and colors sped like a kaleidoscope twirled by a monkey. Hopping out quickly, Fedelm hoped to avoid any mindbends or flashbacks.

During the whole occupation of her subconsciousness, Eileen barely rustled. She recalled the sensation of having a double vision, her dreamworld operating on two planes. Pleasant enough aboard her Macha tripping the light fantastic on a psychedelic journey, but the tagalong second dream was like simultaneously reading two comic strips in the funny papers or following a text overrun by its footnotes.

In the palimpsest story, an old-time sword-and-sorcery guy out of *Game of Thrones* was getting ready for another skirmish. Dead and wounded were littered all about, and the poor horses wandered aimlessly, looking for their owners. Our hero comes into focus. He's a good-looking movie-star sort, tall and strong, long blond hair, a red cape snapping in the wind. One of three identical sisters, Eileen comes up to him in a violet tunic. She can see that he's interested, but before he can get out his best opening line, she is quick to parlay.

"I love you, I love you, I love you," Eileen says. "I've heard great things about you, and I will help you in your battle." She sweeps her arm to indicate a herd of cattle and a heap of treasure.

"No," says he. "I appreciate the offer, but I cannot lie with a woman whilst a battle rages." Fidgeting with his holster, he barely looks at her.

"C'mon," she says. "You've time for a quick roll in the hay."

"No," says he. "I did not join this fight for sexual rewards, though you have quite a rump on you." Toying with his broadsword, he cannot give her the courtesy of a smile.

"If that's the case," says she, "I'll be nothing but trouble to you, mister. When you're knee-deep in the fight, I'll turn into an eel under your feet so's you slip and fall."

The soldier wiggles the armor girding his loins. "Then I'll trap you between my toes and crush your ribs, and you'll have that mark on you forever, unless it is lifted by a blessing."

"Okay then, I'll shift into a wolf and chase your cattle away."

"And I will knock out your eye for your troubles. That, too, will mar your beautiful face. Only pirates and priests will lie with a patch-eyed doll."

"Aren't you full of yourself, Mr. Big Stuff. I will become a red bull and have my herd stampede and force you into the water."

"Lass, I will chuck a stone at you and break your leg. Now, go away, you bother me."

Rejected three times over, Eileen snuggled into the reassuring warmth of the other hags and went back to her own private wonderland. Soon enough, she was snoring like a kitten.

The leap of faith

Useless, Fedelm thought. *Today's teenagers aren't worth a wet hen's fart.* Nothing but sex, sex, sex. To gather her wits, she wandered through the graveyard complaining to the stones. She knocked on each one but heard not a single reply. Where are the dead when you need them? Her third try would be her final chance, since it was not likely she would find another living soul about at this hour, this place. And three is a lucky number, although three times three can be better, and three times three times three the best of all. Even these so-called Christians knew as much. Wasn't it St. Patrick himself who explained the concept of the Trinity, father, son, and holy ghost, three gods in one, by the simile of a three-leafed shamrock? Three is also the best way out of a yes-and-no situation. The alternative between this and that. The third color between green and blue. Third man between him and the other fella. A charm, the third time. She talked herself into the third jump. The bog girl resumed her position by the three Red Hags, counted to three, and leapt.

Siobhán was waiting for her on the other side. Their thoughts slammed into each other with a brutal bash, knocking them both senseless and unaware of their own individual subconsciousness. A sensation akin to the moment of birth when the child is separated from the mother and blasted into the sensory world of bright light and clear noise and the awful first independent gulp of breath, drowning in air, put on notice that we are two, no longer one. Or truly like the last moment of life when the spirit takes leave of the body, so long, nice to know ya, and in that half of a half of a moment is found the grim and welcome resolution to the nagging question since day one. *Hello, goodbye. Hello, I must be going.*

Two minds fought for mastery. Fedelm held the advantage of wise experience over derring-do, but every teenager has a mind of her own. In their shared shadow vision, Siobhán wrenched a gravestone from the ground and hurled it like a Frisbee, nearly taking off Fedelm's head. The bog girl snapped an iron bar from a graveside fence and flung the pointy spear, missing Siobhán's eye by dint of a deft bob-and-weave. They hollered in each other's faces. They called each other hoor and bitch. They lobbed their best curses.

"You are as orange as an Ulster carrot," said Fedelm.

"You shrew, you bag of bones, you are as thin as a sapling but not as strong. A whisper would knock you over."

"Blatherskite. You are as proud as a cat with two tails. You know nothing about life."

"And what would you know? There's no hope from the grave." Siobhán brought her hand to her mouth, wishing to reel in the insult she had cast. "No, I'm so sorry."

Their mixed thoughts forked into two streams. Siobhán's ragged breathing slowed, and she stopped twitching beneath the blanket. Fedelm hid in the corner of the girl's mind to regain her composure. The streams slowly bent back to each other.

"What is it you want, bog girl?"

To be asked that question after all these years. She sighed. "I want to be with my people. Hours ago, I was freed, but then I feared the Hound of Ulster was on my trail, with his terrible swift sword and the spear of a thousand points. No matter what else, I am of Connacht, and he may think me merely another enemy to vanquish. In the hut by the lake, I heard his weapons slicing through the air. Cúchulainn was my dread. But when I saw the royal chariot drawn by the pure white horses of Medb and Ailill, I knew I was wrong. They have come to welcome me home at last. They have forgiven my prophesies." Her grin deflated to a frown. "Yet I cannot go back to my people in this wretched, forlorn condition. They will not recognize me looking like a weathered piece of leather, this fiery hair—"

"Hey now," Siobhán said. "Take care of who you are talking to."

"A hundred thousand apologies, Red."

"You have to learn not to be so sensitive about the red hair. People are secretly jealous of it, that's all. Makes you stand out. Be proud."

"I have to admit that on you and the other two hags, those shades of ginger are most becoming."

"You're too kind."

"Think nothing of it." Fedelm sought to slow her runaway train of thought. "I need a new body, something more suitable for the queen and king. Someone like you."

Launched into the dialectic, the notion rolled back and forth along a Möbius strip. They chased after it, but the thought could not be caught.

"And what is it you wish for, Red Hag?"

"To be a real witch," Siobhán said. "Not a make-believe or a cosplay witch but the genuine article. Spellweaver, dreamwalker, seer of things to come. I want to be like you."

"Perhaps we might strike a bargain," Fedelm said. "When the time comes."

Like a sneeze in the brain, the bog girl's spirit left her, and Siobhán woke at once. She nudged Eileen, who sat blinking for her bearings. It took some shaking to raise Emcee, who complained of feeling oh-so-tired. The Red Hags threw off the animal hide, and the damp air slapped them in their kissers. Fedelm had separated herself and was standing in the middle of the ruined chapel, facing the way they had come, listening for signs.

"What a night," Emcee said. "I had the strangest dream. About a boy who sees a bunch of girls naked in the locker room, and he is burning up with all these feelings he does not understand. They had to throw him into three barrels of ice water to cool his hankering."

"I had a dream, too," said Eileen. "About a woman who made three offers to a gladiator, and the brute turns her down three times. I coulda killed him."

They expected Siobhán to share what she had dreamt, but she told no tales. Braiding her hair at her right shoulder, she quietly wound the knot.

17

The Banshee

MULLANEY SEARCHED HIGH and low for the missing body. A damp slick of mud on the tarp and stringy hunks of peat scattered about the floor were the only clues. He retraced the events of the late afternoon when he'd stashed the girl in the shed, but she was not where he'd left her. She couldn't have walked away on her own, he told himself. Someone must have broken in and stolen her. But who could have known? And for what ends? Lumped against these riddles was a generalized anxiety over leaving Burke for so long with those two madmen. Cúchulainn and his crony would be furious when they realized, at last, that Mullaney was not nearby looking for the discarded pipe. And Burke would be livid if he showed up empty-handed. How would they ever manage to escape without the diversion of the corpse?

Panic often revises the best-laid plans. The original idea had been to drive over, dump the girl, and speed off with Burke while the Ulster lads were having a gander, but now he would need some decoy. He found a bundle of thatching rushes to roll up tightly in the blue tarp and tied both ends with triple knots. Lifting the package in his arms, he saw it drooped approximately in the middle like a body. In the dark, he might be able to fool those he-men, more brawn than brain. If Burke reacted quickly enough, they could be on their way to Westport before the jig was up. An elegant solution, he told himself, check and mate.

He carried the dummy to the truck and laid it in the bed. Confident, nearly cheerful at his own ingenuity, he climbed into the driver's seat and inserted the key into the ignition. Concentrating so thoroughly on his deceit, he failed to notice the person next to him. A woman wailed mournfully, her cry like a pencil shoved into his ear.

"Jesus, Mary, and Joseph. What the devil?" He nearly hopped through the roof.

Scrunched into the passenger seat, an old crone, no more than five feet tall, fiddled with the glovebox, poking her chipped fingernails into the latch. Her skin was the color of spent ash, gray as her ragged clothes and the mess of her mangled hair. Her bloodshot eyes were rimmed with red, as though she had been crying for a long time.

A sharpness radiated from his chest, so Mullaney grabbed the steering wheel to fend off a heart attack. The creature, who smelled of sulfur and blood, panted through her long nose and shook her shoulders, filling her lungs before another outburst.

"Who the hell are you?" he asked.

She let loose a yelp crossways between the bleating of a goat stuck in a fence and the long scritch of nails clawing a blackboard.

"For the love of God, quit your caterwauling," he said. "It's all right. You just gave me a start is all. I'll not hurt you, missus. Nothing to fear. Tell me who you are and how you came to be in my truck at this time of night. Is there some reason for your carry-on?"

"Bah," she spat at him, trying to calm herself. Her face was a rictus of grief.

"Listen, dear, I've no time for a sob story. You seem like a decent person, and I'm sorry for your troubles. Why don't you go inside, the door is open, pardon the mess. Make yourself a nice cup of tea. Feel free to use the telephone and call someone to fetch you. A daughter, maybe, or a friend? I need to run a wee errand and am already late as the March Hare."

Waterworks exploded, and she blubbered madly, her nose running, a string of syllables choked off by each sob. Her hands mimed an accompanying sign language known only to her. Through clenched teeth, she wept, the ropy sinews of her neck taut as clotheslines.

"Now don't cry, darling. It cannot be as bad as all that." He pawed through the clutter between the seats and found a paper napkin to offer her.

She blew her nose loud as a honking goose. He toyed with the idea of driving off with her but decided she might prove a bit too much of a diversion. And what would they do with her on the road to Westport? Dump her by the bridge in Leenaun?

With one last mournful refrain, she settled herself.

"Now, love," Mullaney said. "What seems to be the trouble?"

"Death," she croaked. "On the road ahead."

"No, lass, I am a careful driver—"

"Death will visit soon." She pointed a claw toward the boglands and let out a heartbreaking wail, moaning and swaying in her seat. With her bony fingers, she tore at her bedraggled coat and pulled at her frizzled hair.

"Bedamn, if you are not one of those professional mourners I've heard about. Is that what you are doing? Keening?"

The little old lady wailed with such force that the glass windows shook. Mullaney covered his ears as she droned on like a siren, the tears splashing out of her and staining the seats and dashboard with a salty rime.

"Quiet now, you'll wake up the dead."

She keened again, and the radio switched itself on, the headlamps flashed, and a disoriented bat, out for a late-night snack, bounced off the bonnet before flying away in sonar-less spirals.

Mullaney started the engine. "What are you, some sort of banshee?"

"Too late, too late!" She unbuckled her seatbelt. Like a toddler worn from a tantrum, she finished with a breath-sucking whimper. The storm was over as quickly as it started, and she stepped out of the lorry. Her little gray head barely reached the open window. "Death," she said with a composed evil smile. "Don't say I didn't warn ye."

He stomped on the gas and left her standing in a cloud of exhaust. In the rearview mirror, she looked like a gran buttoning her cardy as she headed toward Burke's place.

On the short trip to the bog, Mullaney pondered how to signal to his partner that they needed to make their escape. Best to leave the motor running, make sure both doors were unlocked. Give the horn a toot and ask the mythological lads to unload the cargo. Then thumb Burke to hop in and zoom like a rocket. Finding a paved road would take a bit of skill, but then go, man, go, he told himself. As fast and as far as you can. But at the top of the rise, the headlights picked out a figure in the distance. He slammed on the brakes and stopped the motor.

A scarecrow watched over the bogs. Mullaney jumped from the truck, hesitating to come any closer to the effigy. He had been expecting Láeg to greet him, but the charioteer and his boss were nowhere to be seen. The butt end of the spear had been jammed into the ground, and the pointy end had been jammed into his friend. Impaled through his bottom, Burke swayed on the pole five feet high in the moonlight. Barbs pricked against his skin from the inside. He looked like a hedgehog on a stick. His eyes were closed, and his mouth hung open, a tiny trickle of blood running down his chin. Dead, he was dead.

Mullaney turned his head and retched. The Guinness came back with a vengeance. Collapsing to his knees and slumping on his haunches, he covered his face in his hands. The banshee had foretold death, but he did not expect to find Burke skewered and dangling from the trick spear. A sudden thought alarmed him. Suppose those fiends were nearby, waiting to finish him off. He was too tired and heartsick to move, even to save his own life. In the stillness, he listened for footsteps.

"Did you find me pipe?" The unmistakable voice came from the top of the spear. The corpse had opened his eyes and was grinning mischievously at him. Mullaney nearly vomited again, but relief got the better of him.

"You're alive?"

"If you could call this living."

"But the many-barbed spear—"

"You have a point there, Mick. By all rights, I should be dead as a beetle in a jam jar, but I find instead I have merely become a sort of hole-y man." He chuckled at his own witticism and winced. "It only hurts when I laugh."

"Let me get you down."

"Not advisable, I'm afraid. I am given to understand that I am to wait right here, or at least that's what the dumb one said. Seems it would exacerbate the internal bleeding if I was to try to remove the many-headed prickle."

"Are you in much pain?"

"I would feel a helluva lot better after a smoke. Did you manage to find my pipe?"

"No, I did not find your pipe. I wasn't looking for your pipe, if you remember. The whole thing was a ruse."

Burke tried to scratch his head but found he could not lift a finger. His range of motion was limited by the rod up his bum. He could swivel his head true left to right, but he could not rotate his shoulders to look behind him. His legs were fine, and from time to time he swung a foot like an infant trapped in a high chair.

Mullaney wondered if one of the barbs had somehow stabbed his chum in the brain, for Burke seemed to have no memory of the plot. "The idea was I would tell them I was after searching for your pipe out there whilst you and the Hound of Ulster were contending for the local chess championship. Instead, I scooted round to the house to fetch the body. We figured they might leave us alone if I delivered the girl they've been looking for this whole night long."

"Excellent plan," Burke said. "But as you can see, they have left the premises."

"Maybe that's a good thing after all, since the body wasn't where I stashed her. I'd wrapped her up in a bit of tarp and shoved her in the toolshed. But someone seems to have stolen the child."

"You cannot find her? No wonder you cannot find my pipe either, for a pipe is a much smaller article than a body. And of a different philosophical nature and function altogether."

"For the love of the gods . . . now they have got me saying it. Forget the feckin' pipe."

"I'll try, but it is awfully dull stuck here. You're saying someone else has absconded with the Connemara Girl and will get all the glory? That's just brilliant." He looked as sad as a runner-up.

"I'm sorry, Tom."

"No, don't you see?" Burke managed to wag one finger. He had found the bright side to their predicament. "We no longer know where the body is. You have managed to elude all responsibility for the crime. If those two come back, we have a legitimate excuse which leaves us off the hook. Not literally, mind, in my case."

Pleased his friend could find humor in the situation, Mullaney fetched the tarpaulin dummy from the back of the lorry. "I had wrapped her up in this. When I discovered her missing, I took a sheaf of thatch to make it look like a body."

From his perch, Burke examined the package. "You wouldn't have fooled them one second, no, sir. They're very observant—not so much Cú, but the other fella, right enough. Always the way, isn't it, with the sidekick? Wasn't it old Sancho Panza who knew the score whilst your Don Quixote was tilting at windmills? Is it not Igor playing the fiddle to lure young Frankenstein? Let me ask, what took you so long getting back? Couldn't have been three minutes' work to fashion that jellyroll."

"I was held up by a banshee."

"You mean to say you were robbed? By a what?"

"A banshee come to warn me that you were dead. She was keening so, I'm surprised you didn't hear it from here."

"I thought that noise was a stuck bagpipes," he said. "Or them giants stepping on the sheep."

Mullaney shook his head. "The things you do not know about your own country. Sure, are you an Irishman at all? The *bean sídhe*, the old fairy woman who appears in the night, wailing and keening to warn of the coming death in the family."

"Well, she was wrong on that score, as you can see. I would not ask her to tout a kiddies' football match. Or whether we'll have rain tomorrow. Listen, though, what were you intending when those lads found out they had been hoodwinked?"

"We would have driven off north by then. Halfway to Westport. Or head for the ocean."

"North would be a mistake, Michael. Those boys are Ulstermen, and their natural inclination is to go north. No, I would not object to an excursion south to Galway City. Find ourselves that nice Italian bistro near the Corrib."

"If we ever get out of this alive, I'll treat you to a lasagna dinner." Mullaney could not help but admire Burke's chutzpah, matteradamn the circumstances. He tried to push in one of the barbs protruding from his friend's belly, but he had to draw back his hand before he could reach the point. Inches before the apparent tip, it drew a dot of blood. A wonder Burke was in such good spirits. Conversation seemed to help distract him from his discomfort.

"So, tell me, Tommy. What went on while I was gone? And how did you end up like a butterfly under glass with a pin through your guts?"

* * *

Láeg had lost, deliberately or not, and Burke asked for a match against the Hound. As expected, Cú was not one to back down from a challenge, and the bone and horn pieces were cast upon the battlefield of squares sewn evenly on the tablecloth. The Ulsterman did not know or observe the conventions of modern chess, preferring to play by an antique set of rules. For example, leaping was allowed, but only by the queens to escape danger. When taking a pawn, it was the custom to shout "Off with your head" and roar with laughter. Bishops were not bishops but priests of the Druidic religion. Cúchulainn had not heard of castling, but once explained, the move was incorporated with indiscriminate gusto. A knight who is captured may be ransomed, but only by a duel of honor among the other knights, in some complex chivalry that was a source of contention between the two players. With the better understanding of these quiddities, Cúchulainn quickly won the first match, though he seemed to be inventing new rules as the game went along. As predicted, the legendary sportsman had too much honor to refuse a rematch. Cú and Láeg joked between themselves while they reset the board, pleasantly acknowledging the new opponent's stratagems. They had grown accustomed to one another's moves like a long-married couple. Cúchulainn whispered a name to his valet.

When the armies had been assembled, Cúchulainn gestured that Burke should move first.

"Thank ye, kindly. Now that I know the rules, watch out."

"Jolly good," Láeg said. "You reminded him of Fer Diad. You know his story, do you not?"

"No, I am afraid that I don't. Your move, Hound. I'm not one for the books and such."

"An epic poetic work about one of Ireland's great heroes."

"Arrah, don't get me started on poetry. The nuns made us memorize pomes long as your arm. Mr. Yeats and Mr. Kavanagh. At least they made sense, had a story. The stuff nowadays don't even have to rhyme. Hold on a tick. I do know a poem:

> There once was a lad out of Derry,
> whose own sister he'd like to marry.
> Oh, no! says the vicar,
> Would it not be the quicker—"

"No, not that sort of thing," Láeg interrupted. "Have you not heard of the Cattle Raid on Cooley? What do they teach in the schools these days?"

"I read that one on the internet," Burke said. "Limericks. net. They call that business at the end a *near rhyme*."

Cúchulainn opted for the King's Gambit, and Burke countered with the Sicilian Defense.

"He paid you a great compliment in comparing you to Fer Diad," said Láeg. "They apprenticed together on the Isle of Skye. Best friends and foster brothers."

"No, I can't say I know any Fer Diads. I read the story about a bull named Ferdinand to my granddaughter Mary Catherine when she was a wee girl, a lifetime ago."

"Fer Diad of the horned skin which no spear or sword point could penetrate versus Cúchulainn of the many-barbed spear. The classic conundrum of the immovable object meets the irresistible force. They met at the ford of the river and fought for three days. None of this rings a bell?"

"Must have been a worthy foe. Three days, was it? I'll have your man in three moves."

Cúchulainn grumbled as he fell into Burke's trap. He laid down his king. "Rubber match?"

While they rearranged the chessmen for the decisive round, Láeg continued his reminiscence. "They were in close combat, you see, sword to sword. Fer Diad gets the drop on him and sinks his blade right into Cú's chest, the blood spurting out and dyeing the river red. My liege hollers for his trick spear, and who floats it downstream to him? You're looking at him. Me, Láeg. Meanwhile, with his left hand, Cú fires a lance at Fer Diad's privates, so the horn-skinned fella lowers his shield to protect his vulnerables. With his right hand, Cú tosses one of his ordinary javelins at his foe's heart, and Fer Diad has no choice but to turn his back. Here's where our man is genius. He picks up the gáe bolga with his bare foot and chucks it with his toes, no less. A thing of beauty, unfolding in slow motion, all eyes following the arc till the spearpoint goes right up the poor fella's arsehole. And it keeps on traveling deeper and deeper, and then the head of the harpoon explodes and dozens of barbs pierce Fer Diad from the inside out. Wasn't that a parry? I will tell you what: that must have hurt."

They were three moves into the final match when it became apparent that Burke understood the game better than his opponent. As more white pieces were removed from the board, Cú's temper sizzled, and he sprouted four extra fingers and four extra toes. But Burke was oblivious, concentrating instead on the sequence of moves he was sure would come. Even Láeg foresaw the endgame, and he tried to calm the hero by creating a diversion.

"Burke, you're a smart man. But you would be smarter still if you read a bit of literature."

"Who needs books when you've got street smarts?" Burke reclaimed his captured knight, gave him a wee kiss, and boxed in his opponent. "Check."

Cú's big eye widened further to accommodate seven irises, and he squeezed the squinty eye till it leaked saltwater. He sacrificed his queen to buy some time.

"Wait a minute," Láeg said. "What's become of your comrade? That fella hunting for your fire-eating mouthstick? He's been gone long enough to carve a set of pipes out of a bog oak."

"Whisht, now, I'm nearly there. I cannot imagine Mullaney lollygagging at the task. Ah, the dear me, I could go for a smoke now that I have you beat like a Persian rug."

The big fella exploded. He pulled the tablecloth and scattered the pieces. "Where is he?" he bellowed. With a startling quick leap, he was on his feet, scrambling in the wilds looking for Mullaney while his second gathered up their weapons. For his part, Burke finally realized his friend was long overdue and how he had been sidetracked by the chess. He panicked and ran, but before he had gone ten yards, the air whistled in curlicues in his eardrum and the spear found its target. Right up the poor man's bum.

For good measure, Láeg planted the butt end of the gáe bolga in the soft peat and hoisted Burke into the air. They left him dangling there as a warning: Do not mess with Cúchulainn when it comes to the pleasant diversions of sports and games. Sore over being so deceived, the Ulstermen marched toward the sea to beat back the tides with their swords.

* * *

Mullaney believed every detail but was stumped by the enigma at the end of Burke's story. "Whyever would they head for the coast?"

"You have heard of the flight of the wild geese?" Burke winked and smiled through the pain. "I told them you were taking the bog girl across the Atlantic to Amerikay in your wee rowboat."

"Hah! You are the crafty rogue. I can see why you were nearly champion of the county with your double feints and tricky moves, but Tommy, you should have let him win. Two out of three, at least."

"It's a grand game. The sport of kings."

"That's horse racing, Tom. Don't worry. We will figure out a way to get you down. Tell me, does your insides hurt any worse? Is there anything I can do for you?'

Burke bravely confronted his misfortune. "I would savor a bowlful of Ole Virginny about now."

18

The Fairies

LIKE THE GLOW of a child's nightlight to ward off the bogeyman, pale blue flickered in one window of the otherwise darkened house. On both sides of the walkway, bushes rustled as Bridget and the screwball couple walked past. An army of mice, perhaps, or hedgehogs on the prowl, warning of the intruders with their wee squeaks. Compared to the chaotic shambles of Mullaney's, Burke's property was neat and tidy. Bridget felt guilty intruding at such an ungodly hour. Back home, she would never have dreamt of disturbing her neighbors, for they would call the Philly police in a heartbeat. Her companions, however, had no such compunction. When nobody came to the door at the first polite knock, Maeve pounded with her fist and kicked the jamb for good measure.

"*Fan go fóill!*" A high-pitched voice approached. "Hold your bloody horses, I'm coming." The porch light snapped on, and the head of a small old woman appeared in the crack below the chain lock. Over her half lenses, she viewed them suspiciously.

"Is it yourselves? Or *taibhsí?*"

"Do we look like ghosts? Don't be silly, Granny, we are as real as you," Maeve said. "Let us in, for the gods' sake. I need to make a visit to your bogs. You do have a water closet in this hovel?"

The old crone undid the chain and pointed her thumb to the rear. "The toilet's on your left." Al followed Maeve down the hall, leaving Bridget alone with the woman of the house. They scrutinized each other in the foyer, perplexed by what they perceived. The tiny old thing stooped slightly at the shoulders, around which hung an afghan in rows of bright colors. Her skin, thin as an onion's, was ash gray, her wiry hair a shade lighter. Dark circles surrounded her puffy eyes. The look of an insomniac of some practice.

"Mrs. Burke," Bridget said. "So sorry to disturb you so late."

"Hah! I knew it. I could tell you were an American by looking at you, but hearing you speak, I am dead certain. Tell me, then, whaddya call a sandwich on a long hard roll with salami and pastrami and capicola, some melted provolone, lettuce, and tomatoes, with a dash of vinegar and oil and a sprinkle of oregano?"

"An Italian hoagie?"

"Hah! Philadelphia, am I right?"

"As a matter of fact—"

"Do youse wanna glassa wooder?"

Bridget frowned at her. "Mrs. Burke—"

"Sure, I am only joking, having a bit of fun. No harm. I could tell straight off. Something about you shouted Philadelphia or maybe Jersey. You ever seen *The Sopranos*? That's a gas show, all right. Too much of your feckin' swearing for my taste, and that ending was a headscratcher. But those characters! C'mon in, bada bing! Never met me a real American face to face."

Shuffling in a pair of oversized slippers, the old dear led her to the sitting room and offered her a spot on the sofa. On the old TV played a black-and-white western with John Wayne and other cowboys rounding up a herd of cattle. Mesmerized by the action, the old woman backed into an easy chair, her eyes never leaving the screen. "Have you ever been on the Chisholm Trail?"

"No, I am afraid that is a long way from Philadelphia."

"So it is. But look at that nice bunch of heifers in it. Go ahead, round 'em up, Duke. I love this part. How much do you think a herd like that would fetch a head? Once upon a time, this part of Ireland was a good place for cattle. More cows than people. For all of them beefeaters over in England." She relaxed further into her easy chair, rested her feet on the ottoman, and raised the volume with the remote.

Bridget had to practically yell to be heard over the yips of the cowboys and the moos of the cows. "Is Mr. Burke around? I have come to speak to your husband."

The old woman tore herself away long enough to give a mock glance about the room. "I don't see himself about." She chuckled to herself.

"But this is his house, right? Did he happen to mention anything to you about the body they found out on the bog?"

"Well, now, that certainly sounds like a good beginning for a mystery fillum. I don't mind a bit of Hitchcock now and then, but if you ask me, this modern stuff is plain gruesome. Show you how the autopsy is done? No thank ye. Turns my stomach when they show you a foot without a body, or a severed head."

"Is he asleep back there? Maybe you could wake him, if it's not too much trouble. If you would point the way, Mrs. Burke?"

"Burke, is it? Well, now, I'm sorry to say you are too late. It would be like trying to roust the dead, dearie."

Maeve and Al barged into the sitting room, faces aglow. Maeve's sundress was inside out, and Al attempted to play a tune with the zipper of his fly. Their attention was immediately diverted by the movie.

"This one is called *Red River*," the old lady said. "John Wayne is the star, with Walter Brennan, a good Irishman, as Groot."

Transfixed, they sat on the arms of the sofa. "I love a good western," Maeve said. "Git along, little dogies. Do you have any popcorn, *a stór?*"

"Help yourself to the treasures of the pantry."

With a nod, Maeve sent Al to the kitchen.

Watching him trail off obediently as a golden retriever, Bridget said, "I don't mean to interrupt—"

"There's Montgomery Cliff," Maeve said. "A good-looking boy."

"*Clift*, I do believe, the past tense," the old woman said. "Heart attack, and him in his forties. Only the good die young, they say. Speaking of which, Miss Philadelphia here is after looking for a Mr. Burke. As far as I know, that fella is dead."

Hearing the sad news, Maeve slid off the back of the sofa and crossed the room to hug the widow around her slender shoulders. "That explains the state you are in. As soon as we came in the door, I says to myself, that woman has been crying her eyes out. I thought it was the movie. Oh, Granny, I am sorry for your troubles."

"You're a dear," the old woman said, patting the arm around her neck. "But it is all unnecessary. Truth be told, death is never personal. I cannot deny, however, a good cry is a tonic."

Settling deeper in the warm spot on the sofa, Bridget rubbed the sleep from her tired eyes. What sort of world had she wandered into? The movie seemed to be on a loop, a cattle drive that would never end. Yet the heartless widow remained glued to the TV. The death of her husband was *not personal*? All day long Bridget had been imagining conversation with Burke, and now, apparently, he was dead. That certainly threw a match into the gasworks. She would have to go back to the inn and give her condolences to Burke's daughter-in-law. Perhaps Natalie did not even know. Never mind the poor man's granddaughter, who would be heartbroken, but Bridget needed that Red Witch to show her the way to the body before anyone else heard the news. Death may not be personal, but it is certainly inconvenient.

"Pardon me, Mrs. Burke—"

The old woman snapped at her. "And that's another thing. You keep calling me missus. I'm nobody's wife. Not Burke's nor any man's."

Whistling a merry tune, Al returned bearing a large bowl of popcorn, proud as if he were coming home with the spoils of war. Before he could set it down, he was stopped by a contemptuous stare.

"Any butter?" the old woman asked.

"Hunger is the best sauce," Al said.

Maeve pointed to the kitchen, and Al spun on his heels to make things right.

"He is such a dear." Maeve quite boldly stripped and turned her dress round right, talking all the while, oblivious to the circumstances. "You will have to excuse my American friend. She does not understand our customs, even though she claims her last name is Scanlon."

The old woman perked up. "One of the Scanlons of Bal-lynahinch, or are your people out of Kinvara?"

"I don't rightly know," Bridget said. "We are Irish Americans, though. You know, green beer and leprechauns, 'Danny Boy' and the St. Paddy's Day Parade."

"I never heard a single one of those things, honey," Maeve said. "Not wonder you don't recognize an old keener when you meet her."

"Oh, for goodness's sake, come out with it," the old woman said. "Banshee is the name on me. If you cannot say it, I will."

"The banshee?" Bridget asked.

With no warning, the banshee squealed through her nose, a mouselike cry that intensified into a rolling whine, and the first tears dripped from her red eyes. The wailing increased into the screech of a fire engine, drowning out the cattle arriving in Abilene with a wall of sound. The sheer mournfulness induced ineffable memories of love lost, kinfolk long departed, and the disappointment of unrealized ambitions. As abruptly as the keening started, she shut off the tap.

"Do you believe me now, Philly Cheesesteak? I am no monster, merely the harbinger of death. If you hear my cry, expect bad news."

"My apologies," Bridget said. "So you know for a fact that Burke is dead?"

"Is." The banshee brightened at the smell of buttered popcorn. "Or will *soon be* dead."

Al dropped the bowl into Maeve's lap. "Soon? Soon? You mean there's a chance he lives still? We must make haste. This lass thinks if we find Burke, we find Mullaney, and Mullaney will lead us to the girl."

"And what girl is this?" the banshee asked.

Bridget said, "The girl they dug up this morning."

"Well, good luck to youse," the banshee said. "There's many things lost on the bogs and never found. I myself had a gray cat once upon a time."

Al leaned in and patted her knee, sending up clouds of dust. "We thought your people might be able to help us look for her."

"Can it not wait till the end of the fillum?"

"No, dear," Maeve said. "Not if we want to talk with Mr. Burke before he's dead and forever silent."

"Good thing I seen this one twenty-seven times. I suppose the ending will not change." Nevertheless, she rose with some reluctance and had to be encouraged through the front door.

* * *

The banshee was spry for a woman her age, and the others struggled to keep pace with her. She cared nary a whit for the obstacles, not even the unholy minefield of the cow pastures. The plate-sized patties were so numerous and invisible in the night that it was impossible not to step in the shite. The two lovers did not seem to mind getting dirty either, but Bridget was disgusted by the smell coming off her shoes.

"Where are we going?" she asked. "Who are 'her people' you keep talking about?"

Maeve linked her arm with Bridget's. "We are paying a visit to the people who foster your well-being. The Cobblers."

"The Folk of the Hills," Al said. "The Good People. The Wee Wauns."

"We are going to the Otherworld, honey. To have a word with the Enlightened."

"For the love of Mike," the banshee said. "We are calling upon the fairies. I am the *bean sí*, after all, woman of the fairies. Have you no Irish on you at all?"

"Right, so," said Al. "The f-f-f-fairies."

"Youse two are so superstitious you cannot say their name and break the taboo. A fine pair you are. The thing you must remember is the fairies have no interest in you at all. Zero. They will not be kidnapping you. Sure, where would they put you, taking all that space and natural resources? On a fine night like this, it seems a grand idea, but where would they hide you in the pissing rain, or how would they keep you entertained in the long nights after Samhain? Sure, they would have to be putting on pantomimes and benefit performances. Not to mention the cost of three square meals a day. No, they have no use for the likes of human beings."

They climbed a stone fence and located the fairy ring, a circle of stones and mushrooms surrounding a hawthorn tree. The old woman gave the secret greeting, a complicated series of whistles and animal calls synchronized with certain hand movements. Code words were exchanged to open the portal from this world to the other.

In sets of three, the fairies materialized out of the darkness, rubbing their eyes with their tiny fists, yawning and stretching, slightly annoyed to be rousted from their beds. They ranged in size considerably. The smallest could sit comfortably in the palm of your hand, and the tallest would reach the cap of your knee. Despite their diminutive status, they were similar to grown adults in most respects. Three or six of them might be considered fairy children, changelings perhaps. Half of the rest were men and half were women, some had beards, and some had red hair. All wore costumes that blended in with the nearby rocks and heather, and one even wore a suit of water. None of them expressed any outward sign of surprise at their visitors, though perhaps this may be accounted for by the presence of the banshee. She had shrunk to the size of a shinbone.

After greetings in Irish, the parties switched to English in hospitality to the stranger from abroad. The fairies assembled in the great circle and invited the people to sit and join them. Dumbfounded, Bridget obeyed without question. Her instinctive anthropological interest outweighed the smidgen of incredulity in her mind, but only just so. Her neighbors on

either side were fascinated by Bridget and could not stop staring at her eyeglasses or her dung-splattered shoes. Two were
selected to be spokespersons for the group: a sprightly gent
who introduced himself as the blacksmith Liam na Sopóige
and a young woman who called herself Corr.

"You are a long ways from Rathcroghan, Your Grace, and
the portal from that world to this at Oweynagat. What can
we do you for?" Liam asked, once the formalities were over.

Maeve took the lead. "Begging your pardon, but we are
on the lookout for two human men, a Burke and a Mullaney,
who are out at this wee hour somewhere in the nothingness
of Connacht."

Liam produced a pipe from his trousers and stuck it in
his mouth. "They must have done something serious to war-
rant the attention of a king and queen. Not to mention the
claustrophobia of passing through the Cave of the Wildcats.
I would not welcome such a tight squeeze. Tell me, did this
Burke and Mullaney steal somebody's shoes?"

The fairies tittered at the question. It was their favorite
one.

"No," Maeve said. "They did not steal any shoes."

"Where they messing about with a slingshot, using a
chunk of cheese for ammunition?"

"No," Maeve said. "I am always on guard for such
flummery."

"They haven't been bothering the sheep?" Al looked
around the circle to see if anyone found this interjection
amusing. They did not.

The wee blacksmith tapped his chin with the stem of the
pipe. "Those lads are not searching for golden treasures at the
end of a rainbow or some other such nonsense."

"I would not put it past Burke," Al said. "But no, they are
not seeking the so-called crock of gold."

Striking a match on the sole of his foot, Liam lit his pipe and gave it three good puffs. "They haven't been cheating at chess, have they?"

Al and Maeve shrugged their shoulders.

"This is a riddle wrapped inside a walnut hatched inside an eggshell. Why do you seek this Burke and Mullaney?"

"They know the whereabouts of the girl that has been placed in the bog," Maeve said. "They dug her up and accidentally set the Whirl in motion."

Murmurs orbited the circumference.

"Why did you not say so in the first place?" Liam signaled the young maiden across from him. "Corr, do your thing, and tell us what there is to tell."

In the middle of the circle, Corr lifted her left foot, bringing it to rest on her right knee. She bent her right arm to resemble the neck of a wading bird, and she closed her right eye.

"What's going on?" Bridget whispered. "Is this some kind of yoga, the posing crane?"

"One leg to stand between this world and the other," Corr said. "One eye to stare into space and time."

"Not everyone can manage the crane crouch," Liam said. "Takes good chakras and special training to transcend the material world."

Swaying to keep her balance, Corr intoned the transcendent chord to unlock her vision. "The world is awhirl this night, black is white, and three times are converged in the one space containing yesterday, today, and tomorrow, available to all. I see the Hound of Ulster in the great ocean, slashing the heads off every ninth wave. I see three druids, heads aflame, atop the bones in the graveyard clay. I see a man rooted like a tree." The seer dropped her foot and opened her eye, grinning bashfully in front of the strangers.

"She always sees visions in threes," Liam said. "For three is the best of all numbers."

"Ask her where that man is," Maeve said. "The one who is a tree. Surely he will have the sap of knowledge from long years rooted to one spot and nothing to contemplate but the meaning of life."

Corr had borrowed Bridget's glasses and was peering through the huge lenses, blinking her eyes. "Everything is out of focus."

"They will never believe this in Dublin," Bridget said. "I am not sure I believe it myself."

As its purposes had been fulfilled, their conference ended unceremoniously. One by one, the fairies disappeared, popping from sight like a string of burnt-out Christmas lights. The banshee whooped a yippi-hoo as she vanished, and Liam glowed like a will-o'-the-wisp as he exited to the Otherworld. After handing back the eyeglasses, Corr pixelated as she whispered in Bridget's ear, "The bog, the bog."

CHAPTER

19

The Isle of Skye

A STRANGE, ALMOST SISTERLY feeling peppered Fedelm's black heart. She had developed a real affection for the Red Hags, an unintended consequence of having leapt into their minds and spent a few brief moments sharing dreams in their souls. They were the same age she had been when the killers took her life, for she would be forever seventeen. But two thousand years in the peat had matured her, brought wisdom and hard experience, and they had so much to learn, standing on the spearpoint between childhood and adulthood. Such tender empathy baffled her, for she had long since expected the worst of people. Yet the girls had been a great help, no questions asked and nothing to be gained. At her instructions, they were making ready for the journey, pulling on their socks and shoes, gathering the small weapons from the chariot.

"So, you three are off to school this fall. Dublin, I suppose. Or over the sea to study with the bloody Saxons?"

"Depends on the Leaving Certs," Siobhán said. "We hope to end up in Galway together, but you never know how you'll do on the exams."

"Ah, well, wherever you choose, it will be the best years of your life. Never again will you have such close friends and limitless freedom. Late-night bull sessions. Parties till dawn. Shall I regale you with my experience in going away to school?"

They nodded eagerly, settling like minions at her feet.

"I had never been on a boat before, so the journey over the sea to Alba was thrilling. The cold salt air in my face, the deep blue mysteries below the bow, perhaps an ancient whale with a mouth big enough to swallow a man on a horse, or the bonny shoals of herring, or a pod of wistful selkies. We skipped from one island to the next, like a flat stone thrown across the surface of a pond. My heart, too, bounced along the further from home we traveled. All my own people had seen me off. Father, mother, and two sisters had traveled as far as the last spit of our beloved land so they could wave their handkerchiefs from the dock. I faced north to resist the temptation to beg the sailors swing aft and take me back home.

"*Eilean a' Cheò*, the Isle of Skye, was our destination. More precisely, Scáthach's castle, renowned for being impossible to breach. As we neared the barricade of rocks, the sailors stowed their oars and raised the red-hand flag. Under that ensign, the boat steered itself through the jagged passage without scratch or jostle and landed at the green peninsula. They put the new students ashore, and our first test was mastering the Pupils' Bridge. As soon as a person stepped on one end, the opposite end of the bridge flew up and slapped them in the face. Some tried to race across but were tossed into the ocean. Others tried to leap quickly before the far side had a chance to react, but that stunt never worked. But I outsmarted the Pupils' Bridge by walking across backwards. My ingenuity earned me bonus points with Scáthach, the headmistress. Once we had all joined her, she signaled to the captain, and the boat slipped away. We were officially on our own at the Fortress of Shadows, all excited to meet the other freshmen and settle into our new digs.

"In the dining room, a large dinner had been laid on the table. Fishes and crabs and lobsters, as you might expect, but also green leaves and herbs in bowls, apples and other pomes, and plenty of groats for those who needed a good filling. As we tucked in, suddenly comes the *skreich* of the Scottish pipes and a man in a flannel skirt escorting two other kilted fellas toting an enormous platter laden with a sheep's stomach stuffed with oats and raisins and suet that had been given a good boil. A great Scot groaned to his feet and made a long speech, not a word understandable, and then all the boys fought over who would stab the haggis. Rounds of what they called Scotch whisky were poured. 'Twas at that first feast I met Cúchulainn and Fer Diad, the big men on campus.

"Those two lads may as well be pups from the same litter. They were inseparable, good-hearted rivals in every pursuit. Take pole vaulting, for instance. It was unknown at the time in Ireland, but on Skye almost everyone had their own pole and was forever leaping left and right both night and day. Not as they do now, to see how high you can jump, what's the point in that? No, back when I was a lass, it was to see what distance you could vault. Can you use the pole to hop over ditches and culverts, or if you were fit enough, to ford a large stream or river? Best ever for me was twenty-two feet four inches, but that might have been on account of my disadvantage in stature compared to the lads. They were always bragging after the size of their poles.

"On Field Day, the contest came down to the two best friends. Fer Diad vaults twenty-four and six, and Cú goes twenty-five. And so on, six inches more at a time, until they both hit thirty-three feet. Up your man Fer Diad goes, the pole snaps in two, and he ends up soaked in the drink. Without a running start, Cú not only bests him by three feet, he starts hopping back and forth from shore to shore like he's on a pogo stick. A real show-off if you ask me, but the girls flocked to him like the best footballer or the captain of the hurling squad. They were all dying to give him a ride, and he could take his pick.

"The Hound of Ulster had not told a soul that he was already betrothed to a girl back home, name of Emer, daughter of Forgall the Cunning. Did he let that little detail stop him from hopping bed to bed? He did not. He even dallied with Scáthach's own daughter Uathach. My point is, watch out for the glamor lads, Mr. Popular, the ladies' man. Nothing but trouble. Some lads have egos wide as the sea.

"Stick to your studies, girls. Under Scáthach's instructions, we learned all the important life skills. How to juggle nine apples at a time. How to hone a sword's edge sharp enough to shave a man's beard without a nick, or how to lop off his head without a drop of blood. We learned the art of making thunder through our bottoms to disperse all enemies. How to hide ourselves beneath the slope of a shield. She taught us the dodge and feint against a poison dart. How to master underwater fighting, the chariot wheel toss, the snapping teeth, and the hero's scream. You must believe in yourselves, hags, fill your lungs and open your mouth full wide to power through the high notes if you want to make your voice truly blood-curdling."

In the back of her throat, Siobhán rehearsed a silent scream.

"Cúchulainn was the paragon of nearly every feat. He could throw a javelin through a space no bigger than a finger and a thumb making the *okay* sign. He could launch a flying lance with one foot and make it stand on its point. The rims of his shield would slice you in two, and the sickles of his chariot wheel would snip off your leg at the knee. He could take the reins between his teeth and ride through the enemy line with nine swords in one hand and three spears in the other. Scáthach showed him the trick of the gáe bolga, the many-barbed war harpoon that kills a foe from inside out. She taught him as well how to use his anger to bring on the riastradh and triple his ferocity. Born for destruction, the Hound of Ulster was champion warrior of our school. For all his warts, he was some hero, and many is the happy memory of watching those gory feats in awe and admiration. But as is said, live by the sword, die by the sword."

A glaze fell over her dark face as she relived her college days. Absent-mindedly, she stroked at the wound at her throat. In the crumbling tower of the chapel, a barn owl screeched and launched its silent hunt. The mouse never knew what hit him.

Eileen asked the question on everyone's mind. "Were you a great warrior, too?"

A wry smile lifted Fedelm's darkened cheeks. "I was no warrior. Sure, I could handle myself in an emergency, needs be, but I was nowhere near proficient at the stabbing game. You have to put your heart into it, each time, to be any good at killing or maiming. No, my passion was poetry, not war. Throughout the western lands, Scáthach was well known in the art of wordplay, and she taught me assonance and dissonance, sprung rhythm, when to throw in the odd dactyl, and how to mind a metaphor. Not in your bockety Saxon tongue but in the melodious Irish. Our mornings were spent on the battlefield, but after our tea, all was poetry."

The three Red Witches could not hide their surprise. A giggle rumbled in Emcee's throat, a spurt of laughter squeezed through Eileen's fingers, and even Siobhán failed to stop her eyes from rolling and her eyebrows from arching.

"You scoff," the bog girl said. "But the poets made the heroes. Poets invented Ireland itself. Cúchulainn would be a forgotten sociopath, just another corpse on the crimson plain, a heap of ashes, or a body pickled in the bog. What is a ghost but an unfinished story? One that desires to be told?"

"Bah, that's all history," Eileen said. "I prefer to live in the moment."

"What would we know of the present without our myths? Don't read too fast and miss the point, girls. In my opinion, we have only our words to translate the past. Only words, in the end, to show we were once here. Indeed, we might as well be made of words."

"My mother would kill me if I went off to study poetry at college," Emcee said.

"Whatever you do, don't be too harsh on your parents; sure, aren't they doing the best that they can, for all their own faults? Besides, you would be surprised by what a mother might say. Even the high art of poetry was not the end of my education at the Fortress of Shadows. For it was through Scáthach that I developed the imbas forosnai, the light of foresight. It is a gift, for such vision cannot be simply learned or bought. Prophecy is sharper than the exploding spear and more powerful than the salmon leap. And if only I had convinced them to heed my vision, I could have saved the men and women of Connacht from undertaking the Cattle Raid of Cooley."

She told them the whole tale of her encounter with Medb and Ailill on their way to wage war against the Hound of Ulster. How three times Medb had asked about the fate of her troops, and three times Fedelm had warned of the slaughter. She had spoken in poetic meter of the crimson and the red, the loss of so many men. Still, Medb had refused to listen.

"I played my small part in the great saga," Fedelm said. "I hid nothing from the queen, though for two thousand years I have wondered, should I have said more? I don't know, been more emphatic in my rhetoric or raised an unholy ruckus? But I was just a green lass coming home from college. She was too proud to follow the words of a woman poet, even one with the foresight. Thank the gods, at last she has forgiven me. Or forgotten how stubborn she was about the bull."

Siobhán stole a glance at the broken chariot in the graveyard. "You think this Maeve character has been chasing us this whole night long? She's come to carry you home?"

"Aye, I believe so," said Fedelm. "At first I thought it must be Cúchulainn come to finish me off. Complete the work of the assassins who murdered me and make sure I was well and truly dead this time around. I could have sworn I heard his singing sword back at Mullaney's farm. But he is far too clever and bloodthirsty not to have tracked us by now."

"Why don't you use your gift of foresight? Look into the future."

"The light was extinguished by the waters of the bog," she said. An inner darkness dropped upon her like a heavy wave, pulling her down into a bottomless despair. She bowed her head, slumped her shoulders, and bent her knees, as if ready to jump back into the grave. The Red Witches enveloped her in their arms, a group hug for their depressed friend, so close they could feel the soft dampness of her body and smell peat smoke on her breath.

"I was never able to use the vision gift to predict my own future," Fedelm said. "It doesn't work like some parlor trick. The light of foresight was always bright and clear, but only concerning the fate of others. I could count the dead men on the battlefield. Or I could have even warned Medb about her own end, bathing in a stream many years later. Hit in the head by a chunk of hard cheese launched from a slingshot. Poor dear. Alas, I could not have saved myself from the killers." She held out her wrists and showed them the scars on her neck.

The thick mist on the ground rose into a fog, as is common during the change of seasons in Ireland. The ragged teeth of the chapel walls had all but decayed, and the faraway hills were but a memory. It was time to go.

"Which of you best knows this land?"

Eileen raised her hand. "I have ridden my horse this way many times and passed this very chapel from beyond the crooked lane."

"Which way is quickest back to Mullaney's house?"

"We could circle round to the main road that goes through the village. If we are lucky, we might find some early riser to give us a lift. I don't know about you, but I could sleep for a week."

"Sorry, but we must foot it ourselves," Fedelm said. "You would have much to explain if we met a stranger on the road, don't you think? *Who is that corpse you are dragging around with you?* Never mind three witches out for a coven at this hour. We don't want to scare the milkman half to death."

"We could go back for the rowboat," Siobhán said. "I will take an oar if youse are too feckin' weak and tired."

"There must be an easier way," Fedelm said. "Those horses did not swim across the lake towing a chariot."

Eileen had a plan. "The western shore runs beside a ridge for a spell, and then takes you on the edge of the bogland."

With her dagger, Fedelm drew in the dirt, calculating the time and devising a strategy. "Are you sure none of you has a chess set upon you? The knights always point the way to trouble when dumped from a crane bag." She scrutinized each face. "No? Then we will follow the lakeshore. Keep alert for the shaking scraws and the quagmires that can eat a body. Follow the fox's trail, quick as a wink."

She tucked her dirk in the fabric of her tunic and showed the girls how to hide small weapons upon their persons. They left the graveyard and sang quietly to keep the line together and avoid the dangerous wet spots. Their repertoire was mostly American songs popular among the lovelorn.

A voice came out of the fog. "Is that what passes for a melody these days?"

Fedelm drew the dagger from her cloak.

"Put away your short sword, poet. There will be no need for a pointed debate."

"Who is that talking in the gloom? Make yourself known."

From the mist, a sticklike shape took form: a crane, standing on one leg in the shallows of the lake. As they drew near, the witches saw that the bird was actually a young girl, holding a yoga pose.

"Is it Corr of the Sióga?" Fedelm asked. "As I live and breathe, I haven't seen you in the age of two whales. How is the health upon you?"

"Smashing," said the fairy. "Poor misfortunate poet. I can see by your complexion and the red knot of your hair that time has not been kind to you."

"You try lying in a bog these twenty centuries and see where it gets you. I am surprised to have any body at all, and consider this leather suit better than bits of dust and atoms swirling in the atmosphere. How are things in fairyland?"

"*Musha*, not as they used to be. The West is full of tourists, Germans and Americans, so you cannot get a good night's rest. And there was the Celtic Tiger, wildly come and gone, sans teeth, sans claws, sans everything down to the stripes of its tail. Dubliners were buying up the land for holiday lets on every scrap and hillock. Then the whole thing goes bust and the hills is full of white elephants, can't be sold or mortgaged. Serves them right, greedy bastards. Aye, globalization has played havoc with the Good Folk, and only now is things settling, so. And who are these three young ladies? Training to be druids, are ye?"

"These are the Red Witches, don't you know? I expect your lot has heard of these hags."

"Word has come of the likes of them and how close they are to the magical ways. Pleased to meet you. Are you the ones what dug up my friend from the peat?"

"No," Emcee said. "That was my grandfather, Tom Burke. And his friend Michael Mullaney."

"And what do these peasants plan to do with this poor child of the bogs?"

No one dared answer at first, but Emcee finally ventured. "They probably want to give her to the National Museum and display her in an exhibition for the plain people of Ireland to see a real Connemara Girl from the Late Iron Age. But we rescued her from that awful fate."

"For now," the fairy said. "Poet, you are being followed this night. The gates at Oweynagat are open. The bullheaded queen and her consort have been on the hunt, and they bring an outsider with them. From Philadelphia in Amerikay. The land of golden streets, if such a thing can be believed, out beyond Tír na nÓg in the great western Aicean."

Fedelm shook her head. "I am not convinced such a place exists."

"Let me assure you it does. But Amerikay is as full of Irish as Ireland itself, though not one in ten know where their people are from. Still, it does not stop them from being sentimental about the motherland, how they love their mothers. I have seen other visions as well. I see a man who is rooted like a tree. And the Hound of Ulster is also about and seeks you. But he is presently busy hacking the whitecaps off every ninth wave."

"So, the both of them are about? Medb and Cúchullain?"

Corr shrugged her slim shoulders. "The old story is well knotted with twists and circulations. Let me just say the Whirl is in motion once again."

"Thank you, Crane Girl, for the warnings. I have lost my imbas and am much obliged to be caught up on the whole plot."

"Make haste. And when the time comes to choose your fate, let the wisdom of the afterlife guide you." Corr stood on one leg and shape-shifted into a bird, then flew into the shadows across the lake. The three girls watched the star-filled sky till she disappeared, and when they looked down, Fedelm was well ahead on the fox's trail.

CHAPTER

20

The Sea

WAVE AFTER WAVE after cold wave pounded against the rugged cliffs of his chest, yet even Cúchulainn could not vanquish the sea. On the strand, Láeg dutifully counted off the triads, and at each ninth wave, he called a warning to his master. Lifting his shining broadsword, the warrior slashed the breakers and sent the whitecaps flying. At first, he roared with each stroke, trying to jumpstart his frenzy, but no go. The sea is an impersonal foe. Perhaps subconsciously Cú realized the folly of his task, or perhaps he was fatigued by the three chess matches. Eons had passed since he had last walked among the mortals, and he imagined each new wave was Mullaney or Burke, those infuriating bumpkins who had deflected his quest. A breeze sent the spindrift scudding like tumbleweeds, and our hero was soaked to the bone, his red tunic a sodden blanket and his magnificent long hair a knot of kelp.

"That is ninety times nine," Láeg hollered from the shore. "While the waves are in terror of your valor, I do not think the Aicean likely to surrender."

A curious dolphin leapt in the air not six feet away. Normally, Cú would have chased the creature and engaged it in underwater combat for pure fun and games, but he could barely shake a fist. The dolphin blew a raspberry through its spout and tail-kicked on its merry way. The next big breaker smashed across Cúchulainn's back and knocked him off his feet. Tumbling in the undercurrent, he was dragged across the sharp shells and rocks, arse over elbows, under two additional pounding waves, and tossed upon the shore. He crawled along the sand like a shipwrecked sailor. A desert had collected in his tunic, and he hated that gritty feeling in his own blowhole. He stood and shook out his drawers, leaving behind small crustaceans and new dunes from the copious sand he had dredged. That is how the place became known as *Snámh-ar-an-Ghaineamh*, or Swims-in-the-Sand.

Out of a sense of decency and propriety, Láeg faced the tides as his boss was wriggling his shorts down around his knees. He had to shout to be heard. "I was thinking, as you showed the waves what-for, that we may have been sent on a fool's errand. They are a pair of hornswogglers. Suppose Burke slyly told us Mullaney had taken the girl to Amerikay as a further diversion upon the first diversion. To get us out of the way whilst the clever one absconded with the girl and hid her elsewhere in Connemara."

To dig out the finer particles, Cúchulainn twisted his pinkie into his earhole. "That is a bold double misdirection."

"Perhaps they planned to rendezvous with the archaeologist we met outside O'Leary's. The fair-haired girl with the glasses over her eyes. I would not put it past the Irish mortals to be in cahoots with the Americans."

"The bold deceivers."

"But we can outmaneuver them by returning to the bog before they slip away."

"I am itchy all over," Cúchulainn said. "Pebbles between each tooth and enough salt in my eyes to corn a side of beef. By the gods, a good rain would be most welcome."

"The hour is late. The Whirl will not whirl endlessly. We must put some acres behind us if we are to complete our business before the rising of the sun."

"Dagnabbit, there is nothing worse than this infernal sand. It is everywhere and has found every hole that's in me." Cú blew his nose and scared a flock of wild geese flying overhead. He fussed with the waistband of his shorts. "Do you not have a decent towel?"

"Please concentrate for a moment." Láeg planted his fists on his hips like a scolding nun. "We must hurry, you fool."

Cú's left eye twitched, and the lines on his brow forked like lightning. "I will not take another step till I rid myself of every last grain. Be a good fellow and lend me your comb."

His valet fished around in his crane bag and handed him a hairbrush. The first stroke teased out a dozen sea lice, which scurried down the Hound's arm and disappeared like tears into the strand.

"Keep it," Láeg said, and waved him away. He then produced the pipe he had found on the bogs and filled it with the chocolate-scented tobacco he had pinched from Burke's pocket as he was hanging on the gáe bolga. He lit a bowl and pondered the shooting stars as Cúchulainn addressed his golden locks, carding his own wool.

*   *   *

Mullaney mulled over the problem of his impaled friend. They discussed the option of calling an ambulance and letting the emergency medical technicians determine the best course for removing the spear from his bottom, but neither of them could devise a logical explanation of how it got there in the first place.

"I can hear you now on the telephone with the 999 operator," Burke said. *"My friend Tom has a spear up his arse; can you help? And furthermore, be careful, for the business end is barbed as a porkypine with deadly exploding spikes . . . One-in-a-million shot, aye . . . Well, it was thrown by none other than Cúchulainn . . . No, I cannot spell it. Let's say the Hound of Ulster . . . Up North, righty-o . . . Tossed it with his toes, he did . . . The why is it? you ask . . . Beat him two out of three at the chess . . . Indeed, Tom was runner-up in the All-County . . . Good question. Would you believe it if I told you we dug up a bog girl this morning? . . . Well, to be truthful, I snuck back and hid her in my shed, and that is why this Cúchulainn fella is after us . . . No, ma'am, we have not been drinking. Listen, could you send someone knows a thing or two about impalation—"*

"Impalement," Mullaney said.

"Aren't you're the right scholar."

"I take your point. I should have left her alone in the first place, but how was I to know removing her from the bog would trigger some disturbance in the space-time continuum?"

"Is that what happened? Well, that's grand. Matteradamn, I will have to Google *continuum* to have the slightest idea of your perplexities. Still, I feel all the better to have a rational explanation for our predicament. Didn't I tell you we should have notified the Gardaí in the first place? Leave the girl be for the anthropologists?"

"Archaeologists," Mullaney said. "And I seem to recall you were the one looking for a wee bit of fame. 'Local Farmers Discover Bog Girl.' Your face on the telly. They should see you now."

"Rub my nose in it, since you have me at a disadvantage. That girl has been nothing but trouble. I could have told you

right from page one that you should not mess with the supernatural, and here you cocked up a whole space-time continuum. Listen, I could text my granddaughter, and maybe she
and them witches could cast a spell to remove this timber."

"Or bring one of those Draught horses to winch it out of
you."

"Ah, Mick. To be honest, I am a bit fearful of those
bastes. Wouldn't a horse-pull hack my guts all the worse?"

Mullaney circled around him, investigating the pattern
of spikes visible through Burke's shirt. "If I could only reach
the tips, I could probably push them back into place. Like
springs on a lumpy mattress."

"Don't you think I have tried that? I'm much too weak to
lift me elbows, even if you offered a pint this moment. I am a
goner, Mick. Do me one favor and ask my Natalie not to lay
me out in one of them open caskets at the wake. Them
undertakers make a hash of a fellow with the makeup and
lipstick and trying to tame the old cowlick. I never fancied
people staring at me while I am alive, much less when I am
dead. Besides, what is the body without its soul? Something
to carry around the person what lives inside. I'll take a Mass
of Remembrance, though. And a good feed at O'Leary's for
the neighbors. Have Mannion whistle up a lament. The lads
will be expecting me to stand another round, and make sure
them roast beef sandwiches are not slathered with the horse-
radish. There's a box of cash under the floorboards and an
insurance policy in the pocket of the green herringbone suit
I never wear. May as well bury me in that fine Irish tweed,
unless you fancy it for yourself. Say *slán agaibh* to the boys for
me."

"Don't be talking rubbish, Tom. Listen, if this pointy
spear hasn't killed you yet, you still have a chance."

"I am murthered certainly, killed like Cock Robin."

Something was running along the bog lane, panting as it climbed the rise of the hill. With three quick barks, Bonnie said hello, wagging her tail and anxious to be greeted and petted. She allowed her man to bend down and hug her closely.

"That's a good girl," Mullaney said. "Where have you been all this time?"

The collie took notice of the human scarecrow and knew at once his predicament was neither normal nor desirable. She flattened herself to the ground and tried to will him down with her best supra-canine stare. When he did not obey, she took three steps toward him, barking to show she meant business.

"Could you call off your bitch?" Burke asked. "For the love of the Holy Mother, she will wake the dead and give ourselves away."

"Bonnie, that's only Tom Burke. You know Tommy. He's my best mate. C'mon up out of that." Mullaney whistled a command to lie low, and she fell to, wagging her tail against her better judgment. "Good to see you, Bonnie. You're real, aren't you, lass. The first real thing we have seen all night, right as rain. Kind of reassuring, isn't it, to know the real world is immediately the other side of this one?"

"I would feel a lot better without this stick up me arse, real or no." Burke wriggled to find a more comfortable position. "Did you mean that business about best friends, Michael? It is nice to hear you say so after all we have been through."

"You were a world of help to me when the missus flew the coop. And when Flannery off and went to America. And you've been a resource around the farm, so, yeah, I suppose we are best mates. Despite all the trouble—"

Ignored as the pair exchanged their fraternal regards, the bitch began to sniff at the base of the pole. Straightaway she pawed at the peaty earth, soon enough started digging like a frantic mother trying to rescue her buried pups. As she worked, the spear shifted, and inch by inch, Burke lurched toward the ground.

"You're on your way, girl. Steady on," Burke encouraged her from the tilting flagpole. "They say the border collie is the smartest dog in the world. Easy now, Bonnie, go slow. Over in America there was a dog who learned the names of over one thousand things. *Fetch your teddy*—he'd come back with his toy bear. *Bring me the blue bone*, and sure, didn't he find the right one, not the red or the white, and drop it with a squeak at your man's feet. Smarter than a five-year-old child is your collie, so the man on the telly said."

The spear had been levered enough for Mullaney to grab Burke before he fell on his face. The old fella rested on his hands and knees, the blood rushing to his head, moaning at the discomfort of his new situation. Most tenderly, Mullaney pressed a point near Burke's belly button, but it did not give a jot. His stomach yowled and complained. They were so engrossed in the puzzle that they failed to notice the soft arrival of a stranger.

"You'll not extract the harpoon that way, lad." A small man with a rough beard appeared out of the dark. No bigger than a schoolboy, he carried a twisted shillelagh and a clay pipe tucked in the breast pocket of his shirt. His appearance caused some surprise, but considering all the other events of the day, he was not entirely unexpected. The little man stood between them, implacable as the Buddha.

"And who might you be?" Mullaney asked.

"Liam na Sopóige is the name upon me. A mere gentleman blacksmith out for an early-morning stroll. Your man seems to be in a pickle. What sort of shenanigans caused this unfortunate state of distress? How are you not dead as dead can be? Have you by any chance partaken of the Beer of Immortality? The brew of Goibhniu, the smith of the Tuatha Dé Danann?"

"Nothing but a few pints of Guinness hours ago," Mullaney said.

"The Beer of Immortality would be pouring out of the many holes in you. Perhaps you were fooling about with what shouldn't be fooled with?"

"It's not what you think," Burke said. With each word, he grimaced.

"It's hardly ever what you think," said the smith. "Tell me, then, what syllogism led to this thesis. I may be able to help you with the right sort of explanation as to why you gentlemen are lurking about the Connemara countryside at this wee time of the moon."

Mullaney stepped in due to Burke's apparent difficulties in speaking for once. "That's the gáe bolga. The spear of many exploding points. You may find it difficult to accept, but the legendary Cúchulainn himself is about this very night, and he threw that javelin with his bare toes into that unusual target. All on account of being bested two out of three at chess."

"Chess? Why didn't you say so in the first place?" Liam asked. "Tell me, then, what was your key move to defeat the Hound of Ulster not once but twice? I am curious, for it is known far and wide on this little isle of green that he cannot be beaten in any aspect of the sporting life."

"I used the Fool's Gambit," Burke said proudly.

"The Fool's Gambit?" Liam was knocked off his feet and sat down by the reek of turf bricks. "Bedad, you would think the big fella would have recognized the maneuver right off. Was he distracted otherwise at the time? Did someone kick a Gaelic football his way? Perhaps a pretty fair maid gamboled by and ruined his attentiveness. He is a sucker for a dish."

"No ball," Mullaney said. "And there were no women about the place."

"You would be surprised," Liam said. "Just because you cannot see a thing doesn't mean it isn't there."

"Sometimes even if you see a thing, it doesn't mean it is there," Mullaney said. "Yourself, for example."

Liam scratched his beard in consideration of that truism. "Enough of your riddles. Didn't yourselves dig up such a woman this very day in this very place?"

From the fringes, Bonnie had gathered enough courage to approach the little man. She sniffed his feet, and Liam offered her the back of his hand to inspect. A dog's nose is often the best indicator of a man's character. The collie laid her head in his lap, and he scratched behind her ears.

Mullaney scratched behind his own ear. "How did you know about the body in the bog?"

"There are no better folk than the folk of the West for keeping an eye on this country. And you would not believe how some of the Good People like to gossip and spread the news. That girl has gone viral. You would be surprised how many demigods are about hunting for her as we speak."

To rest his weary knees, Burke lifted one leg at a time and gave them a good stretch. "I told you we should have reported it to the authorities straight off."

"You said no such thing," Liam said. "Mister-me-man, you are up to your arsehole in this mess. And you are to blame as well for taunting Cúchulainn so. You would have let him win the rubber match had you any sense."

Liam then scolded Mullaney. "And you should have given over the girl at the first request. Why would you tempt the gods or dally with the great legends of Ireland? Have ye one brain between the two of youse? Listen to the natural world and respect what the signs are telling you."

The little bitch whimpered and wagged her tail in agreement.

"Cannot you wave your magic wand?" Burke asked. "There's nothing I would like better than to be free of Ireland's own and be asleep in my own bed. I take it you are one of the fairies—"

"There you go again," Liam said. "Rules is rules. Established and articulated for your protection as well as ours. Don't go around saying our name. Don't beat the heroes of Ireland at their own game. And don't be digging up bodies from the bogs and setting the clocks whirling to let the dead rise from history. Be careful when you untie a Celtic knot. Tell me, then, what were you planning on doing with this Connemara Girl?"

"Donate her to the National Museum," Mullaney said. "So people could take a good stare and understand what life was like back in her era."

"Dangerous," said the fairy. "Ill-advised. Haven't we problems enough than to be clamoring for the simpler times? Make Ireland great again, is it? Bah, there is just the present and that's all there is."

Burke cleared his throat. "We don't even know where she is anymore. Lookit, somebody else walked away with her. Now, you said you might be able to help with this tricky spear if we provided a proper explanation. That's our story, beginning to end."

Liam rose to his feet. "Tell me, then, which foot did he use when he hurled the barbecue spit into your rump roast?"

"His right, I believe. Me back was facing him."

"You had better be certain. Give it a twist anticlockwise till you hear a click, then it will slide out. But if you guess the wrong foot, then it will cut all the strings inside you. Your heart is in your stomach and your kidneys is where your lungs ought to be."

"Can you lend me a hand?" Mullaney asked.

"Ah, no. A bit squeamish, don't you know, and I desire to be elsewhere should your friend be mistaken in his sense of direction. You're sure it was not to the left? I have overstayed my welcome in any case. *Slán*." Liam na Sopóige walked off with the dog close on his heels.

*   *   *

At Swims-in-the-Sand, Cúchulainn and Láeg conferred over their plan of action. The ocean, relieved to be free from the Hound's terrible sword, rolled on pleasantly, the waves sighing as they broke upon the shore. Pieces of the moon gleamed on bits of broken shell and nacre, making the shore sparkle. A restless gull laughed at the comedy and flew above the two men as they drew maps in the sand, soon to wash away.

"What do we know?" asked the charioteer. "And what remains a mystery?"

"Well, we don't know what we don't know, so we should focus on the known knowns."

"Very wise, as usual. We know that Medb and Ailill are seeking the girl as well. I can smell those Westerners from miles away, the scent of the bull forever on them. We know as well those two eejits who uncovered the girl are still out on the bogs. Or at least the one who is pinned to the spot by your tricky spear. What we do not know: the whereabouts of the other fella, and the whereabouts of Fedelm herself. We do not know who took her and why."

"You have too many whys and wherefores," Cúchulainn said. "Dawn waits for no man nor demigod. It is often better to act than to think."

"I know it is late," Láeg said. "But we could have left an hour ago if you weren't so set on making yourself more presentable. The vainest—"

"Do not lose your head, old friend."

A ninth wave roared over the strand.

"Forgive me, but we have no more time to spare if we are to do what we set out to do. There are three spiral journeys from the same starting point: ours, Fedelm's, and the queen and king of Connacht's. We cannot keep spinning away from the center."

Cúchulainn shoved one thumb in his mouth and set the other in the middle of the sand drawing. They were ready to go back to the beginning.

CHAPTER

21

The Magic Eyes

After the last fairy had vanished, Bridget tried for a long while to reconcile what she had seen with what she believed. She had questions, but nobody to ask. She could rationalize the eccentricities of Al and Maeve and their weird argument about the legendary past, and the little gray lady might be simply a throwback to the older ways and customs of the West, but nothing in her archaeological training had prepared her for the fairies. Her studies of ancient cultures relied upon tangible evidence and the empirical record. Sure, every mythos had stories about supernatural visitors, the Irish as much as any, but there was never any concrete evidence. The most fanciful artifacts had plausible inspirations. Even the treasures in her beloved Mütter, the Soap Lady, the American Giant, and other anomalies of the natural world, had empirical, rational, scientific explanations. What she wouldn't give to have one of these "fairies" to question under controlled conditions.

Like many an Irish American child, Bridget had heard of the fairies in an oblique way from her grandparents, who warned that the fairies would kidnap her if she wandered too far from home. The fairies were responsible for a missing coin or the broken heel of a shoe. Little kids believed in the tooth fairy's weird pastime of collecting lost teeth while they slept. These inventions were no more real than Santa Claus or the little green men of Mars. Fairies lived in books and movies as tiny, winged pixies adding colors to the autumn forest or painting the windows with ice. But those were Americanized fairies. The Irish fairy, it turned out, was a different being altogether. For one, they ranged in age and gender, shape and size, not a wing on them, unless you counted the girl who morphed into a crane. But the truly strange thing: they seemed more concerned with metaphysics than in any pot of gold at the rainbow's end. There are no such things as fairies, yet they had materialized from the ether, sat beside her, and spoken. One of them had even tried on her glasses.

Al crept close and sat beside her. "I cannot help but notice that you have two sets of lovely eyes, one pair you can remove and hand to someone else. Do you have the imbas on you? Is that so's you can share your vision of the future? Are you some sort of sorceress or enchantress?"

"My glasses?"

"Made of glass, are they? Will wonders never cease? Mightn't I?" With a delicate touch, he removed the pair from her face and held the spectacles at arm's length, afraid of trying them on.

"Go ahead," she said. "They won't hurt you."

He wriggled them in place. Blinking like an astonished owl, he marveled at the dark shadows of the faraway hills, the rolling pasture, and the beauty of the women in front of him. "*Feicim*," he said. "Maeve, I can see! So, this is how the earth truly looks, sharp and clear, as if each thing in it had lines drawn round. There's a whole other dimension, for feck's sake. You have got to try these on, babe. By the gods, look at all them beautiful stars."

"Lemme see," Maeve said as she ripped them off his face. Behind the thick lenses, her eyes seemed twice as large, and she considered the view like a canary that's flown out the parlor window to see a wider world. "These are magic eyes, babe. I can see it all like it was brand spanking new. Why have you been holding out on us, honey? Did you get these marvels in Philadelphia?"

"I've worn glasses since I was a kid, but I bought this pair in Dublin."

"Oh, I've heard great things about that place," Al said. "Teeming with beautiful women. I bet they have all the latest modern conveniences."

"Sure, you get your magic eyes there," Bridget said. "And magic ears, too, in case you are hard of hearing."

"Do they have anything for selective hearing?" Maeve asked. "This one can pinpoint a maid unbuttoning her blouse from a mile away, but ask him to take out the rubbish, and he claims to have never heard a peep."

"They have magic hair in Dublin too," Bridget said. "In case you are going bald. And a magic voice that lets you talk to anyone you like, wherever they may be. There's a big magic bird that can take you and a whole battalion across the ocean in a few hours. And a magic web that will allow you to see what's happening everywhere in the world. Twenty-four seven."

The ancient queen and king were thunderstruck by the information. From her back pocket, Bridget retrieved her phone and powered it on. She toyed with the idea of calling someone to come help her, but what would she say and whom would she awaken from their bed? *I am out here in the middle of nowhere with a pair of legends talking to the fairies.* Her dean would think she was drunk or stoned. She thumbed through her cache and found the photos from the Red Witch of the West.

"I can even show you an image of the bog girl taken earlier today. A magic drawing, if you like, only from real life and not some artist's imagination." She stood between them and scrolled through the files. When the close-up on the girl's face appeared, she froze the image on the screen.

Unaccustomed to looking through spectacles, Maeve bent close till her nose nearly touched the glass. "No, sorry. That's not the girl we are looking for. This is a gnarled lump, the color of old oak. We met the real poet on the way to war. Fedelm had a broad forehead and a narrow chin. Her eyebrows were black as darkness itself. Her lips were scarlet as Parthian silk. She wore a speckled cloak, not this drab frock, and a tunic embroidered with fine red threads, the whole ensemble brought together with an oakleaf pin. Her hair was as golden as the weaving rod she held. Not this strange reddish color. And she wore three lovely, long braids, not this punk look, cut ragged on two sides. Her eyes had three irises to see the past, the present, and the future. You can't even see her eyes in this drawing. This thing is a withered hunk of leather."

"She has been in the stew these past two thousand years, her skin pickled by the peat, her hair hennaed from blond to red by the chemicals in the vegetation. Of course the girl's looks would have changed, but I find her as beautiful, in her own way, as this Fedelm you described. It would be extraordinary if we were looking for two different girls in the bogs." Bridget zoomed in on the pin at her collarbone. "What about that brooch? How many young women wore that design? What more can you tell me about this Fedelm?"

With a shrug, Maeve handed the phone to Al for his inspection. By intuition, he figured out how to swipe between images and to use his two fingers to zoom in and enlarge select details. He was quickly enthralled by the noose and the wound at her neck. "From what I remember hearing about her killers, they wanted to make sure she was well and truly dead. A real professional hit, though I have seen plenty of stiffs worser than her. Might well be her. Take another look, babe."

"I was not acquainted with her all that well," Maeve said. "Back in the day everyone sorta knew everyone else, at least by reputation, for Ireland was a small country. We only met Fedelm the one time. The girl was coming back from her training on the Isle of Skye, and we had summoned thousands of men from all over for the Cattle Raid. The odds were stacked on our side, no matter he was the Hound of Ulster. With no hand to help him, he was not going to beat the best fighting forces of the nation.

"I don't know why I bothered stopping her, but I figured it isn't every day you bump into a poet. So, I asks her to use her light of foresight to tell us how the war would end. I thought she'd say our soldiers would overwhelm the paltry defense, we kill Cúchulainn and capture the Brown Bull. Case closed." Behind her glasses, Maeve's eyes teared up. "But no, she says the green fields will be dyed crimson and red with the blood of the soldiers of Connacht. I asked three times just to be sure, but she would not vary her answer. You would have thought a Connemara girl such as herself would have had the decency to be more encouraging about our chances. Was she rooting for the other side? Was she a double agent of those dirty Red Handers?"

"Most disloyal," Al added. "You are either Team Connacht or Team Ulster. If you cannot say anything nice about our side, 'tis better to say nothing at all. But that poet went on and on, as they do. Crimson and red, red and crimson. Let's just say she had a haughty, intellectual demeanor. Gave a right fright to the men. Sure, Cúchulainn was a stone-cold killer, but we did not need such dismal cheerleading for our boys."

"There's only one way to know whether this bog girl is Fedelm or if she is someone else entirely." Maeve fiddled with the spectacles on the bridge of her nose. "Do these magic eyes allow you to see the future?"

Bridget laughed. "Of course not."

"Then you don't mind if I hang on to them for a spell. They make me look more sophisticated, wouldn't you agree, Al?"

"Babe, you look like a sexy librarian," he said. "You are gorgeous with them on or with nothing on at all."

They left the fairy ring, intending to spiral back in search of Mullaney and Burke. Without her glasses, Bridget had to hold on to Al's hand and let him guide her over the unfamiliar terrain. Falling under his intoxicating spell, she rather enjoyed feeling the pulse of the king in her hand. The new spectacles on Maeve's face slowed their pace considerably, for the natural world distracted her in its novelty. Crossing the field, the queen noted every cowpat and remarked how each shape reminded her of something else, like camels or sailboats in the clouds. A bat spun after a moth. Tattered bits of wool clung to old wire fences. The heather and furze danced under the moon and stars. A scream in the night stopped them dead.

"By the gods," Maeve said. "A cunning little vixen."

The white tip of a fox's tail sent her careening into the hedges to interrogate the trickster. Relentless in her pursuit, Maeve wandered out of sight and beyond hearing as well, leaving Bridget quite alone with the charming cad.

"Never trust a fox, says my gal. Maeve will be half the night following that sly boots." Al squeezed her fingers and patted the stone wall, inviting Bridget to sit by his side. "She gets her mind fixed on an object and cannot be shaken. The gods know how I tried to dissuade her, but we all remember how that ended up. Half the good sons of Ireland gone. Never follow the rump of a misguided woman."

"That's awfully chauvinistic," Bridget said. Ordinarily everything about him would have been a nightmare, but he held some mysterious sway over her. Her logical mind said no, but she was well past logic. She enjoyed the heady aroma wafting off him, a mix of burning oak leaves and verbena. He smelled like a lit candle.

He wedged his fingers into the space between them. "I suppose it might come across that way. Don't get me wrong, Toots. I have no problem with a strong woman, if she knows her place. A herd led by a mare will often stray and come to ruin."

She felt the wriggle of his thumb drawing spirals at her hipbone. "She knows what she wants, and she goes after it. You beast."

With a pleasant sigh, he offered her the pillow of his shoulder upon which to lay her head and shut her eyes. His hand wandered the distance from the seam of her jeans to the tent at the back of her shirt. The touch of his fingers against her bare skin startled her and raised the hairs at the small of her back.

"You make a fair point," he said. "There is much to admire in a person in pursuit of her passions. You are as soft as the insides of a rabbit's ear."

Bridget was not used to such attention. Certainly not from the men in the archaeology department, who were of two types: converted rockhounds shy around real women or would-be Indiana Joneses who paid her scant heed. His fingers walked up her vertebrae. They would not believe this in Dublin or Philadelphia. She lifted her head from his shoulders to look at his face as he kept on caressing her back. "But what about your wife?"

"You don't need those glass eyes. Your gaze is magic without them," he said. "I would not worry about Maeve. She has numerous transgressions on her side of the ledger. Everyone knows the story of how she lured Fer Diad to battle his best friend Cúchulainn."

She stared into his eyes, noticing at certain angles three irises in blue and green and brown.

"We were losing men left and right on the Cattle Raid of Cooley. First she sent her ambassadors to recruit the horn-skinned hero, but Fer Diad would not agree to meet us. Next she sent poets and bards, but their songs did not woo him to the fight. Finally, she sent the satirists to mock and make fun of him. With his cheeks vermillion from ridicule, Fer Diad could no longer resist. But to keep him in the camp, Maeve had her own daughter Finnabair sent to his tent."

"You do not look old enough to have a daughter."

"And seven sons as well. After Finnabair plied him with her favors, Maeve came over herself and poured him wine, and with every cup she gave him three kisses. At her neckline, she had daubed the scent of fresh apples." Al unbuttoned the top of Bridget's blouse and leaned his nose close to her skin. "You smell as sweet. Do I detect the aroma of cream from a milk cow?"

"Just soap, I'm afraid."

He kissed the top notch of her breastbone. "She offered him a golden chariot, a choice plot of Connemara farmland, a lifetime supply of wine, and no income tax for himself and his ancestors."

"Sold," she said. "You could have had me right there."

He nuzzled her neck again. "Her best golden brooch, and Finnabair to be his wife. And finally she says, 'and a long night between my own friendly thighs,' to clinch the deal. Can you imagine such a thing, and me in the next tent over? As if I have no feelings. Well now, what's good for the goose is sauce for the gander."

Bridget let herself be kissed once more, right behind the ear. "Was it worth it, in the end, to have Fer Diad on your side?"

"Worth it? Is any slaughter ever worth the prize? No, the only lesson I take is you must live to the lees whilst you may. Won't you give us a little kiss, darling?"

She hopped off the wall and fumbled to button her blouse. Her cheeks were blazing, and a thin film of perspiration clung to her brow and the back of her neck. Without her glasses, she could barely make out the disappointment on his face. Bridget was embarrassed for letting things get so far. Behind her, Al kicked his feet like a schoolboy and whistled a sad song about a love gone off to America.

Like Frankenstein's monster, up tromped Maeve, her arms straight out to save her from any obstacles in her path. Her lenses had fogged over completely. "Is that you, Al? I cannot see a bleeding thing through these magic eyes any longer. They are not worth a tinker's dam. Help me out here, Philadelphia, for I am going blind surely."

Bridget rushed to the rescue, removed the glasses, and wiped them clean with the tail of her untucked shirt. Immediately thankful for her restored vision, Maeve gave her a big smooch square on the lips.

"That's merely some condensation," Bridget said. She put on her glasses and widened her eyes. "See, right as rain."

"Wet as rain, you mean, like trying to walk underwater. I never did find Miss Fox, but I heard voices out there, all kinds of strange things. I was nearly done for by some class of monster. Has either of you ever seen a three-headed púca? Scared me witless with its hairy red back and six eyes peeping through the gloom."

"I've never even seen a regular pooka."

Maeve threw her arm around Bridget's shoulders and gathered her bosom to bosom. "And what were the pair of you doing whilst I was nipping like a bat over hill and dale? Did he try to take advantage of you, honey?"

"He was telling me all about your daughter and your other promises to Fer Diad."

"Daughter? We have a daughter?"

From the background, Al chimed in. "You remember Finnabair."

With a pensive gaze, Maeve searched the hard drive of her memory. "Ah, right, so. There were so many chiselers about the house in them days, is it any wonder a mother might forget one or two. She was class, though, half as pretty as meself."

Al clucked at her. "And don't forget the invitation for Fer Diad to warm his weapon between your welcoming thighs."

"Don't be jealous, Al, it doesn't become you. Fer Diad was just another disappointment in the end, outwitted by that half-wit Cúchulainn. Who slept with whom was more fluid in those pagan days, honey. The war between the sexes wasn't any easier, but then again, the battle is half the fun."

"I don't know if I could have done what you did," Bridget said. "The things you were willing to give up because he was a hero."

"Ireland, my Ireland, what would I not do for thee?" Maeve chuckled ruefully and stole a glance at her longtime partner. "Listen, darling, I am an equal-opportunity briber. You help me find this bog girl, and I will tell you where all the treasure is buried. You could not get a better offer if you came across a leprechaun. And I can make you famous from Donegal to Wexford, from the Ring of Kerry to the Giant's Causeway. Who wouldn't pay to have tangible proof?

"In the end, we stole that brown bull and staged a fight against our white-horned champion. Those two beasts tore the stuffing out of each other, leaving bits and pieces strewn all over the countryside. Sure, aren't half the places here named for some part of an Irish bull? I could give you authentic evidence of one of the great myths of Ireland. You could be one of the most famous archaeologists in the world. For I have the horns of the Donn Cúailnge, encrusted with gems and gilt, with the Ogham on each side testifying to the tale. I'll tell you what: they can be yours, if your Connemara Girl we have been chasing proves to be our Fedelm. Once she is safely delivered to our possession."

"Go ahead, lass," said Al. "A bull in the barn is worth any number of heifers."

"Honestly," Bridget said, "I have as much interest in finding her as you do."

"Let us go then, we three, and tarry no more. The world is in a state of chassis, all is awhirl. While I was out in the wilderness blindly chasing that fox, I heard other voices in the distance from three points of the compass. The armies are on the march. We must be first to the girl." Clasping Bridget by the wrist, Maeve drew her close enough to reveal the nine irises in each eye. There was no longer an apple smell upon her. The queen of Connacht reeked of ashes and blood.

22

Close Encounters

A FOX STOPPED DIRECTLY in front of them, and Fedelm and the witches halted on the path. The trickster sized up the visitors. The three gingers were a familiar sight about the parish, but the strange shadowy stick figure was another matter. Bold as you please, the fox trotted and stopped three feet away, sitting in front of Fedelm as though she had something to say.

"Little red dog," the bog girl said. "Do we know each other?"

With a cock of its ears, the fox followed her voice, attentive to its rise and fall. They stared at each other, trying to remember through the ravages of time. Wagging its bushy tail, the fox yipped and laughed. Fedelm smiled as if finding a lost dog after centuries of searching.

"You go on ahead," she told the girls. "I will be a few minutes in colloquy with this fox. I had such a familiar when I was your age, and I am led to wonder whether this bitch is related or no. Best handled on my own."

The hags hesitated to abandon her for even a few minutes.

"I will be along presently. The *madra rua* is a messenger and often the best ally, for they are aces at subterfuge and cunning. After all, she is your double, a ginger and a fellow traveler. Keep to the path alongside the lake and mind the slippery ground. Do not set foot in a quagmire, lest you be stuck there the rest of your life. Eileen knows the way."

They walked on. Every so often, one or the other would peer back over her shoulder to see if the bog girl was following, but in the last tableau she was squatting on her haunches, engaged in some conspiracy with the fox. It felt strange to be on their own. So much had happened in the hours since Fedelm appeared, and now she seemed like an older sister. Across the empty countryside, the setting moon cast long shadows, and the only sound was their own footsteps until Eileen signaled to freeze and listen.

Crashing through the bush ahead, zigzagging from lakeside to bogside, a woman in a bright-turquoise sundress bumbled toward them, blinded by her steamed spectacles. The gaudy miss was talking to herself in Old Irish, a choked panic in both sides of her monologue. The moment she became aware of their presence, she stood tall and still, nearly facing their direction. Craning her neck, she tried to discern what was ahead on the path.

"*Cé thusa?*" she demanded. "Are you a person or a thing, or what sort of fiend are you altogether?"

The hags kept their distance, hoping she would go away or that Fedelm would return to deal with the stranger. The peacock feathers on her dress had mysterious eyes that winked conspiratorially as she swayed in place.

"She's pissed out of her mind," Emcee whispered.

"Don't try any of your shenanigans," the woman said. She shook her bangled wrists at them. "Is there one of you, or are you in threes? I am warning you, my man is just around the corner and will easily dispatch you with cold iron. Will you speak or run away? Are you a good spirit or an evil púca meant to do me mischief?"

The mad woman spun on her heels, and in her confusion, took one step east and two steps west before electing the direction whence she came, toddling like a youngster learning how to walk. Ten steps away, she hollered over her shoulder. "Old púca, old pal, by any chance, have you seen a chariot drawn by two white horses? Lost your tongue? Arrah, never mind, you foul smelly wretch."

They were still in place moments later when Fedelm arrived. "Why are you not further along? Morning is coming, and we have ground to cover."

"There was a crazy lady in our way," Emcee said. "Stotious as a clam in wine sauce."

"No, I don't think she was drunk." Eileen shook her head. "It was the eyeglasses on her. She could not see three feet in front of her nose, and she hadn't the sense to wipe off the fog. A right peculiar bug. An older lady. Thirty-five, maybe forty."

"Insulting us," said Siobhán. "Thought we were some class of pooka, or one girl with three heads. And then she asked if we had seen her white horses and chariot. Do you think she's the one who lost her team? I was about to point her north to the chapel."

"Blind drunk, I'd wager," Emcee said. "Stumbled out of O'Leary's. All tarted up for the night and stinking of apple brandy from three meters."

"Show me exactly where she stood," Fedelm said.

On the spot of soft ground, the woman's spiked heels had poked a set of impressions like the stars in the constellations. Fedelm squatted and dipped her finger in a tiny hole to gauge the weight of the walker.

"She was flash," said Eileen. "Wore a skimpy dress with lots of peacock feathers. Bracelets up and down both wrists and three gold rings on each hand. She works out too. Arms like ropes. A big blond horsey type, by the way she carried herself."

With her black tongue, Fedelm tasted the air. Fresh apples. The same sweet aroma as that night long ago when she had met the queen on the road home. Apples masking the scent of blood and ash. Fedelm remembered the woman's persistent questions and desperate need for reassurance about the fate of the army's Cattle Raid, and she recalled as well her own powerlessness to deny the truth of her awful vision, the crimson and the red, the apple, the blood.

"You Red Hags had a close encounter with Medb, the queen of Connacht. She who intoxicates."

"No wonder then," said Emcee. "The smell of drink."

Fedelm remembered. "She enticed a nation, made men crazy by her honey-mead breath and the apple scent of her skin. Four men were fool enough to marry her, including no less than Conchobar mac Nessa, the king of Ulster, and later his bodyguard, Ailill mac Máta, the father of her seven sons and their lovely daughter Finnabair. Each of those young men brought troops of three thousand to the war, but that was not all. She had her own soldiers of twice three thousand, and hordes besides from the kings of Munster and Leinster and even a few turncoats from the North. More men than could be counted. On the other side, the loyal men of Ulster had been laid low by a sleeping curse and had to rely upon one young hero. You can read for yourself how Cúchulainn slew the many thousand. All the gory details, heads on spikes and exploding spears, men cleaved in two, and temptresses sent to divert the hero with sexual favors. It's all in the book *Táin Bó Cúailnge*, which surely they have taught in that school of yours."

The girls looked at the ground.

"Medb gets a bad rap, if you ask me," Fedelm said. "Sure, wasn't it men who recorded the saga? How many of their kind fell for the shape of her lovely bottom or the beauty of her eyes? It was men who laid the blame at Medb's feet, conveniently forgetting that every one of those thousands was free to follow his own mind rather than his desire. Don't ever forget, hags, how readily men fear a woman in power. And how wrongfully man-written history can heap scorn on our kind. Suppose she slept around? What man hasn't rutted at every chance? At least she had a reason beyond pure lust. Sex was her secret weapon. What matter if she was stubborn and bullheaded? Any man as bold as she would be called ambitious and determined. Write your own mythology, girls."

The bog girl was shaking after her oration. Her tanned fingers clenched into fists, and the wound at her throat throbbed anew. Siobhán laid a sisterly hand upon her shoulder, and the girls rallied around her.

"I will have a great subject for my college application," Emcee said.

"She couldn't have gotten far," Eileen added. "We're not ten minutes from Mullaney's claim on the bogland. Over the next hillock, you should be able to spot her easily in that peacock dress."

They secured their weapons and climbed the ridgeline. Below, the boglands stretched across a valley hidden by a low mist. Out of the obscurity, shapes began to take form, and a low rumble of distant sounds could be heard. Faint at first, a whinny and an answering neigh. A warning snort through the nostrils. All at once appeared a magnificent herd of warhorses, heads down to munch on the sparse vegetation or ears pricked at the sound of any approach, dotting the plain to the horizon. Scattered among them were unhitched chariots resting on their yokes. Small turf fires glowed on the ground, beside which lay unmistakable human forms at ease, a multitude of men. Sentries and early risers chatted quietly or fortified themselves with flagons of mead. Many other warriors snored under animal skins. A young boy took a piss in a hole in the bog. With a flint, another soldier scratched a last Ogham letter to a sweetheart in Dingle. One rutting man bent over a camp follower to make his carnal farewell. A silversmith sharpened a broadsword at a grinding stone. Spears had been gathered in pointy bouquets. Shields sparkled. Breastplates creaked with the men's yawns and sighs. The great All-Ireland Army whittled the last anxious hours before battle.

Fedelm squatted to consider the scene. The Red Witches covered their hair beneath the black cones of their hoods and sat on the ground beside her, dazed by the spectacle.

"I don't feckin' like the looks of this." Eileen shook her head. "Where the bleeding hell did those boys come from?"

"Medb's troops," Fedelm said. "Caught in the Whirl, doomed to repeat their tragic history."

With a rough catch in her throat, Emcee addressed the others. "I have reached my limits. It is one thing to be finding Mullaney's house stabbed with a thousand knives. Or to be hanging around with a walking corpse half the night, or chariots in a graveyard. And I could take the talking birds and foxes and even the queen of Ireland in a peacock sundress and stilettos. But it is too much to ask to be facing down this lot. How are we supposed to do battle using these wee letter openers?" Reaching in her jumper, she extracted a small iron dagger. "Dammit all, Fedelm. Can't you chant some spell and get us out of this mess? We're not witches at all, just three girls caught up in your personal drama. You're a real danger, that's what you are. I wish my pops had never dug you out of the ground."

The bog girl did not take her eyes off the troops during the entire harangue. Calculating the odds, she drew a map in the dirt and a spiral outlining their journey. She stuck her thumb in the center of it all. "Listen carefully. We must find a way to reach the queen before the battle begins, for I do not doubt the vision in crimson and red. I have no way of knowing what those lads might do if we try. You three might pass by with no more than a few wolf whistles and a pinch on your bums. I cannot risk it. They will not recognize me from bygone days, for I have changed too much. One overzealous lookout might run me through or lop off my head. As I see it, we have two choices: Go back the way to the rowboat, hike to the little shed, and wrap me again in the blue sail. Home to your mammies and forget the whole night. Or we run the gauntlet and take our chances on finding the queen and king. Medb will eventually return to the heart of the camp to command her men."

The witches mulled the options, conferring with one another in the silent looks and language of longtime friends. Eileen and Siobhán applied delicate peer pressure. Emboldened by such solidarity, Emcee finally nodded her assent. Never underestimate the trouble your friends can get you into.

"We could sneak you by," Siobhán suggested. "In disguise. Take my hoodie and keep your face hidden and your hands in the pockets. You and Eileen and Emcee pretend to be three druids, and I will be the girl leading you on."

"You play the poet?" Fedelm gave it a moment's thought. "Aye, it just might work. You will have to lose your daggers, for they would kill you at the first whiff of iron."

Eileen brought up the small barrier of language. "Suppose we run into a sentry who desires a wee chat? None of us are halfway decent in today's Irish, much less the Old Style."

Fedelm struggled into Siobhán's jacket. "I'll teach you enough. Simply memorize 'I am a poet here to see the queen, and these are my priests,' and I guarantee those men won't give you a second glance. Superstitious at the mere mention of poetry or religion."

"But what about the bog girl's blackened legs?" Emcee asked.

"Shove your hooves in my shoes." Siobhán kicked off her trainers. "The soldiers will fancy you are wearing black tights."

"They won't be looking at me," Fedelm said. "Not with your gorgeous red hair."

After the Irish lesson, Siobhán led them down from the ridge to creep single file into the camp. The cooks boiled the breakfast in great vats, the porridge bubbling and steaming, and a grand fry was on as well—a gross of eggs, rashers of bacon, and chains of sausages hissing in long iron skillets. The men chatted among themselves in a forced lighthearted manner, their bonhomie concealing terrible dread. Some of the boys bantered over a round of cards and did not even notice the new arrivals. Off in a dark nook, two lads stripped to the waist were wrestling in front of men lazing on animal skins, pints of plain in their meaty hands. A few warriors were curious about the quartet, particularly the flame-haired beauty leading three shrouded druids, but the girls managed to pass thirty yards into the congregation before encountering any resistance. A dark-haired Celt beseeched them to stop with one raised palm. Out of his mouth poured a torrent of Old Irish, which sounded vaguely like a question.

As she had rehearsed, Siobhán answered in his language. "I am a poet here to see the queen. And these are my priests."

He pointed his thumb over his shoulder and muttered a desultory comment. They were well past him when Siobhán whispered to Fedelm. "What is it he said?"

"Talk to the Maines."

"Who are the feckin' Maines?"

"The seven sons of Medb and Ailill, each given a new name of Maine because a druid prophesied that a Maine would kill her ex-husband and sworn enemy, Conchobar mac Nessa, the king of Ulster."

"That girl got around," Siobhán said.

"Put your tongue in your throat," Fedelm said.

A pair of curly-headed warriors sauntered over, one as fair as wheat, the other dark as oak. Each brother carried a silver shield with scalloped edges, one with three horses entwined, the other with three knotted wolves. They wore matching tunics trimmed with red and gold.

Siobhán delivered her line, but this time the men did not move, for they were fixated on her strange costume and her long red hair. The fair one reached out to touch it, but drew his hand back quickly. Surprising herself, Siobhán cooked up and cast a spell upon them in that moment, and the dark-haired one spoke in perfectly reasonable English.

"I am Fedlimid, now called Maine Athramail, or Daddy's Son. And this is my brother Cairbre, called Maine Máthramail, or Mama's Boy. We have not seen the likes of thee before in these parts. What art thou whose hair is aflame but does not burn?"

"I am a poet—"

"Ah right, another bleeding poet," said Mama's Boy. "Speak no further. The queen will deign to see thee and hear thine prophecy. Yonder thou will find her fire and her tent, but I venture thou art no poet but a beauty sent to light our passions afire." He pointed to a safe passage through the camp.

Past the curious soldiers they progressed for thirty yards more. On a dry spot near a stand of heather, two additional curly-haired brothers abandoned their chess pieces and rose to block the path. One was fat, one thin. Each brandished a short sword with a black handle and one pommel in bronze, the other in silver. They wore the same tunics as the other brothers, red and gold to indicate their tribe.

"Halt, who goeth there?" said the fat brother.

"I am a poet here to see Queen Medb. Who dares to hinder a poet with the light of foresight?"

The thin brother said, "I am Eochaid become Maine Andoe, the Swift. And this is Cet become Maine Mórgor, the Steady One. Our mother may be found at the exact center of things." Swift and Steady let Siobhán pass but crossed their swords in front of the other three girls. Steady scrutinized them carefully, hunching over to peer into their dark hoods.

"Wait! We are on the lookout for spies and ye could be thou, disguised as womanly priests."

"We are not the druids you are looking for," Eileen said, enchanting them with a mind trick. With no small satisfaction, the party waltzed past the bewildered twin generals. Fedelm tugged Siobhán's shirtsleeves and advised her to lead them in a more circumspect fashion.

A third set of twins in red-and-gold tunics, also mad for the chess, were in the way. They had long spears and threatened to poke Siobhán.

"I am a poet. I demand to see your mother."

"Charmed," the charming one said. "I am Sin, become Maine Mílscothach, the Honey-Tongued, and this gloomy lad is Fergus, or Maine Taí, the Quiet Man. Where hast thou been all mine life, thou gingersnap?"

"I have no time to dally with you. Save your honey words for the bees." Siobhán then spoke to the Quiet Man: "Do you know where your mama is, little boy?"

Honey-Tongued spoke for his silent brother. "Say, that is some beautiful hairdo on thine head. Where did thee get such coppery tresses?"

"From the milkman," Siobhán said. "I won't ask you again. Your mother is expecting us to prophesy the fate of all these men."

Tossing a pawn in the air, Honey-Tongued lost interest in the game. "All right, sis, have it thine way. Keep on thy path. Thou cannot miss her."

The party hurried by, and the bog girl swore that Quiet Man had recognized her but let her pass with a wink. Siobhán dropped back to consult with Fedelm. "What is the deal with these lads? Have they never met a ginger?"

"You forget your history, schoolgirl. The Vikings brought the recessive gene to the west coast of Ireland, but much later than the days of the Cattle Raid. You have appeared seven hundred years too early. You have beguiled their poor hearts with your lovely locks."

Another man in a red-and-gold tunic snuck behind Fedelm and stood a whisper away. This one did not have curly hair, nor brother for a companion, nor weapon in hand. He put a finger to his lips to alert Siobhán and the others not to give away the surprise. He clamped his hand on the bog girl's shoulder. Her eyes danced madly in the dark shadows of the hood, and she dared not turn her head as he spoke. "I am the youngest of the queen's sons, Dáire, become the Maine Móepirt, or Beyond Description." He licked his lips and grinned. "We have been expecting thee."

23

Keys to a Killing

O F ALL THE strange incidents of his long and odd day, none disturbed Mullaney more than watching his own dog willingly trot away with a new master, Liam na Sopóige. Bonnie was a link to his old life, and he was sad to see her go. His daughter, Flannery, had chosen the runt of the litter, and she often accompanied him to teach the young sheep-dog the art of herding sheep. He knew nothing at all about the business, and his neighbor Burke hindered rather than helped, save for the odd bit of half-correct advice regarding the basic commands. The little bitch reminded Mullaney of happier times, yet he could not begrudge her choosing the Otherworld. The Folk of the Hills had more suitable work for an aging collie—gathering the wee ones back to their forts before dawn or minding the changelings whilst the old folks went out for a bit of craic and a couple of pints. It is a dog's life. He would miss their daily walks over the bogs.

"Was it clockwise or anticlockwise?" Burke asked. "I cannot remember the which for certain."

"A man is liable to have a dominant foot just as he has a favorite hand. The wee blacksmith advised us to turn in the opposite direction," Mullaney said. "Do you remember, then, if the Ulsterman played chess right-handedly, or with the left?"

"Let me think. He was sitting across from me, so it is hard to picture the scenario without a mirror. Let's say the right."

"So, anticlockwise till we hear the click. Can I ask you a personal question? Do you not think this whole business is, well, a bit homoerotic? With the spear and all?"

"I do not," Burke said. "Remember, we are talking about a great Irish hero and a paragon of Celtic masculinity."

"The monks who first wrote down the story of Cúchulainn back in the medieval days, weren't those boys secluded from the womenfolk? I would imagine that fraternal environment might have an effect on their stories."

"If I start in squealing, you will stop. And if there's any blood, I cannot stand the sight of it. I nearly fainted when they took the head off me earlier."

"I noticed it didn't stop you talking."

"Go on then. Anticlockwise. Be gentle, Michael."

Mullaney grabbed the base of the gáe bolga and rotated it slowly until a soft but audible click of tumblers felt like the winning combination to a lock. He took a deep breath and pulled. Freed of his impediment, Burke fell to the ground no worse for the experience, feeling, in fact, a greater sense of purpose in his emptiness. Even the seat of his trousers was magically repaired. The ball of barbs had retracted into the pointy end, and Mullaney tossed aside the javelin and lifted his friend to his feet. The dizzy world bobbed on, free of its axis.

"Are you yourself, Old Burke? Good as new?"

"Restored utterly. I have had worse visits with the proctologist down in Galway."

"Let us arise and go now," Mullaney said. "Before those lads realize the trick was on them."

"Wait a minute, wait a minute, wait a minute," Burke complained. He scraped the muck from his knees and steadied himself. "Where do you reckon we should go?"

"Hop in the lorry and drive as far as bloody possible. Sligo, Donegal, the ends of this cursed island."

"Now, there you have me. I don't think I would be able to sit for more than five minutes," Burke said. "Not in my sensitive condition. Besides which, it may be too late. When I was above it all in the crow's nest, I could see them coming on the horizon."

"Cúchulainn and his charioteer?"

He pointed north. "No, a whole flock of horses."

*　*　*

The two warriors were racing against dawn. The natural world knew the hour. Flowers tensed in blooming anticipation of the warming sun. To get a jump on the competition, birds sang in the darkest hour. Creatures of the night made ready to punch the nocturnal clock and hie themselves to bed. Cú and Láeg were running late, wheezing and cursing at all the setbacks to their mission.

Flying due west, the crane spotted them on the road and landed gracefully on a stone bridge ahead on their path. Crawling out like a troll from beneath the arch, a wee blacksmith and his new dog joined her at the highest point of the span.

"You're not concerned that he might salmon-vault right over us?" asked Liam na Sopóige. "Those lads are in an awful hurry. I can see the headline now: *Mad Dash Tramples Fairies.*"

"I shall take the form of an irresistible woman," the Crane Girl said. "Who shall it be? Would Cúchulainn stop for Cathleen ni Houlihan or the Shan Van Vocht?"

"Definitely the younger of the two," Liam said. "In truth, though, either one might be a bit too chaste for our purposes."

Corr scratched her beak with her foot. "Sheela na gig?"

"The one with the big—"

"The fertility hag, right."

"Wouldn't that lass scare him a bit? Spreading her legs to give birth to the wide world. Oh, I don't know. Quick now, come as you are."

As soon as he saw the pair on the bridge. Cúchulainn drew his sword and indiscriminately chopped the air as he ran toward them. "Out of the way, fairy, if you know what's good for you. And you, too, dog, or I will treat you like Cullan's own beast and have your insides meet your outsides."

"Hold on, you big galoot." Liam held out the flat of his small palm. "Didn't your mother never teach you not to run with a scissors? You could poke an eye out."

Stock-still, Cú simmered, letting his spasms roil. "Don't say a word about my mother."

"Typical. Don't the Irish all just love their mothers? My mother, the saint. Had to put up with the grief of seven children and the bandy-legged old man besides. My mother doesn't deserve the likes of me. My mother could do no wrong."

One of Cúchulainn's eyes nearly popped out of its socket.

"Oh no, Hound of Ulster," the Crane Girl said. "Mind your temper. We are here to tell you what lies ahead."

"Get on with it then," said Láeg. "Can't you see the first rays of sunshine making ready to peep over the Twelve Bens? We must go faster than the speed of light."

"What do you seek?" Liam asked.

"We seek the girl Fedelm," said Cú. "Poet and prophet."

The crane morphed into a beautiful young girl, who balanced on one leg above the roiling stream. "You are not the only ones on such a mission. I see a man who has had a tree removed from his backside. I see a four-eyed woman conniving to lock up a girl and throw away the key. I see three red witches, murder on their minds."

"Your riddles are all very well and good for another day," Láeg said. "I see this and I see that and never a straightforward answer. Up North your kind are much more reliable than the folk of the West. Out of the way, egret, before I make a bag out of you and a footstool from your little friend's head."

"Well, I never," said Liam as he popped away, cursing like a stoat. Bonnie, ever the old dog with a new trick, disappeared with a double wag of the tail. But the girl on the bridge could not sprout a single feather before the ancients roughly pushed her aside into the water.

* * *

"Horses?" Mullaney asked. "Is it Sean Mannion's Connemara ponies on the loose again? Good fences make good neighbors, especially when the neighbor's horses are in your field."

"No, it's not them ponies. Nor any equinity seen around here. Warhorses, Mick. And those two-seater chariots besides. And plenty of men, too. An old-fashioned army like that Dungeons and Dragons lot from back in the day. If you could climb on my shoulders, you could see over that hillock for yourself. They are assembling in the valley at the bottom of the bottom of the bog."

"I don't believe it. C'mon, let's have a gander."

"No, thanks, I am paralyzed. My legs are shot from under me, Mick. I'll hold the fort."

The ground quivered under Mullaney's feet, the bogland a fluid, living organism, unstable and dangerous. A man could vanish into the wet center and become part of another layer of the story. Like the girl behind all their troubles, the young lass uncovered from the bowels of Ireland. She was the key to an epic saga told century by century, shifting on the cycles of life and decay, forgetting and remembering again. Rooted in the West, Mullaney had long felt he was disappearing into Old Ireland, as organic as the water and moss and the accidental victims buried there. Ashes to ashes, muck to muck. He wished he had paid better attention in school when the Christian Brothers had recounted the bowdlerized version of the old bull story. At the moment, a little more Irish would be advantageous.

How astonished he had been as a young boy to learn that the army of Connacht was led by a woman. After school one day, over biscuits and milk with his mum, he outlined the story of Medb, queen of Connacht. "Why wouldn't she have an army of her own?" his mother had asked. "Sure, what makes you think women are not the strong ones after all? Forget carrying you chiselers around nine months and the pangs of bringing babbies into the world. Forget working hard as a man with none of your 'days off,' from your first hour to the last. Who has every problem laid at her feet? Mothers."

For the first time in many years, he wished his mother was around to have one of their heart-to-hearts where she might listen patiently to his troubles and share some sensible advice, all the while sipping at a whiskey poured into the camouflage of a teacup. But the old folks were long gone, and he had to climb the hill on his own.

He was taken aback by the sheer number of horses, men, and munitions stretched over the plain. Charioteers led horses to their halters and yokes. Men donned horn helmets, chain-metal shirts, and bronze breastplates. They painted each other's faces and slapped red handprints above each other's hearts. Young boys scurried about, fetching spears and battle axes, javelins, and large stones for slings. A great hubbub and commotion had landed smack upon them. And for what? A different day, a different bull, or was it all happening then and now simultaneously, awhirl forever all the time, every moment, every triumph and mistake, every birth and death, always happening at once? His mind scattered questions like chessmen spilled from a crane bag. Mullaney thought of his hapless friend Burke at the gravesite. The mass of men was heading their way. It was all starting once again, and they would be caught in the fray. The poor unearthed girl had been the caulk to the crack in time.

* * *

Ever since he realized he had grown old, Tom Burke wondered what news awaited him from the distant shores of his body. One day it might be a mysterious soreness in the elbow. Another morning brought a lingering stiffness in both ankles. Overnight, a purple bruise had bloomed on his left hand. Tingling in his toes if he sat too long. A hacking cough. Fingernails cracked and splintering. A toothache to numb with whiskey. Spots of blood on the pillowcase. Parched, the mouth dry as the Gobi. Blind in one eye for ten frantic seconds. More hair on his brush than on top of his head, and more hair in places he'd never imagined hair could grow. Not one day without a leak in the teapot. He needed a nap, yet he could not fall asleep. He was hungry but could not stomach a bite. Feck all, getting old.

He was surprised, therefore, to be giddy as a schoolboy on a weekend, despite the labors of a long day. Minding his own business, he had been coerced into helping extract the girl from the bog and then spent the evening digging a thousand empty holes. Despite having his whole head lopped off and bouncing across the lino. Or the hours stuck on the sharp end of a stick in the middle of nowhere. True, there was a list on the positive side of the ledger. He and Mullaney had found what was sure to be a national treasure and the making of a name for themselves. Grand as well to visit with Mary Catherine and her two ginger friends. *Witches*—the thought brought a smile. God love 'em. And he had bested the Hound of Ulster, two out of three, even though many years had gone by since he had so much as looked at a chessboard. The Fool's Gambit to bury a fool. They weren't bad lads, Cúchulainn and Láeg, a couple of boyos that under other circumstances might have been his regular drinking buddies in the rare ould times. But it was Mick he felt most grateful for, a true friend despite all the guff. Sure, what wouldn't he do for the poor soul. The plaque would engrave their names for the ages: Connemara Girl, discovered by Michael Mullaney and Thomas Burke. He would insist upon second billing. Anti-alphabetical order, anticlockwise. He laughed at how happy he felt.

"You there," a familiar voice called out. "I thought I told you to stay put." It was the charioteer back on the scene. Reflexively, Burke covered his backside and stepped away from the returning warriors. Their skin shone with sweat despite the cool morning, and the big strong lads stopped and put their hands on their knees to catch their breath. From beneath his mop, Cúchulainn smiled at him, the tiles of his perfect teeth as white as a bull's horns. Armor clacking, he lumbered over to Burke.

"You are a most formidable foe," he said. "Not only have you managed to free yourself from the many-barbed spear, you are crafty as a red dog at the chessboard. It takes a fine man indeed to beat the Hound of Ulster."

"Thank you," Burke said. "I got lucky. You would not be so bad yourself if you learned a bit of patience."

Láeg stepped between the pair. "You must have had some help to foil the spear of many spurs. Is your friend about?"

Confident that he had finally won them over, Burke pointed to Mullaney atop the hillock. "He is counting the horses and men gathered on the plain. They appear to be getting ready for battle. I know you are supposed to be larger than life and all that, but I can't say I like your odds against the lads of the West."

From a holster round his hips, Cúchulainn drew two small knives, blades thin as paper. The steel flashed in the moonlight as he performed the *preabadh na gaoithe* or chop of the wind, fluttering his two wrists in a quick and intricate series of slashes. Burke was reminded of the lightning-quick knife dexterity of a tableside chef down at the Japanese steakhouse in Galway. Cuts faster than the eye could follow.

When Cú was finished slicing, he put his forefinger on Burke's collarbone and carefully pushed out a neat and perfect block of the old boy, leaving behind a square hole. He peered straight through the opening, spying Mullaney far away on the ridge. "Your turn," he said to Láeg. "Be careful or it will all fall down."

Exasperated at having to play yet another game at such an inopportune time, the charioteer slid a block out of Burke's right knee.

"Lord have mercy," Burke said. "What have you done? I am all in pieces like a human Jenga."

"Thirty-two bars, to be precise. Don't move a muscle." The Hound considered his strategy and carefully removed a chunk of Burke's left hip.

"We really don't have all night for this," Láeg complained. "The great armies are assembling on the plains."

Trying to keep his balance, Burke swayed where he stood. "What, am I to fall apart like a jigsaw? You are a poor sport, and I have known some sore losers in my day, but don't this beat all? Haven't I treated you like a son? Taught you how to smoke a pipe? Showed you the King's Gambit and the Fool's Defense? And this is the thanks I get? Well, no wonder the ordinary people of Ireland are so reluctant to claim you as their national hero. You have a temper on you that does no good in the public relations department. A mean-spirited lout and murderer. Breaking bad since I met you. One thing does not go your own way, so violence is your first resort, when a few diplomatic words would do wonders for your reputation."

"For the gods' sake, would you be quiet?" Cúchulainn could bear not another peep. He wriggled out the block at Burke's belly button, and the man collapsed in a clutter.

*　*　*

As he surveyed the field, Mullaney was not surprised when Láeg joined him at the ridgeline. From his crane bag, the charioteer removed a primitive scope without lenses, and through this tube, he assessed the strength of the troops in the valley. His lips moved as he counted the divisions, and at the end of his calculations, he tapped Mullaney on the bicep and motioned for him to silently follow. Back at the gravesite, Cúchulainn was trying to rebuild Burke's body but had fitted several pieces out of order.

"What mischief have you got yourself into now, Tom?" Mullaney asked. "I leave you alone two minutes, and you look like a reek of turf fallen into a jumble."

"He cut me into one of them towers of blocks," said Burke. His mouth had been shoved where the middle of his backside should be. "I told him he should save the swordplay for the assembled militia."

"It is Medb's army, all right," said Láeg. "I saw six of the seven sons named Maine, and all the usual adversaries from Leinster, Munster, and Connacht. All are gathered save the queen herself. She was not at the center of the camp, and it gives me hope that she has abandoned the field before the battle has begun."

"More importantly, where is the girl?" Cú asked.

"I saw no poet, no beautiful woman with three golden tresses and seven irises in each eye." The charioteer hung his head. "Fedelm was not among the armies of Connacht."

A notion leapt into Burke's mind and wriggled through his nether lips. "Hold on a sec. You mean to tell me you are looking for some blond girl? That's not who we found in the bog. I have proof on my phone, but I will only show it if you put me back proper."

"It's true," said Mullaney. "I know it. I seen it."

"Oh, allow me," Láeg said, shaking his head. With the aggrieved reluctance of a longtime lieutenant, he quickly rearranged Burke into completeness, the seams disappearing as the last piece of the puzzle slid into place.

Burke shook his arms and did two deep knee bends to ensure he had been faithfully restored, and then from his back pocket he took out the phone and scrolled to the pictures from the dig. The body in the photograph was a dark and shrunken thing with a knot of red hair off to one side of her skull. The image flickered to black as the last smidge of power drained from the battery. "I don't know who she is, but I cannot imagine she is the girl you are looking for."

With a grunt, Cúchulainn waved off Burke's objections. "You are a sly fox. You and this other citizen. No more of your magical diversions. I know she is out there, matterad-amn your primitive drawings."

Mullaney sucked in his breath to join in his friend's objections, but Láeg stopped them both. "No use to complain. The Hound has made up his mind, and it cannot be unmade by good sense or a hundred thousand entreaties."

A hint of the war spasms shone in Cúchulainn's eyes. "I will spare you still, for we have other needs of your services. You will have one last chance to redeem yourself, canny man. If we are to plow through this army, we cannot go on foot. We require a chariot and two stallions to pull it. Use your wiles to secure us wheels and the necessary horsepower. I would prefer a deluxe white model with gold trim. Oh, and if you could manage it, one armed with sickles at the spokes to slash through the knees of our enemies. And the horses should be black, don't you think, more threatening and fearsome."

"And how are we supposed to do that?" Burke asked.

"Take these dirks." The hero of Ulster removed two small swords from the inside of his red cape. "Remember there are three keys to a killing: be quick, be decisive, and be precise. Some of those lads will wear breastplates, so you'll have to find a weak spot." With the flat of his hand, he made the universal throat-cutting sign.

Mullaney stared at the blade. "I don't think—"

"Not thinking is all for the best. The hour nears. Do not mess with the Maines, if it can be helped, for they are vicious characters who do not know their own names. Stay clear as well should you encounter Fer Diad the Horn-Skinned, for his Achilles' heel is where you would not expect it. Beware of all them western cowboys over there, for they are nothing but brutal killers who will take your head or heart if you let them. And should you not return, remember you died for Ireland." He pushed the two men toward the battlefield.

Mullaney and Burke ambled up the hill. Behind them, the warriors jauntily waved their swords and spears, urging them to take courage and get moving. Like two tardy school-boys sent to fetch the parish priest, they dared not disobey, but at the same time, an overwhelming sense of doom came over them, a despair so profound it left no choice but blind acceptance, knowing the end was near and would come mercilessly.

"Let's pretend this isn't real," Mullaney said. "That we are not conscious characters of free will. From the beginning, none of it never happened. I never found those toes in the sod. I never even went out digging peat in the first place. What use have I for a turf fire? The house has central heating and a gas cooker. You were not complaining that my Bonnie was pestering your sheep. There is no girl wrapped in the tarp, no lunatics dressed up like Braveheart and his Scots out for blood. It's all a lark, Tom. We are not here at all but comfy in our beds, waiting for another morning to come. No horses, no chariots, no fairies or banshees, no Cattle Raid, no bull, no body. You have not been murdered thrice this day. All a nightmare from a bad piece of last night's fried cod and chips. An existential crisis brought on by a deep and abiding dread of our age. All a bad dream, and we have but slumbered here—what do you think, Burke?"

"Bollocks," he said.

Heavy dull thunder rolled across the plain despite the cloudless sky. Voices rose, the men in their war wagons eager for the maddening assault. Their song echoed across the bogs of Connemara.

CHAPTER

24

A Hard Bargain

AQUILINE NOSE TO aquiline nose, Maeve leaned in, her features flattened and out of focus, an animal heat radiating off her skin, so close that Bridget feared she was about to be kissed or eaten. The queen's words roared in her ear like the ocean through a nautilus shell. "What can I offer to sweeten the deal? Would you take my husband as well, or is he too old for your appetites? Let me assure you, honey, Al's spear flies true. Or would you fancy one of my seven sons, the Swift or the Steady, or better yet the one truly called Beyond Description? I might even persuade Finnabair to lie with you, if you so desire. Or any of the men or women under my thumb. Indulge your fantasies."

Bridget pulled away. "As attractive as that sounds, I will have to pass. I am no Fer Diad you can tempt to do your dirty work. Frankly, I don't understand why you are bargaining with me. I don't know where this girl is, whoever she is."

With a cluck of her tongue, Maeve countered with her disapproval. "Ah, but you can find her, can you not? Isn't that why you have come to this godsforsaken sinkhole? You are a bone digger and a graverobber. We had no other reason to drag you around with us all night."

"First of all, I am an archaeologist. Even so, I have no divining rod that points to where the bodies are buried. I am only here on account of a tip on the internet. I've been telling you all along that in order to locate the body, I first have to find Burke or Mullaney."

"No more time for games, sweetie. We must get to the girl before the Hound of Ulster does. Three times I asked her to tell us that our side would win, and three times she denied me the answer." She kicked off her heels and headed toward the ridgeline.

"What's the big hurry in reaching this girl before this Hound of Ulster?" Quickening her pace, Bridget matched her stride for stride. "That doesn't seem like much of a crime. She was being honest, and she was right! You must admire her for telling it like it is, and you don't honestly believe her prophecy had anything to do with your defeat, do you? That's the worst kind of magical thinking."

Al caught up and insinuated himself between the two women. "Magical thinking! Now, that sounds intriguing."

"Magical thinking is when you put your ego in the center of cause and effect. Like a superstition. Knock on wood and you will get your wish. If I bring my umbrella, it will not rain."

"What else?" he asked. "Boil a flint arrow in milk to cure a bellyaching calf? Never buy an egg on a Tuesday. Spin yourself three times anticlockwise if you are lost. Spill the chess pieces from your crane bag, and the knights will face your trouble."

"I'm not sure—"

"*Dún do bhéal!*" Maeve had heard enough. "Stop your blather, you pair of eejits. I'll give you magical thinking with the back of me hand. We've a war on, or have you not been reading the signs?"

From the path, the everlasting moors spread to the sea. Giddy flames danced near the ground, hovering like small ghosts. From her earth science classes, Bridget knew such bioluminescence was a chemical reaction caused by the decay of organic matter releasing compounds of gases that ignited with the oxygen in the air. Scientific name *ignis fatui*. But she much preferred the name *foxfire* or *will-o'-the-wisp*. Blinking over the dark bogland, the effervescent flames slowly joined together to form larger objects. Horses appeared first, greenish white changing to dun and chestnut, and then the chariots and the tents, and finally the men themselves materialized. Hundreds of young men in tunics and capes, brother recognizing brother. *Hello, good to see you again, it's been a long time.* Sounds floated from the field: hooves stamped, wheels creaked, and iron hammers clanged on anvils as blacksmiths forged weapons of war.

With tears of pride, Maeve and Al joined hands at the top of the ridge and watched their army come together. They were young again, ready to launch a great adventure into the fray of blood and ballyhoo, teetering on the edge of glory. For two thousand years they had been waiting for a second chance. But they failed to see trouble at their feet. A bright red fox darted from an ambush spot, yipping and snapping at their ankles in a vicious and dizzying display. The sly familiar had followed Fedelm's instructions, using a blend of herbs to froth at the mouth. She entwined herself among their feet, crossing and double-crossing until they were hopelessly caught in the same plot.

"Mad dog!" Al said, and in his haste to elude the varmint, he lost his balance and reached for his beloved, tripping and pulling his unwitting queen over the edge. Together they plummeted pell-mell down the steep ridge, arms and legs swinging for balance, oopsy-daisy, helpless to stop their downfall. Jarred loose of his boon companion, Al skidded uncontrollably through the scree, each bump accompanied by a grunt or a groan. Maeve came tumbling after, a perfect somersault over the laughing vixen, her skirt taut as a kite, revealing her bare bum with the bull tattoo. Arse over tea-kettle they rolled, scratching through the furze, knocking against rocks sunk into the soil, bones snapping, blood gush-ing, slippers flying in the air, all the way to the bottom, where they landed in a tangle of arms and legs and torn cloth, motionless as two rag dolls. Its mission accomplished, the fox barked with satisfaction and trotted away, content that she had played her part in the epic saga.

A short "oh" was all Bridget could muster as she wit-nessed royal deposition. The sabotage had played out in slow motion and quick time all at once. Drawn to the scene of the disaster, she carefully scooted down the hill, slipping, regain-ing her balance, and wending her way to the victims. To her entreaties, the king managed a low moan, but the queen said not a word.

Loitering nearby, three soldiers witnessed the catastrophe and were stunned to find the royal pair at the bottom of it all. As professional warriors, they were trained to perform the necessary first aid to the unconscious monarchs. They staunched the royal blood with strips of cloth torn from their skirts and wrapped the victims' bruised skulls and bones in gauze from the linings of their capes. One man checked for pulses while another tried to find a heartbeat through a hol-low ram's horn.

A stout fellow in a tunic trimmed with embroidered red crosses took charge of triage. He called for two litters, and the medics laid the injured monarchs upon crude stretchers and carted them away. Grave expressions on their faces, bystanders milled about, speculating in muted Old Irish. Bridget had no idea what they were saying, no clue as to the condition of her two companions. The corpsmen were pale and upset and, with nothing else to do, made a fuss over finding the queen's high heels and collecting all the chessmen that had spilled from the king's crane bag.

After the commotion had died away, the stout red-cross man finally took notice of the woman crying on the lip of a ditch. Unholstering a flint axe from his belt, he plodded over to her. Bridget cringed at his size and threatening demeanor, but as he drew near, she found herself unable to stop chuckling. He bore an uncanny resemblance to chubby Oliver Hardy of the Laurel and Hardy comedy team, right down to the unfortunate moustache bristling like a black toothbrush under his round nose.

"I cannot speak a word of Irish," she said. "Except '*Cá bhfuil leithreas na mban?*' though I don't suppose that's of any use at the moment."

Hardy scrunched his mouth and fiddled with his collar. His cogitations flustered him, but he soon found the English. "Who art thou? What hast thou done to the queen and the king?"

"I am Bridget Scanlon, from Philadelphia."

He nodded as though he knew where that was.

"Except now I am with the University College, Dublin. Lecturer in archaeology, here on fieldwork."

His continuous nodding unnerved her. She had no confidence that he understood a single word.

"I am friends with Maeve and Al. Queen Medb and King Ailill," she corrected herself.

"Didst thou push them down the hill?" Hardy frowned and looked at her crosswise.

That comment put her Irish up. "Of course not! What sort of person do you take me for? They got excited, seeing all the soldiers and horses, and rushed to the edge of the ridge. That rabid fox appeared out of nowhere and deliberately tripped them, and they came tumbling down, and next thing I know they are knocked out cold as two fish in the market. Are they going to be okay?"

"Thou best come with me." Hardy took her by the arm and led her through clumps of soldiers, who were amused by their determined beeline to the camp's headquarters. A few of the men winked or whistled at Bridget, and one poor chap pretended to swoon at the mere sight of her, but most bore a confused expression, wondering perhaps at the woman's resemblance to the queen—the blond hair, the long nose, a certain rambunctious swing of the hips. Depositing her outside a large red tent, Hardy ordered Bridget to wait, and then he disappeared inside for several long moments.

Across the way, in front of the mess tent, a little boy stared at her, fascinated by her glasses. Bridget smiled and waved from her hip, and he scurried away to gather another boy, his brother perhaps, and lead him by the hand. The second child had a sweet face, but his eyes were not on her, for he was blind. She hunkered down to their level to be more approachable, and the brothers were won over. The older of the pair tried his Irish on her, but Bridget shrugged and shook her head. He mimed trying on the spectacles, so she handed over the frames, and the boy immediately put them on his younger brother's face.

"Sorry," she said. "Not magic enough."

Piping mad, Hardy appeared and strode to the boys, yanked the glasses off the poor lad's face, and handed them back to their owner. "Scat," he said. "Urchins are the curse of this country."

"Don't be so hard on them, they are only children," she said. "How are the queen and king?"

"Thou art called Philadelphia?"

She smiled. "Yes, that's my name."

"His Majesty hath been asking after thee," the soldier said. "Queen Medb, I am afraid, hath not yet awakened."

As she followed Hardy into the tent, Bridget noticed that his hemline did not cover his stout backside. He soon blended in with the crowd of well-wishers hanging around the bedside. Several doctors and nurses in matching green tunics checked charts and wound bandages. One man fussed over a bowl of leeches, and another honed a straight razor on a leather strop. A druid cast sticks on a night table and, dissatisfied with the pattern, collected and threw again till he reached the preferred prediction. In an obscure recess, a pair of curly-haired men conferred in brotherly whispers. On a primitive chaise longue rested Al, his right arm in a sling and a nasty goose egg rising in the middle of his forehead.

On a queen-sized bed covered by elk skin lay Medb, helpless and diminished, unconscious as a clock. Her head was wrapped in white linen, both wrists encased in plaster. Someone had removed her makeup, and she looked tired and hurt. Her cracked lips had a nasty red split, and a purple-and-yellow shiner circled her left eye. Bridget went to her side and caressed her free fingers.

From his pillows, Al called her over. "C'mon, sit next to me. I need some lovin', too."

She had no one else to trust, so she reluctantly crossed the room and knelt beside him. After the accident, someone had cut Mullaney's secondhand clothes off Al and replaced them with regal robes of green and black.

"Have those boys been giving you any trouble, Philadelphia?"

"You could tell Hardy over there to lose a few pounds or get a longer tunic. He leaves far too little to the imagination. Is Maeve going to be okay?"

"Time will tell, my dear." Al stroked the back of her neck. "Unfortunately, we have so little left. She will be as mad as a castrato when she awakens if we have not found the girl."

With the crook of his finger, he bade the two generals to come out of the shadows. Traipsing to the chaise with military precision, they offered a smart salute to the king. Al pointed to his right arm trapped in the sling, and they dropped their hands.

"These are two of my seven sons," he said. "Maine Athramail—"

"Begging your pardon, sir, but I am Maine Máthramail."

"By the gods." Al sighed. "Whatever possessed your mother to call the lot of you Maine? Let's say this is Mama's Boy and the other brother is Beyond Description. Now that I think of it, that is a confusing name indeed. Why did she not call you the Straight-Haired Fellow? Had she run out of names entirely? Beyond description, all right, bold as an uncracked egg. The tales I could relate about this lad. Used to wake up early to eat his brothers' shares of the flapjacks. Or threaten the smartest lads in class if they refused to do his homework for him. Filched his mother's jewels once and gave them to some strumpet in exchange for a peek at her you-know-what. Beyond Description is right, if we are talking about the nerve of an all-time chancer." Roaring with laughter in remembrance of those early family days, he gave his son a hard, affectionate pinch to the right deltoid. "When she wakes up, remind me to ask your mother how you come to be the only one of my seven sons without curls."

Standing at attention, the two soldiers surreptitiously poked each other in the ribs, looking as though they might start a brouhaha.

"At ease, lads, chill out. This comely lass is Bridget of Philadelphia, or the Woman With Four Eyes. She has been most helpful in our pursuits. Well, not all of my pursuits, but let's say the most important one."

By now everyone's attention was focused on the colloquy of the king's circle and the blond with the glasses. Had nurse or doctor, priest or bodyguard been paying attention to the queen, they might have seen the flutter of her lashes as she gallantly tried to open her eyes from the depths of her nobility. Let it not be said that she made no effort on the battlefield. Whatever flaws she had, she fought the good fight in the mirror of her mind: Cúchulainn cleaved in two, the bull of Cooley being led by the ring in its nose, a victory parade of rose petals. We are all heroes in our own dreams.

"Go on then, boys," Al said. "Tell her of our offer, good only if you sign today."

Beyond Description cleared his throat. "Thank thee, Father—"

"Enough with the *thees* and the *thous*," Al said. "Try to get with it."

"Thank you, Father," his son said. "We have consulted with Fer Diad mac Damain and with Fergus mac Roich. We have polled our chiefs and commanders, the two Crúaids, two Calads, two Cirs, two Ecells, three Croms, three Cauraths, three Combirgs, four Feochars, four Furachars—"

"Right," said Al. "We don't need a litany, and she does not need to know the whole alphabet or that we consulted Awful Man or Jag Off or Little Sprout and so on. Let's say we ran it by all the boys and they agreed."

"Very well," said Beyond Description. "Although it is highly irregular not to name the names of all the brass in a negotiation."

Mama's Boy spoke up. "The resemblance is uncanny. If we could get you out of your clothes and into hers. Now that I am hearing it aloud, it does sound peculiar, but we would like you to be our mother."

Bridget blinked at the audacious request.

"For pretend." His brother was not pleased to be usurped as the lead salesman. "We are prepared to be most generous. Mademoiselle, in exchange for your services for the interval, we are prepared to offer you a choice of any parcel of land at:

Caisleán Gainimh, the Sandcastle,
Tuaim Móna, the Mound of Turf,
Sceith an Aill, the Vanishing View,
Uisce Cos, the Dripping Backwater,
Dumpáil Truflais, the House of Truffles,
Gríos Súil, the Sunshine Grotto . . ."

"Again," said the king. "You do not have to list every possible piece of property. The clock is ticking."

"If you insist," said Beyond Description. "Perhaps the señorita is more interested in a villa in Meath or Roscommon. Anyplace your heart desires."

"And you can always keep your Dublin address," said the king. "Think of our offer as a retreat in the country, a pied-à-terre in the wilds of Connemara. We have a nice flat above the best Italian restaurant in Galway City and a bedsit in Westport—lots of good shops there."

Every eye in the tent was upon her, anxious for her answer. Bridget felt as if someone were trying to sell her a time-share, and she did not know how to elude such aggression. She jumped from the couch to pace the floor. "I am flattered," she said. "But I don't think—"

The other brother leapt into the pitch. "You drive a hard bargain. What would it take for you to say yes, today, this very minute? How about we throw in a paddock with a nice string of Connemara ponies? Who can say nay to a horse?"

"What is it exactly that you are asking me to do?"

"It's only for the once," Mama's Boy said. "While Mammy is out of commission and the old man is flying with one wing."

"You wouldn't have to do much," said Beyond Description. "Battlefield maneuvers are always at the generals' discretion. Yours would be a symbolic role, leadership behind the scenes, making the grand strategies, pushing around the miniature horses and chariots on the big map back at HQ whilst our boys slog it out with the Northerners."

"We need a woman's touch," said Mama's Boy.

"Once more into the breach! The West's Awake!" shouted his brother. "All that sort of esprit de corps palaver to cheer on the boys."

Al raised his hand to hush his two wayward sons. "We are asking you to be Queen for a Day, Bridget of Philadelphia. Make the rabble think you are Medb, ready to win us the bull this go-around. Take off those glasses and you would fool even the Hound of Ulster into believing he was in combat with the real head of the army of Connacht."

"But it is a phantom army," she said. "You saw yourself, Al. It is nothing more than a will-o'-the-wisp. None of it is real, no horses, no bull. Not even you."

The king was stunned. His roguish charm petered out, replaced by worry and wrinkles. His boys looked blankly into the distance, pretending they had not heard.

The druid cast another lot of pixie sticks, and all the medical attendants halted their useless procedures. Everyone was crushed by disbelief. The mood was so quiet and somber, you could have heard a fairy sneeze or the wings of a real moth beat against an imaginary tent. When Bridget realized what she had done, she was flabbergasted, too. She felt as if she had ruined Christmas or told an impressionable child that the sun would one day explode and dissolve the whole solar system in a supernova. The folk gathered round fidgeted with disappointment and were afraid of what she might say next. They were her people, all right, death-obsessed and melancholic to the core, but nevertheless they expected something grand to happen at the next tick of the clock. The fatalistic optimists. She felt sorry for their naïve investment in her no or yes. Empathy erased the doubt that usually paralyzed her heart. *Yes*, she said, *yes*. A great Irishness filled her heart and lifted her bosom.

"Sure, I was only kidding you," she said with a bright smile. "Yes, of course, I will do it, on one condition. The bog girl is mine, should we find her. And if you should chance to see any red-haired witch on the battlefield, bring her safely to me." Bridget stole one last look at the body in the sickbed, bandaged like a mummy, and then she went away with her handmaid to the queen's private dressing room, chattering about what might be suitable from her wardrobe.

Her decision lifted every spirit in the tent, and the news quickly leaked and spread like a virus through the camp. *The queen lives; long live the queen.* The troops broke out in joyful song, and even the horses displayed a renewed vigor in their hoofsteps. Such is the delicacy of morale among armies; the scale tips from fear to valor if the fight is for a good cause, even if the new leader is merely a public relations stunt. Bridget threw off her ordinary clothes and let herself be clad in royal weeds, anointed with the smell of apples, and changed into the queen of the West.

Behind the tent, delighted at the sabotage, the red fox held her tail high as a flagpole.

25

Fools' Gambit

A s they shared a smoke from the purloined pipe,
Cúchulainn and Láeg watched the two men of Connacht marching to their doom. In any battle, someone must
make the first move, fire the first shot, or send out the first
patsies to draw fire. Even the most coldhearted make such
decisions with misgivings. Even the most calculating might
ask themselves when such sacrifices suffice. But the most suc-
cessful champions are not sentimental about their pawns,
and their thoughts are many moves ahead before the first
pieces fall from the battle. Endgame is all.

"Do you think they have any chance?" the charioteer
asked as he passed the bowl.

"Medb's army must be lured to give chase. We will take
the first chariot that comes rolling over the plain. I may have
softened my heart on those two had Burke been more pru-
dent on the chessboard."

To warm his fingers, Láeg cupped the bowl. "Burke has
proven indestructible to this point. Perhaps he is too full of
the Beer of Immortality."

Cúchulainn chuckled, pleased with the memory of combat. "Sure, I was only having fun with the fool. We will see how they fare against a merciless foe."

"What if after all this we fail to find the girl?"

"Fail, fail again, fail better." The Hound seemed to savor the possibility. "There is always tomorrow."

* * *

"Do you have a plan?" Mullaney asked. "It is the two of us with these bottle openers against all the roughnecks of three provinces. Like a football match where we are the only pair of eejits in the visitors' wrong colors. We will be creamed."

Burke tapped his temple with the flat of his blade. "Strategy, my dear lad. You forget that as a mere lad of sixteen I was the champion of the Four Provinces Chess Tournament."

"Your story gets better at each telling."

"Kindly remember how I outdueled the hellion of the North, two out of three, and me not touching a queen nor bishop these past decades. Half the battle is anticipation. You have a number of options move by move, but if you are looking only at your pieces, you are playing against yourself. What is your opponent thinking? He knows that you know that he has ideas, but the point is that you know he knows."

"I am a little bit lost here on who knows what."

"Try to follow the plot of my thinking. I am asking, in laymen's terms, what do you want him to do? A forced error is deadlier than a random mistake."

"Your analogies are getting the better of me."

"Look for the lacunae in the other fella's logic. Cúchulainn is all instinct and lets his temper rule the long game. He would not see a hole in a ladder. All I had to do was step where he least expected. Make it look like I was walking into his trap, d'ye savvy?"

THE GIRL IN THE BOG 269

"I suppose, but leading a whole army is more complex than matching chess wit. How often do your theorems work when faced with an exponentially larger foe? There's a lot more than sixteen chessmen, in case you hadn't noticed."

"Exponents, is it?" Burke laughed. "Simply ask yourself: What is the one subterfuge those slaughterers down there would not anticipate?"

Mullaney gazed upon the mass of soldiers. Despite their misgivings, the Western warriors were singing and whistling at their work, hitching up their wagons, and shining their iron blades. The many moving parts of a great mechanism were gearing up for havoc and destruction. A slouching beast getting its legs under itself to stalk and strike.

"Can we get around somehow to its backside," he asked, "and surprise it from the rear?"

Burke tugged at the waistband of his trousers, which had been sliding off his bony hips. "That's exactly what they are expecting us to do, and even as a double feint, they would still reason such a tactic is our only possible move. If nothing else, a rear attack offers us some protection against total and instant annihilation. And that is why we are not going to do it."

"You said it was our only chance."

"Ninety-nine point nine, nine, nine percent of the time, but where is your imagination, Mick? What they cannot possibly fathom is two lads walking straight up to their teeth till we reach the gooey center of it all and hop aboard the finest chariot they have."

"They will kill us, Tom. Or they will die laughing at these butter knives we brought to defend ourselves."

The truth lasted but a single beat. Any longer and it would have prevailed.

Burke chucked his small sword into the moor. "Odds are slim, let's admit, and these daggers won't do us any good and might be seen as an unnecessary threat. Maybe we are a couple of pawns, but we have courage in our hearts. I've been killed thrice this night, and that's what we know that they don't know. These boys have yet to meet the true immortal heroes of Connacht."

There was a scintilla of fact in his fallacy. Although Mullaney himself had not suffered a single scratch, he had seen Burke without his head and Burke skewered like a kebab and Burke jigsawed like a puzzle. He should have died already three times, yet there he was, blathering away. Perhaps he could not be killed at all. Nonetheless, Mullaney tucked his dagger into his jumper as they walked straight into camp.

A few men of lesser rank nodded as they passed by. A pair of Galway hookers gave them knowing winks. Local farmers tried to entice them to buy, at heavily marked-up prices, piles of withered turnips and hunks of graying meat. A druid, consoling a confessor, smiled in a sinister manner. A hairy-legged sentry, chewing on a red apple, lowered his spear to waist level and casually signaled for them to stop. With his mouth full of applesauce, he asked if they were there to see the blacksmith. Strained through the mush, the Old Irish was more or less intelligible. Mullaney simply repeated, "Here to see the smithy are we," and they earned safe passage from the edge of the bivouacked camp followers and into the paddocks fragrant with the not unpleasant odor of horseshit.

"There's nothing imaginary about that smell, now, is there, Mick?"

"Whoever is in charge of arranging this panorama paid attention to the incidentals, I will grant you that."

"The Lord cares about each and every sparrow," Burke said.

"And the devil is in the details."

The Irish Draught horses idled, preening, thick at the withers and athletic enough to pull the two-man chariots into battle. Mechanics checked wheels and greased axles. Laden with swords and shields, a blacksmith's apprentice ignored the two strangers. Boys with rasps as big as themselves tended to ragged hooves. Groomsmen smoothed the horses' coats with currycombs and tied knots in their manes to provide each warrior a handhold during a skirmish. A farrier trimmed hooves while an apprentice beat nails to affix new shoes still warm from the forge. Army gear lay about the corral, and in the blacksmith's shops hung rows of leather aprons. A perfect disguise if they could get past the fierce watchdog sleeping near the anvil. Even at rest, the cur looked like he would chew first and ask questions later.

"What would Cúchulainn do?" Burke asked. "Too bad we were not armed with that trick spear. One good toss and the pooch is turned inside out."

"You haven't a pork chop in your pocket? Or a hurley stick or ball he might chase? What is the plan, Tom, to outfox this shepherd?"

The dog yawned, exposing the daggers of his teeth. He rose and gave himself a good shake. Like the horses, he was bigger than today's breeds, with the wolf not entirely filtered out of the genetic mix. Hard to believe, thought Mullaney, that this slathering monster was the same species as his Bonnie, but a dog is a dog. He played his gambit and whistled. The shepherd tensed immediately.

Walk up, Mullaney signaled, and the dog instinctively moved toward the horses and waited for the next command. *Wheet-wheeo-wheet-wheet*, Mullaney tried, and the dog obeyed his *Get down*. Agitated by the aggressive watchdog in their midst, a half dozen horses looked as if they might skitter off. *Way to me*, Mullaney whistled, and the mutt ran around the herd to turn them anticlockwise. *Take time*, he was forced to blow, and when the animals calmed, he tootled *That will do* and ended with one last blast for the shepherd to lie down and rest. With nothing guarding the foundry, Burke snuck in and stole two aprons. The incognito interlopers went from unnoticed to nearly invisible in their new kits, blending right in with the hammer-and-tongs crowd.

Amiable as jockeys before the race, the charioteers began arriving at the stables to claim their teams and wagons. A lanky graybeard field manager took charge and gave the lads their assignments. Young boys hurried to position the horses in their traces. Whips cracked as drivers tested their elasticity. The whole operation happened quickly and efficiently, a marvel of precision. Within minutes, the first chariot rolled off the line, and one by one the war wagons departed to join the legion assembling on the plain. In the end only the graybeard with the clipboard remained, shaking his head beside a beat-up jalopy and a mismatched pair of nags, not fit for battle. With a scowl, he scanned the yard and settled on the faux blacksmiths. He bade them to report to his side.

Purple-faced and livid, the sergeant cursed in words that had not been uttered or heard in nearly two thousand years. Burke and Mullaney took his meaning to be *Get that heap out of here*. At once, they hustled to the empty chariot.

"This is our chance," Burke whispered. "We drive it off the lot and back to Cúchulainn."

"Are you crazy? Do you even know how these things work? Because I surely do not."

"How hard can it be? Follow my lead," Burke said, and he stepped onto the back of the chariot and reached for the reins. The cart swayed on its two wheels, and he danced a jig to keep it steady. "Hop on and help me find the parking brake."

No sooner had Mullaney set foot on the running board than he felt the whole vehicle teeter and totter. He lost his balance and fell to the ground with an *oomph*. The horses spooked and charged ahead without warning, throwing off Burke beside his friend. The watchdog sprang to his feet to chase the runaway chariot, but teeth nipping at their hind legs only spurred the horses to race faster. In a flash, the rickety war wagon vanished into the darkness in a cacophony of barks and whinnies and the shudder of worn wheels. The would-be horse thieves could only watch from the dust.

Berating them in a flurry of *fecks*, the sergeant pounced upon them. He pulled them up by their apron strings to take a good look at their faces.

"Easy there, my good man," Burke said.

"I'll be a son of a gun," the graybeard said in English. "Saxon spies. Off we go, lads, to the brig with the pair of yis. I shoulda shoulda guessed. What sort of Irishman doesn't know his way around a horse?"

He grabbed each man by an earlobe and bullied them through the crowded camp, Burke and Mullaney yowling like a pair of truants caught skipping school.

*　　*　　*

Láeg heard the hoofbeats first. He raced for the abandoned gáe bolga and shouted a word of warning to his boss. Exploding out of thin air, the chariot and horses ran straight for Cúchulainn, and at the last instant he flattened his body to the ground and covered his head against the stomping hooves. Once the spinning wheels had cleared him, the Hound vaulted in his renowned salmon leap to land abreast of the crazed team. Under the horsepower of his two feet, galloping without a care, he matched their reckless pace, and grabbing the yoke in one mighty hand, he brought the chariot to a screeching halt. The horses reared, whinnying and kicking, and the axle nearly split in two, so great was the strength of his grip. Láeg flew to his side and found the reins, whispering soothing words to the frightened animals. Once the thrill had worn off, they looked under the hood and inspected the horsepower.

The old nags were past their prime. One was a sorrel with a blaze on its blond nose, and the other was a dun marked by zebra stripes on its hind legs—hardly the jet-black pair as requested. Dented and patched, the dilapidated cart was several years outdated, the upholstery threadbare and dirty, and the left wheel had a suspicious crack and serious wear on the tread. The number of weapons stored inside was a joke. The basic arsenal lacked a spare shield and a stabbing lance. Láeg tried to put bright paint on a disappointment. "So, the wagon is not perfect. It's a wonder they were able to send us anything at all. They are a most improvisational pair. I thought those two lads would be chopped to mincemeat in five minutes flat."

"This is embarrassing," Cúchulainn said. "I am the Hound of Ulster, the greatest hero of the Ulster Cycle, and I cannot be seen going about in a rickety jalopy. It is not even gilded, for the gods' sake. And those two ponies are fit for glue."

"You have to learn to let go," said Láeg. "Don't let trivial matters ruin your life. So, it isn't your dream chariot. Two bumpy wheels are better than none at all."

Cúchulainn considered this bit of wisdom. With the nail of one finger, he scratched the part in his hair, and the anger on his features slowly relaxed through the power of a blank and inattentive mind. A serene smile tugged the corners of his lips as he patted the dun horse on its rump. "Aye. Let's go get the girl."

*　*　*

Each time he saluted an officer of rank, the cavalry sergeant had to let go of one of the miscreants' ears, but that was their only relief from the tortuous walk to the command center. A fat man with a bristly moustache on his baby face stood guard.

"Hardy, me bucko, I caught two Saxanachs," the graybeard said. "Out stealing horses."

"That is a serious offense in a time of war," said Hardy.

Burke could not resist an aside. "That's another fine mess you have gotten us into."

"Silence, you English dog," the sergeant said.

"And that's one more ting," Burke said. "All this Saxon business and thinking us English. I am as Irish as a pint of plain or a sad song on the harp. What business have you calling me and my friend otherwise? *Fad saoil agat, gob fliuch, agus bás in Eirinn!*"

Mullaney expressed his surprise. "I thought you said you hadn't a word of the mother tongue."

"Trying times sharpen the memory. Before completely losing his marbles, my old *seanathair* used to shout that motto. What does it mean, anyways?"

"Something you might hear at the pub. 'Long life, a wet mouth, and death in Ireland.' A kind of toast, if you will, after a late night of drinking."

"Truer words were never spoken."

A quick red fox emerged from behind a hedge, ears erect to catch the last snatch of their conversation.

The sergeant's chubby cheeks turned pink under his steely whiskers. "English or Irish, neveryoumind. They are enemies of the nation, I tell you, and should be sentenced and executed by herself, the queen."

"Nation?" Burke said. "What ish my nation? Who talks of my nation? Sure, we are as Irish as any of you villains and bastards, you knaves and rascals."

"You are a right philosopher," said Hardy. "But the night is slipping away like a greased pig from the butcher. The queen will know what to do. Follow me, lads."

Burke nudged Mullaney in the ribs so that he would not miss the sight of Hardy's big bare bum. "Your man is no top and all bottom."

Inside the tent, the air was close and tepid with the unpleasant aroma of so many ancient people. A druid stood by the front door, tossing conjuring sticks on a table that could pass as a barstool. Several medicos in matching tunics were jawing amongst themselves, taking sides in a dispute between a leechmonger and a barber with a rusty razor. Far from the maddening crowd, a curly-headed man in a tunic trimmed in red and gold daubed his eyes with a matching handkerchief. His wet pink face showed evidence of a long crying jag. At the center of it all reclined a neglected patient with a white bandage around her head and two apparently broken wrists resting at her sides. Hardy pushed the prisoners past her and delivered them to a nattily dressed gentleman stretched out on a short couch. He had been reading yesterday's news etched in Ogham on a long wooden stick, and on an end table sat a pitcher of mead and an oaken tankard.

"A pair of spies, Your Honor," Hardy said. "They claim to be on our side, but we have not seen their like before."

"Gentlemen," said the man on the chaise. He welcomed them with a sweep of his free hand. "Won't you prostrate yourselves before your lord and liege? You are not from these parts, I take it."

Encouraged by the point of a lance, Mullaney and Burke knelt like altar boys.

"Au contraire," Mullaney said. "I was born in Connemara and left for the city, only to come back to run my father's place after he passed away. I own the next farm over, and this is technically my land you are camped on."

"Your land? How curious. Why would anyone lay claim to this barren bog? Small wonder you emigrated. Bigger wonder you immigrated back. And you, sir. What is it you do? Are you a gentleman farmer as well?"

"I am a man of the West," said Burke. "Never the once left this island, I am proud to say. I live right next door to Mick, though to be honest, neither one of us farms much these days. The government pays us not to produce a thing. Aside from a few odd sheep, you could hardly call it farming at all. More to maintain appearances. I try to grow tomatoes in the back garden, but it is forever raining in this land, and those red bastards adore the sunshine."

"A man of leisure, I see. Not unlike myself." The reclining man poured himself a flagon of mead. "I am Ailill, the king of Connacht. But it is the missus what runs the show. I am a bit of *arm candy*, is that the phrase? A trophy husband?" He broke into a taste of a song: "*I'm just a gigolo; everywhere I go, people know the part I'm playing . . .*"

Burke interrupted his number. "So where is this queen of yours? I have a few choice words for her."

On cue, in walked a tall and beautiful young woman, with an elegant face and cascades of yellow hair. The courtiers and servants bowed to her, even the doctors and the priest. The curly-haired man stopped his bellyaching. Favoring his broken arm, the king struggled over to kiss the largest ring on her many-spangled fingers. She greeted him with a confident smile. Something of a fashion plate, she wore a crimson tunic, over which was layered a hooded cloak in deep-purple velvet. Embroidered on each shoulder was a fierce bird of prey, and on her back in the same luxurious thread were five pots of gold coins. In one hand she carried a light-flashing spear, and in the other fist was an iron sword. She was the perfect embodiment of an ancient queen, except for the pair of glasses slipping down her aquiline nose.

CHAPTER

26

The Final Battle

THE THREE RED Witches began howling, and three hundred of the Connacht warriors dropped dead from the awful fright. Another three fifties and three thousand cowards fled the camp for the long journey home. The hags were unsparing in their warnings of the fate awaiting those who remained. Ravens and rats would gnaw at dead men on the battlefield, the blades and spearpoints sunk into their bodies. Their widows and children would wail and search for years to come, unable to find enough bones to bury. Awhirl in his manic torque, Cúchulainn would soon plow through the troops, dealing death and destruction. The witches sang loud and long murder ballads and dirges, often in a haunting minor key, relentless as a siege. "Hail Ulster, woe to Ireland," they chanted. This bold advice came courtesy of Fedelm, designed to attract attention and win the girls' release.

In their patchwork disguises, they had nearly made it to the center of Medb's camp before being found out by the youngest of her seven sons. Beyond Description and his goons had deposited the four young women in a small tent adjacent to the royal headquarters. The fake druids were blindfolded, bound in ropes, and forced to sit on three three-legged stools. Siobhán, the make-believe poet, was hitched by her wrists to the central post supporting the canvas roof. Junior-level guards lit three torches, and Beyond Description paced gleefully, enjoying a coup that would win him favor from the queen. While the druid spies were a fine catch, the real prize was the poet in the middle, for a redhead had not ever been seen in all of Ireland. Rarity of rarities, her glorious hair signified mystery and prestige, truly magical to the very roots. Mulling questions for his interrogation, Beyond Description circled like a scald crow, arms folded behind his back. He pictured every stripe he would lash across her pale skin, and he rehearsed in the theater of his imagination how she would cry for mercy. His depravity was matched by the genuine fear he felt in the presence of such a woman.

A fat man with a short moustache poked his pale head through the opening. "It's your mother," he said. He was trembling more than usual. "And your father. They have been injured."

"Wait here," Beyond Description said to his prisoners. "Don't move a muscle."

A clamor rose in the next tent over, multiple voices talking over one another with no one taking control. Stretcher bearers delivered two patients. Doctors argued over best treatments. A druid muttered last rites. Two men cried in a far-off recess, and one voice rose above the others: "Will she be all right? Will the queen live?"

"What do you think is going on over there?" Emcee asked.

"Listen, Medb has been hurt before the battle has even begun," Fedelm said. "I sent a wily fox to make mischief and waylay the royals, but perhaps she has exceeded her remit."

No sooner had the bustle of the first incident subsided than another ruckus arose outside. Voices offstage hollered at each other, angry men cursing and flinging accusations. From the tentpole, Siobhán called out to her friends. "They are saying they have caught two more intruders. Did they not accuse us of being spies?"

"The place is thick with them," the bog girl said. She laughed to put them at ease. "The mice have gnawed a hole in the granary."

Siobhán asked, "What will you do once the queen has set you free?"

Wistfulness nearly made Fedelm weep. She thought of the days before her troubles. "I will go back to my people where I belong. There are no folk like the folk of the West. Despite all the black murder and mayhem in Connemara, this is where I belong."

The tent flaps burst open, and in strode the fat guard, Beyond Description, and a man with one arm in a sling and an apple-sized lump in the middle of his forehead. Ailill strode to the red-haired girl and stared lasciviously at her. Clearing his throat, the prince tried to steer his father's attention. "These are four more spies I have caught, m'lord. The ginger one at the post claims to be a poet. Is she the one you and Mother have been looking for? Is this not Fedelm, the prophet of our doom?"

"What sort of witchcraft is on these ginger drops?" The king twirled one of Siobhán's curls around his pinkie and then unwound it as he gazed into her eyes. "No. This is obviously not Fedelm. Medb put no bounty on this girl's red head."

The word caught in Fedelm's throat. *Bounty.* Betrayed. She had not known for sure that Medb had planned to kill her once again. The old woman at the edge of the woods. *That murdering bitch.*

Failure registered in Beyond Description's voice. "Then what we do with these spies?"

"Kill them," said the king. "First, kill the poet. Kill her anyway, as if she were Fedelm. And then execute her Saxon hags. And make sure they are dead indeed. Not thrown in a bog but burned or sealed in a stone tomb."

With a wink at the redhead tied to the post, the king hurried back to his own tent.

Beyond Description turned to the fat guard. "You heard His Majesty. Eradicate them with due haste and leave their bodies for the scavengers. And when you are finished here, rid us of those two tiresome spies who would steal our horses." He paused at the entry. "Get busy, fool."

Bowing to the departing prince, the chubby mustachioed fellow in the short tunic raised his head, his eyes wet with fat tears. With his dagger he cut the blinds from the three druids, for he did not like to murder someone without giving them the chance to face their fate.

"Wait," Eileen said. "You wouldn't want to hurt a girl, would you? Think of how Cúchulainn spared Medb when he caught her unawares as she tended to her time of the month. He had a noble spirit and pardoned her life."

The guard hesitated. His moustache twittered on his dancing lip.

"What is your name?" Fedelm asked. "I feel we have met before."

"They call me Hardy, miss."

"Well, Hardy, you know how the story ends. Same saga every time. Cúchulainn is right now heading this way in his deathly chariot with seven swords in one hand and the gáe bolga flashing in the other. He will thresh the Connachtmen like wheat in the field. And there will be nothing left of the least of you but crimson stains on the ground and the crows picking the gore."

"I have me orders, lass."

"Is a bull worth your life, Hardy? We are all victims here, you included. Shall you be led by a ring through your nose? Think for yourself. Think of the missus and the seven wee Hardys back home. A little farm in the glen, is it? A few sheep, a milch cow, a crop of potatoes you will never slather with clots of fresh Irish butter. You cannot escape the mad frenzy of the Hound of Ulster. Slip away while you can, there's no shame in it."

"You will give me a head start, will you?" Hope rambled in his realistic breast. "I cannot untie you, for they would have my hide."

"Fair play, Hardy. *Slán abhaile*, and safe home to you."

Despite her anger at Medb's betrayal, Fedelm kept her word to the executioner and gave him time to make his escape.

Hardy was not five minutes away when Siobhán felt a stab behind her eyes, sharp as a migraine. The image started as a pinprick circle and then slowly spread into focus across the field of her mind. A wattle hut, with a sow in the back room, and children playing in the rushes. Five, six of them, and then the careworn mother, a wee one at her breast, looking anxiously at the Killary road heading south from Leenaun. Chickens pecked in the yard for insects; one chased down a grasshopper churring in the potato patch. The woman brightens at the small fat figure clomping into view, and the children see him too. All six of them, black haired and blue eyed, little roly-polies, miniatures of their daddy, sans moustache. Hardy coming home to the Hardys, all running down the road to bowl him over at the bridge with hugs and kisses.

The scene dissolved like an old-time silent movie, the circle narrowing slowly to black. Siobhán breathed deeply and opened her eyes. "He makes it. I can see Hardy and his family as clear as if they were all standing right here. He gets home to the kiddies and wife."

Tears of joy glistened on Fedelm's leathery cheeks. "You have it, just as I thought: the imbas forosnai. Not bad for your first prophecy. You are a real witch after all."

"Do me, do me," Emcee said. "Tell me if Billy McKenna will ever make a move—"

"It's not a toy, Mary Catherine," said Fedelm. "It isn't a party game for figuring out boys."

But Siobhán had already swooned into a second trance. "I see a lake, black as coal. We are all on the shore. You, me, even Mr. Burke and Mr. Mullaney, and some other woman who I do not recognize. Ah, no, don't—" She blinked and fluttered her eyelids, ridding her mind of the awful vision.

"Go slow at first," said Fedelm. "You have a dangerous power. As for you, Eileen, your talents lie elsewhere. An herbalist, perhaps, a painter. And Emcee, you may not ever know how to see the future, but that should not stop you from weaving your magic. You are all more wonderful than you think." In the quiet of their minds, the captives reflected privately on the gift, considering what they might request when free to live their lives.

Now, Fedelm had other matters to attend. "Shall I tell you all how to cast a spell to make men go mad and run away like mice?"

For the next five minutes, she instructed them in the fine Irish art of cursing, and they practiced how to control the hidden power of the lungs—singing from the diaphragm, positioning the mouth properly for the o's and a's, how to handle the clash of consonants in a good Irish wail. They rehearsed their chant about the ravens and war-torn men and the crimson and the red.

"The key to a good prophecy is to be quick and decisive and committed," said Fedelm. "There is one last screw to turn. At the end of the second verse, we will switch refrains— 'Woe to Ulster, long live Ireland'—and those eejits will think the war is good as won. It is child's play to fool a man into thinking he is certain about two opposite notions at the same time. Sure, I have never met one who knows his own mind better than a good woman does."

The three witches cackled, and then they began to howl at the setting moon.

*   *   *

Flitting at his father's ear like a gnat, Beyond Description kept trying to whisper some juicy tidbit of information. Al shook his head and tried to swat him away, but at his son's further prodding, he rose from the couch and bowed to the new queen. Feeling mighty foolish, Bridget curtsied as best she could.

"My love," Al said, as he took her hand in his. "You are the spit and image of her twenty bygone years. We were so happy then, and I am sure that you and I will be happy now. I won't be a minute. My boy here reports of more foxes than hens in the coop. A poet and her priests. While I am dealing with this trifling business, perhaps you might handle these two saboteurs caught in the royal paddocks absconding with the royal chariot and a pair of our finest horses." He gestured to Mullaney and Burke kneeling by the couch as he made his exit.

Bridget handed her sword and her spear to two hand-maidens and then pushed her sliding glasses to the bridge of her nose. Everyone forgot the old queen stiff on the hospital bed, for they could not take their eyes off the new queen, wondering whether she would fail in the first three minutes.

She had no idea what to do or what the others expected of her, only that she was supposed to serve as a sort of project manager for the pending battle. It was like being a junior lecturer one morning and the head of the archaeology department the next. The men kneeling in the dust fidgeted. They did not seem to fit with the sword and sorcery types. In their leather aprons, they looked like the couple who ran a cupcakery across from her flat in Dublin.

Mama's Boy poked his sword at their bottoms. "Stand, peasants. Stand before the queen."

Bowing and scraping as she passed, the onlookers gave her wide berth. With a flourish of her robes, Bridget sat on the couch as if it were a throne, leaning like Cleopatra against damask pillows. A pared apple had been placed on the end table as she arrived, so she munched on a slice, nearly swooning at the delicious first taste. She had not had a bite of food since hitting the road from Dublin. When she had finished feigning indifference, she graced the prisoners with her attention.

"Who sent you here?" she asked. "Are you spies?"

"By the hokey, you are a Yank," Burke said. "I knew it from the minute I clapped eyes on you."

Every ear in the tent was now listening intently. Bridget glowered at him for ruining the illusion. It is good to be the queen, she had decided, and now this peasant was spoiling everything.

"You are not Irish at all." Burke was indignant. "You sound like you hopped off the airplane at Shannon this afternoon. Playacting the queen. Well, you forgot about your specs, your highness. And your quare accent."

Mullaney tried to calm his friend, but his efforts were met with raw resistance. Burke's face flushed red as the apple, and he went all squinty in the one eye whilst the other bulged in its socket. He shook with rage.

"It wasn't my idea," she said, in a confidential whisper. "They asked me to do it on account of the accident. The real queen fell down a hill."

Enough was enough. Burke had endured three deaths—his head severed from his neck, been gored through the middle from stern to stem, diced into pieces like a chessboard, and on top if all, he had been nearly run over by a chariot—but now here was an American usurping the role of an Irish queen. "I demand to know what the hell is going on."

"Settle down, Tom," said Mullaney. "You have half a dozen spears pointed your way. And let's not forget your high blood pressure."

"Who are you?" Burke thundered at the poor woman.

"All right already. Geez, that's enough," she said. "I am Dr. Bridget Scanlon from University College, Dublin, a lecturer in the field of archaeology, which is the study of ancient cultures—"

"We may be from the West, but we are not thick."

"Apologies. I came down here this evening looking for a girl who calls herself the Red Witch of the West. Something Burke. I don't have her real name, but we've been texting back and forth after she posted some pictures on the internet. And somehow I got caught up in this . . . epic . . . or whatever is going on."

"The Red Witch of the West?" Burke asked.

"Never trust social media." Bridget slumped against the curved arm of the couch. "She's the one who started all this with her posts about the man who found a body in the bog."

"That was me," Mullaney said. "Long ago, yesterday morning. Me and my friend here. We are no spies or horse thieves at all. Just a couple of farmers digging in the wrong field. I am Michael Mullaney, and this is Tom Burke."

"The Burkes of the village inn? Natalie Burke's father?"

"Father-in-law, to be exact, though she is like a daughter I never had. And that Red Witch you are looking for is my granddaughter, Mary Catherine Burke."

"Selfie man," said Bridget. She flashed an imperial grin. "We meet at last."

"Under highly dubious circumstances," Mullaney said. "A hundred thousand welcomes and all that. And you are from America?"

"Philadelphia, originally."

Burke laughed. "Next he'll be asking if you know his daughter, Flannery, gone off to the States. I keep telling him America is a big place."

She lowered her voice to ward off eavesdropping. "Your daughter is the one with the peacock room? I've been in your house tonight, Mr. Mullaney, and I hate to tell you it looks like a hurricane came through. Knives and forks stuck into the walls. Your home has been hacked to bits."

"Those two hooligans," Mullaney said. "Went on a stabbing spree."

"And at your house, Mr. Burke, there was an old lady watching cowboy movies, only she turns out to be a banshee, and that's not half of what's happened. Fairies, can you believe it? Real fairies. One even turned into a bird. And there was a trickster fox who deliberately tripped the king and queen, the real queen, and sent them thumping down a hill. It's like we are all caught up in some ancient fairy tale."

Burke kept his voice low, too. "Mr. Philosophy over here thinks it is some loop in the cycle repeating itself. We could tell you stories of our own, Bridget of Philadelphia."

"I never should have done it," Mullaney said. "I hid the body in my shed, but when I came back, she was gone. We have spent the night with these other odd characters, Cúchulainn and his charioteer, who are searching for her, too. As far as I can tell, she is an old acquaintance of theirs by the name of Fedelm."

Like a Celtic knot, the plot kept twisting back on itself, one loop interconnected with the next, knitted into a nearly impenetrable yarn.

"Everyone is after that girl," Bridget said. "Even Maeve was looking for Fedelm. The queen of Ireland over there, asleep in the bed. They asked me to take over when she was hurt, and now I am supposed to lead the Cattle Raid on Cooley. I don't even know where Cooley is."

With a violent snap, the tent doorway flew open, and in stomped Ailill and Beyond Description. The king had a peevish mien, and his son had a look of chagrin. As he passed by the hospital bed, Al patted Medb on the forearm and nodded to Mama's Boy, faithful at her side. Satisfied that his wife was still unconscious, he walked over to the alcove, a big grin on his face. "And how are you, my blushing bride?" He bent awkwardly and kissed Bridget's forehead before squeezing beside her on the couch. "Spies everywhere. Witches and traitors. They won't be giving us any more trouble. What fate have you decided for this pair of rogues?"

The air hummed with the faint sound of molecules crashing, the noise growing to a monotone of static, and then the howling bored into their eardrums. The weird song of the three Red Witches filled the valley. A great keening full of woe and misery. Doctors and nurses ran off, moaning and groaning. The druid collapsed, dead as a doornail. Hundreds of men outside the tent bayed in agony. Like an air raid warning, the volume increased in spirals of wailing and screaming and gnashing of teeth.

"What is that bloody noise?" Ailill asked.

"Our fate," Beyond Description said. "You can hear it in the twisting verses. They are saying 'Hail Ulster, woe to Ireland,' and men are dropping like birds stricken in midair."

"No, wait," said Mama's Boy. "They do not say that at all. The chant is 'Hail Ireland, woe to Ulster,' and surely the battle is as good as ours."

"Who is making such contradictory claims? Are we to win or to lose?" Ailill shouted above the caterwauling. "What women are behind such deceit?"

They covered their ears with pillows. They fell to the floor cursing and praying and making vain promises to the gods. This was not a good night.

*　　*　　*

Bonfires and constellations illuminated the battlefield, a wee corner of Ireland glowing in the dark, and brightest of all was Cúchullain's frenzied halo, the bloody hero's radiant starlight.

The horses realized they were pulling the great hero of the Ulster Cycle. Battle-weary old veterans, they summoned reservoirs of strength and courage. A gentle slap of the reins and the two nags were flying, the wagon wheels banging over the rough terrain, the charioteer deftly steering a course through the murky and dangerous bog. On the wind, a mad song blew fierce as a winter storm. The first wave of men Cúchulainn and Láeg encountered were those driven bonkers by the Red Hags' howling curse. The retreating Connacht soldiers barely recognized the maniac charging into their midst, and all those who abandoned their chariots and battle gear were spared their lives. Cúchulainn would not deign to fight scaredy-cats.

The second wave of sound came from the North in a mad stampede through the valley. As if fleeing from a conflagration, great herds of deer and hares and wild boars, even wolves and badgers and tree cats, all the beasts of the forest and field, ran smack into the battle. The mass of animals split forces, and half detoured south to Munster and half forked east to Leinster.

Moments later, the source of their panic became clear. Having been stirred from their sleeping curse, the hard men of Ulster descended on the plain, a mob of soldiers headed their way—a bloodthirsty horde, the clatter of chariots and the glint of many weapons. *To arms! To arms!*

In their haste to join the fray, the Ulstermen had not bothered to take time to dress, and so those bold ruffians charged into battle wearing nothing but swords and shields. Company after company arrived on the plains, wild looking and handsome in their fierce nakedness. The unexpected arrival of his fellow Northmen brought a song to Cúchulainn's heart, and he led the savage, nude battalion into the cowering army of Connacht. With a renewed panache, he hacked and stabbed and killed with glee, and he suffered the stabs and slashes of his foes, the wounds gathering like badges and his shield thick with spearpoints and broken blades. But the Hound did not falter. He spasmed and went into his frenzy, which alone was enough to frighten any milquetoasts. He tossed the gáe bolga and had his charioteer retrieve the many-pointed spear from the punctured bodies. His enemies died in the many ways there are to die. Chopped and lopped, skewered and whacked, by lance or dagger or sword or the sharp edge of a flying shield, they gave up their spirits. Some expected a different outcome, but death always comes as a surprise to each man. For there is only one war, the same war, over and over again. Without notice or care, the men kept surfing the red wave, and Cú fought and killed them all, including Fer Diad, to whom Medb had given a ride between her thighs as a prize. Even her sweet daughter, Finnabair, dropped dead from the shame of such pointless sacrifice. The bogland soaked in the blood and the land was stained crimson and red. Too many others were slain to list here, though these deeds are recorded in the *Táin Bó Cúailnge*, the oldest story of them all.

A lull in the killing allowed Cúchulainn and his charioteer to knife through to the heart of the enemy camp. The two valiant horses, nicked and flustered from the many skirmishes, slowed to a quiet trot. The chariot wheels groaned, and Láeg tossed a few slingshot rocks and boulders overboard to lighten the load. Torn flags fluttered over the few remaining tents. Fires dwindled to embers and ash, and a mist of smoke and fog hung like a droopy ceiling over the ruins. Now and then a figure emerged from some hiding place and, frightened by the sight of the Hound, scurried away like a mouse. A boy consoled his brother with a stick of rock candy. A mother carried a jug of water to her perforated son. A three-legged dog barked once before retreating. Far off, a tin whistle tootled a lament. Crows and ravens, hunched like contemplative monks, scoured through the tatters.

Láeg pointed to a group of tents at the center of the camp. Holes and slashes had been cut in the canvas by various projectiles, and the nearby latrine had its top sheared off completely. They parked the cart and solemnly regarded the ruins. All through the blood sport, Cúchulainn had not forgotten his search for Fedelm. Amidst the rubble, he allowed himself one last hope. He vaulted from the chariot and patted the bay on its sweaty rump. With a hardy wave, he sent Láeg to water the horses and dispatch any stragglers. His charioteer offered him a parting salute and then steered the wagon anticlockwise.

The biggest red tent appeared the most likely headquarters, but Cúchulainn feared it might be housing a few last desperadoes. He drew his broadsword from his belt and cautiously slipped through a portal in the canvas, only to find it had been abandoned in haste. A blue dress with peacock feathers lay draped over a couch. A little overflowing jug sat forlornly on a table, and he allowed himself a bellyful of apple mead to quench his prodigious thirst. Someone had left behind a nice crane bag, its chessmen randomly scattered on the floor. In the dim light, he almost missed the most obvious thing in the room: on a queen-sized bed lay a woman, bandaged around the head, her plastered hands clutching at the elk-skin blanket. She had seen him enter and spoke his name in a weak and raspy voice. Bending close to her face, Cúchulainn recognized her at last.

"What misfortune has befallen you?"

She managed a wry smile. "Foxed again."

From beneath her pillow, she reached for a fingernail razor, but he grabbed her wrist and gently released the weapon from her grasp. "Medb," he said. "I would be within my rights to kill you."

"I am at your mercy."

"Not for the first time." He put away his sword and knelt beside her. "Tell me, did you find the girl?"

She took his bloodstained hand in hers. "I was about to ask you the same question."

"We are yet awhirl this brief time. Where have your people gone and left you all alone? Where is the king?"

"Dumped me this cycle, honey." She looked past him to the holes in the roof. "Though they could not have gotten too far. If you hurry, you might find him quivering in one of the pup tents nearby. Or he's already lit off to Oweynagat at Rathcroghan, to wait for me on the other side."

He kissed her gently. "Goodbye again."

"*Slán go fóill*," she said. "Till next time."

27

Blue Hour

MAMA'S BOY WAS the first to make an Irish goodbye. Without a word, he slipped through the back of the tent, as everybody else had been unnerved by the witches' howling. One by one, the others abandoned their duties. Two nurses lifted the dead druid priest and deposited him outside by the rubbish before sprinting away. With no one left to do the dirty work, the doctors split for the coast. Beyond Description stuffed his ears with ram's wool and could not be persuaded to stay. In short order, the king was left alone with the old and new queens and the two horse thieves. He considered himself outnumbered.

Sniveling next to Bridget, he tried to lay his head upon her chest. "Goes to show you, if you want someone killed properly, you need to see to it yourself. How sad I am to leave you, but I must go. My darling Four Eyes, you will always be the one who got away." She brushed him off, of no more consequence than a flea.

With a shrug, Ailill made his way to his unconscious wife, pausing to wish her farewell. "A pity, indeed, were I to fall in the thick of battle. We will rendezvous on the Other Side, babe."

She had no more endearments for the disgraced coward.

As soon as the king had departed, Mullaney showed Bridget his hands behind his back. "I have a dagger in my pocket, if you will cut these ropes."

"Why would I need your puny blade when I have Medb's sword of fire?" She lifted it above her head. "Who am I kidding? Where is that knife of yours?"

The howling outside eased to a mere screech, and then to no sound at all. The soft snoring of the sleeping queen broke the eerie stillness. The eye of the battle was over them, a momentary calm in the bloodstorm.

"What do we do now? How do we get out of here?" Bridget asked.

Burke took off his blacksmith's apron. "The first question to consider is, what move does the enemy desire? If I was them, I would expect myself to stay put, hide beneath the bed until someone comes to our rescue. But never take the clear path, for the road to victory has many switchbacks and is often blocked by a flock of sheep. No, our foes would never expect us to risk all and step onto the pitch against such odds. Unless they are bluffing and counting upon an unforced error. In which case, we make the double bluff and stay put. Or perhaps the triple bluff—"

"For feck's sake," Bridget said. "Make up your mind."

"I think the safest thing is to do what is the least safe." Burke was already at the front door. "What are yis waiting for?"

"Goodbye, old girl." Bridget stroked Medb's hair splayed against the hospital pillow and then followed the men as they exited. The profound silence of the tent was no match for the preternatural emptiness outdoors. It was quiet enough to hear smoke rise and ashes fall.

"Which way, Bobby Fischer?" asked Mullaney. "Is it to the left or the right we are headed?"

Burke studied their position, spinning to the cardinal points of the compass till he faced north. "Those Ulstermen would never guess we would walk straight into their arms. The Fool's Gambit is no tomfoolery."

From out of the dark sky rained a slew of javelins. Three fifties or more, the spears screamed in an unholy barrage. The points thudded into the bog, ripped through tents, and pierced the war drums and wine barrels scattered about. Bridget and the men checked their persons for any puncture marks. Behind the deadly hail came an unholy roar let loose by a horde of naked warriors pouring into the camp, crying "Woe to Ireland!" and retrieving their tossed weapons to have another go.

Amid the flop and flap of the passing soldiers, Mullaney looked for haven from their persistent masculinity. He led Bridget and Burke to the adjoining tent, quietly evading the Ulstermen and their pointy sticks. Another surprise awaited them.

Inside the makeshift brig, they found a red-haired girl tied to the central support pole and three other captives bound to three three-legged stools. Burke instantly recognized the closest prisoner as his granddaughter in a dark hoodie.

"Saints preserve us," he said. "Is it Mary Catherine? What the divil are you doing here?"

As they set about freeing the captives, Bridget was immediately drawn to the third girl on the third stool. "I have finally gone mad. You are her, Fedelm, the girl in the bog."

Nervous as a first-time mother, she bent close to touch the girl, embrace and enfold her, feel skin against skin, breath to breath, apprehensive and excited in equal measure. She could not help herself and ran her fingertips lightly on Fedelm's cheek and stroked the contours of the braided red knot. The bog girl allowed her the caresses—indeed, she enjoyed the sensation, matched pulse to pulse. They held each other's gaze, a momentary truce, until Bridget realized the advantage she was taking and withdrew.

"You're alive," she said. She thought of her grandfather's story of the island of the eternal ancestors. A thousand questions danced in her eyes, the frantic marvelous disbelief and recognition of love. Bridget bent to untie the ropes.

Free at last, Fedelm rubbed her wrists and stretched her thin legs. She slipped off the druid's jacket. Bridget and the two farmers stared at the living corpse, the darkness of her skin and clothes, the architecture of her braid and shaved head, the ancient scars. Old and new, real and hallucination, in the flesh and of the spirit. Her smoky-sweet aroma of peat filled the space. When she flinched, her leathery skin rubbed and squeaked.

"You're alive?" Mullaney asked. He was gobsmacked at the revelation. "You walked away. Here I thought I had been keeping you safe, all wrapped up, so to speak. But you left me."

"As she lives and breathes," said Burke. "If this night has taught me anything, it has led me to conclude you should believe what's right before your eyes as easily as what you cannot see nor prove."

"We found her," Emcee said. "In your old shed. She was moaning under the blue tarp."

"We have been out all night with her," Eileen said. "First, we were running away from Cúchulainn, and then we stepped right into the camp of Medb and Ailill. This is Fedelm, the prophet who tried to stop the Cattle Raid of Cooley."

Burke took one step closer. "So, this is Fedellum—that's a quare name, though not the strangest one I've heard this night. Can you speak at all, Bog Girl?"

"Wait just a dang minute." Bridget held out her arms to stop everything. "I know I am just an American, but what the hell is going on here? What's the deal with this whole reenactment of an epic saga? How can you trust these fairy tales and folk legends and myths full of anachronisms? Men and women who act like gods, fairies coming through the hellmouths between the Otherworld and this one. Now we have this time traveler from the Iron Age? Go ahead, Bog Girl, say something."

"If you would all stop your blathering," said Siobhán. "Give her space of a word."

During their interrogation, they did not notice the man who had crept into the tent, quiet as a devil's cat. Only Fedelm saw her old college friend standing in the entry, his tunic torn with slashes and spear holes and dagger pokes, his red cape tattered and smudged, his golden hair spiked with briars. On his arms and legs, he bore the wounds of his many skirmishes. His hands were red with the blood of three fifties, three hundred, and three thousand Connachtmen, but his features softened when he spotted her, and the seven irises of his eyes sparkled.

"Cúchulainn," the bog girl said, under her breath.

The others parted to make way, and he sped forth and took her scrawny body in his arms, like a giant oak embracing a weathered sapling. Tears etched jagged paths through the filth on his cheeks.

"Fedelm, Fedelm, what has befallen you?"

"On my way home from the Isle of Skye, I warned Medb not to fight you. I begged her not to pursue the Brown Bull of Cooley. I told her there would be nothing but crimson and red. Out of spite at that prophecy, my own people killed me and packed me in the bog, preserved like a bad memory."

"If it isn't the Hound of Ulster," Burke said. He clapped the great hero on the back and raised the dust of a thousand vanquished foes. "My old pal."

"Ah, there is my friend now called The One Who Cheats at Chess, and his crony, Bold Deceiver. Thank you for those two fine horses and speedy chariot, if that was indeed your doing."

"Arrah, don't mention it," Burke said. "It was simply a matter of the unexpected triumphing over anticipation."

"It would surprise me if your every word was not a surprise."

Through the open door and the slits and slashes of the canvas, the blue hour reached this part of Ireland. Night became day as the stars faded and sunlight peeked over the arc of the spinning world. What had been pitch black lightened to navy, an ambiguous and malleable moment, the indistinct gloaming, the *bánú an lae.*

"We must go," said Cúchulainn as he set Fedelm down on her own two feet. "I have traveled far and looked high and low for you."

"And here I thought you were my foe," said Fedelm. "When it was Medb all along."

"Some are born fighters, and some are born poets. You played the part of seer. Now come with us to the bonny North and be free."

The bog girl cupped his chin. Her eyes followed the mad dance of his many irises. "You know I cannot leave my people. I am of Connemara in the province of Connacht, and I would rather have no side at all than to be a part of the timeless dispute."

He was too proud to ask again. With one last look at the mortals, he pivoted on his heels and strode outside. A bright ring of daylight bleached the blue hour, and the eastern rays began to wash away the men and horses, the chariots, and the whole camp. The others followed to see off the great hero, but Fedelm quickly dashed into the queen's tent while it was still in shadows. She did not witness the erasure of the Hound of Ulster.

Medb opened her eyes to find Fedelm standing by her bedside. She had no more honey-words, only guilty silence. The poet held a smothering pillow in her hands, poised for revenge, or for the sunrise to come and whirl the queen back into the old story.

* * *

"It will be a fine day after all," Burke said. "Your turf will have a proper chance to dry."

The others were too flustered to remark upon the weather. As the sun spread over the bog, the ancient world melted. The tents and smoldering campfires, the stacks of ruined swords and shields, the tired horses and the tattered crows, the men living and dead, even the Brown Bull himself, all dissolved like the mist. When the queen's borrowed robes disintegrated, Bridget was left with nothing but her own briefs, so she bustled about looking for a cover-up and slipped into the first thing she could find, the blue dress with the peacock feathers. Mullaney gasped when he saw her, reminded of his lost daughter. The suffocating pillow collapsed to goose down and left Fedelm empty-handed. Even the feathers melted like snowflakes. The queen of the West crumbled to dust. Morning had broken the Ulster Cycle and turned the Cattle Raid into a lonesome trail. The war was over, and the likes of it would not be seen again. Until the next one.

After such an epic night, they were at a loss about what to do in the morning. To a person, they were exhausted from their excursions, yawning, hungover without the benefit of drink. The Red Witches kept close together, trying out minor spells, making a stick dance a jig and a rock roll like a hurley ball. Out on a hard patch of land, Bridget and Fedelm watched the sun become a full orange circle as it rose above the mountains. Mullaney and Burke scanned the endless and empty horizon for something new or different.

"I wish I had my pipe," Burke said. "A nice smoke would be a pleasant way to welcome the day."

"I wish I had my dog," Mullaney said. If the weather remained fair, he thought, he might have a wander about the many limestone fissures and caves in the area and look for possible openings to the Otherworld, with Bonnie's favorite squeaky toy in his pocket.

"You will not find the likes of such a collie again," Burke said. He laid a comforting hand on Mullaney's shoulder. "What shall we do with this lot?"

"Send those girls home to their mammies. Their parents are probably half out their minds with worry. But not before we give them a decent feed. I'm famished, aren't you? Is that pain in your guts any easier?"

"Best in ages." Burke wiggled his bottom. "Funny, but I could eat a horse."

"You're rejuvenated then, old fella?"

"My mind is as clear as the bottom of an empty glass. Well, weren't we the ones for taking the grand chances, the divil mind the risks to life and limb?"

"Last night's not the first time you lost your head."

"Well, let's hope it's the last I sit on the wrong end of a sharp stick. Or am banjaxed to pieces with a sushi knife."

"Some night, wasn't it?" Mullaney said. He waved to get the attention of the others. "Who's hungry after all that? C'mon to my place for a nice Ulster fry for breakfast."

Emcee jumped to the front of the queue. "A cuppa would do me right."

As the party left the empty battlefield, Bridget lingered at the rear with Fedelm. The bog girl took her arm, and Bridget felt the jolt of her hand in the crook of her elbow. The morning birds sang, and a single white cloud floated lonely as an island in the sky. Anyone chancing upon the peaceful scene would have never found a trace of the carnage and mayhem that had occurred mere hours ago. The whole saga had sunk into the bog.

"I want to hear your story," Bridget said.

"What is there to tell? I had a life that ran into trouble through no fault of my own. It is a sad story, but one that many suffer."

Bridget could not contain her enthusiasm. "Ever since I was a little girl, I have been interested in what the dead might tell us. As an archaeologist, I examine traces of history, the physical evidence in bits and pieces of whole civilizations, but we never get to see the whole picture, not really. You were there."

"I don't know if I am a spokesperson for ancient Ireland. Mine is but a wee slice of a complicated tale," Fedelm said. "In fact, each life has many stories in it that whirl around inside the space of memory."

"To begin, tell me this: Are those legends real? Are all those other tales from the *Táin* accurate, at least in their outline, if not their particulars? Is it true what they say about Cúchulainn?"

"Every word. As far as words can be trusted. Though I am not sure what you are after regarding that ancient hero.

Real or no? Sure, isn't the past just another story we tell our-selves, no more factual than our stories of the future?"

Bridget slowed her pace to lag further behind the others. "Well, if you cannot attest to the Hound of Ulster or Queen Medb, maybe you can fill in the record about what everyday life was like. I want to know all about you—what you ate, what clothes you wore, life in the village, what you felt and believed."

"Those are mighty personal questions, seeing as we just met." Fedelm laughed, her teeth bright against her black throat. "Tell me, are all Americans bold as peacocks?"

"I just want to understand the past."

"It is remarkably like the present, only earlier. Sure, we had different customs, funny clothes, our own philosophy and religion and science, but deep down we are you. Full of doubt and hope, the same old loneliness, but sure, everyone enjoyed a good joke, loved a story to pass the time. You could never tell if my father was dead serious or was having you on, stone-faced either way. My mother was a good listener and a comfort for the little passing sorrows. A boy once loved me beyond what I could tolerate or deserve. When I was the age of those witches, I dreamt of writing poetry. What else is there to know? I might as well conjecture about your life in the modern world and would only fathom it if I could be you for a while."

"And what I wouldn't give to be under your skin."

Fedelm gave her arm a playful squeeze. The others had reached Mullaney's place and were waiting by the front door. The house had been restored to its bachelor glory, not a hole nor rip in it and every sharp object safely stowed where it belonged. Bridget put aside her questions for another hour, for we all think there is time enough later for one more talk.

"By chance, do you have any of that Beer of Immortal-ity?" Burke asked.

"A Guinness will have to do," Mullaney said, and he held two bottles in his hand. The taste of victory.

The guests took over the kitchen, frying the bacon and eggs, slicing tomatoes, opening a tin of beans, carving slabs of brown bread to toast, and boiling the full kettle for great lashings of strong Irish tea. Bright sunshine filtered through the curtains, illuminating their party, and Mullaney was glad for the sound of female laughter again in his home and the simple domestic joy and hum of a fresh start to another day. They moved outdoors to savor the glorious weather. A spread large enough to feed an army was laid upon an immaculate picnic table, and when it was time to tuck in, they all sat down and filled their plates. All except Fedelm.

"I couldn't eat a bite," she said. "My stomach has shrunk to the size of a new potato, but don't let me stop you. I could go for a flagon of water."

Over the meal they swapped narratives, and by the time the last crust was claimed, they had pieced together how both Medb and Cúchulainn had been chasing the bog girl for their opposite ends, and they'd learned how a simple message on the internet had led Bridget to stumble across Ireland into a confederacy with the king and queen. Mullaney and Burke regaled them with tales of matched wits and exploits on the chessboard, not to mention a head bouncing on the floor and the other two escapes from murder. Their jokes and tall tales were infused with a warm nostalgia for the adventures of the recently passed hours. Nursing their second cups, they deliberately avoided the question on everyone's mind. Of course, no qualms against propriety can stop a determined old man.

"Tell me, Fedelm," Burke said. "Why did you not go with the Ulsterman when he offered you the chance?"

"I do not want to be part of their whole cycle, or any cycle of history, for that matter. Being out of time is better than being caught up in it." She laid her hand on Mullaney's shoulder, nearly taking his breath away. "And who knows, next go-round Cúchulainn might be my foe and Medb my friend. No, thanks. I am not a prize bull, am I? No more than you."

The hags piled the plates and cutlery to take to the kitchen sink, but Mullaney waved them off. "Leave it for later," he said. "I'll do the washing up. A sunny day is rare enough."

In the glade behind the garden, bees hummed their gauzy melodies and birds sang their love songs in the blue-washed sky. Nearby, the lake water lapped with low poetry. The Red Witches noticed the missing rowboat and promised to retrieve it from the distant shore. "We're champion at the oars," Eileen said. "Bar Siobhán." The redheads favored the shade so as not to burn, but the others sat facing the sun, working on their Irish tans. Time passed, having nothing else to do, till all were fit for a nap.

Without warning, the bog girl let out a raspy cough. "I am toughening," she said, her voice crackling with the ravages of time.

"No doubt," Burke laughed. "I feel much stronger since the beginning of this ordeal. We are all a bit tougher after going through the wars."

"No, my skin is drying to chalk. I am dehydrating." She could feel the change coming over her body. Fine lines splintered audibly and tightened her lips and the corners of her eyes. Her limbs ached and her joints and muscles had lost their elasticity. Two thousand wet years were evaporating in the rare sunshiny day.

Bridget jumped up from her lawn chair to feel the bog girl's arms and face. "Dear Lord, we must get you out of the sun. Your skin is deteriorating rapidly. Exposure to the air will dehydrate you in an hour. Quick, you need moisture, a climate-controlled space—"

"You're not putting her in a glass case," Mullaney said.

"Nobody is talking about that," Bridget said. "But I know scientists at the university—"

Fedelm stiffened and cried out, "I have to go back to the bog."

Everyone fell silent, realizing the sad truth of her statement. She was withering to death before their eyes. Shrinking like a raisin.

"No, no," Burke said. "We can't do that. Maybe some sort of terrarium, or surely there's another way to save her. Run her under the shower till we figure it out. A kiddie pool?"

"Are you not listening?" Siobhán shouted. "She needs to go back to the bog. She is dying all over again. Can you not understand that she knows what is best for herself?"

Helplessness nearly paralyzed them. The bog girl creaked and moaned, her fingers and remaining toes hardened at the tips, and her windpipe constricted, too narrow for one more story. The rough scars at her neck and wrists blanched to white, and a few strands of red hair escaped the knot. She coughed and hacked up dried bits of old grass and moss.

"Do you not know a spell I could use to save you?" Siobhán said.

"There is no magic to stop time," Fedelm said. Her eyes searched the girls' faces, pleading to her sisters. The witches finally realized what must needs be done. Consent went unspoken by the ginger sisters. Emcee and Siobhán lifted her and set her on unsteady feet, fanning away the heat. Spurred by a deeper knowledge, Eileen went to the toolshed and fetched a shovel to bury her once more. They all felt sad and hopeless in the face of the hard dry facts.

"Will you not help us, Pops?" Emcee asked.

Poor old Burke hadn't the heart to answer.

"She needs to be put back where we found her," Mullaney said.

"No, not to the same wretched hole," Fedelm croaked. "Somewhere new. Deeper and wet as it was when first they buried me."

Her breathing slowed with the pain in her chest. She was shrinking before their eyes, collapsing into herself. They laid her gently in the blue tarp and carried her out onto the bog. Well beyond the original spot, they found the wet seep of a sunken pond, already choked with a layer of sphagnum moss floating atop layers of decay. Burke and his granddaughter chopped some hazel branches and fashioned three withy pins. Mullaney helped her to her feet, and a moment of kindness and gratitude passed between them. He did not want her to go, but he understood that she must. "Goodbye, *a stór*." He smiled. Fedelm turned her back on the mortals and took three agonized steps to the edge of the bog.

"*Go raibh maith agat*," she said, staring into the brackish water. "I cannot do this on my own." She hesitated, her words filled with apprehension. "I need someone to fill the gap between the story and the deed. Be quick and be sure. Do not warn me. Make certain I do not float back to the surface."

Mullaney searched Burke's face for some clue that was not there. Despite their slapstick courage on the battlefield, their constitutions were designed to avoid confrontation. The three Red Witches looked away, tears in their eyes, unwilling to strike their sister. No one could bring themselves to act instead of talking and more talk.

"I thought you Irish knew how to swing a shovel," Bridget said. She grabbed the handle, closed her eyes, and made her wish. With a single blow, she felled the bog girl. The body collapsed to the ground, dead again, and glad to be back between the two worlds, ready to be wrapped in a blanket of peat. Bridget fell to her knees, her mind reeling. The jolt of what she had done tingled in her blood and nerves, spun her so dizzily she nearly forgot who she was.

The others knew she had acted to end the old girl's suffering, and indeed, they were grateful to Bridget for having the courage and gumption. Still, it was not easy to stand at the water's edge with the poor creature at their feet. Each person played their part. Bridget removed her glasses and wiped the tears from her eyes. With their slight burden shared between them, Burke and Mullaney waded into the pond, and the Red Witches ducked beneath the water and pinned the body in three places so it would not rise.

* * *

Six people know the true story of the girl in the bog, and six is a good number, being twice three, though not as perfect as three times three. Burke took up competitive chess again, winning the senior division of the All-County Mayo Tournament later that summer, though some would say that he was bewitched and used unprecedented moves drawn from mysterious sources unavailable to mere mortals. Nothing he enjoyed better than an outdoor match under sunny skies. He was a ruthless player, jittery at having to sit too long. After his opponent laid down the king, he would stand his foe a pint or two and chat contentedly, smoking his pipe and counting the magpies that regularly came to watch him play. A week after the events of that night, Emcee was the first to bob her hair, and in solidarity, Siobhán and Eileen followed suit, donating their long red locks to charity for children in need. Without their bright manes, the Ginger Sisters seemed less frightening somehow, but hair grows back in time. The whole village was astir when, as if by magic, Emcee was accepted to Oxford and hopped over to England that fall. Eileen went farther still, heading to Canada to study art and music in Montreal, sad to leave her friends and horses behind. Only Siobhán stayed close to home, matriculating at the national university in Galway to pursue Irish literature, which she loved with a passion that surprised her with each crack of a book. On holidays and breaks from school, she would borrow one of the Magills' Irish Draughts and ride out to the boglands.

Often, she found Mullaney and his new border collie tromping around the old battlegrounds. They liked to visit the pond and watch the sunlight reflect off the waters, dark as a secret. Through the power of her imbas forosnai, she advised him precisely when to make the trip over to America and reunite with his faraway daughter.

Waking in the blue hour back in her Dublin digs, Bridget sat up suddenly in bed, breathless with excitement. She knotted a braid in her golden hair and popped in a new pair of contacts. The dead were finally speaking to her. At midday she left her flat to ride the train into town and meander across Stephen's Green. She thought of the girl she had left buried in the bogs and wondered how she might be getting on these days. In a used bookstore by the Ha'penny Bridge, she found what she needed, in translation from the Irish, no less. Staring into the Liffey River's black pools, she had hatched a radical new thesis and made plans for an exploratory archaeological dig. In her heart's core, Bridget knew exactly where to find the jewel-encrusted horns of the bull and other artifacts that would prove the authenticity of the *Táin Bó Cúailnge*. Ever since that short leap of imagination, she was certain who had been buried in the West.

ACKNOWLEDGMENTS

THIS IS A book about another book, and I am in debt to so many writers and storytellers. *Táin Bó Cúailnge* is a compilation of stories extracted from a group of interrelated texts known as the Ulster Cycle. Drawn from an oral tradition and assembled from partial and complementary (and contradictory) tales written over the ages, it has come down to us from monks and scholars. The two English translations I relied upon are by poets: Thomas Kinsella's 1969 Dolmen Press edition and Ciaran Carson's 2007 edition published by Viking. I recommend Seamus Heaney's bog poems, Flann O'Brien's *At Swim-Two-Birds*, Manchán Magan's *Thirty-Two Words for Field*, and *Bog Bodies Uncovered: Solving Europe's Ancient Mystery* by Miranda Aldhouse-Green. Karen Russell's fabulous short story "The Bog Girl" made me nearly abandon the project altogether, but she and I are talking about different girls. A toast to Robert Mahony, Paddy Meskell, Grainne Fox, and Fiona Mackintosh for reading earlier versions and providing useful suggestions. I am grateful beyond measure to my brave and bold editor Sara J. Henry and the stellar team at Crooked Lane, and to my agent Peter Steinberg for never giving up. The book was made better by

Melanie Pugh Donohue's creative contributions and encouragement. Thanks to my family and friends, who listened to my blather about gods and bogs for ages. Apologies to the Irish people of all sorts for any mangling of the Irish language or culture, but we have long since left that island and rely upon the generosity and good nature of its readers.

Thanks a million.